Terrorbyte

Cat Connor

9mm Press
New Zealand 5018

All names, characters, places, and incidents in this publication are fictitious or are used fictitiously. Any resemblance to real persons, living or dead, events or locales is entirely coincidental.

ISBN: 978-1-6921725-3-4
ISBN: 978-0-9814256-3-4
ISBN: 978-0-9869731-4-7
ISBN: 978-1-7386219-7-2 Draft2Digital

Cover design by *9mm Press*
Book design by *9mm Press*
First published in South Africa by Rebel ePublishers.
Now published in New Zeaaland.

Acknowledgments.

I would like to thank the following people.

Chrissy Gordon – Long time best friend, legal advisor, connoisseur of chocolate.

Sara J Henry – intrepid net buddy, copyeditor, marvelous author, missing twin with a chocolate stash in the freezer.

Graeme Johns – cheerleader, novelist, Australian (but you'd hardly notice).

Simon Burnett – voice of reason, kiwi-at-large, author, lover of my ham sandwiches.

Jayne Southern – Editor extraordinaire, with a wicked sense of humor.

Joan De La Haye and Caroline Addenbrooke at Rebel e Publishers – for making this enjoyable all over again!

Caleb, Bex (& Deaglán, Caeden, Connaire), Trish (&Victoria), Jo Jo, Joshy, Squealer, Tink, & Breezy

Mum and Dad – thank you.

To Josh, Caoilfhionn, and Brianna.
For the laughter and sparkle, you bring to my days.

Chapter One

If That's What It Takes

"Are you sure this is the alleyway?" I stared down the dreary lane, hoping Lee would say no.

The whole place reeked of urine and discarded syringes. With a sense of foreboding, I pulled my badge from my pocket and hung it around my neck by the lanyard. My eyes flicked up and down the close walls of the alley, looking for cameras. I spotted a bracket that may have once held a camera. How handy.

A heavy bulletproof vest hung from my arm. Begrudgingly, I pulled it on. They were uncomfortable and I preferred not to wear one unless absolutely necessary. Lee already had his on. They were definitely better suited to male bodies.

"This is the one she said," he replied, and slung his badge over his head. Lee didn't seem in any hurry to venture in.

"This is exactly how I imagined my Saturday morning would be," I said with a wry grin.

"Yep, me too. Life is good."

"Where's the nearest camera?" I asked.

"The bank, beside the alleyway. They have two cameras located on an outside wall, both covering the street."

"If we don't find anything we'll go visit the bank. We might get lucky with their footage."

Lee nodded. I was tempted to abandon the alley in favor of the bank right off.

I pulled the hair tie from my ponytail, scraped my hair back off my face and retied it higher and tighter. I felt a prickling sensation in the pit of my stomach. Adrenaline surged.

"Ready to rock?"

"Right with you, Ellie."

I stepped into the deep shade of the brick buildings that surrounded the alley, took a breath of cool air and decided it might be a pleasant place to spend an hour. A blast of strong urine odor hit the back of my throat and I changed my mind.

Lee flipped out his notebook and scanned a few pages. "The girl, Rose Van den Berg, said she looked back and saw a blue door with chipped peeling paint."

The door nearest me was a rusty red so I continued walking. Lee caught up in two strides and fell into step. The next door was a faded green showing patches of pink undercoat. We glanced at each other and moved on, noting two large dumpsters against the opposite wall just past the green door. At the end of the shadow-shrouded alley were two more dumpsters. I took an unfortunately large breath – stale, foul air caught in my throat, making me choke. I coughed into my elbow, trying to limit the noise and not hack up a lung.

I looked left: a blank brick wall rose up blocking out the sky. No windows or doors broke the monotonous wall. I kicked at discarded fast-food wrappers tangling around my boots.

"There it is." Lee said. His notebook was gone, in its

place a Glock 22.

We were about ten feet from the door. Above our heads were small frosted louver windows. I counted three windows. The door appeared to have an opaque glass panel at the top, but on closer inspection, it was dirt that obscured the glass. I removed my gun from my hip holster: it was time to see if this was the place the girl remembered. The place she said she was held captive and the last place she saw her older sister.

We approached the door with caution. If the shit hit the fan there was no cover. We'd be in the open until we reached the dumpsters.

Lee knocked. We both stood to the hinge side of the door, against the grimy brick.

Inside, someone shouted. The words were unintelligible. Maybe it wasn't English.

Lee knocked again.

Another voice called out.

Again, I couldn't understand the words.

I shook my head at Lee.

He reached over and knocked again, this time he followed up with a deep bellow, "FBI. Open the door."

Noise erupted. Yelling. Shuffling. Panic.

It is peculiar how some people react to us. You'd think the bad guys would learn to control their outbursts and better disguise their guilt. But not so much. Few people we come across are pleased to have us knock on their door.

Lee kicked the door in and stepped inside. I followed.

Two men sat calmly at a filthy table. Not a sign of the panic we'd heard.

"FBI. Who else is here?"

They shook their heads. Language flew from the older man's lips as he gestured wildly with nicotine-stained fingers. Some things are universal.

"English?" I asked.

They shook their heads.

I had no idea what language they were speaking. I took clues from their appearance: swarthy, lined and leathery skin, dark eyes, dark curly hair. Mediterranean maybe. Greek possibly.

I lifted my radio from my belt and called in our back-up. Sam and a few other agents, in a concealed position out of the alleyway, were waiting for my call. Lee cuffed the two men and sat them back-to-back in the middle of the room on the rickety chairs.

He showed them the photo of Rose.

"Seen her?" he asked.

One man flinched; the other stared with cold dark eyes. Somewhere in the back, I could hear movement.

"Leave them," I hissed. "Let's do it."

I opened the inner door. A long hallway stretched away from us with a bare light bulb hanging from a wire. It gave off enough light to see four doors in the hall. We stood for a moment, listening.

"To the right," Lee said. "Could be Albanian." He cocked his head back towards the other room.

I nodded. I'd considered Greek, so I was geographically close.

I lifted my radio off my belt once more and updated the situation; our backup had already rolled into the alley. A smile flickered across Lee's face as he heard Sam's voice in the room behind us. It gave me a sense of security knowing he was there; it was probably the same for Lee.

Lee and I moved fast yet silently. The inner hallway was filled with hot sticky air, the kind of air that hurt to breathe. We located the door from where the noise seemed to be coming. We looked at each other from separate sides of the doorway. I held up two fingers. He nodded.

Lee turned the handle. It wasn't locked.

A scream bounced off the walls. Lee shoved the door open. In front of us, another swarthy man held a blonde girl against him, one hand clamped on her forehead, his free hand holding a knife to her throat. The blade pressed into the white flesh of her neck. Tears slid down her face. A trickle of red ran down her neck.

I trained my weapon on his head. Lee looked for a body shot, through the hostage if necessary. The girl looked like Rose.

"FBI," I said in a clear voice. "Drop the knife."

"No," he replied and shook his head.

Whatever.

"Have it your way," Lee snarled.

The girl sobbed. The man's grip tightened.

My palms were sweaty. He pressed the knife harder

against her. I pulled the trigger. It seemed to take forever for the bullet to leave the chamber and hit the mark. A hole appeared in his forehead; his expression didn't change. He fell very slowly. Lee grabbed the girl and lifted her clear. He took her straight out of the room and handed her to a waiting agent and was back within seconds.

I stepped forward, kicked the knife away from the body and checked for a pulse. It seemed pointless as a pool of red grew quickly around his head and threatened my boots.

I rifled through the pockets of the dead man. No wallet, no identity information, not even a driver's license. Being close to him was unpleasant. I felt myself gag as his body odor and the smell from the pooling blood mingled into a cloying stench.

"Nothing," I said to Lee. "This fucker hasn't showered for a month. I can't believe the air in the alley is preferable to being near him."

Another voice sounded behind Lee. "You okay in there, Ellie?" It was Sam.

"Yep." I pulled my phone and snapped a picture of the man. "Search the rest of this place and call in the forensics team. Is there an ambulance for the girl?"

"Called already, she's with the paramedics now. We're already searching," Sam replied.

Lee checked his cell phone then spoke to me, "Caine wants to see you, Ellie."

"He text you?"

"Yeah."

"Imagine that?"

Caine had been adamant for the last few years that he wouldn't be texting any of us, ever. In his words, he preferred to call and hear our delightful voices. And here he was texting. The old dog was learning new tricks and life was twisting on the weird scale. I was happy to leave the rapidly building stench coming from the dearly departed. My body craved oxygen, even the urine-filtered air of the alleyway would suffice for now.

I strode through the door, leaving Lee with Sam. They headed off to help with the search. Caine was waiting in the outer room by the alley door. We stood just inside the doorway.

"That kid, she's the sister of Rose Van den Berg. They're Dutch nationals, both reported missing six months ago," Caine said.

"From where?"

"They went missing in Johannesburg."

I sensed a backstory worthy of taking a few minutes to hear. "I'm listening," I said.

"They were traveling with their grandfather from the Netherlands to Johannesburg. At O.R Tambo International airport, immigration officials questioned the grandfather, saying they believed he was trafficking the girls. He produced their travel documents and assured the officials they were his grandchildren. Yet he was told he would have to go to the police station. The girls were not allowed to accompany him but he was guaranteed that customs officials would watch them. He never saw them again."

"Clever."

"When he arrived home, empty-handed, police in the Netherlands told him he was not the first person to fall victim to this particular scam."

"Interpol?"

"That's where we got the information."

We walked out to the ambulance.

"You're okay?" Caine asked.

I removed my vest, rotated my shoulders, working out the tension from the adrenaline that had flooded my body before and during the takedown.

I nodded. A wave of relief hit me, knowing we'd re-united the sisters and they were alive. Alive is good. Sometimes it's not all bad news.

"What condition is the body in?"

"You're going to need to use prints to identify the perp," I replied.

"That bad?" He raised an eyebrow.

I grinned. "Nah, he had no identification on him. My bullet hit him right in the middle of the forehead. Plenty of face left for family to view, if he has any here."

"We don't negotiate." His tone conveyed no room for what-ifs. "These idiots need to learn that and learn it well. Was the kid in immediate danger?"

We stopped in front of the ambulance, where Caine could see the girl receiving medical attention for a small neck wound. She'd need one or two stitches. I could see a

Hudson mask on the gurney next to her and wished I could reach in and borrow it. Clean, cool oxygen would rid my lungs of the foul air I'd breathed.

"Yes, she was," I replied. I angled my body away from the scene in the ambulance.

He nodded. "Then it was the right call."

"How the hell did they end up in Washington?" I had questions.

"I'm hoping the girls can tell us."

"How'd the first kid escape?" The first two men we came across in the rooms weren't exactly spring chickens, and probably wouldn't be running after anyone. But the knife guy – the putrid smelling man – I knew he wouldn't let his meal tickets escape without a fight.

"She was left alone for a few minutes and discovered the door unlocked," Caine replied. "That indicates carelessness, and lack of experience in managing teenage kidnap victims, to me."

"An unlocked door? That was one lucky break and one feisty kid."

"Yes," Caine replied.

"Are we handling this?" It didn't seem like a case for Delta A.

"No, I'm passing it over to another team."

It was what I expected. We had dedicated teams that specialized in finding lost kids and dealt with trafficking. A joint task force with ICE sprang to mind. I was immensely pleased to be out of that loop. I'd come across a particularly offensive Immigration and Customs Enforcement agent during another case. I certainly didn't want to repeat the experience. It begged the question of why we were called out in the first place.

"And we received the call – why?"

"I thought it might have been something else."

I shot him a questioning look. "Like?"

"We've got an ongoing case." He proceeded to explain. "Delta B team is working on a case involving an Albanian crime syndicate. So far, five dead: all with ties to the Albanians. When the kid described how she and her sister were taken and gave a description of the men that held them, the perps sounded Albanian to me."

The penny poised but didn't drop. Albanians were linked to human trafficking in both the United Kingdom and Belgium but, as far as I knew, here in the United States they were involved in drugs and general thuggery.

"Have the Albanians spread their human trafficking wings to include South Africa and here?" I asked.

"Not as far as we can tell. Everything we've seen so far suggests that this is an anomaly," Caine replied. He seemed certain, yet there was something ticking away under the surface. I could feel it.

My left eyebrow rose. "And, is this connected to Delta B's case?"

Caine's mouth twitched. "Different Albanians, but might be good for some information."

"I take it we're the only team working in Northern Virginia?"

We may all be Delta, but we were often separate teams.

Caine was Delta's Special Agent in Charge. He moved between us, helping whichever team needed him. Sometimes we all worked together but mostly the nine of us made up three teams to give better coverage.

"Yes, B is in New Jersey. All the murder victims were found in Long Beach." The sides of his mouth twitched so violently he almost smiled. "C is offering assistance down in Georgia where some market gardener dug up a few bodies."

I checked my watch. I really needed to get going. "I'll write my report then head home," I said.

"We'll all see you tonight," Caine said. "How's Mac coping with the fuss?"

I smiled. "Badly."

"He's probably made the connection between speeches and microphones," Caine said with a massive upper lip spasm.

"I'm sure he has." There was no stopping the smile on my face. Caine twitched his lips into a frightening grimace. "I don't know that we've helped him any by razzing him about the things he said while under the influence."

"I think you'll find it wasn't 'we'," Caine replied, pointing at me, then himself.

"No, it wasn't you," I agreed.

It was me, Sam and Lee. Mostly me. Memories of Mac spaced out on Ketamine, courtesy of the Son of Shakespeare, were never far away. Memories of Mac and his rainbow people amused me on a daily basis; in the main, I kept them to myself.

"Wipe that grin off your face, Ellie. It's hard enough for him to move past calling Sam 'Mr. T' as it is."

Then I saw it. Suppressed amusement. He did find it funny.

"See you tonight," I said.

"Let me know if you need a persuasive escort," Caine said. His voice dropped to barely a whisper. "I'll have Mr. T and his pal, General Lee, pick him up."

I imagined Mac handcuffed and escorted to dinner. It was amusing but possibly necessary.

"Will do."

Chapter Two
Someday I'll Be Saturday Night

Mac lifted his head, his hazel eyes meeting mine with the determination of a man searching for an out.

"Why?"

"Because we are required to attend." I tugged my tee shirt free from my waistband, letting it hang over my jeans. The early evening was warm, bordering on muggy. I felt hot and tired, and my mood teetered on the edge of nervously peeved and ornery bitch. I pulled the tie from my hair and shook my head, ran my fingers through the length of my hair and massaged my head with my fingertips. Even my scalp felt irritated.

Irritated was the new happy.

I could still smell the dead guy, even after showering at work and changing into clean clothes. The clothes I'd worn all day were in the garbage. I felt like I needed to shower again.

He shuffled papers across his desk, without looking up at me. "I have a lot of work to do."

"I know." I steeled myself for the string of excuses that seemed ready to fall.

"Do we really have to?" he implored, looking up at me through the dark hair that fell over his eyes.

"Yes, we really do," I replied, weary beyond belief.

"You know I hate this ..."

"Yes ... I know you hate this."

I remembered exactly what I was doing the day the publisher rang to tell me our book made the New York Times bestseller list. I dropped one of the crystal glasses I was washing and it smashed in the kitchen sink. I never dreamt the book would sit at number three for two months and I still hadn't found a replacement glass.

We have to do this.

FBI agents who write poetry: we were big news, especially after the Son of Shakespeare case and the whole world found out about the sucky little poems he left for me, artistically stuck to dead bodies. Personally, I think people only bought the book to check out my warped mind. I hoped they were disappointed but sales indicated they weren't. I think I'm fairly twisted. Finding parts of people in your car and bath tub and hanging from the ceiling will do that to a person.

"Who'll be there?"

The answer rambled in my head: about two hundred people we've never met; half the FBI; all our family; most of Mauryville. Mauryville is the small town I'd lived in before moving north to be with Mac.

"People." I crossed my fingers and hoped my next comment sounded convincing. "It's a dinner function, so probably not many." I was trying hard to make it sound like a small intimate gathering, the sort that wouldn't require a microphone.

Mac's eyes met mine. "You're a terrible liar, Ellie."

He passed me a pile of papers. Flipping through them, I realized they all said similar things: 'Congratulations.

See you at the dinner.'

"There's even one from that friend of Simon's and dad's, GW."

"So is it that GW?"

"I think so. Look at this." He handed me the email. I glanced over the contents and noted the Secret Service brief at the bottom.

Just when I thought I'd taken his mind off things, he snapped at me, "I cannot speak in front of people ... with a microphone in my face." Mac's eyes shifted back to the paperwork on his desk. A thin scar from a knife fight ran along the side of his face, almost obscured by his hair. A scar on the bridge of his nose, from a maniac with a baseball bat a few months ago, was still pink. A reminder that Mac wasn't afraid of wading into trouble even when there was a real possibility of physical injury and yet, here he was about to bury himself in work rather than face a microphone. The Son of Shakespeare had really screwed him up. I saw the little lost boy behind his eyes. Before I realized what had happened I found myself wanting to smack him good and hard upside the head and tell him to get over it.

"I don't want to do this either." That was the truest thing I'd said all afternoon. You do what you have to do.

He looked up. "Then let's not; let's turn off the phone, lock the door and stay home."

That's not going to happen. "Barring our deaths, we have to attend."

"Don't tempt me like that."

"Mac, we're going, everything is going to be fine." It was a white lie for a good cause.

He shook his head. "No, it will be dreadful ... I will make an ass of myself." He sighed a long, theatrical sigh. "And it will be embarrassing as hell."

Speculating that it might well be, I injected a smile into my voice and said, "First, let's just get there and do the mix and mingle thing, sign a few books, have dinner ... I'll read a few poems, you feign illness and we'll leave."

I kept my fingers crossed that what I was actually thinking wouldn't pop out of my mouth: Suck it up, princess!

There are worse things in life than speaking into a microphone in front of a crowd of people. I couldn't think of any, offhand, but I knew there were worse things.

Then it dawned on me, the smell of the dead guy was worse. I wanted to scream, 'I shot someone today.' But I sucked it up and moved on. There was no sense in letting that scumbag ruin my night, not with Mac so keen on doing the same.

"Oh, I won't be faking the illness and remember, you're a sympathetic vomiter."

It took vast amounts of willpower to hold myself in check. I knew he had a genuine phobia of microphones but, man, he was standing on my last nerve.

Mac must've realized how close I was to biting off his head. He smiled suddenly and asked, "Afterwards, can we string up your brother and that no-good-best-friend of yours for publishing this fuc'n thing?"

"Good – progress! At least you're coming with me now." I grinned. "Stringing up my brother sounds like a plan."

Mac's eyes were on me and I seriously considered making a call to Caine to have Mac escorted. I sensed his intention to back out at the last minute.

"What time does this fresh hell kick off?"

"A car will pick us up at seven-thirty."

"A car," he said, barely above a whisper. "They're sending a car?"

"Yeah."

Mac frowned as he read something on the computer monitor. It made me uneasy seeing his brow crease like that. My reaction was a hangover from the past, which didn't help allay the feeling of foreboding. Experience told me this particular expression usually foretold an exclamation of horror, followed by a dead body.

I swallowed hard. I knew it would take some getting over. I told myself that the killer sits on death row, that Mac was simply frowning. The Son of Shakespeare was a memory and not my reality anymore. Unfortunately the memory of him lay intertwined with our poetry book; I doubted I'd ever escape that. My idiot brother, Aidan, had compiled the book during that case and it contained the first poem Mac ever wrote for me, the one the Son of Shakespeare stole and used.

No wonder I had a killer on my mind.

Our front doorbell buzzed. I started to walk in the direction of the hallway when Mac leapt over his desk to head me off. My hand shot out and fingers wrapped themselves in his shirt as he attempted to pass. He came to an abrupt stop.

"I'm not letting you out that door," I said, twisting the fabric in my hand.

"I'm just answering it," he said indignantly, attempting to brush my hand away.

And I came down in the last rain shower.

"You arranged this," I accused.

"I did not," he scoffed.

The person who'd been ringing the doorbell began knocking loudly. I reached the door one step in front of Mac.

"Let me," I insisted, reaching out and twisting the door handle. With a sharp pull the door swung open.

Eddie almost fell into the hallway.

I was somewhat surprised to see Mac's older brother: lifelong tormentor and now something new. Savior?

"Mac, I've got a ..." Eddie started then wisely stopped.

"... very small brain?" I offered.

He scowled as he processed my comment, which didn't improve his looks. It took nearly a minute before he spoke again. "No, it's mom. She wants Mac."

I smiled. "Of course she does. Funny that she hasn't called. Usually there are upwards of six calls a day."

Eddie floundered; his mouth flapped.

"On your way, Eddie. We have a prior engagement."

I closed the door. Mac leaned back on the hall wall. He had the good grace to look sheepish.

"I have no words!" I said, shaking my head.

"I bet you find some," he replied.

"You think now is the best time to get mouthy?"

The corners of his mouth turned up. "No, ma'am."

"That's what I thought. We should get ready."

I couldn't imagine Mac asking Eddie to save him. It defied reason. He held an intense dislike for his older brother.

Mac grinned. "After you."

"I don't think so."

I took his hand and we walked together into the living room.

I knew about his nervousness. I understood how badly he was affected by the knowledge that complete strangers had heard him rambling over a surveillance audio link about rainbow people, when he'd been doped, but this was a different situation. Glancing at the clock on the wall told me we had two hours before the car arrived.

I knew I would regret my words but it didn't stop me; it never stops me. "You could do with a Valium." Or a bottle of bourbon, or maybe both. Okay, bourbon was a bad idea; it is too easy to sniff it out on someone's breath. Maybe vodka. My sense of professionalism took over: even in my worst moments I would not turn up to such an event plastered. We'd survived a hellish year. Taking the edge off tonight with a little yellow pill sounded good.

His arms tightened around me. "Valium?"

"Yep."

"Where did you get Valium?"

I replied, "The doctor last week."

"Are you okay?"

Of course, I'm okay! I'm always okay.

"Yes, I am okay."

"Then what's with the creepy smile?"

"What's with the close, suffocating observations?" Instantly, I regretted being so sharp.

"Do you feel better?" he asked.

"No, I'm sorry. That was uncalled for." I really was sorry. "I was just thinking about Aidan and the whole fundraising thing tonight at The Aquarium."

"You were planning his demise!" Mac accused with amusement.

"Maybe."

"Maybe's ass."

"He swam with the fishes," I said, without even trying to hide the satisfied smile on my face. The subject had successfully moved away from Valium.

Mac steered it back. "Does this have anything to do with those nightmares?"

I smiled and kissed him. "I'm okay."

I was okay, just so long as no more bodies turned up near me and I didn't think too much and no one ever publishes anything of mine ever again.

"Does it?"

"I've mentioned them, therefore I guess it does." Nightmares. Flashbacks. It's all semantics and hardly worth quibbling over. I didn't believe that for a second but I tried. If I tried harder, it might even be plausible. I looked at the clock again. “We have to get ready.”

Chapter Three
Bad Medicine

I stood in front of the bedroom mirror fussing with my hair.

"Did you get a call today from dad?" Mac asked from the bathroom.

Both our fathers were heavily involved in our Butterfly Foundation project. They both retired over ten years ago and had volunteered to take over the brunt of the day-to-day work created by the Foundation's existence.

I'd spent the last few years telling myself that one day I'd have more time. One day there will be fewer freaks to track down. One day I will be able to let the FBI go. Yeah, right! One day pigs will fly. So for now, our fathers take care of business and we take care of criminals.

"Mine or yours?"

"Mine."

Mac's dad, Bob, had called me that morning while I was in the office. We had discussed the upcoming board appointments. I nodded. "Bob told me he wants my dad to take the chairman of the board position."

"Will the announcements be made tonight?"

"Yes. During dinner, the chairman will be announced, and so will the trustees." Guess he now had a reminder about the speeches. Something outside caught my eye. I moved to the window. On the balcony railing sat a large Monarch butterfly. So very beautiful.

Mac had a reminder for me, too. "Tomorrow you and I are flicking the proverbial switch, the server is up and running. The Foundation goes online officially at midday."

The Monarch fluttered its orange wings then soared skyward. I watched until it was gone from view. We had a vision and that vision now had life. No matter how much I hated having our poetry published, the proceeds from sales had made possible the Foundation that supported the kids of bipolar and schizophrenic parents. Okay, not entirely; I'd used my trust fund money, which had been sitting in the bank since I was eighteen, the insurance money left to me when mom was murdered, as well as half the insurance money from when my house burned to the ground.

Oh, the life I lead.

All in all, life was good. We were making a difference. Even if it wasn't a huge difference, at least some kids had a safe place to talk and get support. Inside the Foundation server, sanctuary was provided by moderators and counselors.

Our mission statement rang in my ears from an internal looped recording: 'To provide security and a safe place for the children touched by bipolar disorder, dissociative identity disorder and schizophrenia.'

Mac whispered in my ear, "Earth to Ellie, we best get into our monkey suits, sweets."

"Yeah ... and take a chill pill." Five milligrams of calm coming right up. I swear I felt it doing me good well before I'd swallowed it.

He kissed my cheek. "Yeah, let's do that first. Let's turn up loaded to a function full of FBI and the media."

"Exaggerate much?" Under my breath I growled, "I won't be loaded and you could do with chilling, dude."

A little while later and in a better mood, I stood in front of the bedroom mirror surveying the dress I wore. Mac came up behind me in his black suit, wearing a platinum shirt that matched the platinum silk of my dress. We looked fantastic.

I stepped back and felt my shoe catch on Mac's. His arm snaked around my waist to steady me. A hundred memories collided all at once and, for a split second, I was back in a car park in Lexington viewing the first body left by the killer known as Jack Griffin.

***

I slipped out the door unseen and quietly edged my way between two police officers. We all stared into the trunk. My eyes struggled to comprehend what I saw.

My brain stuttered. "What the fuck is that?"

"I'm not sure," Doug replied. "It's hard to tell."

There was a mass of flesh and fabric, no obvious beginning or distinguishable end. It didn't resemble anything in particular. I glimpsed a flash of something silvery.

"Gloves? Flashlight?"

Alex handed me a pair of latex gloves. He took a flashlight from his belt. I carefully lifted a piece of bloodied fabric and revealed what I figured was an arm. “Shine it here for me.”

Alex directed the beam of light over my shoulder.

“Looks like a bracelet,” Doug commented. He was right. Not only that, it looked familiar.

I leaned in and read the inscription.

“Oh, man.” I gulped for air. My legs threatened to buckle. I staggered slightly as I turned away. I managed to unload the meager contents of my stomach by the back wheel, preserving the integrity of the crime scene as much as possible. Someone pulled my hair back and had hold of my shoulders. A tissue magically appeared in my hand as I straightened up.

“Thank you,” I spluttered, wiping my mouth.

“You’re welcome.” Alex’s voice sounded just as smooth as Doug’s. “Go on back inside. Do you want me to call someone for you?”

“Give the forensics team a hurry-along.” I was facing the café and sure as hell was not going to look back at the car. I pulled my wallet from my pocket and handed over my card, “My number is on here, ask for SAC Grafton.” I took a breath. “Tell him ... we found Carter.”

Alex frowned at me. “He’ll know what that means?”

“If he asks, tell him he’s in the trunk of my car.”

***

Suddenly a night of fund raising and celebrities didn’t seem so bad after all. It was a relief to get into the limousine.

Chapter Four
Ordinary People

The evening could have been worse. There were no dismembered bodies and no Post-it note poems. I was not covered in blood nor was anyone else.

Mac smiled at my surprise in having enjoyed the evening.

"I'm going to change out of this," I said, sweeping my hand down my body.

His eyes followed my hand.

"You're sure we shouldn't make some babies? They'd be damn cute!"

I could see the laughter in his eyes as I replied, "Cute they would be, insane most certainly. You know our gene pool needs cleansing, babe."

I fervently hoped the laughter in his eyes wasn't masking something deeper; an actual desire for children. Breeding from our combined genetic line was not a great idea. On the grand scale of ideas, it ranked right up there with bamboo shoots under fingernails or a stint in Guantanamo Bay.

Mac turned me to face him, kissed me, and said, "You're sure?" The smile in his eyes faded.

A sinking feeling hit me. I couldn't tell whether he was joking or not. Suddenly it didn't look or feel like a joke. Damn. We'd agreed a year ago that having kids would be a bad idea.

We had agreed.

I didn't want to have that conversation again. Ever.

"I'm sure." I changed the subject. "Make some coffee, will you? I'm going to change."

Wearing the more comfortable attire of jeans and a tee shirt, I settled on the sofa with my laptop and checked my email.

We had fulfilled our duty to the publisher and the kids. It was almost fun playing dress-up and grown-up. Even so, I was relieved to be back at home and away from all those pretty people, most of whom lived far from the reality I saw every day.

I had a hard job imagining what their lives would be like. It's not that those people are immune to crime; they just seem to not notice it. I suspected I was being somewhat unfair. Few people saw the side of crime I dealt with, and it was my choice to work violent serial crime. I could've chosen a less gory job, with more congenial hours, but I hadn't. My choice.

Several times during the evening, I thought I saw the singer Rowan Grange. I didn't recall him being on the guest list but, then again, I didn't see the final list. I considered that we should've had him and his band, Grange, perform. What a coup that would have been: one of the biggest bands (next to Bon Jovi) to come from New Jersey. That sure would've made the night more fun.

My mind wandered off to the last Grange concert I attended. Normal things like attending rock concerts were rare gems in my life. I tended to hold those memories tightly. Another Rowan Grange memory edged to the forefront. He was gorgeous and smiling in the lobby of the Marriott, while I, the recipient of the smile, was shoeless and disheveled. Such is my life. One day it would be nice to run into him when I'm behaving normally. I'm not entirely sure I ever do, so it could be a long shot. I realized I had Googled him while daydreaming. Cringing, I closed the browser.

Dad's smile floated into view and evoked more amusing thoughts. We'd finally met the famed former President, GW. I'd noticed the presence of the Secret Service immediately. I'd also noted that the security was about as low key as those guys get; bit of a giveaway that someone important was around and it wasn't the current President. I shouldn't have been surprised at who it was. Our fathers had known him for years but would neither confirm nor deny the identity of the mysterious friend they'd told us about before my father's heart surgery. GW seemed to enjoy the evening; I doubt he understood any of the poetry. It's not that we write flowery prose, or even particularly intellectual prose for that matter, it's just that he was once photographed reading a book upside down and he can't say nuclear.

Enough said.

My brother survived the evening without me feeding him to the sharks; I allowed myself to dip a toe into a shiny puddle of my earlier fantasy. Watching him twitch in a tank of electric eels would've been most therapeutic. My mind conjured up a delightful image of Aidan struggling to swim to the surface in a deep glass tank, his plight exacerbated by deadly Sea Wasps and Portuguese Man of War jelly fish. A stingray or two appeared, moving ever closer; other sea creatures were attracted by his fearful flailing. Oxygen bubbled out of his mouth as his last remaining breath escaped.

I blinked and imagined Aidan sinking to the bottom of the tank, eyes bulging, mouth open, one small bubble floating to the surface.

Back to reality. We hadn't fed him to the sharks or even dropped him in the tank with the electric eels. I felt a smile creep across my face. Tossing someone into a tank of sea creatures is not something one should attempt in evening finery. But I knew that had a suitable moment presented itself, I would've succumbed to temptation.

"Ellie!"

I dragged myself from the email screen I was staring at. There were no emails from Rowan Grange. I was mildly disappointed.

"Uh-huh?"

"Phone, sweets."

"Thank you." I leaned over and kissed Mac as he passed me the phone.

He whispered, "It's Caine." He grinned as I rolled my eyes. Mac's boss never called him in the middle of the night. He had taken a position in the FBI's Cyber Division. I never thought he'd join up but he said he found stock trading a little too tame after running around the countryside with me, scared half to death and avoiding a bad poet. Now he spent his days dealing with email scams, viruses and Internet threats. Guess that floated his boat, although I can't say I found his field terribly exciting. Part of his job was monitoring certain chat rooms and chat formats, especially if complaints were received about the conduct of patrons and such. He was also an expert in social network sites. His Twitter page had more followers than Oprah and he'd garnered quite a following on MySpace and Facebook. They don't have emergency midnight callouts in Mac's part of the Cyber Division.

"Problem?" I used my most pleasant telephone voice. I knew Caine wouldn't call this late if it wasn't urgent.

Mac turned to leave but I grabbed his sleeve. He sat down.

Caine's raspy voice came back at me, "Yes, there is a problem."

His tone bothered me. I'd become accustomed to grumpy but this time, there was something else, an edge I hadn't heard in a long time. Fear?

My stomach twisted.

We'd only been home an hour and a half, so he couldn't have been home much before us. Trouble comes quickly. In my experience it's usually stomping a blood trail across a pristine floor.

"What?"

"Been called back to the office. We have a possible new case."

If he was calling me from the office, he hadn't been

home at all. He must've gone in to do something when the call came through.

"Since when?" And since when does he say a 'possible' new case? If we received a call, that alone meant there was enough concern to make it a probable case.

"I got the call thirty minutes ago. It's an unusual one, Ellie."

"How unusual?"

"You might find elements of this case familiar." Caine stopped speaking, leaving a hollow sound on the line.

A groan sounded in my head. This was hard work. He wasn't giving me a lot to go on.

"Okay ... What do you want me to do?"

"I want you to run the investigation." He paused. His words idled in space, then he said, "Lee says there's a poem."

My blood suddenly felt cold. Thoughts swirled in my head. A poem: we hadn't encountered a poem in a crime scene since The Son of Shakespeare case.

Coincidence?

I'd been thinking about him earlier.

Coincidence?

Focus, Ellie, focus. I tried. I really did but something else surfaced, triggered by the thought of a crime scene poem – or maybe the Valium had worn off.

***

"We found this on the body in your trunk." He removed a yellow Post-it note with the tweezers and showed it to me. The writing was smeared with blood but still legible.

" 'Cream of the crop, he's missing his top, no more meals *à la gourmet*. Breakfast of champions is not Special K.' " I read it aloud. "I don't even want to ask if that means his head was hacked off."

"It was removed from the body. We found it under his legs," Caine said. "Now get out of here," He dropped the Post-it back into the bag. "Stay in touch. Stay safe."

***

"Ellie?"

"Right here," I replied. "Where and when?"

I listened to a long stretch of quiet before he spoke again.

"I want you in Alexandria A-sap. Lee and Sam are on scene. Lee called this to our attention. He took a call from the local police asking for assistance."

"You coming?"

The entire conversation seemed punctuated by Caine's silences. I didn't like it.

"Caine?"

"This is yours, Ellie. You're Supervising Special Agent on this one. I'll be with the Director for a while." He paused and before he spoke again, I heard paper moving on his desk and knew from experience he was pulling an all-nighter on something for the Director. "I'll meet up with you as soon as I can."

Part of me wanted him to walk me through this. Another part knew I could do it and there was no way Caine would let me loose if he didn't have faith in me. He'd promoted me over the phone. Now that's bizarre.

"Take care, Ellie."

"We'll see you soon, yeah?"

"Yeah."

The line went dead. Mac took the phone from my hand.

"How bad?"

I shook my head. "I don't know yet; it's my case, that's all I know. Well, that and Caine just told me I was a Supervising Special Agent, not an acting SSA."

I could see no sense in worrying Mac with the poem thing until I'd viewed it for myself and had a handle on what was happening, so I tried diverting us both with the Supervising Special Agent thing. Was I ready to go up a pay scale?

I watched his face. He was concerned. But then: "SSA," he said, with a grin that wiped away all remnants of concern.

"There's a crime scene in Alexandria; Lee and Sam are there."

Mac's brow creased and his voice dropped to a hoarse whisper as he said, "You want me to come?"

"It's late." I glanced at my watch. It was already past two in the morning. "I may not be home for hours. I'm sure your mom has plans for your day off and I'd hate to interrupt!"

I could ask Mac to join the team if we needed him. I

was sure Caine could wrestle him out of the Cyber Division to help. He'd done so numerous times before but not at my request. Mac had worked on cases with Lee and Sam and the other Delta teams, but not with one led by me. The request would depend on what was waiting for me in Alexandria and whether or not I felt we needed a cybercrime specialist on board.

Did I want that? Did I want us working that closely as well as living together? A quiet voice in my head reminded me they were bridges to cross in due course. I just bet trolls lived under those bridges: evil, fat, drooling trolls, ready to cause all manner of trouble. It didn't matter right now; the trolls and bridges would wait.

I pushed away thoughts of us working together and focused.

Mac tapped my arm and said, "That's not an acceptable answer."

I saw the spark in his eyes; I knew he'd come if I asked. Good to know. It was possible that he didn't want to find out what his mother had in store for him, and that was why he was keen to help out.

I told myself the new case couldn't possibly be the Son of Shakespeare/Jack Griffin/Charles Boyd, so there's nothing to worry about; nothing at all. I'd worked at least nine cases since the Shakespeare thing. This was just another case. No reason to expect anything as bad. No reason to expect that anyone was targeting me or leaving bodies for me to find. No reason whatsoever.

Just another case.

"I might not be back until tonight," I replied with a smile. "You know how unpredictable my job can be. Until I get there and view the scene, I have no way of knowing how this investigation is going to go, or what I'm going to find. Could be a long day. No sense you wasting your day off."

"Sure?"

"Uh-huh."

The truth was I did not want this case. I wanted nothing to do with poems. I could have happily lived my life without ever seeing another poem at a crime scene.

I tried my trusty 'I'm okay.' The results were less than convincing; nothing felt okay.

Dang!

Chapter Five
Social Disease

The early hours of Sunday morning found me standing on the pavement looking up at a building, the exterior lit by the rolling lights of five police cars parked out front.

From the second I stepped through the outer door and into the foyer of the apartment building, I could feel it.

We stood in the atrium of what used to be a high-rent, architect-designed apartment complex. Diffused red and orange light spilled from a grubby stained-glass window high above us. Odd. It was dark outside, yet I saw colored light falling inwards. The colors did nothing to brighten the drab interior. I peered past the colors and glimpsed spotlights on the roof beyond. The building had fallen into disrepair over the years; it was as if no one cared or remembered the architect's intentions. I didn't think he intended his dream to end in this sorry state. Yet someone cared enough to make sure the spotlights still worked.

Oppression hung heavy in the air. Terror seeped from the walls: years of abuse cradled by the all-seeing, all-knowing, all-absorbing building. It had the makings of a great haunted house.

I squeezed my eyes tightly shut, then opened them fast, making the atrium blur; an old habit. Reality blurred into a functioning calmness.

"Supervising Special Agent Conway?"

The voice belonged to a tall, broad-shouldered, brown-haired police officer not much older than me. He stood about four feet from the external doors, bathed in an eerie, orange light.

"Yes."

He stepped forward. "I'm Officer Josh Konstram, your escort," he said and offered his hand.

We shook briefly.

"Pleased to meet you, Officer Konstram."

"Likewise, Agent Conway. Call me Josh." He offered his hand again.

I smiled. We shook. I replied. "I'm Ellie."

Five doors opened off the atrium. Police officers stood on either side of one open door indicating where we should go. Josh stepped forward and led the way.

A fluorescent light down the hall flickered, flashed and went out. The absence of the light created an even creepier atmosphere. We walked down the wide hallway and past several other apartment doors as we went, eventually stopping next to another police officer. He handed us protective shoe coverings and latex gloves. I pulled on the shoe coverings, then the gloves, as did Josh.

Josh held the door open and said, "This way, Ellie."

The officer by the door cleared his throat.

Josh corrected himself, "This way, Agent Conway."

I glanced at him. "Ellie."

He grinned and the more senior officer on the door nodded.

Josh stayed on my right, guiding me away from bloodied footprints and possible trace evidence as we walked down the dingy hallway to find Lee or Sam.

The home was in disarray but the impression I gleaned was one of permanent turmoil and disorder. Nothing I saw indicated the mess was attributable to the current situation: clutter piled high; junk stacked on every flat surface and piled on chairs in the rooms we passed. Possessions lay heaped along the entire length of the interior hallway: books, clothing and newspapers. Stuff. This was the home of a hoarder. Josh stopped at the end of the junk-filled and untidy hallway.

I felt a rising desperation brought on by a pervasive feeling of menace that seeped from the apartment walls. I felt suddenly claustrophobic. I took some slow deep breaths and wished I hadn't – the air was none too fresh.

Stemming my own panic as best I could, I called into the rooms beyond, "Lee?"

His deep voice filtered through my defenses, leaving warm security in its wake. "Ellie, check this out."

I'm okay.

I glanced at Josh. He said, "I'll be right here."

"Thanks."

I stepped over strewn garbage as I made my way to his position, somewhere on my right. The clutter spilled everywhere but became overshadowed by garbage and general filth. As tempting as it was to cover my mouth and nose with my hand, I resisted.

The smell of death permeated the room that may once have been a dining room.

I found Lee in the kitchen.

"I'm here." I flicked my eyes quickly around the room, getting a sense of the scene.

Lee pointed to the cabinets and something written in marker pen. Writing extended all the way around the kitchen, putting the body in the center of a bizarre circle of words. It took me a few moments to discover the beginning.

"A poem?" Lee's manner was tentative.

I knew by his tone he didn't want to go there again either.

I read it twice, forcing down bile and swallowing as hard as I dared. It wasn't just a poem. Not a whole one anyway: just the first two lines of a poem I knew well. I surveyed the scene. I could feel there was something else here, something that may hold a clue or two. The more I looked, the more the feeling began to seem like wishful thinking.

Lee was waiting for an answer.

I bent over the body of the woman. Around her neck was a gold ribbon, the sort used on gifts; a ribbon tied in a pretty bow. There was no obvious blood smeared on the bow or the ribbon. I leaned closer to her face. I could smell chlorine.

I felt Lee's eyes on me and answered his question.

"It's not a whole poem."

"What then?"

I smiled. I knew he was so going to love this as much as he loved middle-of-the-night crime scenes.

"They're the first two lines of a poem I wrote to Mac."

"Get out of town!"

I flashed him a damn-I-love-this-job smile. "Yep."

Lee rocked back on his haunches. Disbelief flashed across his face, then a more thoughtful look took over. "There's something else. I found a Post-it note addressed to you."

I heard his words but no meaning filtered through; my brain had switched off.

"Ellie, did you hear me? I found a Post-it note."

It flicked back on. "Where is it?"

"Bagged and tagged by the crime scene investigators."

"Do we have a copy?"

"Yeah, I copied it and sent a copy to Caine."

"Great." That explained why we were involved. A note addressed to a special agent is enough to get us an invitation to what is usually police jurisdiction. I really didn't want to get into the whole Post-it thing. "I hate Post-its. I haven't used one since we arrested Jack Griffin."

Right after I arrested the so-called invisible man I switched to memo cubes and magnetic whiteboards.

Lee stood up, slowly stretching his legs. "What do you think? Copycat or whole new situation?"

"He's not copying anyone that I know of, even with the Post-it, Lee. This is not a repeat of the Son of Shakespeare."

Something else worried the hell out of me and trying not to think about it was not a happening thing. The ribbon was familiar.

"Didn't we have an unsolved rape a few months back where the assailant tied the victim with gold ribbon?"

"Yes."

"I think we got trouble."

Lee nodded. His already dark eyes seemed darker and his face held a grimness I didn't often see.

"Can you smell chlorine?"

Lee leaned closer to the body and sniffed. "I can now."

He clenched his teeth and frowned but made no further comment.

"You got pictures for us?" I asked.

The crime scene photographer would get all the evidential pictures needed. I wanted something we could peruse now, without waiting for the actual photographs to be processed. That's why we carry digital cameras.

"Uh-huh."

"Swap memory sticks with the camera."

"Sure."

I removed a spare memory stick from a small plastic case on my key ring and handed it to him, then slid the one containing our crime scene photographs back into the case. It was so much easier working with memory sticks and thumb drives – we didn't need to find a secure line to transfer information. The twenty-first century was full of great inventions and I embraced every single one as soon as it became available.

"Will you let the local police know we are interested in this? Have them copy me on the forensic reports from the scene. Let them know I am especially interested in the writing, the ribbon, plus the placement of the body." Until I said it, I had done well not to acknowledge what we were looking at. My mind had carefully blurred most of what was in front of me and reduced it to a professional context: nothing more than another case. I knew I had to do it, so I took a breath and scrutinized the body in front of me.

Female aged between twenty-five and thirty, shoulder-length blonde hair, wearing a red tee shirt. The woman was lying on her back, naked from the waist down. Knees bent, legs apart. A bottle of bourbon lay by her right thigh. It still contained some of its contents although the top was off. I could see no obvious wounds but there was a great deal of blood on the floor, mingled with bourbon. Bloodied handprints, smudged on the woman's inner thigh, partially concealed bruising. I pulled back, stopping my thought processes before they fixated on the pain suffered by this victim.

I indicated the bottle. "I want to know the significance of that."

"You got it, boss."

"How long ago do you suppose she died?"

"Maybe as long as eighteen-to-twenty hours. She was last seen yesterday morning."

"Any thoughts on the cause of death?"

He shook his head. "We got a lot of blood but no obvious wounds. She could've bled out from penetrating wounds we can't see," Lee said. As an afterthought and thinking out loud rather than imparting vital information, he added, “Feels like murder to me.”

It sure didn’t look like an accident or natural causes. “Yeah, I’m figuring she didn’t do this to herself. Any weapons found?”

“Not yet.”

“My money is on stab wounds in her back. This pose bothers me, feels staged and I suspect it was done after death.”

My eyes roamed the countertop and stopped on two plates with toast, partly eaten. Behind the plates were two glasses, half-full of milk.

“Where are her kids?” A chill ran up my spine as someone walked across my grave. I looked over my shoulder expecting to see a person standing behind me. There was no one there, yet eyes drilled holes into my back.

“We don’t know.”

I saw a ripped bag of some kind of animal feed leaning up against a wall. I lifted a handful of pellets and let them fall through my fingers, back into the bag. Chicken feed. Why would she have chicken feed?

“You seen any chickens?” I asked Lee.

His puzzled expression suggested not. “Should there be chickens?”

I indicated the bag by my foot. “Well, something must eat this.”

“Strange thing to have in an apartment.”

I changed the subject. “Who found the body?”

“Neighbor found her. Sam is next door with the neighbor."

"Well, that explains why I haven't seen him yet. I'll have a quick look through the rest of this place then head over to Sam. Which apartment?"

I was struggling not to puke and wishing I were Samantha from *Bewitched.* One good twitch from my nose and everything would disappear. I wouldn't even mind having Endora as my mother. I doubt I could stand being married to Derwood though.

"Fifteen, back one."

"Thanks."

I skirted the body and left the room. It didn't take me long to find out what ate the chicken feed. In a back bedroom, I found a small cage and a bedraggled bantam hen. Poor thing didn't have much of a life. The water dish was empty. I filled it in the cluttered bathroom next door. The hen stared at me with beady black eyes.

I stopped at the kitchen on my way out.

"Hey, Lee, there's a sorry-looking chicken in a cage back there. Please get it taken to the animal shelter."

"Will do."

I glanced at my watch – it was nearly morning proper. The watery yellow stuff leaking in through the ragged curtains must be sun. Damn, it got late fast. I chuckled to myself. My mind sent out a warning that this was all too unnatural and it was ready to snap at any moment. But no time for fractured minds; we had a sicko bastard to track down.

This was no copycat killer. Admittedly, when I first

heard about a murder with a poem it was easy to let my imagination be carried away and even propel me back in time. But Jack Griffin didn't pose bodies like this. He got his thrills by chopping them up and leaving them for me to find. I let go of an internal sigh of relief; at least I think it was internal. I glanced around quickly. No one near me reacted. Jack Griffin wasn't his real name, but I never thought of him as Charles Boyd. He was Jack Griffin, the invisible killer. A bad poet who wanted to be Shakespeare.

It was damn sucky that the sicko used my poem. I shuddered at the thought that some psycho had bought our book. I wasn't exactly bursting with joy about a Post-it note addressed to me, either.

That was all it took for me to find myself back in the kitchen confronting Lee. I remembered the look on his face when he smelled the chlorine; him not telling me what the note said. There was something he didn't want to tell me and I'd nearly let him get away with it.

"What did it say?" I asked, from the doorway.

He flipped back a page or two in his notebook and read aloud, " 'Special Agent Conway, Gabrielle – We need more chlorine.' "

"That's it?"

"Yes."

"Chlorine ... So I'm thinking that it's no coincidence that I could smell chlorine on the body."

"I'd say not."

"It's not concentrated; it smells more like she's been

swimming recently. Let's find out if she liked to swim and where."

"On it," Lee replied.

"I'll see you later."

I left the apartment, no happier and no closer to knowing what had happened inside.

Standing alone in the hallway outside number fifteen, images of the dead woman swirled through my mind. Vomit rose in my throat as I forced the images back into context, but I held it down. I clicked on Sam's number in the contacts list of my cell phone.

He answered on the second ring. "Hello, Ellie."

Caller ID was one of my favorite inventions. "Do you want me?"

"At the risk of losing my job ... you mean that in a professional way?" Sam quipped.

My eyebrows shot up. I was glad there was no one there to witness my surprise. "Yes, I do."

"Too bad."

It was hard not to laugh. "Yeah, yeah ... do ya?" I really enjoyed working with Sam and Lee. They had a way of maintaining a sense of balance and clarity no matter what was happening around them. Somehow it turned out that we always got the worst cases. I remembered my father dishing out wisdom when I mentioned a tough case once, 'We're not given anything on this earth that we can't handle.'

"No, I got this." He paused. I swear I could hear his mind working. Sam eventually said, "Unless of course you're still wearing that little silvery dress you wore to dinner."

"Jesus, Sam! It was platinum and that's Supervising Special Agent Chicky Babe to you."

"Is there anything you want me to do, SSA Chicky Babe?"

"Find out if the neighbor knows where the victim's children are."

"They went to their father yesterday for the week. Parents split over a year ago."

"Send someone to interview the father and the kids." I leaned back on the wall behind me. "Do we have a name for our victim yet?"

"Christine Campbell."

"I want to know if there are any prior police callouts to this address: domestic violence, loud arguments, anything in the backgrounds of either Christine or her ex-partner."

"Will do."

"Thanks, Sam."

"No worries, Chicky Babe."

"Sam," I warned, then laughed.

He struggled to keep his voice even. "We'll call you if we need you, Supervising Special Agent Chicky Babe. Go home. Tell Mac I said 'hey'."

"Will do."

"This has the potential to be a shitty investigation. Go back to bed, and get some sleep."

We had a murder to solve, which meant there wouldn't

be any sleeping, not yet anyway. It was sweet of him to care.

I slipped the phone back onto my belt and headed out into the weak daylight beyond the oppressive structure. More happened here than this murder. The building, with its once-beautiful stained-glass atrium windows, hid more violence than one attack. It had history. I wondered if the ex-partner knew anything about that history. That was certainly something I would be finding out.

My mind considered the lines of the poem as I drove home and took little notice of the emerging day as the words played in my head, as if on a looped video:

When the world has done
Lost in time too tired to run.
A safe place came to be.
Feeling your words surround me.

I wished I could remember the rest of the poem. I think it was called *Stolen.*

Mac's red Toyota Tacoma double-cab truck was still in the driveway when I arrived home. I was pleased to see it and happy to know he hadn't decided to go out. One glance at the time on the dash told me it was very early; apart from the gas stations and convenience stores nothing much was open, and where would he go? I sat in the car for a few minutes, resting my head on the steering wheel, while I tried to convince my face it wanted to smile.

Slowly I lifted my head, flicked my hair back over my

shoulders and checked my reflection in the rearview mirror. Satisfied that I had something resembling a smile on my face, I slid out from behind the wheel.

I gave the car door a kick and it clicked shut. Another Monarch flew by and landed on the back of Mac's truck, then flittered away into the woods. I felt eyes upon me and looked up expecting to see Mac watching me. A random sunbeam bounced off the house windows obscuring everything beyond. I could've sworn someone was watching. It had to be Mac.

Again, I checked the smile on my face. It felt okay; in a few minutes, it would settle and become real. Mac opened the back door as I climbed the steps and *voilà,* my smile was real.

"Didn't think I'd see you till tonight." He pulled me into his arms.

"Me neither."

"You okay?"

"Of course." Silly question! Anyway, he knew the answer already; when was I not okay?

"I've gotta do some stuff." I leaned back in his arms and looked up into his eyes.

"Want a hand?"

I shook my head vehemently, ensuring a hair sandwich for Mac. He extracted several strands from his mouth then smoothed my hair, sweeping it behind my shoulders again. "I'm home today. Let me know if you need help."

Unlike me, Mac usually had weekends off. We tried to make Sunday our day. It wasn't going to happen this

Sunday.

"Is there coffee?"

"Damn straight there's coffee; go settle yourself. I'll bring it." He kissed me and gave me a gentle push towards our shared home office.

I slipped off my jacket and hung it on the back of my chair then leaned across the desk and pressed the power button on the computer tower.

I yawned.

It'd been a long night; would be a longer day. I heard a muffled noise and recognized it as the kitchen phone ringing. A few minutes passed while the computer ran through its start-up sequence and I readied myself for work.

Coffee arrived with soft footsteps. "Here you go." Mac placed the steaming mug on the desk beyond my keyboard.

"Thank you."

"Mom called, she'll call back any second."

I glanced sideways at him. "Printer problems? Computer problems? The second coming of Christ at hand?"

Mac crowed. "No, this time she wants me to come over and string Christmas lights."

"O-k-a-a-a-y." His statement sank in, revolved around, and jumped back out. Nope, not even I could rationalize that. "In August?"

"It's mom."

"Silly me. That now makes perfect sense and that's all I needed to know. You going?"

He was quick to reply, “No. I said I was home today. It’s Sunday, Ellie, and I will be home.”

I saw something in his eyes, something I hadn’t seen before. There was something he wasn’t telling me. Whatever it was he had going on in his head was nagging at him.

“Mac?” I could hear that little voice, warning me against asking questions when maybe I didn’t want to hear the answer but, as usual, I plowed on anyway. “Is there something you want to say?”

“It can wait, Ellie.”

Obviously, it couldn’t wait or he wouldn’t look like he did. He was sad. That’s it. I found the look deep in my memory bank: he looked sad.

“Just tell me.”

“I’d like us to discuss the possibility of having our own children.”

He obviously wasn’t joking last night. At that moment, I saw right into his soul and I saw Mac as a child. I saw the vacuum cleaner pipe strike his head and heard his mother screaming obscenely as she brought the metal pipe down on his skull a second time. Damn! I pushed the vision away and looked up at Mac. “Okay, we’ll talk once this case is over.” No harm talking about it later. Much later. By then I was sure I could come up with clever and irrefutable evidence to dissuade this line of thought.

Mac smiled and pulled his chair over to mine. “So what have you got?”

"A nut job on the loose is a distinct possibility."

Mac's fingertips ran down my spine, distracting me with tingles of pleasure.

"I don't know what I have, not yet anyway," I said, taking the memory stick off my key ring. I plugged the stick into a USB card reader and opened all the pictures, one on top of the other. The last picture was a shot of the victim's face.

"Damn," Mac said.

"Yeah. This is Christine Campbell. And this is not how she thought her day would go."

"Damn," he uttered again. It wasn't like him to be lost for words.

"Check there is photo paper in the printer, will you?"

Mac scooted to the far end of the desk. He removed the plain paper from the printer and replaced it with photo paper from the drawer underneath the desk.

"You're good to go."

The printer hummed and whirred and the machine began to print.

Ten minutes later, we were studying the gruesome pile of photographs in silence. Twenty minutes later, my phone rang.

It was Sam.

"We have another similar crime scene. It's possible it's the same killer."

The edge in his voice told me it was more feasible than he intimated.

"I'm on it. Where?"

"Herndon. I'm sending the map to your phone."

"Thanks. Sam, notify local law enforcement. They invited us in on the other case, but now we need to direct this investigation. Let them know we're taking point on these murders. I think we have a sexual predator out there. Get someone to liaise with us from the local police. I want to make sure we keep everyone in the loop. We're going to need somewhere to work close to the scene. I want somewhere visible for anyone in the neighborhood to drop in with information." What was I searching for? The words I needed: what were they? From the blank hole where they should've been, they emerged. Mobile command. "Set up a mobile command center."

I leapt to my feet, dragging my jacket with me. By the time I'd struggled into it and was at the door I realized Mac was waiting with keys in his hand. "I'm driving."

I didn't argue. The prospect of driving in the morning rush hour traffic wasn't a pleasant one.

"You got your cell phone?" I asked, as I passed him in the doorway.

"Nope."

"But your mom ..."

Mac smiled. "What? Won't be able to reach me?" He smacked himself lightly on the forehead with the heel of his hand. "Duh!"

I had to smile. "Just tell me she doesn't have my new number."

Mac locked the door behind us. Spits of rain flew in the wind.

Chapter Six
Gotta Have A Reason

Revulsion washed over me, leaving a prickling sensation in my eyes. Mac turned slowly. His mouth opened then closed. His expression was one of horror, which he couldn't hide.

I squeezed my eyes shut, both to curb the sensation and to blur my vision. The smell of bourbon mingled with blood was overpowering and fresher than the last scene. The same spine-tingling feeling crawled over me. I looked at the deceased – maybe *she* was watching me. Kneeling on one knee next to the body, I breathed in. Chlorine again.

I whispered to the deceased woman, "Who did this to you?"

Gold ribbon was wrapped around her neck and tied in a pretty bow under her chin.

"Special Agent Conway?"

Startled, violently, I jumped to my feet. I stared at the woman's lifeless face, not convinced that she hadn't spoken. I half expected to see her mouth move as the voice repeated, "Special Agent Conway?"

As my heart thumped loudly I realized that the voice came from behind me. I looked over my shoulder and saw a uniformed officer. Not a ghost.

"Yes."

The officer stepped forward with a slight grimace on

his face. "Sorry," he said.

"It's fine, Officer. I didn't expect anyone to be behind me. You wanted me?"

"Special Agent Jackson would like you and your partner to join him outside."

"Thank you. We'll be right there."

"I'll escort you, ma'am."

Here we go with the ma'am stuff. I felt I should enjoy it while I was relatively young and it was somewhat flattering.

I shot a glance at Mac to see how he was faring. His greenish pallor suggested we should leave. I didn't want him to throw up and contaminate my crime scene.

"Let's get out of here," I said. "Sam is waiting." I slipped my hand into Mac's. "I needed to view the scene to satisfy myself we're dealing with the same killer."

Mac shook his head. "It's so much worse in person."

"Ain't it, though?"

We followed the police officer out of the apartment, down the narrow walkway and into the open air. It was difficult not to gasp as the fresh air hit me. The wind forced the stench from our lungs.

Rain spattered onto my face mixing with tears I couldn't suppress. I was grateful for the camouflage. I tried to lighten up by thinking of how something like crying would ruin my tough chick reputation. Well, it could, if I had one. That's something I should cultivate; maybe it should be my goal for the year. I could fully embrace my new role as SSA with a fresh new don't-fuck-with-me persona. My teeth sank into my lip as I curbed the urge to laugh. I didn't think I could do cold-hearted bitch.

The officer stopped just in front of a mobile command center parked at the curb. I could've sworn it wasn't there when we arrived. The door opened. A gust of wind caught it and flung it back against the side of the truck. The metal-on-metal clang vibrated through my head, setting my teeth on edge.

A booming voice came from inside. "Weather's turning. Come in."

Mac helped me up the steps, into shelter. The uniformed officer exerted a fair amount of effort and successfully closed the door behind us. I looked around the confined space. It was tight but reasonably comfortable. It was a good thing I'm not claustrophobic.

Sam handed us a coffee each and motioned for us to sit. Mac stepped to the side so I could reach a chair. It still amused me that none of them ever sat until I did. Chivalry was alive and well within Delta A; elsewhere it labored under emancipation. Sam gave Mac a light slap on the shoulder. I saw coffee slosh precariously in his mug.

"You okay?" he asked Mac, scrutinizing his still-pale face. It was rather unusual for Mac to appear pale. He had a hefty dose of Cherokee blood from his maternal grandmother and about the same amount of Black Irish from his paternal grandfather.

"Yeah."

Sam nodded and moved on. "We have a witness who

saw a male leaving the apartment."

I closed my eyes for a second. It was good news.

"Where is our witness?"

"Lee has her through there ..." he said and pointed to a door, partly open, about five feet from us. "They're going through mug shots."

"Credible?"

"Upstanding citizen, without as much as a parking violation in all her ninety-four years."

"Ninety-four?" I felt my mind whir. Do people live that long? In real life, did they actually live that long? Imagine that! How awesome to live almost a century. She surely had some stories to tell.

"Yes, ninety-four."

"Faculties?"

"Hearing aids; very strong prescription glasses; she was wearing them when she saw the male." He managed to say this with a straight face.

"She's sure about the male?"

"She said it was either a male or a butt-ugly woman."

"I like our witness already."

Without warning, my mind skidded over the appearance of the same writing on the walls, while trying not to take it personally. What if it was some kind of voodoo, hoodoo or black magic? What if using my poem could take something from me, part of my soul or something?

Sam gave me a knowing look. "Give!" He kicked my booted foot.

"Nothing."

"Bullshit."

Skirting the steaming verbal pile, I asked, "Who's the victim, do we have a name?"

"Laura Amos, a thirty-year-old teacher's aide."

"Was there a note for me anywhere?" I hadn't seen a note. Maybe he hadn't written one this time.

Sam nodded.

Damn!

I felt Mac's eyes boring into me. Maybe I should have said something about the last Post-it; I had pretended it didn't exist. So far it had worked for me.

I moved on and hoped he would too. "Has anyone done a statewide on the signature?"

"Not yet."

"I got a bad feeling."

"You want go national?"

"Yes. Load this into the ViCAP database; who do we know over there?" I stared at Sam, hoping to jog my memory and it worked. The *A-Team* theme song roared into life, bringing screen shots of B.A. Baracus, Faceman, Hannibal and 'Howling Mad' Murdoch. "Special Agent Murdoch."

Sam shook his head. For a split second I thought he'd heard the music too.

"Murdoch went, he's training recruits now."

"We know anyone else who can keep an eye on things for us?"

"Jamison went over from our division."

I'd wondered where she'd gone. "Cool, get hold of her

and explain the situation."

"I'll get on it, boss. Anything else?"

"Yeah, hit the backwater towns with faxes or emails or whatever they can cope with, circulate the signature as widely as you can within Virginia. I want to know if there are any unsolved cases involving gold ribbon, alcohol, rape or sexual assault, knife wounds and, most especially, any cases with poetry written around the crime scene. And chlorine ... what's with the chlorine?"

This killer had pulled together many elements to create something unique. These crime scenes didn't just happen. It felt like he'd been at this for a while, tweaking, perfecting his skills, deciding what worked best for him. The ribbon and the poem were not necessary to commit the murder. They were an important part of his signature. I didn't know if he needed the alcohol to commit the crime, if he drank any, forced his victims to drink any, or just liked to pour it around for effect. The chlorine was odd, could be signature, could be necessary – but I couldn't think how – or could be coincidence.

"You smell more chlorine?" Sam asked.

"Yes. Stronger than on the previous victim. It was like a thin fog around her head."

Mac spoke. "You are incredible; how you could smell anything over the bourbon and blood is beyond me."

"It was under it. It was an underlying aroma. Think of the smells at the scene as layers. The chlorine was first."

"Still amazes me that you can do that," Mac replied.

It amazes me that no one else seems to notice the

smells I do. "Do we know if our victim had kids?"

Sam spun to face a desk and grabbed his notebook. He turned back while flicking through several pages. He looked up and said, "The crime scene unit found evidence of children, two unfinished breakfasts and a school bag."

I looked at my watch. The kids should be in school.

"Find the children; see if our witness knows which school they attend."

A low buzz emanated from my belt. I stopped its vibration swiftly and checked the display on my phone. 'Unknown Caller' flashed above a number I didn't recognize.

"Mac, any ideas?" I passed him the phone.

He grimaced and sighed. "My brother, that's his work number."

We let the call go unanswered. Mac voiced my thoughts, "It's too early in the case for him to think he's been targeted by the killer."

We all sniggered unkindly. Now that's something I never wanted to see. An image of Eddie's overweight donut-stuffed body tied up with golden ribbons!

"You'd think," I replied. My mind was now playing reruns of the life of Eddie Connelly: Eddie the Hero; Eddie the Victim; Eddie on the Run; and all of it in his own private fantasy world. I halted the amusing memories; it wasn't the time. "Where were we?"

"I'll get on with a nationwide search on the signature," Sam replied, "while we wait to hear back about any possible felons or similar unsolved cases in ViCAP."

"Excellent. Stick a bulletin on LEO as well. Another

agency or law enforcement community may have something that ties in." In my opinion Law Enforcement Online is the best thing since Stephanie Kwolek invented Kevlar back in 1971. LEO is this groovy intranet for the law enforcement community. Everyone can keep in touch, send out bulletins and read updates to bulletins and announcements quickly. It probably saves as many lives as a bulletproof vest. I stood up and checked my watch. All morning I'd had this feeling there was something I had to do but couldn't narrow it down to a particular thing.

"I'll be somewhere," I said, unsure as to where somewhere actually was.

Mac, with an indulgent smile, said, "We'll be in Fairfax. You can reach us on Ellie's cell phone."

"Good to see you again, Mac." Sam shook his hand firmly. "I mean it, man. It's good to have you on board. You are in, yeah?"

"No formal request. It's supposed to be our day off, so thought I'd tag along."

"I'll get something in writing."

"Cheers, just let me know when you get sick of me ... I'll hustle on back to Cyber and get paid to spend all day on MySpace and Twitter."

Sam gave Mac a friendly jab to the upper arm. I knew from experience it was some male bonding thing and given more time and different circumstances, they'd wrestle each other to the ground or something equally grown-up.

Mac drove again and again I didn't mind. The radio

hummed underneath the whine of traffic. Mac leaned forward, cranked the volume and sang along as Bon Jovi's 'Have a Nice Day' blared forth. The volume did little to disguise Mac's voice. The next *American Idol* he was not.

He broke off from singing a few times to curse fellow drivers. The song gave way to the latest offering from Grange. My two favorite bands in a row – we'd stumbled upon a good radio station. I let my mind wander happily with the song and drift with the hunky lead singers.

More cussing brought me back to the present.

The car stopped. I expected Mac to leap out and accost whoever it was he last swore at, instead he opened my door for me.

He announced, "We're here."

I half expected *here* to be his mom's house but it was a parking lot. This was a confusing development. I looked around until I saw a sign that read Inova Fairfax Hospital. Which didn't help my confusion any.

"Why?" I asked.

Mac gave me one of those disbelieving looks. "Your appointment with the neurologist."

"On a Sunday?"

He may as well have spoken Manchurian for all the sense he made. I searched my memory and still had no idea what he was talking about, which I think he realized.

"Ellie ... it's a follow-up from your smack on the head last year."

Damn, we still on that? I thought we were over the

whole fractured skull/coma thing. I didn't remember having an appointment.

"On a Sunday?"

"We thought Sunday would be better than midweek, and the doc works weekends; who knew?"

"Oh, right, now I remember," I said, trying to sound convincing.

He grinned at me. "You still have no fuc'n idea, do you?"

"Not a one," I replied. "Works Sundays? Sees patients? Man, he's dedicated."

"He's seeing *you*. He's usually only here Sundays to do rounds."

We made our way to the doctor's reception desk and then through to the waiting room.

I sat. Stood. Paced. Repeated the cycle several times.

My watch said we'd been waiting for half an hour. Thirty-minutes! Surely, it wasn't that difficult to run on time; why didn't they just allow the correct amount of time per patient? I remembered what Mac told me about Leon working weekends. If he was only here doing rounds and to see me, then I really expected punctuality.

I checked my watch again. "Five more minutes and we're out of here. I don't have time for this waiting shit."

I leaned on the windowsill and glowered through the hazy film that had built up on the outside of the window. I knew Mac was grinning. I also knew he hated waiting as much as I did. My phone hummed once then silently vibrated on my hip. I checked it, hoping it would provide me with an excuse to leave.

“You’re not supposed to have your phone on inside the hospital,” Mac reprimanded, his voice barely above a whisper.

“Tough. I’m sure they’ll get over it. If we hadn’t waited so long we’d have been out of the hospital by the time he texted me anyway.”

He nodded, as if he agreed with me but I knew better; he was being agreeable.

“Who is it?”

“Caine, he wants us in the office A-sap.” I started for the door only to find Mac’s hand firmly on my elbow.

“No you don’t. You’re having this check-up.”

“A-sap,” I said, attempting to extradite my arm from his grip. “He said A-sap.”

“He’ll wait. He wouldn’t want you to miss this either.”

Damn! No escape.

A young nurse poked her head around the door. “Gabrielle Conway?”

Mac’s hand squeezed my arm, prompting me to reply to the nurse. “Yes,” I said.

She smiled, revealing teeth covered in colorful braces. “Dr. Kapowski will see you now.”

“Great.” I sucked in my impatience and tried to ignore the thoughts generated on seeing braces. Since when did they hire twelve-year-olds as nurses? “Excellent,” I said, and gave her a quick smile.

The theme song to *Doogie Howser, M.D.* rampaged through my mind as we followed the teeny-bopper nurse to the doctor's office. I finally succeeded in quelling the dreadful music with a deep breath and an internal 'Shut up!'

A door opened and the nurse stepped aside, allowing us room to enter. Leon Kapowski stood up to greet us.

"Mac, good to see you again." He leaned forward and clasped Mac's hand, giving it a good hearty shake, then turned to me. "Ellie, how are you?"

"Okay."

Mac's smile didn't escape me. I gave his upper arm a flick.

Leon gestured to the chairs by his desk. "Sit."

Surprisingly, his command wasn't accompanied by a hand signal. I had a quick look at my own hands; yes, I had hands, not paws. Opposable thumbs. No fur. I hadn't suddenly become a puppy in obedience school.

"Have a seat? Is that what you meant to say?" I spoke without barking.

"Ellie, please have a seat," Leon corrected.

We sat. The chairs were close enough for Mac to take my hand and give it a reassuring squeeze. I don't like doctors but Leon was almost okay. Maybe the green scrubs made him seem less scary. He looked very like Hawkeye.

Damn, I'd done it again. Now I'd be stuck in Korea. Rain, mud and misery, here we come. Why couldn't I have flashes from *Grey's Anatomy* or *ER*? Even *Scrubs* would be a step in the right direction. And why does it always have to be old television programs?

Leon sat behind his desk and read quickly over my notes. Then looked at me. “Is there anything unusual you’ve noticed, Ellie?”

“No.”

“Headaches gone?” He came around his desk, pulled a black pen-like object from his upper pocket and without warning, shone a super-strength light into my eyes.

“Until you did that.”

He stopped shining the annoying light. “Headaches gone?”

“Mostly.”

“You don’t make this easy, do you?”

“I’m answering your questions.”

“Tell me about these mostly-gone headaches.” He rested back on the edge of his desk.

“It’s no big deal ... migraine-type headaches, occasionally.”

“Describe what happens.”

“Oh ... I get a numb or tingling arm, some gaps in my vision, sometimes I feel sick, the pain is intense and usually only on the right side of my head.”

He nodded. “It’s not uncommon for migraines to follow a head injury.”

“So it’s no big deal, right?”

He frowned. “Normally it’s no big deal.”

I didn’t like the sound of that. ‘Normally’ had a nasty ring to it.

“Anything else I need to know about?”

Hawkeye never frowned like that. Doctors shouldn’t

frown, it's unprofessional. Why was he still frowning?

Leon reached for my file, flipped it around, and skimmed a few pages. He asked a series of questions. I answered as well as I could. If he'd asked them about Mac, I could answer in detail but I don't take much notice of myself. I know I should, but who has time? And Mac's so good at watching over me.

I nodded. "I'm fine." Mac nudged me and mouthed the word 'nightmares.' I attempted to silence him with a single crushing look but failed. My heart plummeted. Now the doc would ask me more questions. We'd never get out of here.

"Ellie?"

My mouth opened then shut before the words could escape.

"Ellie?"

I tried again and this time succeeded. "I have been having nightmares."

"I think that is understandable considering what you both went through." He paused and seemed to scrutinize me. I'm sure he did: doctors do that penetrating look thing that makes it appear as though they can see inside you. "How are you walking up or down stairs?"

Wow, didn't expect that.

"Stairs? Usually with my feet – one after the other in a vertical motion."

"Usually?"

"What? You've never felt the need to crawl up the stairs?"

Leon smiled. "No, have you?"

"Only when I'm really toasted." After a tequila session.

"Are you going to answer my question regarding the stairs?"

Mac squeezed my hand. Jeez! "Okay, look, a couple of weeks ago I had trouble walking down some stairs but that was because of a migraine the day before."

"Trouble how?"

Leaving the doctor's office anytime soon felt like a fading notion. "I couldn't see the edge of the steps and my balance seemed off."

He frowned again. He was less Hawkeye-cute when he frowned.

"Have you been walking into things more than usual? More klutzy than you used to be?"

Mac raised one eyebrow at me. He'd been telling me for months that there was something off about my sense of where I am in relation to objects around me. I had been telling him he was talking shite. I'd been subjected to him going on and on about how I am spatially challenged. I am not spatially challenged. I refuse to be anything that makes me sound retarded.

"Maybe."

Mac looked at me in amazement. "Maybe's ass."

"Okay ... I have more bruises from walking into desks than I usually do." I sensed the truth welling up inside me and spilling forth, unchecked. "I get dizzy for no reason and sometimes there's a ringing noise in one ear. Lying down makes the dizziness worse ... tipping my head also makes it worse. It seems to cause nausea. But it does go away. Then it comes back."

I'm a freak. I dumped a lid on the freaky stuff: no need to mention the odd sensation of eyes watching me at crime scenes. Who needed to mention dead people watching me?

"I want you to have an MRI and a head CT."

"Both? Isn't that overkill?" Something behind Hawkeye caught my eye: a teddy bear, a brown teddy bear lying on a shelf under the windowsill.

Oh, my. He wasn't Hawkeye at all; he was Radar O'Riley impersonating Hawkeye. No wonder he ordered an MRI and CT; he can't know what he's doing! There was no way he was a real doctor.

An uncanny fear gripped me. Maybe there really was something wrong.

The fear gave way to panic. I found myself standing. "I'm on a new case. I need to be at work now." I didn't have time to listen to someone who was obviously an imposter.

"I'm going to schedule the tests. I will get back to you this afternoon." He looked at my file again. "I have your work numbers and cell phone."

"Great, good, wonderful," I replied. Within seconds I was out the door, trying to find the colored line on the hallway floor that would lead me to the parking lot. Mac should've noticed he wasn't the real Hawkeye.

A hand grabbed my arm. "What?" I shook my arm to dislodge the hand.

"Honey, it's me." Mac slipped his arm around my waist. "It's going to be all right, it's just tests, no one thinks there's anything major wrong with you."

"What if there is?"

He grabbed my shoulders and spun me to face him. I staggered as my body came to a stop. "You're still Ellie, you're not a different person, no matter what the tests show."

"I don't want to have the tests." Then I remembered: this guy couldn't order tests if he was not a real doctor. Whew!

"I know, and I fully understand how scary this is. But it is better we find out if something whacky is going on."

How could anything be whackier than Radar impersonating Hawkeye? Why didn't Mac notice?

I decided it wasn't the best time to bring up the whole Hawkeye thing. I had a sneaking suspicion that I might be wrong about that. He may have been the real Hawkeye.

Mac whispered, "It'll be okay."

"What does he think it is?"

"Something called benign paroxysmal positional vertigo."

It sounded bad.

Mac kept talking. "They think it is caused by debris collected in part of the inner ear. It often follows a head injury. It is treatable. Leon said he'll do something called the Epley Maneuver and that should fix it. He wants to be sure nothing else is going on, hence the tests."

Somewhere inside me, I decided he was only saying that to make me feel better. If he knew dead people were watching me, what would he say then?

I breathed in his cologne, let the soft pressure of his hands melt away the panic I felt and fully believed him. Sometimes you've just got to have a little faith. It would be okay. Then I had the strangest feeling, as if I had missed something. I pulled back a little and looked at Mac.

He spoke quietly, "You okay?"

"Uh-huh. Let's get moving, we have to meet with Caine."

There was something else we had to do. Something important, that I couldn't put my finger on, nagged at me. I was sure a switch needed flipping somewhere.

Chapter Seven
Misunderstood

Caine's office door was open. I could see his cantankerous self sitting at his desk writing long hand, while his computer sat idly by. I knocked on the doorframe. Light reflected off the top of his balding head as he raised his eyes to mine.

"You made it," Caine said, sounding as cranky as ever. "What are you standing out there for? Close my door behind you."

It was very tempting to reach out, slam the door and walk away; but I resisted. We entered the spacious office. Mac shut the door behind us and took a seat next to me.

"You in on this, Mac?"

"Looks like it," Mac replied, with his usual calm assurance.

Caine gave him a stony look that an outsider would interpret as hostility – to us it was equivalent to a warm embrace – then turned his attention to me.

"How are you, Ellie?"

"I'm okay."

Caine's eyes narrowed to mere slits. "And again. This time the truth."

"I'm okay," I reiterated with more conviction.

I saw his eyes cut to Mac's then he let it go. "Who do we like for these new homicides?"

"No one, yet." I let my mind bring up the scenes, then

continued. "This feels like an escalation: whoever this is, he's been out there raping and assaulting women for some time and now that's not enough."

He rocked back in his chair, lacing his fingers together behind his head.

"And the words? The poem?"

"It's my opinion that he staged the scene before placing the woman in the center."

"What makes you say that?"

"The writing is fairly even; he took care and attention. Possibly he even copied the lines from something. He was in control." I smothered that thought with a fire blanket, not wanting images of our poetry book at a crime scene. "If he'd just murdered, I would've expected to see evidence of high adrenaline, maybe shaky writing and malformed letters. All we have to indicate his state of mind, is his self-control. He was calm and unhurried."

"Interesting observation."

"I get the feeling he had time prior to the arrival of the victims, time to stage his scene and plan everything. He was waiting for them."

"Mmmm."

"He also had enough time to position them afterwards, so he was sure no one was going to disturb him. Could have stalked them, or at least had them under surveillance for a short period."

Caine nodded but said nothing.

"I could be way off but that's my impression."

The hard line of Caine's mouth blurred. I recognized

that as his equivalent to a wide grin. "I think you're probably on track."

Nice to get a vote of confidence from the boss: enough of a boost for me to carry on with my observations. "Our killer has perfected his talents, he's experienced."

"You're doing okay so far, kid." The right corner of Caine's mouth twitched.

"Kids." I said. "You've just reminded me, both women had kids. We're still trying to locate the children of the second victim."

"Let's hope they're at school and safe."

I nodded. "Did you get a report on any weapons found?"

"No. The medical examiner copied us both on his pre-autopsy findings. He found stab wounds in the back and defensive wounds on the arms of both women. It appears that both the victims died from the wounds inflicted; they bled to death. From now on, all correspondence regarding these deaths goes to you and your team."

Bled to death. That phrase dragged out a word that all the crime shows like to throw out: exsanguination, the fatal process of total blood loss. We'd best stick to 'bled to death.' At least we can all spell those three words. I thought some more about our killer and opted to share my thoughts out loud. "He's organized: bringing his weapon with him, displaying the bodies, the writing on the walls, limiting our trace evidence. He knows what he's doing and he's taking his time to do it." I leaned back in the chair, then sat forward to stretch my back. "How'd he get in?"

"Tool marks were found on the locks of both victims' homes."

"So he may have lock-picking skills too. Isn't he the talented little freak?"

Caine slid a baggie across his desk at me. "Take a look at that."

I could see it from where I sat: a small paper evidence bag. I read down the chain of evidence documented on the front of the bag. Lee's writing was first, along with his signature, a lab stamp and signature, then Caine's. It wasn't a copy at all; it was the original evidence.

"I can see it."

He handed me a sterilized packet containing disposable forceps and a pair of latex gloves.

"Open the bag."

I put on the gloves, opened the bag and pulled out a piece of square blue paper with the forceps. It was the Post-it I'd heard about.

"Read it."

My stomach flipped as I held it in the forceps and read the words aloud.

" 'Special Agent Conway. Gabrielle, we need more chlorine.' "

I dropped the note back into the bag and resealed it.

"The chlorine reference is interesting," Caine stated. From his desk drawer he retrieved another bag. He dropped it on the desktop.

Again, I was in no hurry to touch it. My stomach

lurched, my heart sank and memories of a not-too-distant past flew into my consciousness. I didn't want to be there again.

"Take me off the case!" Even I heard the hysterical tone that edged into my voice but I seemed unable to prevent it.

He completely ignored me.

"Two messages, Ellie."

"I know."

Mac reached for a pair of latex gloves as Caine held them out. He took a fresh pair of forceps and opened the new baggie. "Is this a fluke? Or did the killer know Ellie would be working this?"

Caine spoke quietly making us strain to hear him. "All he could know was there was a chance Ellie would work the cases. The nature of the crime means we would be included. This falls within our task force perimeters and we're currently split between two other major cases, in Maryland and Georgia. With only Delta A still in Virginia, we don't publicize who is in which team."

Mac read the note aloud, " 'Gabrielle, cleaning takes time.' "

"That seems fairly personal to me," I muttered.

Mac lifted his eyes to meet Caine's. "Do you think he committed these heinous acts to get Ellie involved?"

Caine pressed his fingertips together. "We can't know that at this stage, Mac."

Mac's voice hardened. "Best guess?"

"It's possible."

"He uses her name!"

"Could be a fluke, could have easily used any of the agents' names in Delta team," Caine replied, his voice low and calm.

I listened as Caine downplayed the little detail of the notes bearing my name. He was doing a good job. I wasn't buying and I knew he wasn't either. The Unsub could've used any of our names. He could have; we're a high profile team. But he fuc'n didn't. He used mine!

"He had me with the Post-it. The use of a Post-it note has to be a blatant attempt at reminding me of the Son of Shakespeare case. That evil son of a bitch left messages on yellow Post-its for me, and now we have messages addressed to *me* on blue Post-it notes," I said. "You still want to sit there and tell me this isn't personal?"

Another thought crashed into the forefront of my mind. Why were we assuming this was a man? Okay, so women didn't usually kill like this. I decided to stick with the term Unsub and not label this killer male or female yet.

My body switched to autopilot and propelled me to the door. I jumped when Caine spoke, "Ellie, where are you going?"

Conscious thought took over again. I realized I was standing by the closed door with my hand on the doorknob. Freedom lay just beyond the pale-grained wood.

"I don't know, home maybe."

Caine's phone rang. I turned to face him, finding myself transfixed as the noise disrupted the air, causing ripples to radiate from the telephone on the desk. They covered Mac, the chair I had occupied and then flowed over me. As I observed the odd phenomenon, the ripples appeared to pass through the walls and disappear.

"Ellie, you all right?"

Mac stood in front of me. I didn't know how he got there.

"What's wrong, Ellie?"

Couldn't he see the noise ripple through the air?

I didn't know what to say. Why couldn't he see them? Then it occurred to me no one could see them but me. I had a sudden flash of this being way beyond eccentricity. Seeing sound? Madness loomed. He can't know.

Be okay.

I said, "I'm okay."

Caine interrupted. "Good."

I looked past Mac to see what was good. "What?"

"Good, you're all right. I can't take you off this. We got a hit back from the bulletin posted through Law Enforcement Online. I want you to go to Richmond. There was a murder forty-eight hours ago. It's similar to what we have up here now. View the crime scene. Speak to the next of kin ... the victim's husband. See what you can turn up."

The unearthly happenings in my head stopped abruptly. I refocused on the case. We had a hit. I swear one of the best inventions yet is the LEO system. Think MySpace or Facebook for police but not as pretty as MySpace and without the time-wasting applications of Facebook. Although, facial recognition software can be a real hoot.

"I take it they know I'm coming down?" Mac and I were both back in our seats, taking careful notes.

Caine nodded. "Mac, I'm going to have you assigned to us for the duration of this case."

He could have asked – Mac may not have wanted to be in on this case. He also could've run it by me first, in private. I didn't know why I wasn't thrilled to have Mac with me on this. I should be, damn it! We worked well together. He was fun, too. I was scrutinizing Mac's face for a clue to his real feelings when he nodded in agreement with Caine's plan.

"I hate to say this, but why? We have no need yet for specialist help," I said.

"Sam put the request in. It's easier to have Mac on board from the beginning than to drag him in and have to play catch-up later."

"That makes sense." If Sam thought we were going to need someone like Mac on the team, then okay. I remembered that Sam and Mac had spoken of this in the mobile command center.

I turned to Mac and asked, "You don't mind having me as your boss?"

His eyes sparkled. "I don't mind. I don't mind at all."

"Good okay, that's settled. It'll be great, just like old times." A cold shiver ran up my spine as the voice in my head hissed, 'Let's hope not.' I pulled myself together and pressed all reservations aside. My focus was the task at hand.

I remembered something else that needed looking into. "Has someone pulled the open case file for the rape a few months back, the gold ribbon one?" I struggled but for the life of me could not recall the victim's name.

"Lee mentioned it, ask him."

I nodded. If Lee mentioned it then he was bound to have all the information.

"Time to get moving," Mac said.

We stood and headed for the door but something made me pause. I turned back to Caine and asked, "Unless there was anything else?"

"Just one thing," Caine said. He stood and came out from behind his desk. "On behalf of the Bureau I would like to congratulate you on the formation of The Butterfly Foundation." He reached down to his desk and picked up an envelope, which he handed to me. "This is from the division."

I opened the envelope expecting to see a check for fifty bucks or so. Mac peered into it as I pulled out a personal check from Executive Assistant Director Owen. Our mouths fell open at the sight of the amount. Words seemed trapped as I tried to get my head around this incredible act of generosity.

Mac found his tongue before I did. "Owen wrote this check?"

Caine's face cracked, his lip curled, teeth showed: it was shockingly close to a real smile. "Yes, Mac. She's not all bad, you know."

"Wow."

Wow indeed. Hard-assed Owen had a heart. I slid the check back into the envelope. "We'll thank her later, then have the chairman do it officially."

I took the check out again and reread the amount: fifteen thousand dollars. With that and the funds raised at the dinner, we could set up many more school programs than originally planned.

I looked at Caine. He still bore the alarmingly real smile upon his face. "I suspect you had more than a little to do with this. Thank you."

Caine hugged me quickly then kissed my cheek. Over all the years we had worked together, Caine had once before surprised me with fatherly affection. It was unnerving, and yet not.

His scary smile faded back to a more acceptable grim facial expression. "It's a good thing you've done."

For the first time it felt like we'd made a difference. Out of the corner of my eye, I saw the paper evidence bags on Caine's desk. Suddenly making a difference wasn't enough.

Our next stop was the Butterfly Foundation offices. With a degree of relief, I realized my earlier thoughts of flipping switches were validated.

Something did need flipping; it wasn't just something I'd conjured earlier in my head.

***

The ceremonial turning on of the Foundation servers

that house the entire Foundation computer system took place in front of numerous journalists, amidst flashes of blinding light from cameras. Just what I didn't need: more blinding lights.

Afterwards I took dad aside. "I need to speak with you out of the limelight."

"My office?"

"Perfect."

Dad linked his arm through mine and mid-smile announced to the media throng that he was having a quiet word with his daughter and would return soon for questions.

He opened the door for me. "Do we need to sit?"

I smiled. "No, Dad, I just want to give you something from the Bureau."

I handed him the check. "But you might need to sit down before you look at the signature," I told him. "Owen wrote it."

He took it from my hand and read the print. "Owen the ballbuster wrote us a check?"

"Stunning, isn't it?" I said. "Best get that in the bank before she changes her mind."

He nodded. "I'll show Bob then we'll go to the bank."

"Good idea. By the way, I like your office."

I hadn't been in his new office before. It was spacious, wood paneled and highly polished. My mother would've loved it. He had a large leather sofa and a small coffee table in one corner. Directly in front of the door stood his antique mahogany desk. He'd had it moved up from

Richmond. On the wall behind his desk hung a family portrait, our combined family: dad, me, Aidan, Mac, Beatrice and Bob. We'd had the photograph taken at Christmas time. Notably absent were Mac's brother, Eddie, and his family. Absent because Mac forgot to invite them to the sitting. Can't say I blamed him. The other notable absence was my mother. I didn't realize I was staring at the wall until dad spoke again.

"You feel all right, Ellie?"

"Of course, Dad." I kissed his leathery cheek. "Why wouldn't I?"

"What did the doc say today?"

So everyone knew but me. Maybe I should pay more attention to my life.

"He said I'm nuts, Dad," I said, with much seriousness. "Nothing we didn't already know."

"No surprise there, then," he replied, raising an eyebrow.

"None at all." I perched on the edge of his desk.

"I heard something on the news about a murder this morning; they said it was the second in two days."

"They were right. I'm heading to Richmond today. There's a murder there that may tie in with these."

"You got this case?"

"Yeah. I'm Supervising Special Agent on this one!"

Dad gave me a hug. "Well done."

"Thanks. Now I'd better get moving. You walking me out?"

"Sure I am," dad replied.

Chapter Eight
The Fire Inside

Monday in Richmond was drizzly and gray. I supposed untimely death should be greeted by gray drizzle. It seemed fitting and more respectful than brilliant sunshine.

No matter how hard I tried to block out the sobs of the distraught husband, I couldn't. He met me outside his home. Crime-scene tape was still stuck to the front door. While he waited with his son, I did a walk-through. Once back out in the fresh air, I witnessed the torment of a broken man. Somewhere inside my mind I heard Elvis singing, 'Don't Cry Daddy.'

The little boy tugged on my jacket sleeve, his eyes pleading with me to help them. Elvis put on a fine performance in my head. His emotive lyrics filled my imaginary auditorium, bathing the mesmerized crowd with each sad and aching line. I stopped listening at the mention of finding a brand new mommy. Sometimes Elvis songs are real weepers.

I knelt down on one knee, bringing myself more or less to eye level with the child who wanted my attention.

"What's your name?" Please, God, don't let it be Tommy. He didn't look like a Tommy. Tommy's have sandy hair with pale, freckled skin and live only in Elvis songs.

"Dakota."

Bottomless coffee-colored eyes, shiny, straight black

hair and fine features on the pretty side of handsome. Most definitely a Dakota.

"I'm sorry about your mom, Dakota."

His innocent eyes looked into mine. "Daddy won't stop crying."

I wanted to scoop him up and fix his world but all I could do was dish out platitudes. I didn't have one that covered a murdered mommy. I opted for 'less is more' and said nothing.

His small fingers pointed to my gun. "Will you shoot the man who made my daddy cry?"

"That depends, Dakota; it depends what happens when I find him." I brushed tears off his cheeks and tried to steer him away from such thoughts. "I think you're very brave. Your mommy would be very proud of you right now."

Stones were digging into my knee. I straightened up.

Dakota's dad joined us. "I'm sorry. I'm not much help."

"Understandable, given the circumstances. Just know we're doing our best, Mr. Trevalli. If you think of anything, call me." I handed him my card. When he took the card from my hand, I noticed something in his eyes and followed a hunch. Maybe a different tack would elicit some usable information. "Had your wife been ill at all?"

"Ill?" He shook his head. "No, not really."

"Not really?"

"Julie is ..." He stopped himself and corrected his mistake. "Julie was bipolar."

"Was Julie taking her meds?"

He nodded. “Yes, she hasn’t skipped meds in four years.” He ruffled the hair of his young son. “He was her world. She’d never skip or stop her meds or do anything that could potentially harm Dakota.”

“Thank you. I’ll be in touch.” I shook his hand and offered condolences, “I’m very sorry for your loss.”

“Thank you.”

Dakota tugged on my jacket again. “What’s your name?”

“Ellie. My name is Ellie Conway.”

He took his dad’s hand; they began to walk away and then Dakota turned and said, “Goodbye, Ellie Conway.”

As I hurried back to my car I realized I didn’t feel the eyes here; no one was watching me. You’d think Julie’s spirit would stay around her little boy. If I’d felt the watchful eyes at the Laura Amos’s murder scene and earlier at Christine Campbell’s home, why not this one? That puzzled me. Almost as much as the faint smell of chlorine in the kitchen. The body was gone but the smell lingered.

Lee was waiting patiently, as he did. I liked working with Lee but couldn’t help wishing he was Mac. He was stuck in Fairfax with a family emergency. Eddie had struck again and sent the family into turmoil. I was sure it was more Eddie bullshit but as always, it had to be sorted out. By Mac.

“And?” Lee questioned as the door slammed behind me.

“This sucks. The husband is not much help, there is a child ... and I don’t have any fuc’n answers for anyone.

Something new came out, though: she was bipolar."

The engine rumbled to life and the indicator ticked on the dash. A few long silences and several bouts of irate curses later, we had crossed town.

Why is it that buildings in cities all end up a dirty, smoky, nondescript color? Is it so hard to make them attractive? The world should be pretty. As we pulled into the parking lot of the FBI field office on Parham Road I decided the buildings here weren't as ugly as others I'd seen, but then it's not exactly inner city. There is quite a large wooded area and even a school very close by. On sunny days the sound of children cheering and laughing on the baseball diamond floats on the breeze.

No one was playing today.

Lee's fingers tapped on the steering wheel as he formulated the question I guessed had been bugging him from the moment I got back in the car, "So is it the same?"

"I think so. I want to check the file. The writing on the walls was certainly familiar. The bourbon, the blood; I want to know about the body and the ribbon. I could still detect chlorine."

I dropped the visor down and flicked the vanity mirror open. With a quick touch of my index finger, I wiped away smudged mascara from under my eyes and ran my hands through my hair. "Okay, we're good."

Lee had already walked around the vehicle and opened my door for me. A violent gust of wind almost knocked me on my ass as I climbed out of the car. Lee's huge hand grabbed my arm. "You need an anchor."

"Thanks."

We made our way into the building and found the special agent who had attended the crime scene. He showed us photographs and produced a small note addressed to me, although he wouldn't have known it was meant for a fellow agent. The note read 'Gabrielle, cleanse the pool.' After viewing the evidence, I wrote my report and emailed it to myself, with a copy for Caine. My case or not, a copy always goes to the boss.

"Lee, did anything come of that old case?"

"The gold ribbon rape ...? No, they got the guy. He'd trussed the victim up like a freaking turkey with gold ribbon."

"Nice. At least that's not a forerunner to this spree then."

Something bugged me: for some reason I couldn't remember the rest of my own poem, so I didn't know where the words at this scene fitted. If this was an earlier death then why did the other crime scenes bear the first few lines of the poem?

It felt like someone had thrown jigsaw pieces up in the air and they were landing in random order. Now I was building the puzzle without the corners to stabilize it. It was also possible that it wasn't the same poem. I left Lee at the office and went back to our motel. I needed to clear my head and going for a run was about the only thing I knew would work.

I changed into my old academy sweats and running shoes then headed out to pound the rain-puddled pavement. The street was mostly empty of people. In the distance I saw a woman pushing a stroller. A courier pulled up near me and leapt from his van; within seconds he was gone again. The woman disappeared through a doorway, leaving me alone on the wet street.

My mind switched to autopilot, lulled by the rhythm of my feet. Every footfall took my mind farther away from the images of the child and his grief-ridden father.

A foot came from nowhere; I stumbled and missed my footing as I tried to step over the obstacle. The dark blue cap fell from my head, releasing a waft of lavender shampoo as my hair tumbled free over my face. In that instant I vowed to never use old-lady-smelling shampoo again.

As the forward momentum continued, my hair obscured the sidewalk and everything around me. I did a fair impression of Cousin Itt from the Addams family.

I thrust out my right foot, corrected my balance with several small steps and giggled to myself. "That was a near miss." I regained my composure and looked at the person who had tripped me. I must've been in my own little world to completely miss seeing someone else on the sidewalk.

He squinted. It gave him a porky, somewhat bloated, appearance. His cheeks rose almost to his bushy dark eyebrows, and his eyes resembled small puffy slits. He spoke with a thick Eastern European accent. "You're all right?"

"Yeah."

His dark eyebrows seemed out of place with the shock

of auburn hair on top of his head, then I realized then he was wearing a toupee. I looked away, hoping I hadn't stared. I hate it when I notice things I shouldn't, they somehow become my total focus.

He handed me my fallen cap and showed disconcerting interest in the yellow initials across the front and back that read FBI. The name on my sweatshirt, along with the FBI academy insignia, was revealed as I shook my hair over my shoulder. His interest in me made my skin crawl.

It took application to remind myself of the Sig-Sauer on my hip safely hidden under my sweatshirt. Extra effort was required to force myself to be polite and upbeat.

"Pleased to run into you, I am Ellie Conway." I proffered my hand and a small smile. With immense effort I stopped my eyes straying to his hair. The last thing I wanted was someone complaining that a person wearing FBI sweats was rude to them, especially when my name was plastered across my chest.

He frowned. The movement pulled his skin taut. He was a sausage about to burst. Someone stick a fork in him, he's done.

"Pleased to meet you, Ellie, I am Markov," he replied. His accent was his only interesting feature, which I picked out as Russian.

A large, fleshy hand came at me and swallowed mine almost completely.

I shook his hand. "Did I hurt you?" I scrutinized his face while extracting my hand from his greasy grip and sausage-like fingers. A memorable accent, a forgettable face.

He shook his head. I noticed tremors. Slight tremors in his fleshy hands.

He pointed at my chest. "Why the G?"

I looked down at my top which read 'Conway G.' "G for Gabrielle. I go by Ellie."

He stared longer than he needed to at the letters. "Ah," he said, still not looking away.

"Are you sure you're all right?" I asked. Something felt wrong. He appeared unduly shaken by the brief collision. Or was it that he appeared way too interested in me? He finally hauled his eyes up from my chest. I wondered if medication had caused him to swell up. I felt the need for a long hot shower.

"Yes, yes, I am fine," he replied.

"Good." I gathered my hair into a twist and jammed the cap back on my head, trapping the twisted hair inside. "I'll be on my way."

Markov nodded, making his chins wobble. The skin tightened even more as the wobble continued internally.

He's gonna blow.

I felt his piggy eyes on me as I set off running down the street dodging puddles, each step taking me farther from his unnerving gaze and dreadful toupee. A smile edged across my face. I staggered into the motel car park laughing so hard I could hardly remain upright.

Chapter Nine
Bitter Wine

I signed into the Butterfly Foundation website and then into the chat room as invisible. I didn't want everyone knowing I was checking up on them. All seemed fine: a bunch of kids were chatting about school stuff, and the moderators were watching. Something flickered on my screen, then I saw Mac's screen name pop up. We were invisible to everyone except each other and I wasn't surprised to see him.

Galileo: *What's up?*

I stared at his question in the purple chat box on my screen. While I was staring he typed again.

Galileo: *Ellie?*

Me: *Did you sort out the problem with Eddie?*

I waited as Mac typed for what seemed like ages. Finally the words appeared in the chat window.

Galileo: *He's left his wife; she and their kids have been over at mom and dad's bleating on about Eddie and what a loser he is. Dad wanted me to talk with Eddie. Mom is frantically stringing Christmas lights. I think she has smoked her way through an entire pack of cigarettes in the last two hours and, apparently, Eddie has a girlfriend.*

Me: *Can you come down?*

I could see my words on the screen: they screamed, 'There's a problem here!' And I wanted to erase them, wishing I hadn't been so quick to press enter. He had enough to worry about back at home. Hadn't I said he could take the rest of the day and try to sort it out? Yes, I had.

I needed him to focus on the case without all the drama going on back home and the millions of phone calls from his mom and brother. I also needed my right arm back. Something wasn't right with the case.

My phone rang. I snatched it off the table and answered it with a calm I did not feel, "Hey."

"Hey, yourself. Everything okay?"

I wanted to say, 'Everything sucks big time and I don't know what the hell I'm doing.' The words caught in my throat and somehow, when they broke free, they were different. Remarkably different. "Everything's okay."

There was silence for a beat or two, "Everything's okay but you want me to come down?"

"Yes." I was really struggling to tell him what was going on but the words were frozen on my tongue and refused to slip through my teeth. Yet again Mac needed to be a mind reader.

I heard him laugh.

"It's not funny," I grumbled.

"Yeah, it's funny. I'm on my way, babe," he said. "Everything's always okay. You could have a partially severed foot and you'd still be okay."

I needed a new word. I wouldn't be okay with a partially severed foot.

"Soon?" I sounded more hopeful than I'd intended, I missed him.

"Very soon." I could hear him moving about the house. "Want me to bring you anything?"

A suture kit to reattach my foot? I wriggled my feet. Neither of them seemed loose. Nope, didn't need a suture kit.

"A copy of our book?"

"I'll bring it."

I paced the room moving ever closer to the motel bed with each pass. "Would you bring my charm bracelet?" Would that protect me from whatever evil was running about killing and leaving parts of my poems? I had no clue but it sure couldn't hurt.

"Anything else?"

"I think that'll do it."

"And everything's okay?"

I bit back a smile. "Yeah, everything's okay."

"Luv ya, babe. Will be with you in a few hours."

"Love you, too."

I hung up and flopped back on the bed still holding the phone in my hand. Countless thoughts fought for priority inside my tired mind. I drifted off to sleep while watching them all struggle. In my dreams, I held a crazy hope that answers would materialize as if by magic and be waiting for me upon waking.

A loud banging at my door startled me from sleep. I stumbled getting up off the bed, tripping over a pair of shoes.

I kicked them out of my way. The banging continued.

I stood a few feet from the shoes, staring at them.

Kicking them should've hurt. Why didn't it? My eyes flicked to my feet; I was still wearing running shoes. I must've been tired to fall asleep with shoes on. Another loud bang made me hurry to the door.

Images of the bloated Russian with his bouffant hairpiece caused a shiver to run down my spine. Peering through the peephole, an eyeball peered back at me. The handle turned in my hand and the door swung open, letting Lee in.

"Took your time," he said, pushing the door shut behind him. He carried a brown paper bag in one hand; his jacket bore wet patches on the shoulders and his hair was damp.

"I was asleep." I wasn't apologizing, I was stating fact.

A giant grin spread across Lee's face. "I thought you would've been researching."

"I will be."

The delicious aroma of one hundred percent Arabica beans wafted from the bag he carried. I snatched it. It smelled so good as I unfurled the top. Inside I discovered two coffees. "Yes!"

Lee grinned. I didn't think he could grin any wider than he had already; I was wrong. "Do I know how to treat you or what?"

I took a cup and passed him the bag. "You're good."

We sat at the small table under the window on the far wall and drank our coffees in silence. After my last swallow I rocked back on the steel-framed chair and asked, "So did you come by to bring me coffee, or do you have another reason?"

"One block over from the first crime scene is another one."

I took a slow breath. "When was it discovered?"

"Half an hour ago. A neighbor grew suspicious and called it in. Apparently no one has seen the victim in three days."

"So this could be before Julie Trevalli was murdered ... and well before the Northern Virginia murders."

"Absolutely."

"You been over?"

Lee shook his head. "I got coffee and came here, thought we'd go together. We've got a weather situation out there."

And I knew I was having an eyebrow situation in here. I could feel my right eyebrow arching. "A weather situation?"

Lee's amusement resounded from deep in his throat. "I sounded like a dork, huh?"

"Oh, yeah." I tried to control my smirk. "Do explain this weather situation."

"Another storm warning. Hurricane Josephine expected to come inland at Virginia Beach within the next four hours. Already we have high winds and torrential rain moving up the state ... tornado warnings in four counties."

"How bad is it going to get?"

"Worse than last month's."

How long had I been asleep? Mac hadn't mentioned

another storm or tornado warnings. He shouldn't be on the road.

"Roads open or closed?"

"Coastal roads are open for evacuation purposes only. Main routes are open but being monitored closely."

I chewed my lip as I considered the news. "Okay, so it's just us then. You, me and Sam."

Lee nodded. "Until the weather clears it's just us." He smiled. "And Mac."

How did he know? "How?" I asked.

"Caine called me, said Mac was coming on down."

Mystery solved.

I stood, stretched, then pushed my chair in. "We best get over to the latest mess."

"Hope you have a decent jacket."

I looked down to find I was still wearing old sweats. I grabbed some clothes and hit the bathroom. It didn't take long to have a quick shower, dress, brush my hair and attempt to look like I hadn't been asleep all afternoon.

As soon as we stepped foot into the parking lot I understood why Lee had enquired about my jacket. Rain bucketed from the sky. I almost missed Mac's arrival with all the water driving into my face.

Mac met us by Lee's car. He gave me a quick hug, followed by a scrutinizing look. To which I replied, "I'm okay. Can we go?" My words swirled away in the wind. Rain splashed against my face, stinging my eyes. A person could drown in this weather. "Now?"

He swung open the car door, holding it firmly against

the buffeting wind while I climbed into Lee's car. The door slammed the minute Mac let go. Sheets of water poured down the car windows.

"Is this the weather issue you spoke of, Lee?" I asked, as the window wipers worked frantically to clear the windscreen.

"It's definitely weather," he replied. "Buckle up, this could get interesting."

It was almost a relief to reach the crime scene, only 'almost' because I knew what was in store. We entered the apartment complex together; dripping puddles onto the foyer floor. Two police officers stood on one side.

Lee spoke to one. "Can we drop our jackets by you two, please?"

The cop nodded. "Sure."

We left our wet jackets in a pile under the watchful eyes of the two young police officers.

"Crime scene that way?" I asked, pointing down a communal hallway.

Both officers nodded.

As I walked along the hallway, it began to feel like all the other buildings we had been in recently: oppressive, painful, way too dark.

A uniformed officer greeted us at the apartment door. "Special Agent Conway?"

"Yes. Do we have an ID on the victim?"

He read from his notebook. "A neighbor told us the apartment is leased to a Sophie Gendell, a thirty-four-year-old mother of three."

"Locate those children."

"Yes, ma'am."

I took a breath before going in. I wanted to hold it as long as possible, knowing the air inside the apartment would reek of bourbon, blood, and decomposition, all built on a thinning layer of chlorine.

The note was stuck to the cabinet above the meticulously penned first line of the poem. It was the first thing I saw when I walked into the room.

"I'm not loving this note," I said. I tried to exhale more than I inhaled. It was tricky. "Nice that I didn't have to go looking for it though; that was real considerate of our Unsub."

Lee and Mac stepped up beside me. Mac read it aloud, "'You could be a carrier, Conway.'"

As I saw it there were two choices: freak out at the note or get on with the job. The job won. More exactly the serene look on the face of the victim won. It wasn't the first time I had a sense that the victims didn't die screaming. That was something worthy of more thought. I stepped back and absorbed the ambience of the room. I pushed away the overriding smells from the bourbon, blood and none-too-fresh body.

The kitchen was clean. Countertops scrubbed. Dishes washed and put away. I opened a cabinet. Tidy. Boxes of cereal in a row. There were notes on the fridge, stuck by colorful magnets. Reminders for swimming lessons, soccer practice, hair appointments, the dentist. Then there was a photograph of the victim laughing with her children.

This woman was a mother. I got a sense of love for her children. And now she lay on her back in a pool of bourbon and congealing blood. Lines from my poem were written around her kitchen cabinets in black pen.

Flashes went off as the photographer did her thing. They reflected oddly in the thick blood pool, casting unusual patterns, swirls and brilliant spots of light with radiating beams. For a second I thought the victim would have liked the pretty patterns. The gold ribbon around her neck made the whole scene appear oddly festive.

"What do you think that means?" Lee muttered, sidestepping to get out of the photographer's way.

"It means this is becoming more personal," I replied. "Or it began personal and we're looking at it out of sequence."

My mind wandered back to a conversation with Mac in our home, the night of the fundraiser. The night he talked of children and I reminded him that our gene pool needed cleansing. Crime scenes with chlorine; notes suggesting cleansing; I am a potential carrier of mental illness. How could the Unsub know that?

"Timeline?"

"We can't be sure until forensics get back to us. But so far, this is looking like the first. So Sophie Gendell is victim one, then Julie Trevalli in Richmond, then Christine Campbell up in Alexandria and Laura Amos in Herndon."

I nodded. "How many days between Sophie and Christine? Just a guess, Lee."

He rocked on his heels, lines of thought working themselves into his forehead. "It's warmish, so maybe only a few days. No more than four, I'd say." The lines smoothed as he smiled at me.

"Four sounds about right." Satisfied that the Unsub didn't somehow overhear a conversation in my home, I turned my attention back to Sophie Gendell. This was not how someone's life should end. I knelt down next to her, carefully avoiding the blood and bourbon mix. I leaned as close as I could to her face and breathed in.

Chlorine.

I whispered, "I'll find the person responsible so you can rest in peace."

Mac's hand reached down to help me stand. "Did you say something?"

I straightened my jacket and shook my head. I noticed how none of us wanted to mention the new addition to the crime scene: an extra gold ribbon lacing the victim's mouth shut and tied off in a perfect bow.

What's with the fuc'n bows?

He'd taken time and care over this crime, more time than he'd taken at any of the others. There was an entirely different feel to it. But I couldn't explain that in an evidential way. Everything pointed to this being the first murder. This is where it started. A series of small electrical impulses caused my spine to tingle and the watching began. Eyes were following me yet there were none to see.

Chapter Ten
Welcome To Wherever You Are

Two hours later, we were on the road. Midnight had been and gone, but it failed to take the horror with it. Tuesday wasn't shaping up to be much better than Monday.

Lee and Sam were a half hour ahead of us because I'd stopped at the cemetery to visit mom. Amidst torrential rain and frenzied gales, I slogged through the darkness and located her gravestone; I confirmed she apparently was still in the ground. It wasn't really a visit; it was more like a curfew check. I conducted them periodically. It made me feel better knowing where she was.

We headed back up north. I hadn't intended leaving Richmond so quickly but the growing storm made delaying travel impossible. I hoped I'd garnered enough information from the crime scenes in Richmond to help our investigation. Poor Mac: packed a bag and drove all the way down to help out with the investigation, only to drive all the way back a mere couple of hours later. Such is life within team chaos.

A familiar tugging in my gut made me very aware of one similarity between Jack Griffin and this new sicko. He seemed to like to travel, to spread his crime scenes over a wide area. I restricted my thinking to the one similarity, because it was easier for my brain to digest. Any contemplation about these murders being personal would overload my delicately-balanced psyche.

My fingers played with the charms hanging from my bracelet and lingered on a small silver angel. Had I thanked Mac?

"Thanks for bringing this down for me."

"You're welcome. Why did you want it?" Mac asked, flicking the windscreen wipers on to high.

"Not sure, it just makes me feel better, I guess." I knew exactly why I wanted it. Each charm was bought for me by my father. Every time he went overseas the first thing he did was find a jeweler and buy me a silver charm. He carried the charm in his top pocket while he was away and put it on my bracelet when he got home. He always came home safe and sound. If one charm at a time protected dad, surely the whole bracelet had more power?

I didn't want the evil to get me.

An hour into our journey, with a murky, gloom-filled, wet dawn well on its way, rain was coming down in sheets. Twigs and small branches tangled in the windshield wipers.

"What's that?" Mac pointed up ahead. I thought I could see a red glow but couldn't make it out clearly. The wipers were going flat out and still I couldn't see much past the hood. Squinting into the dim light didn't help.

Suddenly I knew what it was.

"Tail lights!"

Mac's foot hit the brake. We both lurched forward, seat belts locked. The car came to an abrupt stop.

Offering a silent prayer to the ABS god, I hit the hazard switch at the same time as Mac. I grabbed a flashlight from the glove compartment and swung my door open. My clothes were drenched through within seconds. The sodden fabric clung to me as I hurried to the shape, which I'd determined was a car wrapped around a tree. I heard Mac call out from close behind me. "Ellie! You want road flares?"

I turned into the sheets of driving rain hoping my voice would carry sufficiently. "Good idea, grab them!" I yelled.

I reached the car and my wet hands slipped on the door handle as I struggled to open it. I kept slipping, almost going under the car several times. The ground seemed to be a giant mud slick. It was sucking at my boots and trying to pull me under.

I tugged at the door again. It wouldn't budge. I shone the flashlight in through the window. I could see someone inside and that the air bag had deployed and collapsed. An awful thought crept up on me: it could be Lee.

"What kind of car is it?" I asked, still fighting with the door.

Mac appeared next to me. "It's not Lee's car. Let me." He handed me his flashlight so he could use both hands.

I breathed a sigh of relief.

He braced himself against the back passenger door and tried forcing the door handle up; the handle lifted but the door didn't budge. Mac shoved his fingertips into a gap at the top of the door and pulled; the metal groaned but stayed fast.

"Crowbar?" I suggested.

"Trunk," he replied. "I'll get it."

He turned then stopped by the back door, which was unscathed compared with the front of the car, which was a twisted wreck.

"Shall I draw you a map to the trunk of your own car?"

A wet finger flew in my direction. "One sec." He pulled the rear door handle, the door sprang open. Mac disappeared into the car.

I pulled my cell phone from my wet pocket and punched in '911'. As the operator answered, the driver's door screeched then popped open. Perfect timing: I had zero clue where we were. I knew at some stage we'd left the highway but my tired mind couldn't recall when or why.

"Mac, what road is this?" The irony of the question didn't escape me. I was asking a directionally-challenged person where we were.

Sometimes I have no idea what goes on in my head.

He climbed out the passenger door and took the phone from me, shaking his head and saying, "This time I do know where we are." There was a touch of surprise in his voice. Directions weren't something I usually had to ask for, let alone something he was usually able to give.

Something was very wrong. I leaned closer to him. Rain poured, taking the scent of chlorine with it.

I grabbed the phone back from Mac and spoke into it. "There is chlorine present at the scene. You will need hazmat gear with self-contained breathing apparatus for the body recovery. We have no way of knowing how potent the chlorine is or the quantity involved."

The voice on the phone confirmed what I'd said and hung up.

Mac stared at me. "I didn't smell it!"

"It's all over you. You have spare clothes?"

"Of course. How bad is it?"

"Take your clothes off, all of them ... and thank God it's raining hard."

He looked at me in absolute horror as he began peeling off his saturated clothes. I returned to our car and found him clean stuff from our bags, plus a large plastic bag for his contaminated clothing.

"How bad, Ellie?"

"It's highly toxic and irritates the respiratory system. It can form hydrochloric acid inside your lungs by reacting with the water in the mucosa." Take no prisoners. "It causes burns especially to eyes, mouths, airways. It's also flammable; just add a spark and it's an instant firebomb."

"And it's in our drinking water and our swimming pools?" Mac said. "That's just fuc'n fantastic."

"At safe levels."

While pondering the scariness of the strong chlorine and Mac's inability to smell it, I donned two pairs of latex gloves – not easy to do in the rain – and went to have a look at the car. Chlorine gas is heavier than air and settles low. I attempted to reach the driver's side of the wreck and slipped in the mud at the edge of the road. Hauling myself back to my feet was difficult. Mud covered my jeans and tee shirt and it began to act like sticky body armor, causing my movements to stiffen as my clothes grabbed my skin.

I stood by the driver. I knew I couldn't bend down near him, because a greenish gas was visible about his knees. His body smelled strongly of chlorine. His head was turned, facing away from me. The airbag was fully deflated so it was easy to reach him. I noted he wore his seat belt.

"Sir?"

I shook my hand hard hoping to dislodge some of the mud. The charms on my bracelet sent mud in all directions. I reached into his neck and felt for a pulse.

I couldn't feel anything.

Moving my fingers under his jaw, I tried again.

Nothing.

I went for his wrist.

"I can't find a pulse."

I sloshed away from the car. The smell was unbearable; it began to irritate my nose. A large puddle near the rear tire gave me somewhere to wash my gloved hands. I didn't want chlorine on me, no matter how little.

I felt Mac's hands on my shoulders. "Police and ambulance are on their way with a hazmat team and all the gear. There are landslides and flooding, so some parts of roads are blocked with debris ... might take them a little while to get through."

"Can you smell it now?" I asked. With the car door open, gas was leaching out into the rainy atmosphere, drifting under the car and around the front tires.

"Yeah, smells like a swimming pool."

"Did you notice anything about the body?"

"No."

"Why was the driver looking at the passenger seat? Maybe he turned his head instinctively on impact – but what if there was a passenger?"

I looked up at Mac; rain ran into my eyes as I did so. It stung. It really stung. The rain had washed the leave-in conditioner from my hair into my eyes. I found a moderately clean piece of my shirt and wiped some of the tainted water from my eyes.

"Was there a passenger?"

Mac disappeared, then reappeared on the other side of the car. He opened the front passenger door with surprising ease and more gas wafted to freedom. "This door wasn't closed properly. Bag's deployed as it would in a crash, but no one is here. Curious, no?"

I joined him, the beam from my flashlight playing upon the front console, allowing me to inspect the airbag. "There's something there."

The smell was too much; after a few seconds I pushed the door shut and pointed through the glass. "See that?"

"Hairspray? Is that what that is?" Mac asked.

"Looks like it. Strange thing for a guy with very short hair to have," I said. He didn't look like the hair product type. I don't know exactly what that type is, but it wasn't him.

"Look at the bottom of that canister."

"It's been blown off ..."

"What would cause that?" Mac asked.

"A small explosion."

I went back to our car and found an umbrella. With the umbrella up to shield my phone from the worst of the rain I used the integral camera to snap pictures of the canister and the driver. I had a good view of the driver's face from this angle. There was a long gash down the side of his face, open to the cheek bone. Blood had run down his neck, soaking into his collar and shirt. The whole side of his face was discolored by blood and bruising was evident across his temple. I determined he was hit by something, maybe a few times. These weren't crash-related injuries. I'd heard of air bags breaking people's noses before but not doing this much damage to a face. I took a closer look at the picture I'd taken of the canister. To me it looked as though the bottom of the canister could have caused his disfiguring cut and maybe the bruising. There wasn't much to see on the canister, which probably had blood and skin tissue prior to the bottom blowing out.

Mac's shoulders dropped as he sighed. "Okay, so it's possible there is a passenger, maybe female, wandering around in this storm."

"Damn!" I surveyed the saturated ground. The heavy rain would have washed away any footprints. I scuffed my foot in the mud, uncovering a glimpse of something shiny. I reached down and picked up the object.

"What is it?" Mac asked.

"A lighter ... a Zippo lighter." The lid was open and the wick full of mud. I wiped one side as best I could on my shirt. "What do you think this is?" I asked, showing Mac the etching I'd uncovered.

"A two-headed eagle," he said, after careful inspection.

"Wonder if it belonged to someone from the car." I looked around for something to put the lighter in. Mac held out his hand. Problem solved. "I doubt there'll be anything useful on the lighter by way of DNA or prints, but you never know," I said. Something else in my head pushed forward. "If someone was injured, got out and walked away from this accident ... why bother to close the door?"

"Instinct maybe; it wasn't properly shut, just pushed to. You get out of a car and flick the door behind you," Mac replied. "Well, I do and I know you do."

It seemed reasonable that this person did so too, or they were in a state of confusion and had no idea what they were doing.

"If you'd set off a chlorine gas delivery system you'd be getting out too fast to be worrying about doors."

"What?" Mac said, with as much horror as a single word can convey.

"Could be my imagination. Or it could be that the hair-spray is a clever way of getting weapons' grade chlorine into the country. I've heard of it before." I ran my hands through my hair, pulling it back off my face; the gloves grabbed and pulled my hair. I peered in through the car windows.

"You've heard of it?" he replied. "You know what, for-get it, I don't want to know how you hear of these things."

I was looking for something that might tell us whether we were looking for a male or a female. I found a handbag on the floor in the back, the contents spilled across the floor. Maybe it happened as the person went for the hairspray.

"That's a passport." I said, pointing. There was no comment. I looked at Mac to find him walking back towards me with latex gloves in his hand.

I watched as he pulled both pairs onto his wet hands, one atop the other. Difficult at the best of times but it helps if you display total concentration.

"I bagged the lighter," he said, then opened the door. I thrust my hand in and snatched up the passport.

I photographed it and had a quick read. "Selena Onslow from Canada. Aged thirty-three." I threw the passport back into the car and slammed the door.

"Want to try the driver?" Mac asked.

"Yep."

Already had gloves on and I couldn't see a problem; the gas was most concentrated on the floor of the car. I could see wisps of greenish-yellow cloud. I didn't need to bend down or get anywhere near the toxic cloud to check the driver's pockets. I made a rapid search of the driver and the glove compartment, netting a wallet and a passport.

"The driver appears to be Jacob Riest from New Zealand," I said holding the passport up to show Mac. There was little resemblance between the picture in the passport and the dead man in the car. Mac took pictures. I glanced at the picture again. I thought I'd seen him somewhere but knew I hadn't come across any New Zealanders recently. I tossed the passport back into the car.

I ripped off the gloves and tossed them in the bag with Mac's clothes. The umbrella was rendered useless by a large gust, its spokes sticking out in all directions, the nylon ripped. I shoved it in the trunk of our car.

I needed to get out of the rain for a while, so climbed into our front passenger seat. Mac got in the driver's side.

"We're going to make a huge mess of the interior," he said, shutting his door and leaning back against the seat.

"Not much we can do about that," I replied. "We're looking for the chick, so we should get to it."

"And she potentially set off chlorine gas? Do we really want to do this?"

I shrugged. "Not especially ... but she could be hurt."

I called Sam and Lee to let them know we were having a quick look for a potential crash victim, who may or may not have set off a chlorine bomb in a car. They were understandably concerned. So long as they knew where to look if something went wrong, I felt okay about the situation.

We had perhaps twenty feet of visibility if we were lucky. Woods ran along either side of the road. I loved the experience of a wet and wild late summer and the effects of yet another hurricane. Wind whipped up puddles of water and mud, tossing it all at the car. Dawn wasn't really happening but it wasn't dark either. The road was lost in an ethereal murk that failed as both night and day. A hefty tree branch slammed against the wrecked car.

I wouldn't want to be wandering around, injured, out there.

"Let's see if we can find this chick, then," Mac said, as he checked his weapon.

I nodded. "We're already wet through; may as well keep going." My flashlight flickered. I smacked it on my hand. The beam brightened then faded. "Let's get fresh batteries for this."

He leaned over and kissed me. "First, change into a dry shirt and put on a jacket."

"Yeah, good idea."

I glanced down at my legs. I was caked in mud. Rivers of it ran from my legs to the floor. I squelched with every movement, no matter how slight. My backside stuck fast to the seat.

Mac leaned into the back of the car and found me a dry shirt from an overnight bag. A portable shower would be handy, especially with the chlorine. But I figured the rain would do a good job of rinsing us off.

We had started leaving an overnight bag in the car after the Jack Griffin case. During that case, I seemed to be bootless and semi-clothed more often than not. The longer we were together, the more like MacGyver Mac appeared to be. I happen to know he does carry string and gum in his pocket and there's duct tape in the glove compartment. I've seen him remove a magnet from a car stereo speaker, attach it to a piece of string and use it to find a key in long grass.

He changed the batteries in my flashlight while I changed my shirt. It literally peeled away from my skin. I held the shirt out the door and wrung out as much water as I could. I think I could've filled a small bucket from the run off. I balled it up and shoved it in the plastic bag with the other clothes. There was no point changing our mud-saturated jeans until we'd found the woman. We donned waterproof jackets and caps to keep the rain out of our eyes.

With the crash area lit by road flares to warn of the hazard and to guide the emergency vehicles, we headed farther down the road on foot. It was a toss-up; she could've gone either way, but we chose to go down the slight rise we were on. Down seemed easiest for a crash victim possible murderer. The longer we searched, the more the hairspray and the dead guy played on my mind.

Every so often Mac called, "Selena."

After half an hour of slogging through muddy puddles, being hit by branches and whipped by wind-driven rain while peering into undergrowth yelling for Selena, we turned back.

"Do you think someone could have picked her up?" Mac asked, shining the flashlight into the trees alongside the road on our way back.

"I'd like to think so, yet I hope not for that person's sake." Ahead, I could just make out red flashing lights. "Let's tell them about the missing woman and get the hell out of here."

"Good plan."

I had a queer feeling about the dead guy and had one last look at him before we left. It could be paranoia considering our alert status, but there was something about him. I used my cell phone to snap another quick picture of him and promptly emailed it to myself with a note to run it through our database. He was familiar, but then on a day-to-day basis I came across a lot of people and they did tend to blur sometimes. It didn't bother me too much. If I'd met him and my mind deemed it important, then I would remember. A little faith goes a long way.

Mac grinned at me as I dripped into the car. I smiled as I asked, "How the hell did any of us manage without picture and email-capable cell phones?"

"No clue." He turned the ignition key.

I waved to one of the officers as Mac drove slowly out of the crash scene. People in hazmat suits and breathing gear headed for the crashed car and a decontamination shower was being set up. I'd pointed out the hairspray and suggested they have forensics look at it closely. I'd also handed over the clothes Mac and I had worn, for destruction; then gave the bag with the lighter to one of the police officers. I was confused; it had a Russian emblem but according to their passports, neither victim was Russian.

A decontamination shower was offered to us. Then someone in a hazmat suit suggested it wasn't necessary. We'd been in pouring rain and changed our clothes; that, combined with minimal exposure to a gas that was already dissipating, meant we were at low risk from any side effects.

Which pleased me. I had no desire to stand under freezing water, naked, surrounded by half the county.

My phone rang as we were leaving the crash scene. Sam's name lit up on my screen.

His deep voice flowed from my phone. "We got another one, SSA."

"Where?" The phone slipped in my wet hands, leading to some impressive juggling before I could get it back to my ear, but I wasn't quick enough to hear his reply. "Say again."

"Arlington."

"On our way." I hung up and looked over at Mac. "We're going to Arlington."

"Good to know we have a destination."

The victim wouldn't get any fresher the longer we delayed our arrival. I really wished I didn't think things like that.

Almost two hours later we struggled to change out of our sodden clothing under the shelter of a deserted gas station forecourt. It was morning and the weather hadn't improved much. Peeling off the wet jeans proved difficult. With my foot stuck in the muddy mess that vaguely resembled denim, I reached into the car for something to help. Using the scissors on a multi-tool thing Mac carried in the glove compartment, I hacked my way through the stiff fabric. All I seemed to do on days off was shop for clothes to replace those ruined by the job. I hate shopping.

"I could've helped," Mac said, stowing his filthy clothing in the trunk.

"I'm perfectly capable of removing a pair of stupid jeans," I replied. I threw the multi-tool into the car.

"Or you could've changed in the restroom."

He was full of brilliant ideas all of a sudden.

"Ever been in one of them? There isn't enough room to swing a cat, let alone for me to wrestle muddy jeans."

He threw his hands up in mock surrender. "Just trying to help."

I tugged off the jeans then faced the muddy leg problem: no way clean jeans were going to slide over mud. I scurried to the restroom with my clean jeans tucked under my jacket and Mac's laughter following me.

I gave thanks as I discovered the crappy gas station restroom had running water and paper towels.

Slightly cleaner and more comfortable, we continued our journey.

Thirty minutes was all it took and then suddenly we were in the latest victim's kitchen staring at each other. We'd seen this sort of mess before: a kitchen awash with blood. A familiar voice inside my head told me it wasn't my kitchen and everything was okay. Seems kitchens are favorite kill zones of the Unsubs I investigate. The overwhelming smell of bourbon was enough for my mind to stay focused on current kitchens and not drift back to my own. I looked back over my shoulder to the doorway.

"Who's been in here?"

A large cop stood in the doorway with his arms folded and a serious look on his face. He replied, "The neighbor who found the deceased; no one else, ma'am."

There were clear, bloodied footprints leading from the victim through the door to the hallway beyond. "These footprints, are they the neighbor's?"

"I inspected the woman's shoes and found the pattern to be the same; I've taken them into evidence to make sure."

I smiled. "Good answer."

He smiled back, his teeth glowing against his tanned face, the staunchness evaporating. "The victim is Colleen Bolton, mother of two girls and a full-time waitress. The children are aged twelve and fifteen; they're at school band practice. I've spoken to a neighbor who will take them until Child Protective Services can locate a family member."

He loved his job, I could tell.

"Thank you, Officer."

"Is this the same as the other crime scenes?" Mac asked. His eyes were watering from the unusually fresh tang of bourbon mixed with the more metallic smell of blood.

I inspected the body and glimpsed my reflection in the crimson blood pool. It might be cool to have red hair.

Mac was talking but I didn't hear the words. "What?"

"Is this the same as the other crime scenes?"

I turned slowly on the spot, surveying the room with much care. Writing on the walls surrounded the body;

the wording was familiar and again scrawled in black marker pen. I made a note to check the poem. I felt the eyes drilling into me from up high behind me. A blue Post-it note was stuck to the refrigerator; a lone blue square amidst a sea of magnets and white school notices. I could clearly see the words on the note from where I stood.

"I feel so loved," I pointed to the blue note.

Mac read it out, " 'Christmas in August just for you.' "

Turmoil and aggravation dueled as I processed the spoken words. Hearing them out loud was so much worse than just reading them.

"What hellish shit is that?"

"I think he likes you," Mac replied.

"I am so damn lucky," I said and turned to observe the victim.

The body was in the same position as all the other victims; on her back with her knees raised. Blood and bourbon mixed on the tiled floor. A golden ribbon tied around her neck in a pretty bow and this time her eyes were laced shut and tied off with more gold ribbon.

"Your question before, about this being the same as the other crime scenes: yes and no," I replied, taking a closer look at the body. As I breathed in the now-familiar chlorine, I could see something lying almost obscured under the woman's right shoulder. "Mac, I think we have a murder weapon."

I looked back and spoke to the policeman. "Have the forensics team and photographer arrived yet?"

"Yes, ma'am."

"Send them in, please."

We waited for the photographer to finish with the body and scene. Then the forensics team began to gather evidence.

"Anyone got a pair of forceps?" I bent down and with my pen flicked out what looked like a handle from under the woman's shoulder blade, until it was in plain view.

A technician handed some green disposable forceps to me. "Ma'am."

"Thank you." With care, I lifted the knife, hoping it didn't drop. The eight-inch blade glinted under the electric light. I watched fascinated, as light reflected from the blade, casting shapes on the walls. Little bright shapes danced, reminding me of a migraine aura. The knife spoke, whispering instructions: 'Hold me Ellie; let me show you how it's done.'

The hilt jerked. It almost slipped from the forceps. 'Wrap your hand around me, Ellie.' It wanted to slide into my hand and guide me. Sparkling lights danced. The knife plunged into the back of a woman, released, stabbed again. The lights faded. The knife remained suspended in mid-air.

How bizarre.

Mac held out a paper evidence bag with an uneasy look on his face.

"You want to drop that in here, handle first?"

"Nope." Why should I? I found it. It spoke to *me*.

"Ellie?"

Jeez!

"Fine." I reached out and carefully let go of the knife over the bag. I watched it drop and wondered if it'd go right through the paper. It didn't.

He inhaled sharply as he secured the top of the bag.

"Thank you."

For a split second, I thought I saw relief in his eyes. How odd.

"You're welcome," I replied.

"Why do you suppose her eyes were shut like that?" Mac asked.

"Maybe he's bored with the whole ribbon around the neck thing." I stared at the deceased. "Last time we had a mouth laced shut, now eyes ... I'm thinking this is a message. Or maybe our Unsub likes to pretty them up with ribbon."

Mouth and eyes laced shut ... smacked of those three monkeys, hear no evil, see no evil, speak no evil.

"Could well be," Mac replied. He was scanning for a tech to take the bag and its bloody contents.

I leaned closer to the victim's head and sniffed her skin to make sure I really could smell chlorine. Seemed like I was being stalked by the damn gas. "Chlorine."

"Pardon?" Mac said. "So it is the same."

"I can smell chlorine in her hair; it's faint but it's there. So yeah, we have all the elements. I believe this is the same Unsub."

We left in the same dreadful weather that heralded our arrival. A grey blanket of gloom, buffeted by wind and debris.

Chapter Eleven
Story Of My Life

Once back at the Washington office, my mind began to run over the night's events and kept stalling over the crash. No amount of prodding would budge it, even though I had more pressing matters to work on. Elvis started up all over again. This time 'Trouble' was his choice of song and I had a feeling I was looking for trouble. On second thoughts, the feeling was more that trouble was looking for me.

In an effort to clear it from my head, I decided to talk it over with Mac.

"How did he die? The bag deployed and he was wearing his seat belt. His legs weren't even trapped, for God's sake. His face was a mess but those weren't life threatening injuries."

Mac took a split second to catch up then shook his head. "Guess the crash investigators will figure that out."

"Guess so," I replied. I stood up and moved out from behind my desk. Mac was looking at the timeline for the murders on the white board across the room. He turned and faced me as I perched on the edge of my desk.

"It does seem unusual though."

"Maybe he died before the impact, of a heart attack or something. Do you know how long chlorine gas takes to kill someone?"

Mac stepped forward and wrapped his arms around

me. “I do not.”

“Depending on the grade and its intended use, it could take only ten minutes. But why would someone continue to drive a car filling with chlorine gas? It’s not like it’s invisible or doesn’t have an overpowering stench ... he must’ve been incapacitated prior to the release of the gas. Probably by the blows to his face and temple.”

“This is going to bug you till we find out, isn’t it?”

My head rested comfortably on his shoulder. “Yep.”

“We’re gonna do something about it, huh?”

“Yes.” I pulled back a little. “We are.”

“What do you have in mind?”

“Some answers.”

“And how are you going to come by those?”

“I’m not entirely sure at this point but it will come to me.” Thoughts were already crystallizing. My lower lip was in danger of being chewed right through. “Does it strike you as odd?” I recognized it probably didn’t seem odd at all to him. “He is a New Zealander, she’s a Canadian and here they are traveling together in Virginia?”

Mac appeared thoughtful for a second. “The world’s not that big a place anymore, sweets.”

He gave me one of his you’re-going-somewhere-with-this looks. His eyes gleamed. I knew he thought I was onto something.

“A clue?” Mac said.

“I am interested to know when and where they came into the country, if they were together or, if not, where they met up. I think it’s also worthwhile checking with the embassies," I replied.

His eyes narrowed as he continued to watch me. "Why?"

"Because, Mac, both New Zealand and Canada are considered safe countries by our State Department. Citizens holding those passports can travel here freely," I said.

"And?" Mac asked.

"And in the recent past Mossad have stolen both Canadian and New Zealand passports."

"Israelis?"

"Yeah," I said, with a small nod.

"Ellie, why would Mossad agents be traveling on stolen passports in Virginia?"

"It's something they do if they are following someone, to avoid drawing attention to themselves or the person, or cell, in question."

"I know you are a chick an' all and given minimal facts, are capable of constructing a life story ..." Mac chuckled and ducked before I could smack him, "... but even for a woman this is way out there, babe."

I attempted a sulky, wounded expression but couldn't pull it off. "Homeland Security bumped up the security alert to orange two days ago, saying there was sufficient intelligence coming out of Afghanistan, indicating an attack was possible ... and we come across a car crash and the dead guy, interesting passports, a missing victim and chlorine gas." I stopped abruptly.

Chlorine gas. I knew I'd read something about

weapons' grade chlorine. Russian. Maybe it was in a reference book or a James Bond-type novel. Then I remembered: it was a documentary on unusual assassinations and carrying unusual devices through customs. A documentary on assassination attempts and the tools used.

"A Russian assassin carried chlorine gas into Britain in her luggage. It was disguised as a spray deodorant. If sprayed normally it was deodorant. When the top was struck hard against something it blew out the false base and released liquid chlorine. Chlorine gas is liquid under pressure; it resumes its gaseous state quickly. It's also flammable."

In my mind I could see a scenario play out. Selena underestimated the force of the rain and the wind as she flung the door open and bolted from the car. While running away she threw the lighter back, expecting it to land, burning, in the car. The flame would ignite the chlorine and dispose of all evidence of her and the crash victim.

But the car door blew shut or almost shut in the wind, as soon as she bolted from it. For whatever reason she couldn't go back to finish the job – perhaps she didn't want to – in case she was caught in a late blast. Or had time constraints.

I was hugely thankful Mac couldn't see inside my head.

"Okay ... What's one and one?"

I smiled. "I have no proof that one and one makes two."

"Reasonable people would say it's two."

"I guess reasonable people wouldn't follow a hunch,

either?" I was trying to hold the sharp edge back from my voice.

"Probably not," he said. "Do you feel that strongly about this?"

"Yes," I replied. "And one more thing ... why the hell did he stay in a car filled with gas unless he was already unconscious and, how did she get away?"

"You said one more thing, that's two," Mac said.

So now he can count?

I offered an idea. "She'd have to have been in the car to release the gas and would need a breathing mask. Somewhere on that road will be a mask and probably her clothing."

"She wandered naked down the road?" There was a touch of incredulity to his tone.

"No, she went up. We went down and found zilch. She went up."

Mac leaned back against the wall and jammed his hands into his jeans' pockets.

"Ellie, you're obsessing. How long can you afford to spend off on a tangent in the middle of a case?"

Mission Impossible music rattled through my head. What tangent? We could be talking national security here.

"I am not spinning off on a tangent." How rude.

"I have a suggestion," he said. He gave me the benefit of the slow, calm voice of reason as he talked me down from the ledge. "You should call Homeland Security and tell them your concerns, then we can get back to this case."

Yes, that was reasonable and sensible. And exactly what I should do.

My eyes met Mac's. Was it possible to literally become lost in someone's gaze?

A voice in my head spoke, 'Snap out of it, Ellie, you're not making sense and that odd glint in Mac's eyes is worry, not romance. Hand this over to Homeland and let it fuc'n go! Just get on with it.'

I looked at his face and my eyes traced fresh lines by his eyes.

Do it now! I told myself, before he looks at you like that again. Make everything okay.

I pulled my phone from my jeans' pocket and retrieved the picture of the dead man. He was familiar. Dammit!

"Mac." I did know something. "As crappy as passport photos are, I think this is the guy who tripped me in Richmond." I scrutinized his face imagining him puffy, with an auburn toupee, instead of lean with very tidy short black hair.

"You're sure? I thought you said he was puffy-faced with piggy eyes and a bad red toupee?"

"He was. What would make someone puff up? Allergies? A reaction to medication? Or could a person do that on purpose to disguise themselves, like the wig," I asked, not expecting any answers.

Mac's brow creased with thought. "You covered some winning ideas. I have nothing to add."

"Take away the puffy medicated look and the toupee,

it's the same person I spoke to in Richmond. He was a foreigner... as in Eastern Bloc ... maybe a Russian. That doesn't mean he isn't a naturalized New Zealander but it's odd ..." I searched my brain, replaying the incident in the street. "Markov. He said his name was Markov. Why would a stranger lie to me?"

His left eyebrow rose. "And we find him dead on the road with a different name. What are the odds?"

This was definitely weird, twilight zone and Stephen King weird. I couldn't gauge the expression in Mac's eyes. Was he humoring me?

I considered what I had said earlier. "I might have been a bit off with the whole Mossad thing."

"Maybe, maybe not ... life isn't like it was pre 9-11."

I realized then that I had seduced Mac into my psycho-prophetic web of theories and decided it was time to act rationally. "The State Police who attended the crash will hand the info on to the appropriate agency – if they suspect something out of the ordinary," I said, with more faith than I really had.

"You're sure?"

"Yes." I nodded. "I've got a killer to catch. But I still think he was the man I met in Richmond: Markov, a Russian. Both of them could be Russian. And we found a lighter with a Russian emblem."

I sat down at my desk and began the arduous task of sorting crime-scene information into manageable chunks and timelines.

I spread photos of the victims over the desk. Mac

marked the crime scenes on the wall map of Virginia.

"Where'd you hide the poetry book?" I asked.

I'd run out of time down in Richmond to read it, or even remember that Mac was bringing it to me.

He pulled it from a backpack leaning against my desk. "Right here."

I flipped through a copy of our book until I found the poem. I read it through four times. The killer was taking passages, out of order, to write them around the crime scenes.

Stolen.

When the world has done
Lost in time too tired to run
A safe place came to be...
Feeling your words surround me
Letting tears cascade...
Hoping my dues in life are paid.

Memories stolen by the night
Time sliding dividing light
Jumbled thoughts trapped inside
Who I was suddenly died...
Flashing pictures on a screen
Unsure reality dripping through a dream.

Darkness folding images like cloth
Wrapping the past in a gilded bow
Storing away the horror show
Letting tears cascade...
Hoping my dues in this life are paid.

Mixed emotions confusion reigns
Holding love in shaking hands
Touching a heart giving hope
Flashing pictures on a screen
Unsure reality becomes a crazy glued dream.

"I have our gold bow."

"Where?" Mac asked. He perched on the edge of my desk and glanced at the book.

"'Wrapping the past in a gilded bow.'" I pointed to the relevant stanza.

"No mention of anything being cleansed?"

"Nope."

"Why this poem?" Mac asked.

"Maybe because of the content, because the Unsub could twist it to suit, or interpret it however ..."

Mac's brow furrowed then he grinned. "I love it when you talk jargon to me."

"Idiot!"

"Say it again."

I trotted out my sexiest voice and repeated, "Unsub."

"Dang, ya give me chills."

A glimpse of a shadow caught my eye in the long thin window in my door. I cleared my throat. Mac turned in time to see Caine open the door.

"How goes the fight?" he asked.

"We're making some progress," I replied. I could tell Caine thought something was going on.

"Did I interrupt something?"

"Nope."

"You're sure?"

"Positive."

"Mac?"

I rolled my eyes, hoping neither of them saw it. Was my word not good enough?

"I was giving Ellie some flack, is all."

"I see." Caine's mouth formed a cold slit in his weathered face.

I diverted Caine's attention from Mac. "Everything okay with you?"

"We're still knocking our heads against the wall with the new budget. I'm going to be tied up for at least a week."

"Okay. I'll copy you on anything of interest."

"You handling this? It's a rough case from what I've heard."

"We're good. Mac, Sam, Lee and I make a good team."

Caine nodded wisely, as if it had been his plan all along. Maybe it was. He was like that: sneaky.

"I'm back into the fray." With that, Caine left.

We carried on with the search for more information, sticking pieces together and hoping they fitted. It was nightfall before we headed home for some much-needed rest.

Chapter Twelve
Memphis Lives In Me

I could feel my inner strength ebbing away. I didn't get much sleep. I was hoping being back at the office bright and early would help. But Wednesday morning brought no answers and there was a live performance in my head. Even though I sensed that I was the only one who could hear Elvis, my mouth opened and words tumbled out, "Shut it!"

Mac's hand landed on my forearm. "Who are you talking to?"

"Elvis."

Without so much as a blink, he asked, "What's he saying?"

"He's singing. 'Marie's the name of his latest flame'."

Mac didn't even flinch. "What does he know that we don't?"

I shook my head. Elvis gyrated across my internal screen.

"I dunno ... but ever since that kid in Richmond, Elvis has been strutting his stuff on and off."

"You run out of old television shows?"

"I hope so." My voice slid into confession mode as I said, "I had a really nasty *MASH* incident during my checkup at the hospital."

Mac draped an arm around my shoulders. I wondered how he put up with my eccentricity, which he always seemed to take in his stride and this time was no exception. One day there would be sainthood in it for him, or a straitjacket. The straitjacket will probably fit me better than him, though.

Saint Cormac, Patron Saint of the Twisted Mind.

"Could be worse, babe."

True, it could be much worse than Elvis. He appeared, butterfly-like, with his capes and jeweled jumpsuits. Sometimes I love the way my outrageous imagination works: a butterfly, a freaking butterfly.

"Mac, we know the first Richmond victim was bipolar, yeah?"

"Yeah."

Rain pelted on the windows as Mac followed my mental meanderings. He took a calculated leap and arrived at the next synaptic stopping point. He pulled the laptop closer and tapped quickly on the keys.

"Anything turn up on the others?" Elvis fell silent. "Anything?"

Mac smiled at my impatience.

"Two others, from what family have said. We need more information; those two were supposedly on medication, both were prescribed Amitriptyline but no traces of any were found in their blood."

"The Richmond woman?"

"She was definitely on her medication. She had Depakote on board when she was killed. There are also traces of Chlorpromazine."

"Thorazine," I whispered. "She was on an antipsychotic."

Mac nodded. We'd both come across Chlorpromazine, under its more common name of Thorazine, thanks to our mothers' insanity.

"Nothing we have mentions Thorazine as one of her prescribed medications."

Mac opened another folder then clicked on Julie's case notes. He scrolled through them and a few seconds later said, "You're right."

"I have a theory," I proffered. "They were drugged. That explained the serene expressions on their faces. They didn't die screaming, they died silently, stabbed while in a drugged stupor."

"That makes sense."

"Of course. Don't suppose the medical examiner found traces of chlorine in her hair or on her skin?"

"There is no mention of chlorine," Mac said. "I'll ask them to double check."

The phone rang. Lee's deep voice boomed through thundering rain, "We have another one."

A calm certainty descended as I formed my first question. "Is her name Marie?"

All I could hear over the phone was the rain. A few moments later the noise eased and Lee bellowed, "Yes!"

"No need to shout," I replied, holding the phone away from my ear. "Where?"

"Sorry. I didn't think you could hear me. It's on Vale Road."

"We're on our way."

"You'll see the police cars out front. A long driveway then there's a dwelling."

"See you in a bit." I hung up.

Mac had already grabbed our jackets and scooped up his handy backpack.

"Where're we going?"

"Vale Road. Seems Elvis knows his stuff. We have a Marie."

I couldn't help thinking that it was too quick. Could be that the Unsub didn't get the buzz he did earlier and decided to step up his pace or someone wanted him blamed. A murder a day brings the Feds out to play. Blood, guts and gore brings me knocking on your door. I controlled myself before a stupid smirk spread across my face. I definitely didn't need anyone knowing about my sick little rhyme.

As soon as we hit the pavement, I knew it was going to take some time to reach the latest scene. Water lapped at the gutters and small waves spilled over the sidewalk. Wind howled and trees bent, almost scraping the soggy ground. It took huge effort to remain upright.

I zipped my jacket up to the collar and pulled my hood as far over my face as possible. We were on the wrong side of the river and the traffic was going to be murder.

In an effort to take my mind off the storm and Mac's driving, I flicked on the car stereo, cranking it up to drown out the rain. Rowan Grange powered through rock ballad after rock ballad, making me wish I could see him play live and soothing me in advance of the horror I knew

I was about to face again. Even though it took forever, time seemed to fly while I was lost in the songs that gave me hope.

Despite spending an hour and a half with Grange music, I was in no mood to hang about making chitchat once we arrived.

Mac hung back to talk with Sam who stood under a large black umbrella. The umbrella was one wind gust off being a collection of wire stalks and flapping torn nylon.

I scurried, head down, through the torrential rain to find Lee and entered the building, happy to be out of the rain. My pleasure was short lived and followed immediately by a heaving sensation in my gut. I made my way into the house and located Lee in the kitchen. The stench turned my stomach slightly more than the scene in front of me. The underlying note of old garbage, with a hint of maggot-infested rotting meat, rose through the top notes of a now-familiar blend of blood and bourbon. Hidden under the stink was the more pleasing aroma of chlorine.

I tried not to breathe too deeply. “How long has she been dead?”

“Three to four hours.”

“Then what smells so freaking bad?” I turned on the spot, both to take in the entire scrawled wording around the cabinets and walls and survey the area. My answer lay all around us. “Her housekeeping skills were decidedly lacking.”

“Check this out.” Lee hit a button on a remote. *Fear Factor* blared from a television set on the counter.

"Maybe …" I gestured at the piles of rubbish and maggot infestation. "Maybe she was training for *Fear Factor*."

He switched off the television.

"She got kids?" I saw a baby's bottle amongst the toxic waste and polluted dishes spilling out of the sink. I kept a weather eye out for rats.

"God, I hope not," Lee replied.

My phone vibrated on my belt as Lee's phone rang. Seconds later, Lee's hand firmly gripped my elbow. "We're out of here, Chicky."

I guessed his call said the same thing mine did. 'We have received a credible threat.'

Two officers waited outside the front of the building and escorted us to two more officers standing by my car. I couldn't see Mac or Sam anywhere.

Lee held out his hand for the keys, indicating he would drive. I dropped the keys into his palm; they seemed insignificant in his enormous hand. I slid into the passenger seat and watched as Lee shoved the driver's seat of my Taurus hard against the backseat, giving himself as much leg room as possible. He still looked cramped. He'd look cramped in a Hummer.

"Where to?" I asked.

"Mac and Sam are meeting us back at your place."

How did he know? I hadn't heard his phone or anyone say anything. At least there would be decent coffee. A white coiled wire was running from Lee's right ear down under his collar. Now that explained his insider knowledge; he was wearing an earpiece. I guessed Sam wore one too. I dragged my phone off my belt and called Caine.

"Have you any more information?"

"No. Not yet." I could imagine his grim expression. "Bomb squad is going in, if there is a bomb they'll find it."

"Where did the info come from?"

"Anonymous tip off: maybe the Unsub. Someone who knew unreleased details of the crime scenes."

"Thanks. You want to take this case?"

"This is all yours. I'm not taking over just because some whacko wants to blow you skyward. You're capable."

"Thanks for the vote of confidence."

I closed my phone. Water poured from the blackened sky, wind tugged at the car, visibility dropped to mere feet. Luckily, we weren't terribly far from home. Lee parked up the driveway. We ran for the house and shelter.

Mac handed us a towel each, followed by welcome cups of coffee. The wet towels magically disappeared. Our dining room hummed with voices. Caine, Sam, Mac and Lee were talking while I still attempted to digest those two disturbing words. Bomb squad.

"Bomb squad," I whispered to myself.

Caine's gray eyes drilled into me.

"Bomb squad," he repeated. "Which of those two words is difficult for you?"

"Both of them." I turned to the others. "Does this strike you as odd?"

They all nodded.

"As I thought. Why after six murders would our Unsub turn to bombs?"

"Maybe he couldn't think of anything new to write on the Post-it notes," Mac replied.

Damn! Was there a note? I didn't recall a note. There was part of the same poem, out of order again. I'd seen it written on the kitchen walls.

" 'Flashing pictures on a screen. Unsure reality becomes a crazy glued dream.' He used a different part of the poem. He used the last two lines."

"And he called in a bomb threat," Mac added.

"Is he done?" Sam asked.

I poured myself more coffee; my head ached. There must've been a note.

"He's not done. Lee, note?" I asked again, "Lee, do you have a copy of the note?"

Lee smiled and passed me his notebook, open at the relevant page. There it was. 'You probably think this is about you.'

Sam and Mac broke in, singing the chorus of 'You're So Vain.' One thing for sure, neither of them will be getting through the auditions for *American Idol*. They'd probably make the blooper reel though.

I ignored the note for the time being. The poem bugged me, really bugged me. We'd missed something. 'Flashing pictures on a screen.'

"Lee get on the phone, I want the television remote from the crime scene."

He did as I asked, then reported, "They'll bag it."

"Excellent." I turned to Caine; with a wave of my hand, I said, "You can go."

His mouth twitched. A note of incredulousness crept into his gruff voice, "Did you just dismiss me?"

"I did." Imagine that: being all grown up and capable and running my own case.

"You know where I am, if you need anything."

"Absolutely."

Caine's mouth twitched; he bobbed his head once and then he left.

I turned to my team, quietly delighted to have *my* team but more elated to actually feel like I was in command and capable. The newfound positive energy of being a Supervising Special Agent felt good.

"He's not done. This is his game. And I suspect he was the one who had that television on *Fear Factor*."

"I'm not liking this, Chicky," Lee said, mimicking my style of speech.

"I'm not liking this, either," Mac said.

These guys have been around me too long.

I waited for Sam.

He poured himself another coffee.

I waited.

He set his cup down.

I waited.

He smiled. His straight white teeth gleamed against the deep brown backdrop of his face. Move over, Denzel, there's a new hunk in town.

"Sam?"

"I'm with the boys on this. If his latest twist is bomb threats, he's going to make scene investigation difficult."

"Difficult. Yeah, that's a good description."

A call from the bomb squad interrupted the exchange and I listened carefully as Sergeant Taylor introduced himself and told me what they'd discovered.

They'd cleared the scene and found a suspicious package in the oven. Honestly, after seeing that house, a demolition order might be the only way to clean it.

"Taylor, did you view the package?"

"Yes, ma'am."

"Any writing on it?"

"Two words, we photographed it before detonation. It said, 'Filthy ho.' "

"What was in the package?"

"C4."

"Thank you very much." I wished the bomber had used something more exotic than C4. "Any idea where the C4 came from?"

"There are several reports of stolen explosives from various demolition companies and military bases. Nothing out of the ordinary."

"Good to know. Thank you."

"You're welcome. The medical examiner has removed the body and the scene is secure."

"Thank you." I had another thought. "Have a security guard posted outside the scene for twenty-four hours."

"Yes, ma'am. I'll see to it."

"Thanks, bye."

"Okay, boys." I had a sultry Mae West moment. "The bomb was a message. It sounds like the Unsub had an issue with Marie's housekeeping too."

Mac's phone rang with an insistent, tormenting whine. We knew that ring tone; Mother Connelly, crisis central calling.

"Hello, Mom." He listened, then said, "Because I knew it was you. What do you need?"

Lee, Sam and I backed slowly from the room. There was no need for us to witness another calamity at the Connelly camp, entertaining though they were. As I started to close the door, I heard Mac say, with impressive patience, "Fourteen strings of lights are too many. You've overloaded the circuit. Dad can fix the fuse."

Uh-oh! Any mention of Mac's dad during a maniac-mom episode resulted in ranting about how useless he was. He was nowhere near useless. She, however, was a nasty, crazy woman.

I shut the door, hoping to keep the crazy out. Lee and Sam waited in my office. My computer was humming. Lee had logged into our work system and was running background comparisons on the victims.

"We'll carry on. Mac will be a while."

They grinned.

"What do you need, Chicky?" Sam asked.

"I need to rule out the possibility that someone else committed this last crime." Judging by the stunned looks on their faces, they were surprised.

Sam folded his arms, rocked back on one heel, and

gave me a thoughtful look. "No details of any of the crime scenes so far have been reported by the media."

"You're absolutely sure?"

"Yes." He nodded.

"Either of you think this could be the work of anyone else?"

"No," they replied in unison.

"Then he's stepped up his attacks; this is the second today."

Their expressions solidified into stone.

An urge to think aloud demanded I went with it. "These are not invisible crimes: someone knows our Unsub. Someone saw something. Or at least senses something is amiss. Did our Unsub go home wearing our victim's blood? Did he go home to someone: parents, partner, kids or roommates?" I stopped and sat at Mac's desk. "Get me a list of victims with a mental illness."

Lee placed a crisp white 8½ x 11 inch sheet of paper in front of me. "Your list of mentally ill victims."

As I read the list, the words from the first note in Richmond became more important: 'Special Agent Conway, Gabrielle – We need more chlorine.'

This time the words were in a bold font splashed all over the inner workings of my mind; at that point I knew exactly what he meant. He meant I had the potential to be just like them. It's possible that I carry a mental illness. Mom was a nutter – no, more a raving lunatic than just nuts – and I could carry that gene. How did the Unsub know that? Didn't everybody know that? Didn't we start the Butterfly Foundation because we'd survived being children of the truly insane? There'd been more than one story in the media on the Foundation and how it came about.

I refocused on the task at hand and read the list again. All our victims to date fitted the mentally ill category. "So how is the Unsub connected to these women?"

"Damn, Chicky, you never said you wanted answers." Lee produced another sheet of paper, laying it next to the first. He tapped it slowly.

I leaned over and read out the single sentence in the middle of the pristine white sheet, " 'I got fuc'n nothing. How about you?' " I smiled at him. "Very funny."

I passed the paper to Sam.

"We've got six murders and five of the victims had a mental illness. What about Marie Kline? What do we know?"

Lee pulled out his phone and made a call. Minutes later he had an answer for me, "Six now, Ellie; Marie was schizophrenic according to the medic alert bracelet she wore."

"Thinking just on the Northern Virginia murders ... could these women have a connection to the same mental health facility, or doctor, or psychologist, even pharmacist?" I paused. "But then what connects the Richmond murders to these northern ones?"

"Good question," Sam said.

"Can you extend the parameters of the comparisons?"

"Sure," Lee replied, as he opened a text box on the

screen and added more data. "This will take a while."

"Do we have confirmation of rape in each case?"

Sam's expression changed from bland to confused in a split second. "It'll be in the post mortem reports."

"We have those now?"

Sam smiled. "We have the Richmond ones, plus two of the northern ones." He nudged Lee. "Grab those reports."

Lee pulled them up on the screen. I peered over their shoulders, scanning the first page. I touched Lee's hand and he surrendered the mouse and his chair to me. I read all the reports. Neither of the Richmond murders involved rape. So far, all the northern ones did.

I stood up and let Lee get back to what he was running.

"So the rape is a progression." I said, not expecting an answer. "How long will the comparisons take, Lee?"

"A little while ... hard to determine exactly."

A while was good. I had other plans and a nagging feeling that wouldn't quit. This dreadful voice inside my head kept telling me there was more to this: winding me up and persistently throwing the Post-it notes and poem in my face. No matter how many times I tried to convince myself this was not personal, the voice came back with another note, my name and a reminder that it was my poem being used. The implication that I carried something was definitely personal.

I didn't want these words to escape and fall from my mouth but they did anyway. "Lee, when you've run that, I want you to run the same thing again but throw me in as the wild card."

He stared at me as if he was hoping I hadn't spoken. Sam wore the same expression. Neither of them replied.

"I need a little bit of thinking time."

"Where will you be?" Sam asked.

"In the living room – I'll be back," I replied and hurried out the door. Mac was still on the phone in the kitchen. I closed the living room door behind me and pressed the power button on the stereo. Mac called it a sound system and it had more speakers than anyone could ever need. I just wanted to play a Grange CD and drown out the crap in my head. I wanted volume.

Music blared, drums pounded. It didn't so much wash over me as pulsate through me, as I stood in the middle of the room, arms outstretched. I turned to watch waves of noise disrupt the air. They flowed from me and rippled across the room, skimming the furniture, sliding across the coffee table and melting into the wall. The air around me was like a pond and the music was the stones, sent skipping over the shiny surface by invisible hands. A monarch butterfly flittered near the water's edge on the story told by a guitar. A bass thump punched the air, sound bounced – the butterfly vanished.

As more music floated and rippled into the walls I became aware that the visual disturbances could be part of a migraine, or something worse. I closed my eyes, it was music I needed, not the visual effects.

I knew an answer lay somewhere. The puzzle before me left clues in music. I guess it's no accident that music has keys. I jerked back to the present. It has keys but no chlorine. A quote by W.H. Auden flowed into view on a stream from a guitar solo, 'Music can be made anywhere. It is invisible and does not smell.'

The desire to explore the crime scenes again rose up strongly. I hit the power button on the remote, turning off the stereo. Music fell to the floor and writhed uncomfortably. I ignored it and called the medical examiner.

He answered quickly. I asked him some specific questions. "Were the victims alive when they were stabbed?"

"I believe so. I've found evidence of a heavy duty antipsychotic drug in all the victims so far. Thorazine was not prescribed for any of the women I've examined but was in their systems in very high doses. They would've been unconscious but not dead."

"Any evidence of chemical burns?"

"No," he replied.

That ruled out chlorine; maybe they really did go swimming.

"Stomach contents?"

"Coffee."

Quick morning swim, coffee, high dose of Thorazine and death. Fun date.

"Thank you." I hung up. Unconscious but not dead was something I needed to mull over.

I found Lee and Sam and announced I was going back to the last scene. The anticipated resistance didn't happen.

Sam jangled car keys. It looked like we were taking his work-supplied Expedition. "Ready when you are. Let's get Mac."

Chapter Thirteen
Wild Is The Wind

It was late afternoon when we arrived back at the scene. Light was fast fading, swallowed by rain and general misery. I wanted Wednesday to be over as soon as possible.

My first observation was that someone was missing. Where was the guard who was supposed to be watching the crime scene?

"Hold up," I said to my team. "Anyone seen the guard?"

They all glanced around the approach to the house.

"On a break?" Lee offered.

I shook my head. "As if."

Lee agreed, "They're not paid to take breaks."

I nodded. I knew the security firm we used. Their reputation was impeccable. We checked the exterior thoroughly. The crime scene tape was intact. The door was still sealed. There was nothing untoward, no suggestion of foul play. It was possible there'd been some sort of communication meltdown and a guard hadn't been assigned.

"Everything's still sealed, so unless anyone has any objections, I'd like to carry on as we're here and it would be a shame to waste this time. Give me a minute to call the security firm now and find out why we don't have a guard posted."

I scrolled through the contacts in my phone and

clicked on the security company. The phone rang and rang, eventually flicking to voice mail. I left a scathing message about the lack of guards on our crime scene and made sure they knew it was going in my report. That'd make them work harder when their contract came up for renewal.

Sam tapped my shoulder. "Come on Chicky, let's do this."

The first thing I noticed as we re-entered Marie Kline's home was that the smell hadn't improved in the absence of her body. The rotting garbage brought stinging tears to my eyes as it assaulted my senses.

Lee and Sam looked around the rest of the house while Mac and I checked out the kitchen.

"What do you see?" I watched Mac's face. I saw concentration and brow furrowing.

We were standing next to each other in the middle of the filthy, creepy-crawly infested room. Things scuttled out of sight. Shadows made noises. Dark recesses filled with garbage moved inexplicably. Our shoulders touched and without warning, Tammy Wynette popped into my head and belted out 'Stand By Your Man.' It was impossible to hold back a smile.

"I'm drawing a blank here, babe," Mac said and turned his face to mine. "You're smiling."

"I'm standing by my man."

He laughed. "Tammy's joined the party, huh?"

The song stopped. Without warning, heavy footsteps ran from the house.

Lee hollered, "Sam's down!"

Everything faded to gray as I ran towards Lee's voice with my phone open in my hand, stopping abruptly in front of them both near the back door. It was as filthy as the rest of the house. Sam was sitting on the ground clutching his side, Lee was kneeling beside him.

"You get a description?" I asked Sam and Lee.

"Neither of us saw anything," Lee replied.

I had Comms on the line and told them to advise all police to be on the lookout for someone running away from the scene. Without a description there wasn't a lot anyone could do, except hope that someone saw the Unsub leave the premises, or noticed a stranger in the area.

I hung up and turned my attention to Sam.

"Sam?"

"It's nothing – a flesh wound." He winced as Lee opened the jacket Sam was wearing. "He hit me from behind, all I saw was a flash of steel in my peripheral vision."

Gray became red, deep velvet red, as it spilled through Sam's cream shirt.

"Your nothing is bleeding all over," I replied and made a decision to get him the hell out of there. We could make better time than an ambulance. Especially since emergency services were stretched to capacity by the storm. "Can you move?"

The dirt around us was a great motivator; the less time our wounded friend spent in the disgusting house the better.

"With help," Sam replied.

Lee applied pressure to the wound. I saw dark, almost black, blood ooze through Lee's fingers. I looked for Mac. He was in the doorway examining something substantial.

"What the hell is that?"

"A knife."

I didn't hear him properly over the pounding rain above us. "Say again?"

Mac gloved up, then carefully lifted the object so I could see. "As I said: a knife."

"Jesus. That blade must be a good eight inches long and," I squinted as light reflected off the surface, "one and a half across."

"Yeah," he replied, dropping it into an evidence bag and handing it to me. "Looks military to me."

Sam groaned, "Good to know I wasn't wounded by some feeble kitchen knife, Chicky Babe."

Lee looked at me and said, "He could have a liver laceration, Ellie. Let's get him out of here."

I raised an eyebrow. "You know this?"

"Medic, Gulf War," Lee replied, by way of explanation. "And I saw plenty of black blood in the field."

The things you learn.

"How serious?"

"It's way up there. You have the knife in your hand, it could easily be worse than I think."

Mac swooped in next to Sam. He looked at Lee waiting for orders.

"Let's move," Lee said. "Lift him to his feet."

Mac and Lee hooked their hands under Sam's armpits and hoisted him to his feet, trying not to spill too much of his blood in the process. With support, he managed to walk to the car. I slammed the door to the house and ran after them. I hurried by them and opened the car. Lee and Mac settled Sam in the backseat.

I dropped the bagged knife on the floor in the front. I leaned down, reached under the seat, pulled out the first-aid kit and gave Lee all the wound dressings we had. The blood was more black than red, as it dripped from Lee's hand when he grabbed the packets and opened a hemostatic sponge. I slid into the front passenger seat. Lee packed the sponge into the wound and applied pressure. Sam groaned.

Mac drove. Visibility was one and a half car lengths at best and the rain came down in sheets. The torrential rain drowned out all external noise and plunged the whole world into the depths of a thick gray murk. We had no idea what the traffic was like. I hit the lights and reached for the radio. A flick of my wrist changed the frequency to an open channel.

"This is FBI Special Agent Conway requesting all available cars for traffic assistance. Officer down! Cut us a path from Vale to Fairfax Hospital on Gallows ... We're in a black Expedition, grill lights active."

The airway flooded with replies. Less than a mile later a police cruiser slipped in front of us. Flashers lit the interior of the car, sirens wailed in the wind. In the wing mirror I saw another cruiser slide in behind.

The radio chirped and a voice burst forth, "Agent Conway, stick to my bumper." The brake lights flashed on the car ahead.

"Will do. And you are?"

"Officer Rich Edwards. Mac, you okay?"

Mac and I smiled at each other. He was an old family friend. Their fathers worked together for thirty years. I depressed the talk button for Mac, "I'm okay, Rich. I'm halfway up ya tail pipe. Go ahead and put your foot down."

I was so glad Mac was driving. Aquaplaning was a definite possibility and not one I relished.

The radio crackled. "All roads are wide open. Traffic stopped to get you through. We'll take you all the way. Hospital notified."

"Ten-four."

I curbed the urge to add 'Rubber Duck'; C.W. McCall's 'Convoy' played through my head. What was it with the country music?

Lee whistled from the back. "Damn, Ellie, you don't mess around, huh?"

"The longer he's in the company car ... the bigger the cleaning bill."

Sam managed a laugh. "You're all heart, Chicky."

I settled back into the seat. Lights flashed even brighter against the gray wet background, causing my head to pound in time with each pulse from the flashers ahead.

I puzzled over Sam's stabbing. Why would our Unsub

go back to the scene? Did he leave something behind? I drifted back to the house. My eyes closed as the scene rolled out. I'll just bet there's a country song there somewhere. Couldn't think of a song about a filthy dump of a house, so I moved further into the memory bank, examining everything about the yard and house.

The outside: mud patches on weed-strangled lawn; overgrown flower beds under the front windows, long since choked with weeds. Closed curtains, ripped and hanging in droops from the top. Initial impression: those who resided there didn't care much for their surroundings. This dank hole shouldn't exist in middle-class America. The cracked glass panel in the front door seemed to fit with the rest of the unkempt exterior. I walked through the door, and it didn't smell any better in my memory. The spartan furnishings were possibly thrift store purchases and had definitely seen better days. A book stack grabbed my attention. She read Stephen King and John Grisham. I walked on.

Why did he go back? I stood in the center of the kitchen. What did I miss? I took careful stock of my surroundings. The poem written around the walls; body; ribbon; bourbon; black Sharpie pen. Whoa! Back up. A black Sharpie on the counter, half-hidden under debris, as if it'd rolled away.

I jabbed at my phone. My fingers hit buttons before my mind caught up, searching for the number for Charlie Coleman, who headed up our forensics team.

"Charlie, it's Ellie Conway; did you process the Vale

scene?"

"Yes, ma'am."

"Did you see a black marker pen?"

"I picked one off the counter, ma'am. Strange writing on it ... foreign ... Russian maybe."

"Process that A-sap."

"Yes, ma'am."

"We have a knife for you, too. Looks military, has Sam's blood on it. Can you have someone meet us at Fairfax Hospital to pick it up."

"Yes, ma'am. Sam okay?"

"He will be."

"Good to know."

'Yes, ma'am' flowed so easily. I knew it didn't mean 'Yes, ma'am!' It meant 'We'll get to it as soon as we can, ma'am. No promises. Might not even be this month, ma'am.'

I felt the corners of my mouth turn up. Finally, we had something useful, not just another body. Bad enough that the assailant stabbed Sam from behind and none of us saw anything.

Until the marker pen discovery, this had looked like a very grim day. Now we had caught a break – maybe even a fingerprint or two. We also had a knife that might reveal more pieces of the puzzle. I crossed my fingers that the evidence would be processed quickly. That answers would be forthcoming.

Chapter Fourteen
Have A Nice Day

We placed Sam in the capable hands of the Inova Fairfax Hospital emergency surgical team. Competent as they were, it didn't diminish the worry or the waiting time. I paced the emergency room waiting area. Lee and Mac leaned on a wall, away from the ill and injured, watching me and talking quietly.

A doctor hurried from behind the double glass automatic door and beckoned to me – Lee and Mac came too. He confirmed Sam's injury was a liver laceration and told us he would go up for surgery as soon as they had a theater available. He was otherwise healthy and strong, which the doctor assured us would work in his favor.

Hospital emergency departments are huge time-sinks. It was late when Charlie sent Adam, a member of the forensics team, to meet us a few minutes after two theater nurses wheeled Sam away to the surgical suite. I handed over the knife and watched as Adam signed the evidence receipt. Satisfied the chain of evidence remained intact, I sent him back to the lab.

Sam's parents were waiting for him in recovery, making our presence unnecessary. Part of me wanted to stay, despite Mac insisting that I would be better off getting some rest at home.

I'd never had to talk to the parents of a colleague before; well, I had, but not to tell them their son was seriously wounded. It sucked out loud and then some.

God, is this what it's like for Caine? A horrible sense of guilt when anything shitty happens? A gut-wrenching need to do penance started eating at my soul, gnawing away on the decision I'd made that led to this unfortunate outcome. How does he deal with this?

"I need a minute."

"You okay?" Mac looked worried. Good going; that was exactly what Mac needed: to worry about me even more than he did already.

"I just need a minute, Mac."

"I'll be here."

When I stopped walking, I was staring through a window into the dark wet parking lot. Lights illuminated large puddles. Wind caused small waves in some of the bigger pools of water. Every now and then, I caught sight of my own reflection. Not pretty. I called Caine.

"It's me. I got a question."

I imagined his face as he spoke, "Yeah, me too. You first."

"How do you deal with the guilt?"

"First you accept that you cannot control other people's actions."

"My actions put Sam in danger."

"No, Ellie, your actions took you all back to a cleared crime scene. The Unsub made a decision."

"But ..."

Caine interrupted me, "But nothing. Would you have done a damn thing differently, if there was a do-over?"

"I would've swept the place before going in."

"Well, maybe you learned something tonight."

"It's one shitty fucking lesson."

"You'll never do it again," Caine seemed quite sure. "You think you're the only one who has ever made a mistake?"

I couldn't imagine Caine ever making this type of fucktarded screw-up. Sam was in surgery. This was big.

"I should've looked for the guard and not proceeded until I'd found him."

"Did anything look out of place? The tape? The seals?"

"No."

"And earlier, did you sign off the crime scene and turn it over for cleaning?"

"No, I turned it over to the bomb squad; they turned it over to crime-scene investigators. I ordered a guard so we could get another look."

"Was there a general duty guard posted?"

"Yes. I told bomb squad to organize the guard. To my knowledge a general duty guard was posted."

"That will be in your report. Obviously we have a competency issue with the security company we're using, or someone didn't relay the instruction."

He had a valid point. I still felt guilty and it was all on me. But he did have a valid point.

"The first thing I was going to do once we'd finished at the house was call the company again and find out where my guard was. Then Sam ..." Saying what happened was more of a struggle than I expected it to be. I braced myself and forced the words out. "Then Sam was stabbed. Everything else went out the window. I did call before we went in but there was no reply." I cleared my throat. "I left a message but have yet to hear back from the guard or the company." My conscience smarted. I couldn't help wondering if the guard had fallen victim to foul play and no one knew.

Caine handed out some decent advice. "Chase it up when you can. If you think he is somehow involved then get to it A-sap."

"Okay. What was your question?"

"Do you need to replace Sam?"

Oh, man. I hadn't even considered replacing him. "I can't make that decision yet. I want to wait on the outcome from his surgery."

"Let me know." His voice softened a little, "You okay, Ellie?"

"Yep."

"You're sure? I can lend a hand if you want."

Absolutely not! "I'm okay, Caine. Thanks."

"Keep in touch, kid."

"Have a nice night."

Rain hit the windowpane, making the evening seem even bleaker than before. I let Caine's words settle; I knew he was right; I knew I could deal with it.

I called the security company and left another message, this time for the boss to get back to me with information on the wayward guard. I felt the prickle again and really hoped nothing bad had happened. This was a company that had a large slice of federal pie; we all used them to guard scenes. The owner, Sean O'Hare, was the twin brother of the Director of the FBI, but that's not why we used the firm. We used them because Sean O'Hare was ex-CIA and really knew his shit.

Before I'd put my phone away it rang in my hand. I glanced at the screen before answering. Sean himself.

"You fielding queries these days?" I said.

"Only for you. I heard. How's Sam?" So my messages did get through.

"In surgery," I replied. "Where's the guard?"

"Dead. We found him twenty minutes ago. Throat cut, body stashed in a nearby alleyway."

"I'm sorry." I was. Now I knew why Sean was talking to me at this hour, instead of putting his kids to bed. He would be notifying the man's next of kin.

"Take care, Agent Conway."

"You, too, Sean."

I stuffed my phone in my pocket.

It didn't take me long to walk back through the hospital and find Mac and Lee stationed by a coffee machine outside the surgical suite.

I told them about the guard and we headed off.

Rich had waited for news out in the emergency department. Mac gave him an update and promised to buy him a beer for his help. Translation: he'd throw a few hundred dollars on a tab at O'Reilly's bar for the officers at the Fairfax Police Department, then whip his ass in a game of poker and my money was on it being Texas Hold 'em. I think I'll be busy that night. A good book and a bubble bath sounded inviting.

The day had been a long one; long and tiring. The ongoing torrential rain threatened to wash Northern Virginia away. Streets were flooded, gardens were swamped, with houses held fast behind walls of sandbags – and a serial killer who preyed on the mentally ill.

It was too much of a coincidence that all our victims suffered from some form of mental illness. It looked as though this was the crucial factor. Man, that sucked out loud.

Lee came home with us: he didn't have much choice. Our cars were sitting in the driveway and he was our ride.

Night darkened, torrential rain gave way to persistent dripping under building thunderclouds and tornado watches.

"Stay, Lee. It's too dangerous to drive all the way out to Alexandria this evening."

Lee nodded. He looked as tired as we did. I made up the bed in the guest room and put fresh towels in the bathroom. Tonight I am supervising-special-agent-Chicky-Babe-hostess extraordinaire.

Mac cooked us dinner. It was good steak and even better salad. We ate like ravenous animals, not stopping until our plates were empty.

"Good food, great company." Lee said and raised his wine glass, "Wine's not bad, either."

"I'm going to leave you two to your bonding. I'm tired." I pushed my chair back as I rose.

“ ’Night, Ellie, sleep well.” Lee said, “We’ll get this prick.”

“Damn right we will.”

Mac stood and said, “I’ll be up later, Ellie.” He gave me one of those unsure looks. I could see his mind working and felt his need to ask before he even vocalized the words, “You okay?”

“I’m fine, babe. Tired is all.”

“Headache?”

“Hardly worth mentioning.”

He kissed me lightly.

“I might not be that tired.”

Mac grinned and kissed me again. Lee barfed. Then I remembered something. “Lee, don’t forget to check the computer, it was running some comparisons when we left earlier.”

He nodded. “Will do.”

On my way to bed, I dropped into the office. The screensaver was on – a black background with a swarm of Monarch butterflies. I searched my jacket for a card I’d left in my pocket in Richmond. I wanted to call Julie’s husband. I needed to ask why she’d joined the Butterfly Foundation.

The phone rang at least ten times. I was on the verge of hanging up with each additional ring when he answered.

“It’s Special Agent Conway, Mr. Trevalli. I hope it’s not too late to call?”

“Just watching some TV. Do you have news?”

I heard the hope in his voice and somehow that made

my questions harder to ask.

"I'm afraid not. I have a question."

He sighed and said, "Go ahead."

"Why did Julie join the Butterfly Foundation?"

"What do you mean?"

I rephrased. "I met Dakota and he seems a little young to benefit from the chat rooms. So I'm wondering why Julie joined?"

"She told me about the forums, so I guess she joined for support. You know, be around other moms with mental illnesses."

That made sense. We had built adult forums to provide support and advice for parents, but there were no adult chat rooms.

"To your knowledge did she ever use the chat rooms?"

"No, she only ever talked about the forums."

"You know of anyone in particular she talked with?"

"Yeah. Some woman with a little girl about Dakota's age."

"Remember a name?" It was getting easier as I went and Trevalli warmed up.

"No, sorry. But I think they emailed each other. I can check."

I heard a computer fire up then he said, "Do you think this has something to do with her death?"

Guarded, I replied, "Due to the nature of this case I am exploring all possible avenues."

"I have it," he said. "SassySelena."

"Any other names?" An alarm bell sounded in my

head. It was the second time I had come across the name Selena since the investigation began. Could the missing Canadian from a traffic crash be this Selena? Coincidence? Who said there are no coincidences?

"No, Julie just called her Selena."

"Thank you, Mr. Trevalli. You've been a great help."

Before I could add anything or ask for the emails and address, he interrupted, "I can forward the emails to you."

"Excellent. Do you have my email address?"

"Yes, it's on the card you gave me."

"If you could send those as soon as possible I'll go through them and see if anything jumps up and bites me."

"I'll do it now." He paused with intent, or at least I sensed intent. "Thank you for trying, Agent Conway."

"You're welcome. Take care of yourself and that sweet little boy of yours."

I hung up and made a note on the desk pad, SassySelena, then went upstairs.

Chapter Fifteen
I'll Sleep When I'm Dead

I escaped to bed with my aching head. All I wanted was to sleep in peace, without internal rumblings, without songs, without dreams; just me and the dark.

I buried my face in the cool, crisp, cotton-covered pillow. Bliss. I could feel the coolness fading my headache away; with it went the background hum left over from the doctor's visit. The hum was an annoying reminder of MRI and CT scans; nothing good could come of those tests. Hawkeye, Radar and the teddy bear fell through the running water in my head. I rolled over. Why could I see stars? The Lone Ranger and Tonto sprang to mind and a stupid joke my brother used to tell. The Lone Ranger and Tonto went camping in the desert. After they got their tent all set up, they fell sound asleep. Some hours later, Tonto woke the Lone Ranger and said, "Kemo Sabe, look at the sky, what you see?"

The Lone Ranger replied, "I see millions of stars."

"What that tell you?" asked Tonto.

The Lone Ranger pondered for a minute, and then said, "Astronomically speaking, it tells me there are millions of galaxies and potentially billions of planets. Meteorologically, it seems we will have a beautiful day tomorrow. What does it tell you, Tonto?"

Tonto fell silent for a moment, then said, "Kemo Sabe, you dumbass. It tells me someone stole the tent."

No, really, why can I see the stars? A voice inside my head replied, 'Because your eyes are open, fool. And you have glow-in-the-dark stars on the ceiling.'

I blinked. Yep: they were open and resistant to closing. Shut, damn you!

My phone rang. The display flashed on the nightstand; the ring tone telling me it was Aidan.

I wasn't asleep so I might as well talk to my brother. "Hey, Aidan, what can I do for you?" I shook off the remnants of sleepiness.

"Who is moderating the Butterfly Foundation chat rooms?" No 'Hi, how are you?' No 'Hope I didn't wake you!' I checked the time on my phone. It was nine-thirty, not exactly late.

I was wide awake and very alert. "We have three moderators, each working a four-hour shift. Dad has a list, why?"

"I'm in one of the rooms. There's someone in here I don't believe is a child."

"One sec." I grabbed my laptop, wrestled it out of the carry case, and flicked my cell onto speakerphone. "I'm jumping in."

A minute later Aidan asked, "You're Otherwisecat, right?"

"Uh-huh. I see ya, Aidan; nice screen name!" There was a deal of sarcasm in my voice: 'Hell_boy.' What was he thinking? What was I thinking? This is Aidan. He's like freaking Peter Pan, the boy who never grew up.

I watched, read and surmised that the person didn't

speak English as a first language, because the syntax was all wrong. There is a registration process for the chat room and a waiting period because we check everyone to make sure they are kids and that they're getting the help they need in life. So this person must either be a child, or be using a child's account. I pulled up the details for that particular screen name. SadlySandy had a Vienna address. She was a sophomore at Oakton High School.

"Aidan, I have this kid's details ... I'm going to get someone to call her now."

"Thanks, Ellie. You're staying in the room, aren't you?"

"Yeah. Lemme get the boys up here."

I called out to Mac and Lee. Aidan squawked over the phone, "It was necessary to holler in my ear, huh?" I ignored him and dressed. It was one thing getting flack from Lee and Sam over a sexy little evening dress, but they didn't need to know what I don't wear to bed.

Several minutes later, they thumped up the stairs. Mac knocked on the door before opening it slowly. He showed a great deal of relief at seeing me dressed, sitting on the edge of the bed, laptop perched on my knee.

"Babe?"

"Aidan is on the phone, he had a query about the Butterfly Foundation chat room."

"Hey, Aidan!" Mac said. He sat next to me, peered at the screen and read everything I had pulled up on the SadlySandy kid.

"Aid, where you been hiding, boy?" Lee asked.

"Working mostly. Keeping away from Ellie and Mac

after that fund-raising bash the publisher threw."

"Man, you should have seen how pissed they were. If I was you, Aid, I'd be leaving the state." Lee grinned at us. He was having fun winding up Aidan.

"Really?" Aidan actually sounded worried but I knew better.

"Hell, yes."

I intervened with a dismissive tone, "Yes, we were pissed Aidan; lucky for you we've got bigger fish to fry. Hang on a minute. I need to show Lee something." I beckoned to Lee to come see the screen.

Mac pulled his cell phone from his pocket and called the kid's home number. He walked out to the hallway to minimize the background noise.

I continued chatting to the occupants of the chat room. Nothing had changed with the person signed on as SadlySandy and she carried on taking part in the room. Talk about multitasking: I guess teenagers are well used to texting, chatting, talking on the phone and probably doing homework. All at once.

Mac came back. His stony expression spoke volumes.

A pang in my gut matched the ache in my head. I just knew she wasn't even online.

"Ellie, run a ping and trace on the ISP for SadlySandy. It's not her."

I clicked the Neotrace icon and waited.

"She's okay?"

"Yes. Sandy Galen is at home with mom and dad playing a video game ... that 'Sing Star' thing."

"Guess even the best multitasker can't play that and sit in the chat room holding several conversations."

We watched the trace program trying to pinpoint the location of this imposter.

"Has she given her password to anyone?"

"She said not; whoever this is probably hacked it."

I forgot Aidan was still listening until he spoke, "Is it that easy?"

"Nope," Mac replied. "They'd need to know what they were doing."

"Could that same person have hacked into the database and have people's personal information?"

Oh, God. Bile rose from my stomach, almost making it to my throat. I could feel the burn. Could this be how the Unsub is finding victims? Aidan didn't even know what we were working on. This was an innocent observation on his part. Was there information about me on that database? I hadn't created a profile or anything.

"Aidan, I'll call you back." He really didn't need to hear this conversation. I wanted to go in and shut down the imposter, close the account and, if necessary, shut down the entire server. But I didn't want to leave the kids with nowhere to go for help. If I shut down the server I'd be abandoning them – just like their parents – sending them out to connect somewhere else. Somewhere they weren't monitored by caring moderators. Then the real horror kicked in: if I shut down the server they'd go somewhere this person couldn't prey upon them, or at least would have to work harder to find them.

Somewhere safe?

The thought that they weren't safe now made me feel ill.

Lee and Mac were staring at me as if I had suddenly sprouted horns.

"Can I help you both?"

They looked at each other but said nothing.

"Speak," I commanded.

"He could have something. It's possible that this person may even be our Unsub." Mac slung an arm around my shoulder and whispered in my ear, "You're pale. Do you need something?"

Did I need something? I needed to stop this killer. "I'm okay."

Lee tapped my hand. "Check it out, Ellie, we're seconds off an answer."

We all watched as the last lines filled in on the list then clicked the Registrant button. I looked at the reply to the trace on the screen. "Department of Defense, Arlington. You have got to be fuc'n joking."

"Christ!" Lee groaned.

"Crap," Mac muttered.

"Could the hacker have hacked the Defense Department, too?" I knew that was a million-to-one shot but, hell, could someone from inside the Defense Department hack our Foundation and pose as a child ... to what end?

Mac interrupted my mental ramble. "Nah. This has got to be coming from inside."

I voiced my first terrifying thoughts, "Do we have our

Unsub, or do we have a potential pedophile?" But wait, there's more. "Do we shut the Foundation rooms? Do we expose this immediately and publicly? Do we find who used the terminal showing on this trace, charge them *now* with hacking and hope this is our Unsub? And that something carrying the death penalty will stick?"

Lee watched the room chatter intently. "Can we see if anyone is using private messages?"

"The only ones who can use them are us. It was a safeguard to protect the kids." Mac replied.

"Could someone change that?"

I picked up my phone and made a call, "Caine, we need a liaison inside the Department of Defense, Arlington."

He inhaled. I heard the air rush past his teeth. "You want in the Pentagon? Oh, this had better be good."

"This may be pertinent to our case, I need someone to go to a particular terminal and tell me who is using it. I need it now."

"I'll get you in. Stand by."

Caine hung up.

I watched Lee hustle from the room. It always amazed me how someone as impressive and big as him could move with such stealth. If you didn't see him go, you wouldn't hear him. Lee's six feet seven inches tall and gives the appearance of a quiet, moving wall of muscle. He wasn't someone I'd mess with if I didn't know him so well. He returned carrying papers and looking serious. He handed the papers to me with no comment. I started reading. He'd given me the comparisons we'd run on the victims. Two had the same doctor. Two had the same pharmacist – both were the Richmond cases. I read on until I came to the one thing that churned my stomach and burned my throat. All of our victims had a connection to the Butterfly Foundation. Technically, that meant they were all parents.

My mind threw out a scene to mull over. Marie's kitchen: the baby's bottle amongst the filth. Was there a baby? No one mentioned a baby. It never came up during the interviews with neighbors. There was no other evidence of a baby but for the bottle. I turned the page and read the last section. All the other victims had children; they lived with them, or the kids were with other family members and had supervised visitation. Seeing the list of names on the cold white paper made me shake. Why wasn't Marie's baby mentioned?

I looked up to find Mac and Lee watching me. Mac accurately read the expression on my face.

"We're not going back to Vale Road tonight."

"Could there be a baby stashed there anywhere at all?" This was where Mac had to say 'No' and believe it. Really, truly believe it.

"No. The bomb squad searched for a bomb; they would've found a baby if there was one to find."

A wave of relief almost swamped me. The person signed on as SadlySandy was still chatting to Aidan online.

Caine called back with a contact and a meeting. We were ready to leave within five minutes and my phone went again. Unknown number. I noted the time on my phone. It was Thursday already. I had my wish: Wednesday was over. The little voice in my head said, 'Be careful what you wish for.'

I answered with, "Conway."

"Ma'am, this is Kelvin Nightingale at the Comms center. Nine-one-one reported a woman murdered in Reston; this fits your investigation."

"When did the call come in?"

"Five minutes ago, 911 are still talking to the person."

"Have emergency services been dispatched?"

"Yes, ma'am."

"Remind them they are not to enter the dwelling without police. Have police verify the condition of the victim and secure the scene. We're on our way ... Kelvin – address?"

I hung up and told my team we were going to Colts Neck, Reston.

I called Aidan back and asked him to monitor the chat room and to notify the moderators that we had a security breach. Until we could deal with it, I wanted everyone aware and all eyes on those kids. Aidan grumbled a fair bit about the time and needing his beauty sleep. I couldn't dispute that. He also conceded that kids' lives were more important and he'd stay in the chat room. No doubt he'll get his own back at some stage. I'll be waiting.

This time I hung up and hoped my phone would stay silent. *Enough with the bad news already!*

I sat on the bed and considered our position. Mac and

Lee were frozen on the spot waiting for me to say something.

"Scratch the Pentagon visit. We've got a fresh scene." I looked at my laptop screen. "And SadlySandy is still in the room chatting to Aidan."

"Reschedule?" Lee asked.

"Yeah. Send someone to find out whose terminal it is; I want to know who we're dealing with."

"Not the Unsub," Lee replied with a soft voice. "I'll call Caine."

'Not the Unsub' rang in my ears like a death knell. That only left 'pedophile' in my mind. At that moment I wished I had a normal job, where people used the Internet to chat to friends, not set up kids and ruin lives. Stop! I was jumping to conclusions and going to drive myself crazy. Pearls of wisdom curled and twisted through the horror in my mind and came out as, 'Better to light a candle than curse the darkness.' Great, my mind was tossing up things grandpa used to say. It rolled around my head a little and began to actually make sense. Damned if grandpa wasn't right; there was no sense in me getting upset about this. I'd just have to fix it A-sap.

Whoever it was in the chat room couldn't do much now we knew there was something going on. We were watching from the inside and out. Breathe, Ellie ... first things first. Caine would find out who it is we need to speak to at the Pentagon, while we checked out this new murder.

Mac and I stood on the top step; water lapped at the

edge of the bottom step. The weather hadn't improved in the few hours we'd been home. Our security lights played upon the watery driveway, giving it the appearance of a dirty river.

"Oh, man." I sighed out of sheer frustration. Even the weather was against us.

Lee sloshed out to the car, water turning the legs of his jeans a dark blue halfway to his knees.

"You want I should carry you?" Mac asked, an evil glint sparked in his eye.

I sniggered. "Nah."

"Oh, you think I can't!"

Uh-oh. "Not at all, I know you can."

He grinned, scooped me up, and whispered, "You think we'll be home anytime soon?"

"I hope so."

Lee coughed from the driver's seat, "Excuse me. Crime scene ... fresh puzzle pieces ... a-a-n-y of this sound familiar?"

I wrapped my arms around Mac's neck and slowly slid to the ground. Mac kissed me quickly and we scrambled into the car. That was why we shouldn't be on the same team: inappropriate behavior in a work situation.

"Let's get this show on the road," he said, shutting the car door.

Chapter Sixteen
Breathe

The sound of jet engines overhead drowned out the sirens on the ground and all other noise. I looked up as a huge plane flew over, its undercarriage lights flashing like the trees at my mother-in-law's house in mid-August. Funny I should think of that analogy. Maybe not. Maybe it's because we're overdue for an annoying interruption. He couldn't seriously want to inflict that woman on an innocent baby. She wasn't grandmother material.

We waited until the plane passed before speaking. My first comment was to Mac. "Make sure your phone's off; I have a feeling mom is gonna try calling."

He grinned. "Yeah, me too. It's at home."

Lee chuckled. "Good thinking, Kemo Sabe."

And that one innocent phrase ran that damn joke back through my head all over again. There were no stars that night, just more rain.

We walked from the first available parking space, down the road and around shrubbery in the middle of the square at the end of the street. Police cars were visible, along with an ambulance. The house we wanted was one of the ones that backed onto a wooded area leading through to a main road. The perfect escape route for our Unsub. Probably how he got in without anyone noticing him.

I took a minute at the front door to clear my head,

readying myself for whatever we were going to find.

Mac's hand brushed mine, our fingers briefly touching in a comforting way. Lee's hulking presence was right behind me and, next to him, a space where Sam should be. I blew out a long breath, pulled on latex gloves and disposable shoe coverings, and walked through the door Mac held open.

We were standing in the living room. The first thing I saw was a child's toy box sitting on top of a large play mat. My heart sank then hit rock bottom as I saw family photographs hanging on the walls: mom, dad and two kids. I guessed the kids were about six and twelve. The pictures were full of laughter and love. Nice.

Mac whispered in my ear, "Don't."

I nodded. I knew he, like me, was comparing these images with our childhood. We walked through the living room, into the dining room. From the dining room, I could easily see into the kitchen: black writing scrawled on the cabinets, blood, bourbon, our victim wearing gold ribbon. Everything as we expected it to be. An alarm bell clanged in my head. Exactly what I expected: why did that bother me so much? He had a pattern: it's as it should be.

My eyes closed. Was I being watched? I opened my eyes and looked around. Two paramedics stood talking to two uniformed officers.

They were engrossed in their own low-toned conversation, not watching me. I could feel eyes boring into the back of my head. I spun around, startling Mac. He looked at me very oddly. I smiled, letting him know everything was okay.

Lee was behind us, taking notes. I went back to my task, forcing myself to concentrate on the scene in front of me and ignore the unnerving feelings. Entering the kitchen, I read the poem lines aloud,

"'Memories stolen by the night,
Time sliding dividing light.
Jumbled thoughts trapped inside,
Who I was suddenly died.' "

Mac scowled. "I have always loved that. Not so much now it's been sullied."

"I doubt I'll ever write another poem."

"I'm less than keen myself."

I turned carefully around on the spot.

"Okay, that's part of my poem, now where's my note?" I scanned the room, avoiding her body as much as possible. A small blue square stuck on the microwave door caught my eye. "Aha."

Cautiously, I picked my way across the room, sidestepping the pool of bloody bourbon and shoe prints. I tried not to inhale chlorine and the smell of bourbon-soaked blood as I went. Leaving the note where it was, I read it to Mac and Lee, " 'Stand By Your Man.' Funny, that's the song I had playing in my head at the last scene."

Then it hit me, a feeling I didn't like, a mix of fear and something unknown. It took a few seconds for the unknown to clarify into abhorrence. I could feel his eyes on me. He'd been watching. He was still watching. It wasn't the victims watching me at all.

And he was listening.

"Ellie!"

I didn't want to do this anymore. My lungs felt like they were going to burst. The air wouldn't go in. No matter how deeply I breathed, it wouldn't fill my lungs. I needed to get out. Why couldn't I breathe, dammit? I pushed something out of my way that offered little resistance – maybe it was Lee. I knew I was moving but the rooms blurred to nothing, then as quickly as it happened, everything stopped. I was standing in the dark. Rolling lights from the police cruisers lit a small patch of the street in front of me. The cool feeling on my face was fresh air and pelting rain. A low buzz of conversation floated in my direction from the street. Even in the dreadful hurricane weather neighbors had gathered to rubberneck. It was the middle of the night, for God's sake, they should have been in their warm beds. Why do people do that?

A hand touched my shoulder. Mac. My knight. My sanity. My security. His hand stayed on my shoulder, his voice was soft. "We're going home. Enough is enough, Ellie."

I uttered two words, "Crime scene."

"Lee's got it. He'll bring all the photographs and everything else back to our place."

I felt frown lines crease my forehead. "Our place?"

“There’s no way we’re going across the Potomac tonight and into the office.”

A stupid voice in my head scrambled his words. My vision distorted the lights of the police cars more than the rain had. Scrambled words and distorted vision, damn! He was watching us. I could feel him. He could even be listening. We hadn’t swept any of the crime scenes for bugs or cameras.

I grabbed Mac by the front of his jacket. “Have Lee get this place swept for bugs and cameras. He’s watching us and he’s listening.”

“He?” Mac asked, as he unfurled my fingers from the fabric of his jacket.

I tried to do calm but it came out panicked. “The Unsub, he’s watching.”

Chapter Seventeen
Save A Little Prayer

Mac rolled over, dragging the covers with him. I latched hold of the edge of the comforter as it slid past me and tugged it back.

He mumbled and rolled over, tangling himself in the sheet. As he fought his way free, his groggy voice surfaced, "What's the time?"

"Four."

He struggled some more with the sheet then gave up. "Why're you awake?" His struggle resumed.

Oh, gee, what could have kept me awake? The latest movie playing on the streets, *Serial Killer does Virginia?* An impending MRI to see if my brain was about to implode? Sam in the hospital? Being watched at crime scenes by the Unsub or possibly by the dead victims wanting justice? SassySelena? Dakota? On the other hand, could it be Mac wanting to talk about children?

Mac wrapped his arms around me and pulled me under the covers with him. "Why, Ellie?"

"No idea."

"You can't lie, you know that."

It was warm and cozy wrapped in his arms and not the time to voice all that goes through my head in the middle of the night. "Just the day, is all. It's nothing."

I snuggled against him and vowed to enjoy the small amount of peace found during a night of inner turmoil.

My eyes burned in their sockets from sheer exhaustion and this time they closed and stayed that way.

The next thing I recalled was Mac whispering, "Wake up."

My eyes pinged open. "I'm not asleep," I replied without moving.

"You look asleep."

I rolled over, "Coffee?" I couldn't smell any coffee. "What are you thinking? Waking me up without coffee? Has the world spun off its axis?"

"Kitchen," Mac said.

I groaned, threw back the covers and sat up. There was no light peeking through the curtains. "Is it even morning?"

"Barely." Mac passed me a sweatshirt and track pants.

"I am not going for a run. First no coffee, then no morning light, and now sweats." I raised an eyebrow.

"Lee."

Mac was a man of few words that morning. I donned the clothing. No sense Lee choking on his Cheerios and spilling his coffee because I was naked.

"What day is it?"

"Still Thursday."

"And we're up – why?" I asked, as Mac held the bedroom door open.

"Coffee first."

Even his expression gave little away. I saw tiredness and another element, not something I was accustomed to seeing in his face. If I had to pick a word to describe the extra element, I'd call it revulsion. I knew this had something to do with the case. We were not up before the birds for the good of our health. As we walked down the stairs, I could almost hear the words in his head. At the last step, I grabbed his hand, our eyes met and words tumbled from me, "There was a baby."

He nodded.

"Marie's baby?"

Mac nodded again. I could smell the coffee now. We walked down the hall in silence and entered the warm kitchen. Lee sat on a stool at the counter, a mug of coffee in his hand and two more next to him.

I thanked him for the coffee. Lee gave me one of those damn sorry looks men get when they know something's broken but can't fix it.

"Did Mac tell you?"

"I guessed."

Lee's mouth turned up on one side, "There you go again with your own special spooky shit. How did you guess something like that?"

"Dunno. Mac thinks loud and I can hear him? Where was the baby?"

Lee swallowed a mouthful of coffee then answered, "In the garbage."

Oh, come on! A little more information was required, please; the whole house was a dump. All that came out of my mouth was, "Where?"

"In the kitchen, among the piles of trash was a black garbage bag, half full. That's where they found the baby."

He took another swallow.

"When was the discovery?"

"Four this morning."

"How'd we miss it?"

"Bomb squad removed the pile after our photographer took pictures. A techie noticed a more potent smell than just general garbage as he began sifting through the trash for evidence. He uncovered the partially decomposed and gnawed remains of a baby."

"Oh, my God. Gnawed?"

Lee nodded. "Rats they think."

The fact that Lee used the plural of rat didn't escape me.

Mac drank his coffee in silence.

"How long ago did the baby die?" I remembered seeing a baby's bottle on the bench. My mind focused on the image, the contents were separated into yellowish liquid and white lumps. That didn't happen overnight.

"The baby has been dead a while, two weeks maybe. It's going to be hard to confirm, what with the heat and high humidity we've experienced the last few weeks."

By the sound of it, the vermin attention was going to confound things even more.

"They're doing a post mortem, right?"

Lee nodded, "The medical examiner has already started."

"Good. I'd like to know how the child died." I sipped my coffee, the bitterness complementing the mood of the conversation. "Boy or girl?"

Mac spoke, "A girl, around three to four months old."

"Damn."

That sure wouldn't have helped the smell in the house; the overwhelming stench would've disguised the decomposition, making it just another layer in an already rotting house.

I looked at Lee and Mac. "So we got a dead momma and a much deader infant. That baby has a daddy out there somewhere. Unless I am very much mistaken, there has been no second coming and no immaculate conception here in Virginia."

Lee smiled.

"Lee, see what you can rustle up by way of hospital records for momma Marie. We might get lucky. She had to give birth somewhere. I really hope she didn't do that in that filthy house and that there were doctors or midwives involved."

"I'll get it moving."

He started to get up. I stopped him. "Finish your coffee. Neither mom or baby are going anywhere now."

Mac placed his mug on the counter and, with deliberation, poured himself another. He must've known I was watching but he never looked up when he spoke, "Lee, can you give us a minute, please."

"Sure," Lee replied. "I'll head on into your office and get making some calls."

I waited until I heard the office door close before speaking, "What's up?"

"You know," he took my hands in his and I just knew it

was bad, "I was serious about us talking about kids."

"I figured that."

His voice softened, the pressure from his hands increased on mine, "How bad would it be?"

"Are you asking if what happened to Marie's baby could happen to ours? Or if what happened to us in our childhoods could happen again?"

"I guess both." His eyes smiled. "We're not our parents, we're especially not our mothers. You are *not* your mother."

"We don't know that, Mac. We don't know if having a child will precipitate the same madness, the same condition."

"Do you really believe you were the trigger that drove her over the edge?"

I didn't want to believe that. I'd never wanted to believe that. I had no proof. All I had was a nagging feeling that it could be true. Here he was standing in front of me, asking me to consider bringing children into our marriage. A year ago, he was asking me to marry him. I could see deeper into his soul than ever before. I saw Mac the father. I saw his love, caring, protection and joy. Then I knew exactly what my answer would be.

"No. It wasn't my fault."

A smile crept into his eyes. "Think about it, Ellie."

I wanted to scream, 'Yes, I'll have your baby,' but at the same time, I wanted to run and hide and wished this would go away. Maybe I could call his bluff. I squeezed his hands. "What if I said I had been thinking about it ...

that I had decided we should try?" The words hung in the air like a flashing neon sign. To me they warned of danger. To Mac they flashed something very different.

He pulled me into his arms so fast I had whiplash. His breath ruffled my hair as he spoke. "You serious?"

"Yes."

"Are you insane?"

"Too late to ask that now, but I believe the answer is ... absolutely. We're both nuts to even have this conversation."

"We're going to do this?"

"Yep." I looked up into his hazel eyes and wondered if our baby would have his eyes or my blue ones. The thought felt alien and uncomfortable as it continued to include hair coloring and skin tone. It held me so completely, there was no escape. Even our dubious genealogy was no match for the total package we could create. There was no guarantee that it'd happen anyway. Plenty of couples can't have children and we might be one of those couples. If there is a God, we would be one of those couples. "Finish this case first."

There was a knock on the open kitchen door. Lee poked his head around, "Safe to come in?"

"Yeah," we answered.

"I'm going to head on into the hospital first thing. I'll check on Sam then go digging through files. Am I going to need a warrant?"

I thought for a minute. Damn, he might. Marie was dead so that wasn't an issue but if daddy's name appeared, there could be a disclosure problem. "Nah. Yeah. Dammit. We need to cover our asses."

I tried hard to keep the cringe from my voice. "We're working with Judge Rubenstein."

"I take it that's a 'yes'?"

I nodded. "Get a warrant. I want to make sure we're covered further down the line."

Sam smiled. "So I gotta wake up Old Ruby?"

"Yeah, tag – you're it!"

Rubenstein was an absolute horse's ass. To get a warrant signed by him entailed jumping through a few hoops. Last time I asked, I ended up making him a pot of tea and toast, then walking his evil little yappy rat thing on a leash. He called it a dog. I failed to see the resemblance.

"I'm heading for the shower, seems like this night is over as far as sleep goes."

Mac kissed the top of my head as I moved to the door. I could hear him and Lee chatting about what the day would bring as I climbed the stairs.

Minutes later, I was standing under hot running water washing the night off my skin with soothing sandalwood soap. It smelt like Fiji. I could almost hear the waves on the shore and feel the golden sand under my feet. Suddenly Fiji evaporated.

The cold rain of the night before pelted against my skin and memories of crime scenes flooded my head. I turned off the shower. If the action replay was going to turn into a full-blown hurricane of a deal, with added blood and bourbon, I'd rather not be lost within it and find myself turning into a wrinkled prune under the hot shower.

By the time I was dressed in fresh jeans and a crisp, clean white tee shirt I felt better. I plonked myself on our bed and attacked my hair with the blow dryer. My, time flies: ten minutes later, it was no longer wet and I'd brushed it back off my face.

I flicked through the pictures in my phone while I waited for real daylight to edge its way through the crack in the curtains. Two pictures in particular caught my attention: Markov the dead Russian and Selena the crash victim. I studied her face. Admittedly, a camera-phone photograph of a passport photo doesn't make for a clear image.

My mind danced around the blurriness. Something in that picture of Markov, or whoever he really was, felt familiar. The eyes remained the same, but my imagination toyed with hair color and style. I was still sure he was the guy I tripped over in Richmond. Time passed more quickly as I played my little mind games, rather than staring blankly at the phone. Funny: a dead Russian one day and a marker pen with Russian writing on it another. What were the odds of that happening in the same week? A missing crash victim on the way from Richmond and a woman of the same name associated with a Richmond murder victim. Chlorine gas in the car and the smell of chlorine on all our victims: what were the odds?

The phone buzzed. I almost dropped it trying to answer the call. I read the caller's name on the screen: Caine.

"Morning," he rumbled. "Meet me at the Defense Department in Arlington, not the Pentagon. Head to Courthouse Road."

"Is that where the computer is?" That just didn't sound right. The ping came up as the Pentagon.

"Yes it is; our person of interest threw us a few curveballs trying to make it look like it came from the Air Force Department inside the Pentagon."

"Smart."

"We'll see." I knew that tone. That gravelly, understated tone Caine favored.

"I'm not going to like this, am I?"

"No, not at all."

I ignored it, nothing I could do about it. "I need a temp to cover Sam. I want someone who'll fit in and do the job without being babysat."

"We'll deal with that too."

I hung up.

My lips felt cracked. Not surprising with all the wind lately. Mac ambled into the room looking happier than I'd seen him all week.

"You seen my ChapStick?"

"Next to the basin in the bathroom."

"Thank you."

"No problem."

I rolled the ChapStick around between my fingers, popped off the top and applied it without using the mirror. I knew where my lips were; I'd had them a long time.

Sometimes it's best to avoid mirrors. Times like this, when my eyes stared at me accusingly, I knew I wasn't getting anywhere fast with this case, and I didn't need to see that in the mirror.

Little Dakota sprang to mind. I needed to update his dad. I needed to ensure there was a total media ban on this case.

Lee bounded up the stairs calling, "Ellie, they found something."

I flung open the bathroom door. Mac stuck his head out of our bedroom door.

"What?" we said.

"You were right, he was watching."

"Pervert," I hissed. "Dirty-filthy-killer-pervert!"

Lee bared his teeth. "We're sending the bug boys over all the Northern Virginia crime scenes, looking for cameras."

"He could have returned to retrieve the camera," I said, thinking about Sam.

"Possible," Lee replied.

At least he wasn't asking how I knew about him watching. I have no answers for why I know half of what I know. Right then, I knew that the missing crash victim had something to do with this case. I couldn't prove it. I didn't even know what the link was, but I was sure there was one.

"Okay, Lee, it's morning; head on over to Ruby's. Ya'll have fun now, ya hear."

Lee grimaced. “Fun? Getting a warrant out of Ruby?” He drawled, “Even a blind squirrel finds an acorn once in a while.”

There was no stopping the smile that spread across my face. He’d been working with me way too long.

The first thing I noticed when I stepped through the front door was the absence of rain. The rain had finally stopped. Things were looking up.

Chapter Eighteen
Good Guys Don't Always Wear White

Caine was waiting for us outside the building. Beside him stood a man I'd never seen before. He wore dark trousers and a long stylish overcoat in black leather – the softest, most covetable, chamois – Matrix style.

"Caine." I drawled out my version of a half-assed greeting.

"Ellie, allow me to introduce Officer Misha Praskovya."

The man stepped forward and grasped my extended hand with both of his. "Ah, the famous Special Agent Conway. It is an honor to meet you."

I was taken aback by his pleasing accent and enthusiastic greeting. I shook off the goldfish expression I was sure I had on my face and animated myself. "Excuse me?"

"I am honored to meet you."

"That's what I thought you said." I doubt I hid my confusion at his remark too well. "That's very nice of you."

He laughed, making his dark blue, almost black, eyes gleam. I felt the edges of unearthliness creep in. He looked every bit as if he'd stepped off the cover of a Mills & Boon novel. A scream resounded inside my head. I didn't do romance novels. Make it stop.

He let my hand go and turned to Mac.

I breathed again.

A car door banged and Lee hurried to join us, just in time to hear Officer Praskovya say. "Even in Russia we have heard of the beautiful Agent Conway."

Now he's just freaking mocking me. Mocked by a Russian: now that was a new twist on my day. How would anyone have heard of me?

Mac and Lee beamed like dorks and appeared incapable of speech. So I spoke. "You've heard of me?"

"Yes, you think the world hasn't heard of you?" It was hard to tell but I think he was genuinely surprised at my reaction. Or else he was good at making fun of people. "We have heard of you and the Delta Team and, of course, your poetry prowess, the way you used the sales of your book to start the Foundation."

Up until that moment, it had never occurred to me that we were internationally newsworthy. It was hard enough getting local media to take an interest in the Foundation.

I dismissed his comments as politely as I could, "That's flattering I'm sure, but right now we have a pervert to interview, you'll have to excuse us."

I shot Caine a get-me-away-from-him look and all he did was twitch. A sneaky suspicion crept up on me. This Russian had something to do with our case. Another Russian link.

I addressed Praskovya, "Why are you here?"

"Destiny," he replied. From inside his coat he produced a copy of our book. "May I trouble you for your autographs?"

Mac took the book, pulled out a pen and signed inside the front cover, then passed the book and pen to me. My brain was racing to fathom the situation. But even to me, standing outside a defense building, signing an autograph for a Russian officer seemed beyond extraordinary. I still didn't have an answer! I signed the book and gave it back to Praskovya. I couldn't see a way out of it.

I shook my head. "No, no, why are you here in front of the Defense Department building?" I resisted the urge to elaborate further by adding, 'Why are you in my face, carrying a copy of our book?'

"Your case and my case share an overlap," he said. Smooth didn't describe him.

"Shall we?" Caine said, walking towards the entranceway. We followed him. I slowed to let Mac catch up and walk with me. Lee caught up with Praskovya. I had the feeling he was going to stick to him like white on rice.

We followed Caine down several corridors and finally into a fluorescent-lit, open-plan office. An armed guard stood inside the doorway. He nodded to Caine. I counted seven workstations with computers. The area was devoid of personnel.

Caine stopped at the fourth desk from the door. It faced out into the office and was unremarkable except that the computer was the only one running. He put a latex glove on, touched the mouse and cleared the screen saver. The picture on the screen was an internal view of The Butterfly Foundation website – not the public access area – but the areas we used, with access to all personal information on clients.

"Certainly looks like our perv used this machine," I

stated. Praskovya stood too close to me. I felt the warmth from his body. To say I found it disconcerting was an understatement. I moved over so I stood closer to Mac.

"Your perv is female," Caine replied.

"Female ..." I repeated, "Does she work here?"

Praskovya spoke, "No. She borrowed an identity to get in here. She needed the use of the computers here to hide herself while she did what she needed to do."

"Why here? I'm sure she could use another computer, one easier to access, for instance."

"When you are on foreign soil you go where you are comfortable. She is comfortable in defense areas."

"We know this how?"

"She's an integral part of a case I have been working on for three years."

"Three years? Who is she? *The Jackal*?" I really wished I hadn't gone there with that comment. Visions of Bruce Willis as a fat greasy Canadian mixed with the more pleasing Richard Gere as the Irishman Declan Mulqueen. I knew who I preferred. Damn my mind and its movie-style interruptions. I wanted to dally on the Richard Gere memory but it was not the time.

"She is not Jackal. Who is this Jackal?" Praskovya said, impatience overshadowing his initial charm.

"Never mind, nineteen-nineties movie ... it's a book too, *The Day of the Jackal*. Frederick Forsyth wrote the original ... a great read. As a state security agent, I'm surprised you haven't read it; it's about the attempted assignation of a European president."

Praskovya smiled. "It is interesting inside your head, I think."

Yeah yeah. "And how does this woman affect our case?"

Praskovya replied, "Whoever she's trying to find has something to do with the Foundation."

"She was found then lost again," Caine said. "Anything about that car crash you called in a few days ago seem off to you?'

I stared at Mac. His inscrutable expression gave nothing away. I swallowed hard hoping to dislodge the lump in my throat before speaking, "Yes. The whole thing. I don't think I wanted to believe it had something to do with us but I couldn't shake the feeling it *was* about us. I was thinking Mossad originally, and obviously that was way the hell off the mark, but my next thought was Russian."

Praskovya perched on the edge of the desk and spoke again, "Markov found her. She killed him and escaped."

"And he was?" Apart from being the guy I tripped over in Richmond. I looked at Mac. His eyes bore the knowing look that came from listening to my ramble earlier about the Russian/New Zealander.

Praskovya continued, "Russian police working with Interpol, tracking terrorists."

I looked at Caine. "You're telling me there are Russians tracking someone in our country and we didn't know about it?"

Caine glowered. "Were and we know now."

Could it be any more complicated? The cloak and dagger shit was making my head spin. Russian police using a New Zealand passport; I was pretty sure I didn't want to know how that came about.

I turned my attention back to Praskovya. "She's a terrorist?"

"Yes, and more; she is finding a serial killer."

"A terrorist looking for a serial killer? To what end?"

"Yes, looking for. We think recruitment."

That one word transmuted my blood to arctic crystals. A terrorist wanted to recruit a serial killer. This was exactly what I needed, not! Fan-fucking-tastic.

Caine's phone buzzed, he excused himself. When he came back he told us Officer Praskovya was working with us and would replace Sam.

It was an announcement more than anything else and there was zero room for my opinion on the subject. Caine left to get back to his meetings and paperwork.

I tried to get a handle on Misha Praskovya. Apart from the whole escapee-from-a-romance-novel thing, he seemed pleasant enough; obviously his credentials checked out and he was competent, or Caine wouldn't drop him into my team.

He addressed Lee, "You are Lee, yes?"

Lee nodded.

"You know computers?"

Lee nodded. "Do bears shit in the woods?"

Praskovya looked confused. It took a minute for him to comprehend, then he moved right along. "Can you check the history on this machine? Can we see everything she was looking for?"

"Probably."

"Do it now."

Lee looked at me. I shook my head.

Praskovya repeated, "Do it now!"

I interrupted, "That's not how it's done here. I need the computer experts to look at this machine." I sensed Mac smiling and could almost guarantee Lee was having a quiet smirk. Obviously, Praskovya didn't know Mac was our resident expert in all things to do with social networking and computers. He could probably have used his skills to uncover some info from the machine in question but although Mac was with cyber, he wasn't a computer forensics technician, which was really what we needed. I couldn't take the chance of evidence being declared unusable for whatever reason. Best to leave it to the experts.

The Russian knocked the desk hard with his leg and the monitor wobbled. Praskovya complained, "Too much red tape: have Lee do it."

Who the hell did he think he was? Mr. Tall Dark and Hunky couldn't just swoop in and start ordering my team around. I needed to stop thinking of him in Mills & Boon terms before the whole scenario took over and led to my inevitable committal to a psychiatric facility.

"That's not how it's done," I reminded him.

Praskovya said, "Ridiculous! Get them now."

"Wait." I didn't care how pretty his Russian accent was: I wasn't about to have orders barked at me!

In an open display of anger, he slammed a heavy sticky-tape dispenser onto the desk, "For what?"

My voice was firm and polite. "Either you wait and shut up, or you leave. This is my case."

"You are wasting time." He banged the dispenser onto the desktop again, the force making the monitor shake. "We must stop her."

"I hate to burst your bubble ... but she is not my main concern."

"She is the best lead you have to your killer, and I know how she thinks."

"Shut up." I couldn't think with his incessant autocratic interruptions. How could someone so annoying have such a sexy voice? Guess there's always a redeeming quality.

I didn't care what he knew about the woman or the Unsub. How did Caine think he was a good fit for our team? Maybe he'd had one too many blows to the head. Okay, so I did care what Mr. Tall Dark and Hunky knows about the Unsub: shoot me. Damn him and his Mills & Boon ways!

Very carefully and properly, I said, "Mac, please call in the Computer Analysis and Response Team. Use the case number; we have Priority Request Status for this case."

Not that it actually meant anything: Priority Request Status or, as we liked to call it, Probably Really Slow.

Mac nodded and walked to the far wall with his phone.

I turned my attention to Lee, "Did you get the warrant?" He didn't seem to be far behind us, and I knew how difficult Rubenstein liked to be.

"Sure did. He was in a good mood and I got off lightly." Lee's face beamed. "I'd say he was a man who'd had a good night." He winked. "His friend looked like he-she would be right at home in a Vegas chorus line."

Not something I wanted to think about in relation to one of our judges; good work regardless. "Good job. Execute the warrant as soon as we're done here."

It didn't matter how hard I tried to ignore Praskovya. I could feel my blood boil every time he moved, which was often. He shifted his weight from foot to foot, impatiently. I hoped he'd misjudge and his feet would somehow slip out from under him. It might have happened if I'd accidentally pushed something under his feet. I looked around but couldn't find anything to do the job. Disappointing.

Mac returned. "Ellie?"

"Mac." I tried not to snarl. I failed. "They coming?"

"Yep, CART said to touch nothing."

I looked at Praskovya. "You hear that? Touch nothing."

"Yes," he replied, kicking the desk leg. He dropped the sticky tape dispenser and picked up a staple gun. He tapped it on the desk and fiddled about with it.

"Praskovya, who is the woman you are after?"

"Selena Vadbolski."

Again with the familiar first name. "And she is who?"

"A terrorist."

I knew that already. I wanted to slam the staple gun into his head. I could feel my hands shaking as I forced them not to react to the instructions coming from my irritated nervous system.

"Why would she be comfortable here?" Being comfortable and being able to borrow an identity to get into a defense department building were two different things in my mind.

"She is ex-special forces."

Lee whispered, "*Spetsnaz*."

"How does someone who is ex-Spetsnaz become a terrorist who is chasing a serial killer to recruit him?" My hands shook even more; I really had to fight to keep myself from smacking Praskovya for being such damn hard work. "How does that happen?" I jammed my hands into my jeans' pockets to try to stop the trembling. I had a feeling I was being shoveled the biggest load of manure yet. With so much shit falling off the shovel, my roses should be exceptional this year. My mind was spinning another thread and it wasn't something I wanted to say aloud: 'What does it have to do with me?'

Mac grabbed my arm and whispered, "Something wrong?"

"Oh, no, nothing." Mac squeezed my arm. I glared at him. "Nothing is wrong, I need some air."

I curbed the urge to flounce off screaming obscenities and slamming doors in my wake. Instead, I skulked away hoping no one else noticed my annoyance. Mac knew me well enough to leave me be for a few minutes.

No one was around. I checked the intersecting corridor: empty. There was a courtyard in front of me and the door stood open. I escaped out into the fresh air. I walked around the garden. Tattered flowers struggled to bloom despite the storm's ferociousness. The grass underfoot was sodden and squelchy. Everything had suffered in the persistent rain; at least the courtyard offered some protection from the gale-force winds. A piece of paper twirled by my feet. Why couldn't people pick up their trash? Did they have to crap on everything? I stomped on the candy wrapper, trapping it under my boot. I picked it up, scrunched it and threw it into a trash can three feet away. Lazy fucks. I could feel profound anger rising. Why was a terrorist in a forum, communicating with a young mother in Richmond? Who the fuck killed her; who killed Dakota's mom? Fuck! I never had a chance to read those emails.

Damn, I was sick of sickos taking a shine to me and sick of this godforsaken headache. Maybe Hawkeye was right and there was something wrong with me. I really didn't feel well.

Think, Ellie. Stop and think: anger, faint headache, feeling generally off: you know this. Oh crap. Everything began to blur and not in a good way. My hands were still trembling. I couldn't get my phone out of my pocket. Something poked annoying holes in my vision – black holes – no matter how I moved my head, I couldn't see around them. Infuriating! The voice came back, 'Brilliant, Ellie, you flounce off and now look what happens. I saw the ground floating and wobbling around me.

A thought manifested. I could see it in a speech bubble, 'This is going to hurt.' I fell backwards, unexpectedly grateful for the dark and the peace that came with the fall into blackness.

Surprising things happen in that muddled place between wakefulness and sleep. Ideas that helped break cases floated in that space. Sometimes seemingly random links that offered hope and direction broke through and stayed with me. I hoped something helpful would materialize this time.

A familiar, worried face swam in and out of focus. When it disappeared altogether, I realized he was shaking my arm and calling my name.

A distant whisper. "Ellie."

"Go away, I'm sleeping."

"Ellie, you're not asleep."

How did he know what I was doing? Get out of my head. I'm tired. A sharp pressure on my arm hurt.

"Come on; wakey, wakey." I could hear him clearly now. I even knew I was in a strange place and there was an earthy smell. Wet earth. I didn't much like that turn of events.

My eyes opened. Mac was in my face.

"You pinched me!" I accused.

"Sit up."

Mac helped me into a sitting position.

I looked around, delighted that the holes in my vision were gone and mumbled a soft, "Sorry."

"How's your head?"

"Okay."

Mac guffawed like a dumbass. "I rest my friggin' case!"

"You what?" I was so lost.

Another voice laughed before speaking, "I owe you five bucks," Lee said.

Now what was he doing? Wasn't Lee supposed to be waking up Judge Rubinstein and searching for files?

"What?" I was still lost.

"Nothing, sweets," Mac replied; he had one hand on the back of my head.

"What are you doing?"

"Despite you being okay, I'm not fussed about your blood running out of your head."

"My blood doing what?" I must've heard wrong. Mac waited for my mind to catch up. "I hit my head?" I really didn't want to hear that.

MRI and CAT scan here I come. I couldn't afford another head injury, even one that wouldn't bother most people. My glass skull and I were fast becoming liabilities. It was bad enough that I'd failed to explain the extent of the optical events, associated with the migraines I experienced, to my doctor and Mac.

Lee smiled. "You still okay?"

"Yes," I replied with a scowl.

His smile widened.

"Quit it! What did I hit?" Please don't let it be stone, concrete or anything else hard.

Mac replied, "There was a piece of broken glass in the grass."

"How freaking typical. Is it in my head?"

"No. You need this checked out though and maybe a few stitches."

I grabbed his arm. "Help me up."

"You feel sick or dizzy?" he asked.

Absolutely. But I wasn't admitting to anything. It would pass; it always does. "Nope. I'm wet and muddy and feel like a freaking fool. Will that do?"

I tried hard not to say that I was okay.

He nodded and pulled me up, holding me by the shoulders while he made sure I was steady.

"Thanks, how much time have I wasted? Are the computer boys here?"

Lee and Mac looked at each other. I sensed a conspiracy.

"Not as much as you're going to; we're getting you checked out." Mac replied, "And yes, they're here, they were here," he corrected himself, "They've removed the computer and taken it back to the lab."

They'd moved a lot faster than expected. But once in the lab things tended to grind to a halt. The computer they'd taken would be added to the end of the queue.

I could feel my jeans clinging to my legs. My butt was wet and muddy. I imagined that the back of me looked like a swamp, complete with twigs and leaves stuck to my hair and clothing. I wondered if I could opt out of the whole checkup process, "I need to clean up before you get me checked out."

There it was again, that knowing look they gave each other. It would be more annoying if my head weren't so cotton-wool-like. They weren't going to let me go home.

Then things rapidly turned a whole hell of a lot worse. My legs turned to Jell-O, black swirled in front of my eyes, vomit sprayed onto the ground in front of me.

Mac cursed as he grabbed me. My vision cleared. My head throbbed. I heard voices and knew Lee was talking to someone but it wasn't Mac.

Mac whispered in my ear, "We're taking you to the emergency room."

Everything in front of me swam in a fine mist. I thought I heard Hawkeye but the accent was all wrong. I had no idea why I thought it was Hawkeye. It was obviously Doctor Luka Kovac. It wasn't Korea. It was some modern American hospital, in Chicago. At first it seemed absurd but that feeling subsided as I listened to Luka Kovac talking to John Carter. I listened, expecting to hear Abbey's voice join the conversation but all I heard was running feet and wheels clicking on linoleum.

At that moment I realized I'd gone from *MASH* to *ER*. At least *ER* was a recent TV show. I should've been relieved; I thought it was way better than *MASH*. I'd take Kovac and Carter over Hawkeye and Trapper any day. There was a good chance George Clooney would appear any second: he trumped them all.

How could it get worse? I wondered. Like this: the next voice I heard said, "Christ, Mac. You want to explain this to me?" Caine. Yep, that was worse.

I looked into Caine's steely eyes. "You're standing in my puke."

A paramedic took my arm. “Watch your step, ma’am.” He escorted me to a gurney.

We were going to leave the courtyard and I couldn’t see any way out of a hospital visit. I glared at him. “No way! I’ll go with you but I’ll be walking!” I swept my arm to encompass the gurney and equipment bag, “This is all unnecessary.”

Caine’s voice bellowed from behind me, “You will do as you are told.”

I yelled back, “Not in this lifetime.”

“Conway!”

“Grafton! I am capable of walking.” I knew his blood pressure would soar and it made me feel better.

The accent spoke from somewhere close to me: Luka. “Gabrielle, let them help you.”

There was an audible collective intake of breath as a cone of silence dropped over the area. No one breathed, not even the paramedics. I turned to face Mac, Lee, Caine and the hunky Luka.

“I’m sorry, for a minute I thought you said Gabrielle.” With an intense, cautionary tone, I continued. “We. Don’t. Use. The. G. Word.”

Mac and Lee were motionless. Caine’s mouth twitched just at one corner.

Luka’s eyes sparkled, he disarmed me with a smile, “I’m so sorry, Ellie. Please forgive me.”

Oh God! Unfair! He looks like that and he apologizes. He closed the ground between us and the next thing I knew, I was laying on the gurney. Mr. Tall Dark and

Hunky had tricked me. Mac was talking to him. Surely Luka would come with us; after all he is an *ER* doctor. Damn, I had to be insane. The corridors moved past me, or I moved through them; either way something moved. It felt peculiar. When everything stopped, Mac touched my arm, "Ellie, what's up?"

I noted he didn't ask if I was okay.

"What's his name, the guy who looks like Luka from *ER*?"

Mac smiled. "At least it's not *MASH* this time. His name is Misha, Officer Misha Praskovya."

I was okay: he wasn't really Luka, which was groovy. Part of me was a little sorry though. I almost enjoyed the *ER* sequence. Mac was right about one thing, it was better than *MASH*. And both were way better than the Mills & Boon romance that wouldn't quit.

I wondered what Praskovya's agenda was. It seemed an astonishing coincidence that he would arrive in our world. Yet another Russian connection. Yet another Selena connection.

Chapter Nineteen
Last Cigarette

I discharged myself as soon as the doctor had glued the small cut on the back of my head. No big deal. I convinced them that I had already scheduled an MRI and CAT scan, so no point getting all bent out of shape trying to set up an emergency MRI. It wasn't a lie. I had several unheard voicemail messages and one of those would be from my doctor's office about the tests. Just because I chose not to listen to them didn't make the appointment any less real. I wasn't in the right space to deal with that yet. Dr. Kapowski was bound to have some kind of aneurism when news of this latest debacle reached him. He'd get over it. The killer wasn't going to wait until I felt better.

Anyway it was just a little stress episode, nothing more than a smallish migraine – understandable considering the circumstances. I was pretty sure it wasn't some kind of transient ischemic attack. I was fully functional and had no muscle weakness, slurred speech, or facial numbness. A few painkillers for the headache before it became significant and I would feel okay.

Lee was searching files and would then visit Sam. Mac and I were taking Praskovya home with us. He needed to learn how we worked. We needed to know what he knew.

Mac made coffee and checked the answering machine. Twenty-seven messages from his mother. I told

Praskovya to make himself comfortable in the living room and joined Mac in the kitchen to listen to the messages. They were the best yet. The first fifteen dealt with Mac's avoidance of her, ranting about how he never answered the phone anymore. The next five were thinly-veiled threats about her coming on down to teach him a lesson on telephone etiquette. We switched off the machine at that point.

"Yeah, she's definitely grandmother material," I said, then hustled out of arm's reach.

"Smartass!" he called after me, "Ask Praskovya how he has his coffee."

Praskovya yelled back, "Black, thank you."

The phone messages lightened my mood. Mac's mom had become the comic relief in our lives. I felt calmer and less bogged down by the case. I really wanted a cigarette. I satisfied the craving by imagining I'd already had one, created from all the secondhand smoke that poured down the phone and into our answer machine, courtesy of my manic mother-in-law. Excellent. Mac's mom was transformed into a nicotine fix. That worked for me. Now to get Praskovya working for me. Darkness, or a sort of dark cloud, edged into my mind whenever his name came up. It billowed like his overcoat in the breeze that morning.

I had to stop thinking in romance novel terms. The billowing had to stop. I knew it was too late when a cloud parted and revealed Praskovya, all dark and mysterious, standing under an old stone bridge. He looked expectantly across the river that tumbled over moss-speckled green stones. White foam gathered in small pools among rocks. A woman with long dark hair and a flowing purple cloak picked her way carefully towards him.

This new madness was getting out of hand. He wasn't even my type.

I sighed, cleared the scene from my head and dropped into an armchair across the room from Praskovya. In my usual fashion I pulled up my legs and tucked them under me.

He smiled.

I smiled back.

"How is your head?"

"It's, oh ... fine." Almost let an 'okay' slip out. Damn men, ganging up on me, ruining my word.

"You have a nice home." He tapped the fingers of his left hand on the arm of the chair. He wore a wedding ring on his right hand.

"Thank you." I still wasn't getting anything from him. I needed to break him out of the small-talk phase and get to the guts. "Do you know who the Unsub is?"

He crossed his right leg over his left knee. The tapping ceased. His dark eyes looked directly into mine. I looked back. It was like looking into a black hole.

"We don't have a name," he said.

"How do you know this ex-officer is after our Unsub?"

"She followed his trail across Eastern Europe and we followed her."

"It's the same person?"

"Yes."

"Who is she?"

"I told you, she is Selena Vadbolski. An officer with Spetsnaz."

"Yes, so you told me. How did she become a terrorist?" This woman was important, maybe not to us, but to him. Why? It irked me.

Mac came in with the coffee and placed the tray on the coffee table in the center of the room. He passed Praskovya's first, then mine. Guests first.

"Thank you, Mac. Very nice coffee," Praskovya said. "Do you grind your own beans?"

He really liked the small talk; quite the Chatty Cathy when it came to subjects other than work-related topics.

Mac said, "Not often, we have a coffee shop close by that makes a very nice blend for us."

I looked from Mac to Praskovya and back again. And blew my theory that Praskovya wasn't my type right out of the water. I prayed that the ridiculous Mills & Boon scenes would cease to interrupt my cognitive processes. The whole intrusion was akin to running with scissors. At any moment I might trip and slice myself on the sharp edges of the book covers generated by my imagination. Would he swoop to my rescue? The Mills & Boon interludes had to stop.

I pulled him from his coffee discussion with Mac and back to my topic of choice, "Praskovya ... how does an officer with Spetsnaz become a terrorist?"

"What drives one to do anything? Why did you become a FBI agent?"

I smiled, but only because I had succeeded in ridding myself of the romance novel connotations. He was less charming now and more infuriating. What if I took my gun and pressed the muzzle against his temple? "Tell me about Selena."

He uncrossed his legs and placed his mug on the table. "Do you know much about the Russian Federation?"

I shook my head, "No, I'm sorry, I don't." A little voice in my head kicked in, telling me to listen and not float off: it wasn't a history lesson, it was pertinent stuff. I hate that little voice; it invariably means it's boring stuff that I have to wade through before the good stuff comes out. It took all the little voices to keep me on track. I listened as well as I could, while Praskovya told us of life in The Russian Federation: the crime, the corruption, the unemployment and how the country was desperately trying to recover economically.

They were fighting fires on all fronts and making little progress. Crimes covered up, or simply not investigated during the communist reign, were oozing like septic wounds. One of those things was the high level of serial killing and serial rape. Yet none of this explained how a Spetsnaz officer found herself as a terrorist. Or did it?

"Praskovya, why exactly is she a terrorist?"

He blinked and looked up, astonished. "She committed an act of terrorism."

It would have felt so good to hold my gun to his temple, or maybe just smack him about a few times. I could break his arm in two and hit him with the soggy end. I sucked it up and remained polite. "Which was?"

"Selena Vadbolski detonated a bomb that blew up a police station, killing forty police officers and support personnel."

"She blew up a police station?"

"And made threats against other police stations. She planted bombs in five stations. The explosive was stolen from the army."

"She killed police, she stole explosives and, okay, I understand how that would piss off everyone. Why the hell does she want our Unsub?"

Praskovya sighed. "We don't know."

And just like that, the blackness reappeared. He slipped back under cloud cover.

"You don't know?" I couldn't believe it. I was back to square one.

Praskovya's eyes met mine. He didn't speak.

"Where are you staying?" Mac asked.

"The Marriott."

Mac smiled. "Which one?"

"On 12th Street I think, in Washington."

Mac nodded. "Yeah, we're familiar with it." It was the first hotel we'd stayed in together, during another difficult case, a lifetime ago.

"I'll get a car to come pick you up," I said. "Tomorrow you'll be given a cell phone with our numbers pre-programmed. Contact one of us if you think of anything that might help find our Unsub and your terrorist." I reached over to a small wooden box on a shelf behind me and took out a business card. "Before you get the phone, you might need to contact us."

I uncurled my legs and stretched them. I handed Praskovya the card, then went out to our office to call Caine. I told him his replacement for Sam sucked. I heard Caine grind his teeth. He made no comment. I suspected his jaw was locked shut from all the grinding. After a brief rundown on the nothing we'd got out of him, I hung up before he could speak. It wasn't necessary to hear him growl: I just wanted him to know how things weren't progressing.

I called and checked in with Lee. He was still at the hospital. Sam was doing well. Lee was manually searching through hospital records. He mentioned that Marie Kline's file was hefty and scattered. Apparently she'd used several aliases.

He was busy tracing all the components and trying to assemble a clear medical history and find the obstetric notes. Lee being Lee, he'd managed to get several of the women in the records department to help.

My last call was to Rich. I asked for a favor: a car to return Praskovya to Washington. He was happy to oblige. The bar tab was growing.

I wanted Praskovya and his dark cloud out of my home. I sat at my computer and began to search for an old friend, an old Russian friend, knowing he'd be online somewhere. I just had to locate him. He wasn't as difficult to find as I'd thought. Within minutes, we'd dealt with the small talk and he had bestowed me with information on Spetsnaz.

Interesting and helpful information that almost made me forget I needed sleep. What I was going to get was a few hours going over all the paperwork. There were things I needed to chase up: that computer for one, the bug boys for another. And the bourbon. I wanted to know about the bourbon. Why bourbon?

If our Unsub had carved a trail across Eastern Europe, had he used bourbon then, or something more country-specific? Was this particular brand of bourbon available outside the U.S.? Questions, questions ... and no freaking answers. All this talk of bourbon made me want a drink. Not bourbon; I doubted I would ever drink it again, although it used to be my drink of choice.

Those last four words reverberated around my brain. He couldn't know that, could he? He's committing crimes in Virginia; lots of people drink bourbon. As the words rattled inside my head, they rearranged themselves and started spelling trouble.

I hurried back into the living room. Praskovya's aura felt so dark and obvious to me, it hung over his head like a thundercloud. I fully expected lightning to fire across the room. I wouldn't have been at all surprised if it had struck me.

"Praskovya, which Spetsnaz group did she work for?" I enjoyed proving I wasn't a total fool when it came to things Russian and that I had sources. Vlad had told me a few vital things in our short conversation. After the fall of communism, some Spetsnaz groups remained intact in the various countries that now had them within their borders. Those left inside the Russian federation, once run by the KGB, were now under the umbrella of the Federal Security Service, or FSB. The FSB controlled the primary counterterrorism and hostage-rescue groups. The initials made no sense to me, until my contact gave me the Russian name for the organization, Federal'naya Sluzhba Bezopasnosti.

The cloud sucked most of the color from his eyes, making them darker and less attractive. "Spetsgruppa Al'fa."

I had heard of Al'fa. It was one of the groups controlled by the FSB, the ultimate crack counterterrorist and hostage-rescue group within FSB.

"So you are telling me that an officer from Al'fa committed acts of terrorism?"

"Yes."

"You are FSB?" It felt good to know something, even if it wasn't a whole hell of a lot.

He smiled. "Yes. I am FSB. We are your FBI equivalent."

I stretched out my legs. My mind moved on. "Did we ever see that witness report?"

"I don't remember seeing any witness report," Mac replied.

"Our nonagenarian."

Mac smiled, amused by my description of the relic from Herndon and the scene of the Laura Amos killing.

Praskovya spoke, "You have a witness? What is nonagenarian?"

"The crypt keeper," I replied.

"What is this crypt keeper?"

I'd lost him and it brought me unimaginable joy. "Our witness is a ninety-four year old woman. She saw the Unsub leaving an apartment building."

"This crypt keeper ... saw the killer," Praskovya said, his voice conveying his mental machinations.

I started to move. "Yes, we think so ... now I must go hunt down the report she made. I'd like a description of our Unsub."

Mac stood a split second before we heard a knock at the front door.

"That will be your car," I told Praskovya. "We will see you tomorrow."

Praskovya rose and followed Mac out. I waited for Mac to return to the living room, glad that the cloud had left with Praskovya.

Mac didn't say much when he came back in. I could tell he was pleased Praskovya had gone and that he was concerned over this whole terrorist/killer/Al'fa thing.

"One second, my cunning wifey," Mac said. He eyed me with a small amount of suspicion and asked, "How did you know about Al'fa?"

I smiled. "Did your father ever talk about Vlad?"

Mac attempted to cover his surprise. "I think ... a long time ago."

"Long time ago, back when our dads used to take those fishing trips?"

Our fathers had a long and colorful history together,

which we'd only found out about just over a year ago. All our lives we'd listened to our fathers saying they were going fishing, my dad with someone called Tank and Mac's dad with someone called the Colonel. Imagine our amazement when we learned that Tank was Mac's dad and the Colonel was what he called my dad.

"Yeah, back then."

"Vlad was a friend they met. He was a diplomat then."

"And you contacted Vlad to get some info?"

"We've kept in touch since dad's heart attack."

Mac's smile became a grin. "I never know what you'll pull out of your sleeve next."

Me neither, except this time my 'next' involved running some background checks on Praskovya while we were checking out the witness description and doing all our paperwork. I wanted to know who we were dealing with.

Music floated around inside my head. It was the opening bars to something familiar, though I couldn't quite place it. I waited with as much patience as I could muster to hear what song my brain would dredge up this time. I didn't have a lot of patience to spare. Lyrics belted forth. I jumped. Who'd have thought my internal stereo was that loud? What did a long cool woman in a black dress have to do with our Unsub? I didn't enjoy the inference that spilled from a nest of bad men and whiskey bottles. I liked even less the reference to the FBI. It was unnerving; if the song had mentioned bourbon and not whiskey, I suspect I may have thrown all my toys from the sandbox.

I followed the song and began searching through our CD collection.

"Can I help?"

" 'Long Cool Woman'," I said.

"I'll get it, it's in my truck."

I watched him leave, then hurried to the office. The emails between Julie Trevalli and Selena had arrived from Julie's husband and were calling to me.

It didn't take long for a few weeks' worth of emails to download. I started at the beginning with the oldest time stamp. After reading the first five I began to skip every other one. There was nothing of any interest. By the time Mac came back in and played the song for me, I'd read almost half the messages. They were normal, if such a thing exists.

The exchanges contained general chitchat and what appeared to be two friends discussing children. Except – if I was right – only one of them had a child.

The song triggered nothing other than a feeling of doom. Usually I gained some sort of insight from the songs that stick in my head, or jump out and scream, 'play me.' I had no idea if it came from me or was some universal cosmic thing.

Either way, I know stuff other people don't.

Chapter Twenty

Someday Might Just Be Tonight

Friday arrived with an early morning phone call. Half an hour later I stood on the edge of the ash-covered sidewalk, peering into the blackened, smoldering shell of Marie's house. An occasional flame burst from the hot rubble. The two fire trucks parked by the curb were empty of personnel. The fire fighters surrounded the structure in front of us, damping down hot spots as they flared up.

Mac hustled over to neighboring houses. Windows were shattered in houses on both sides and in the house directly opposite the site. I stood in silence watching the fire fighters. Mac was only gone a few minutes before he came back with information.

"Neighbors heard the explosion; there's a fair bit of damage to surrounding homes. A nine-year-old boy, hit with flying glass, is being treated at Inova now."

"Nice," I commented. "Whoever set this did a damn fine job."

Praskovya stepped up beside me. His black coat swished about his legs, matched only by the swirling thunderclouds above his head.

"Unpleasant," he said.

"I've seen worse."

"Really?"

I turned to face him. "Really. I am sure you have, too.

Anyone who has spent more than a few weeks in Israel has seen worse."

He replied with studied calm. "You've done your homework."

Mac touched my elbow. "Fire service says there was someone inside."

"Who?" Now that was discombobulating. We'd found no evidence to suggest Kline had had housemates.

"Male, approximately thirty years old, identification pending," he replied.

"Cause of death?" It seemed ludicrous asking that when we were standing looking at the mess.

"Hopefully the smoke got him before the flames did," Mac said. "We won't know for sure until the autopsy is completed."

I nodded and wondered how much was left to autopsy.

"You think our Unsub really wanted this place cleansed or is this a happy twist of fate?" Mac said, rocking back on his heels as he surveyed the smoldering wreckage.

"Cleansed, how ironic." I smiled.

"Forensics will come through once the smoldering has settled," Mac said. "We're not going to know much until then."

"Let's hope they find something." I turned to Praskovya. "Your terrorist favors bombs, yes?"

He nodded.

"Our Unsub enjoys them too."

"Another happy coincidence?" Mac asked.

"Oh, I doubt it," I replied. "Just like I doubt our Unsub set this explosion."

Another flame shot skyward.

"So who was caught inside?" I was thinking aloud rather than actually asking.

My gut's opinion was interesting. It thought it could be the baby's father. Maybe he'd heard about Marie's demise and come for the child. Alternatively, maybe he'd killed the child and tried to make sure no one discovered his secret. Bet the crime-scene tape and sealed doors were a nasty shock.

"Penny for your thoughts," Mac whispered in close proximity to my ear.

"Speculation not worth repeating."

As always, Mac was on my wavelength. "You'd have to be pretty dumb to get caught in your own explosion."

"That's true."

He continued, "How smart is someone who knocks up a crack whore?"

"Not the brightest crayon in the box."

"Can't argue with that."

Praskovya cleared his throat. I didn't know about Mac but I had almost forgotten Praskovya was with us.

"Did you have something to add?"

"We are being watched," he said. Pensive.

Mac and I turned to Praskovya. The three of us stood, heads bowed in a tight group.

"Where is our watcher?" I asked. "Could it be a nosy neighbor?"

"Could be." He sighed. Experience told me people were nosy like that no matter where you were in the world, although I had a feeling that in some places they would be more discreet.

"Direction?" Mac asked.

"Fifteen meters behind you, in the trees across the road."

I did the conversion in my head. Sixteen yards. Then flipped my phone open and passed it to Praskovya. "Make like you are texting someone and get a photograph."

He did as I asked and then handed me back the phone. Mac and I kept facing the burnt wreck of a house. I emailed the picture to Lee and to myself, with notes to compare it to the description we had of our Unsub. It was only a possible description and not much help. Our nonagenarian witness was awesome and did her best to supply us with a usable description. Male, approximately six feet tall, short brown hair, square chin, sharp nose, unattractive in her opinion. Within our huddle, we all viewed the photograph.

"Anyone you recognize?" I asked Praskovya.

"I don't believe so."

"Is he still there?"

"Yes."

I nodded and turned to Mac. "We'll carry on. Get the fire department to let us know when they release the scene to our forensics team."

Mac strode over to the scene commander, then met us back at the car.

Sometime later, we met up with Lee in the Hoover Building. I slid into my desk chair and waited while everyone made themselves comfortable. Lee had a possible name for the father of the baby; some poor unfortunate called Kadin Bowen, listed in Marie's records as primary contact during her stay after the baby was born. He also paid the hospital bills.

"Can you get someone to go by his last known address? If he isn't the father then he may know who is."

"I asked Mednick and Charles to drop over and make inquiries."

"Good." I guess.

Mednick was an experienced agent, which is a polite way of saying he could've retired five years ago. Charles had a few authority issues and had been partnered with Mednick to learn some manners. The perfect pair to dig up some background on Bowen.

"Have we got usable DNA from the baby and from the fire body?"

"I don't know," he replied.

"I'd like you to find out and have them compared. That might be the only way to ever know if our crispy critter is related to that poor baby."

I watched Lee's shoulders tense. "Won't bring the little soul any happiness."

None of us quite knew where to file the dead baby. It wasn't something we usually came across. The horror of it would live on in our collective psyche for a long time to come.

"Was there a name in the records?" I asked.

"Crystal was written in the margin of the birth notes."

Mac spoke to him. "She's in a better place now."

He was right. I had no doubt that the short life of that innocent child was miserable and filled with pain.

I shoved thoughts of the baby aside. Back to the killer: enough sidetracks, clever though they are. Our Unsub couldn't have had a better distraction if he'd engineered it himself.

I spun my chair slowly in a circle; as it came back to face the room I said, "Don't you wonder where our Unsub is and who his next victim will be?"

The strangest feeling followed. Someone walked over my grave and back again. I shuddered.

"How many people have signed up with the Butterfly Foundation?" Lee asked.

"I have no idea."

He was right: that was a good place to start to look for our next victim; maybe get there ahead of time. I realized suddenly there was an odd silence in my head, no songs, no old TV shows, no random voices dropping clues. I suspected that the revelation had just jinxed it. Anyway, I was still processing the last song. It had definitely unnerved me.

I swiveled to Mac and asked, "Any idea?"

"No. I can find out." He pulled his laptop from the backpack he carried. "Scoot over." He slid his chair around the desk. We share well.

Lee made himself at home on the sofa and started

making calls to get the DNA ball rolling. Praskovya stayed on the periphery. I knew he was taking notice of everything that went on. He kept his interest mute, which worked for me.

"Is there any pattern at all to the deaths?" Lee asked. He plonked his phone down on the low table in front of him and yawned. "Apart from the women all being mothers? I mean Butterfly is all about kids, so wouldn't they all be mothers?"

"Yep, they would," I replied, as I watched over Mac's shoulder. "There must be a pattern or a reason he chose these particular women ... and a way to predict his next victims."

"He's been tossing out bodies thick and fast, so time is something we don't have a lot of," Mac said.

I had an idea. "Lee, get your laptop, we're going to drop you into Butterfly to chat as a ten-year-old girl whose mommy is going on a rampage."

"I don't know if I can be a ten-year-old," he replied, firing up his laptop.

"Mac, make him a profile. Give him a really interesting background."

Mac grinned. "I'll use yours."

I slapped his arm. "Thanks."

"I have a good reason. We can help Lee better if we know the background."

Mac emailed Lee all the information he required to begin chatting. Lee called out, "Thanks. Did you have to give me such a goofy name ...? Do I look like a Charlotte to you?"

Nope, he did not. He looked like someone you wouldn't fuck with or, in the right light, a rock star.

He was on the other side of the room with a laptop on his knee.

I looked over and said, "Absolutely, Lee, I so see you as Charlotte, maybe Lottie is the pet name your friends use." I nudged Mac. "Was that a bird? Did you see something fly my way?"

He laughed. "You're mighty brave when Lee's across the room."

"Kemo Sabe ... I am in the chat room. Now what?"

"Dig deep. Act like you're a harassed ten-year-old taking refuge from your rampaging screwball of a mother."

We watched Lee's progress from Mac's computer. He wasn't half bad as a scared kid.

Praskovya piped up with a surly question. "And your point to this game is?"

"Your terrorist was in here looking for someone. If the killer is choosing victims from the Foundation, we need to know his criteria. This is as good a place as any."

"But isn't this a protected chat room, outsiders cannot be there?"

"Yes."

"So how does he do it?"

"He needs to be posing as a kid, like your terrorist did. He's hacked into the website or tricked someone into handing over their password and other information."

"This is what Vadbolski was doing too, yes?"

"We think it was similar. She seemed to have information that suggested our Unsub is connected to the Foundation ... she was looking for him inside the chat rooms."

"Was there a record of what she did on that machine?"

"Oh yes. We know every key stroke. Fortunately for us she used a Defense Department machine to do her hacking."

Lee scratched his head. "That report on the Defense computer should be in your email, Ellie. Unless they're still messing with the thing." He glared at the screen in front of him and scratched his head some more.

"I'll check ... you okay over there?"

Mac tapped my arm and showed me the conversation Lee was having with another girl. I tried hard not to laugh. Really, really, hard. It didn't work; I could feel uncontrollable mirth bubbling up.

"He's in deep, babe," Mac said, his voice heavy with amusement.

Lee glared at me. "You so much as smirk and I'm outta here!"

I bit my lip and forced normality into my voice. "What you need to say to her Lee, is that you're pretty sure you are both too young for such things yet."

He floundered, his face contorted; eventually he spoke, "I can't believe ten-year-old girls worry about whether or not they'll need boob jobs later in life!"

I swallowed the rising laughter and replied, "Ten-year-old girls are susceptible to all manner of concerns. It's something to do with the whole pre-pubescent thing they have going. All I can say is don't piss one of them off."

Lee grinned and moved on with his conversation.

Praskovya spoke again. I liked it better when he was an observer. "This may take all day, it may take all week. People will die before you find him."

"Patience," I told him, then called out to Lee, "Hey, step it up in there ... I want you talking about how your mom is today and how she nutted off last night. Say you need to talk but are too scared in case she catches you."

He sighed. "It's not easy being ten you know, what with the pressure to grow boobs and a screwy mother and a boss who is way too pretty to be doing this shitty job for a living."

I smiled at him. "Keep it up."

I carefully shut out everyone and the distractions around me and opened my email. Thirty-seven messages since yesterday. Didn't take me long to scroll through the in-house bulletins and general business communiqués and locate the latest from the computer forensics team. There was a sizable attachment. I opened the twenty-five page document, which appeared to be a room transcript, and began to read.

Our hacker had been busy. Some of the time she had mixed with the kids, chatting and offering advice. It was sensible and well thought out. From the things she'd said I gathered she hadn't caused any harm to the kids. Some of what she told them may have helped. I scrolled down, reading pages and pages of chatty advice and teenage small talk. About five pages in, I found code: a lump of computer code just sitting there in the middle of a conversation. Odd.

"Mac, what does this do?" I pointed the code out.

"Copy it to a doc file, I'll check and see when you're done."

I did as he suggested and carried on reading. A few more pages of chitchat, then a new person arrived in the conversation, someone called Firebug. So far, I knew the woman Selena never used the instant message function within the chat room; good to know because only Mac and I are supposed to be able to initiate instant message conversations within the room. She'd chatted to several people at once. The Firebug person rarely spoke but always replied to Selena.

I started paying careful attention to every word they'd said to each other. There was absolutely nothing that seemed out of place in the conversations. I kept reading. Four pages later, I came across unusual activity: Selena had copied and pasted a block of conversation from the chat room window into a word document, highlighted the entire area, changed the font and the color. She'd then highlighted parts of the conversation. A message appeared. And there we had it, proof that she'd spoken with the Unsub in the room, or at least with the killer Praskovya believed she was hunting.

I summarized for my team, "He's in Northern Virginia and in no hurry to leave. She told him to stop. He replied that he was having too much fun. She told him of Markov. He said he didn't care: no one would catch him.

She warned him his actions were open to viewing and someone was displeased with his behavior."

"Viewing?" Lee questioned.

"Looks as though she's warning him about a superior, perhaps someone senior to him in the cell. Could be a double warning – she could be trying to tell him we're getting closer." I certainly didn't feel we were any closer.

"Any mention of where his next victim is, or where Selena is?" Lee asked. "By the way, what is his screen name?"

"Firebug."

"You are fuc'n joking!"

All eyes were now on the chat room screen scanning the room list for Firebug. SadlySandy popped in. You could hear everyone inhale at the same time.

I looked at Mac; he frowned at the screen. "Mac?"

"It's not the kid. We made her a brand new log-in, screen name and profile; one of the moderators spoke to her and her parents."

"So this is?"

"Not the kid," he replied.

Praskovya moved to sit next to Lee. He watched the conversation.

"It's her," he said.

Mac already had a trace program running. "We'll have a location soon."

Praskovya's fingers tapped on the arm of the sofa. Lee kept on chatting to the kids and Selena. My jacket pocket buzzed then rang. I read the screen – Urgent. Something about the ring tone suggested bad news. I decided I'd best answer it. "I'm taking this outside," I announced and walked out the door with the phone pressed to my ear.

"Conway, it's McNab."

"And?" I guessed he had some information for me.

"Can we meet?"

"How much will it cost me this time?"

"Fifty ... heard something about those gold ribbon cases."

"Where?"

"Meet me at Tulley Gate in an hour."

I hung up and went back to my desk.

A chat window popped up on my computer screen. There was Mac sending a smiley face.

Praskovya asked, "Have you located her yet?"

Mac shook his head. He sent an instant message to my computer.

Mac Connelly: *Get the feeling we're working for him?*

Me: *Yes. I am less than impressed.*

Mac Connelly: *I have the location. It's coming from Fort Belvoir.*

Me: *Interesting place of historic value; maybe we should visit it soon.*

More interesting than Mac realized: Tulley Gate is at Fort Belvoir.

Mac Connelly: *Field trip?*

Me: *How accurate is that signal?*

Mac Connelly: *She could have thrown us like last time;*

maybe not Belvoir at all, won't know until we get there.

Me: *Say nothing. At this point Praskovya could destroy our investigation by taking her too soon.*

Mac Connelly: *Belvoir isn't a small area. We need to narrow it somewhat. I'll get a van out there to do moving signal detection.*

Me: *Good thinking, dude. Keep it quiet, if she's on the move this could be a waste of time.*

The only thing about being the Supervising Agent I didn't like was the thought of having to account for every cent spent once the case reached its conclusion. Waste of time equals waste of money equals Ellie's head on a platter.

Mac Connelly: *Would be a good place to hole up.*

"You two are quiet over there," Lee commented. His harried face looked up from the computer. An inkling flashed in his eyes. I knew he couldn't use an instant message with Praskovya watching.

"Just going over some data," I replied. "This reminds me of something."

Lee's interest was piqued. "Do tell, Chicky."

"It's almost as if we're playing hide and go seek." I made eye contact with Lee briefly, "When Aidan and I were young we used to play hide and go seek out at Fort Belvoir."

A fleeting smile. "Some good hiding places out there."

Praskovya interrupted, "Who is Aidan?"

"My brother," I replied.

"Is there a location?" His tone was curt.

I heard Mac sigh under his breath as he said, "She's re-routed this signal so many times my computer is dizzy. Northern Virginia."

"You have nothing?" He failed to hide his annoyance. I sensed his anger fizzing to the surface, or maybe I saw his jaw clench; whatever, he was angry.

"She could be down the hall, or in the office next door. It's not always straightforward."

I loved Mac with all my heart. The ease with which he lied to Praskovya and the convincing performance was pure poetry. How were we going to get away? We could go one by one and meet downstairs. Or I could just go and meet McNab and do a little recon while I was about it. I dug into the case and wrestled alligators to try to find something that would allow me to disappear without suspicion.

I sent an instant message to Caine.

Me: *Cover for me. There's something I need to check without FSB in tow. An informant of mine has something to tell me.*

Caine Grafton: *Related?*

I crossed the fingers on my left hand while I typed.

Me: *Only to our case.*

Caine Grafton: *Uncross your fingers, Ellie.*

How did he know?

Me: *Not crossed*

Caine Grafton: *I'll alibi you for three hours. You're with me.*

Me: *Thanks*

Caine Grafton: *If this goes horribly wrong, kid, I'm not going to be happy.*

I closed the instant message window. If this goes horribly wrong none of us were going to be happy. Moreover, I was about to lie to Mac.

"Caine wants to see me." There it was, the lie, free for everyone to hear, but worst of all, for Mac to hear. No one had time to comment on my escape route before my phone buzzed insistently. I read the message twice: it still made no sense and caused my over-taxed brain to attempt a meltdown. I needed to talk to my team minus the Russian factor.

"Praskovya, can you do something for me?" I flicked through messages on my phone trying to make the request seem important as I asked, "I need someone to fetch some notes for me; head to the forensics lab on the fifth floor."

"It's necessary?"

"Very. We may have a lead."

Long ago I stopped feeling frightened by the ease with which I could lie while working. It was par for the course, unless I had to lie to Mac. That was different.

"I will go if it is important. You are all busy and I am the third wheel."

Praskovya left. As soon as he was out of earshot, I told Lee and Mac what the message said: "Selena Vadbolski is a double agent working with the US military."

"That is the single dumbest thing I have heard this week," Mac said.

"You and me both, Mac." Lee had stopped typing at my announcement.

It was good that we three agreed on the height of the absurdity. We heard humongous amounts of stupidity some days.

"Definitely Tuesday, more whackos about on Tuesday," Mac said, with his best Dustin Hoffman impersonation.

"Chill, Rain Man," I replied.

Lee roared with laughter. "So it's true, Mac is special."

"I think idiot savant is the term you're reaching for." I kissed Mac on the forehead as I moved past him, intent on escape.

He grabbed my hand and said, "Definitely a smartass."

"Only on Tuesdays."

Lee spoke. "Focus."

"Can't focus on dumb: it makes my brain ache," I told him from one step closer to the door.

"Mine too, but under this pile of stupid, there has to be something usable."

My brain swirled the remarks around and out popped: not much. "Praskovya said she goes where she's comfortable. Defense Department was comfortable apparently, which may hold true for Belvoir too, *but* ..."

"Don't choke on that 'but'," Mac quipped.

I ignored his comment. "That doesn't mean she's working for our military! That seems like one hell of a stretch to me."

Mac feigned astonishment, "I am stunned. I have known you to create an entire history for someone based on a strand of hair and a piece of gum ... and you think this is a stretch?"

I glared. It was half-hearted at best and sadly, he wasn't wrong.

"There's more; I have mail from someone called Sassy underscore Selena, this person was communicating on a regular basis with the first Richmond victim."

"You think it's the same Selena?" Mac asked.

"I think it's one hell of a coincidence if it isn't."

"Anything in the exchanges point to any involvement in the cases?" Mac asked.

"Not a damn thing," I replied. I knew I still had a few to read but I had waded through the majority and they contained nothing more exciting than a recipe for home-made play dough. Had it been plastic explosive I'd have been interested.

Lee added, "We have no evidence to suggest she's working for anyone, not even this terror cell."

I kicked myself back on track. "True enough ... as I said, this is one hell of a stretch."

"And this random statement came from where exactly?"

"I sent a query on both passports. Vadbolski's came back flagged 'Military: Top Secret'."

"Goody," Mac grumbled. "More shit."

"I think we hit knee depth some time ago; best put our waders on, it's just going to get deeper."

I considered the information and its source. I was building a Mossad life story for them both and, after viewing their passports at the crash site, had them chasing a terror cell. So was it really that big a stretch? I'd built that little fantasy because they both used passports from safe countries. Now our military was involved.

I pulled myself up before the word conspiracy popped from my mouth and caused ripples in our already murky pond.

"I've got that meeting with Caine." There was the lie again. I kissed Mac. "I'll be back when we're done." And left without making eye contact; I knew he'd see through the ruse if I did.

I didn't really have a reason for wanting to go alone, except that it was easier for me to slip out than for all of us to disappear. It was fact finding, nothing too difficult in that. I'd meet McNab then go for a wee foray; all I intended to do was observe. If I kept telling myself this was routine and there was no need to go charging in with the cavalry – it might be true.

I was as okay as I was going to be with this. What were the odds of me going out to Belvoir to meet an informant and the signal coming from there, too? Don't think about it.

As I drove I flicked on the radio, the first song I heard was 'Long Cool Woman in a Black Dress.' I switched off the radio and tried to dispel the feelings of unease generated by the song.

Chapter Twenty-One
Out Of Bounds

Why would anyone be following me? I checked the rearview mirror for the tenth time in three minutes. Two cars back I saw the same silver car I'd seen twenty minutes earlier. It had dropped into the flow of traffic two cars behind me as I left Washington. I smiled to myself – this case is causing paranoia – just because the same car has been behind me for twenty minutes doesn't mean it's following me.

Yeah, right.

I saw a gas station sign ahead and decided to pull in there. Maybe the car would keep going, so I could get the plate number, or maybe it would pull in and I could take a look at the driver. Deciding there was no harm in either option, I pulled in.

I cruised slowly past the pumps and stopped on the far side of the forecourt. The other car didn't stop. It carried on but slowed, and I wrote down the numbers.

As I called the tag in, a dark blue car pulled in behind me. Simultaneously, the silver car returned, this time approaching me face-on and turned into the gas station. The single male occupant smiled. I estimated his age to be forty, forty-five. He had short dark hair with a sprinkling of gray, tanned skin – possibly spent a lot of time outdoors – green eyes, a long nose and a generous mouth. In my rearview mirror, I saw the occupant of the dark blue car, also male, wearing a baseball cap pulled down low over his forehead. I couldn't see his eyes and his face was in shadow. No hair showed from around the cap, indicating it was very short or non-existent.

The silver car pulled up alongside me. The driver indicated I should lower my window. I shook my head as I turned the key in the ignition. He'd angled his car into mine. I doubted he wanted to ask directions: most people don't try to block you in such circumstances. I planted my foot on the accelerator and rammed into his car, shoving it aside as I exited.

If they were genuinely in need of directions then the driver could've asked at the gas station. No need to behave like jerks and make my trigger finger itch and heart race.

I took a deep breath and picked up the car phone and called in both cars and descriptions of the drivers.

"There are two State Police vehicles in the area, Special Agent Conway; we'll have them look out for these cars."

"Have them hold the drivers until FBI can question them."

"Yes, ma'am."

As I replaced the phone in its cradle, I knew I should have called Mac and Lee. What stopped me? The lecture they'd fire at me, that's what. And I was almost in Belvoir; what they didn't know couldn't hurt them, or me.

Several times on the drive I questioned the wisdom of heading out alone, but each time I told myself this was just a quick look-see. Selena had probably rerouted the signal and was miles away.

There was less traffic on the road now and I saw a familiar car approaching. What were the odds? I wondered as Mac's dad waved. I waved back. My car phone rang and I pulled over to answer the call.

"Where you off to, Ellie girl?" Only Bob called me Ellie girl. I liked Bob Connelly. He was an older, more weathered version of Mac. Like father, like son.

"Checking something out, Bob."

"Beatrice wanted me to invite you two over for dinner Friday night."

"Sounds good to me." To be honest, it sounded like some exquisite torture; the thought of time spent with Beatrice had that effect on me. "I'll check with Mac and get back to you."

I watched the traffic pass me, looking for those two cars from earlier. Yep, I was paranoid.

"Where is he?" Bob asked. "Thought you two were joined at the hip."

"He's stuck at the office babysitting an out-of-towner."

Bob laughed. "See you Friday."

"Sure thing." I hung up and dropped my phone on the passenger seat. It bounced and hit the floor. We both knew that checking with Mac was nothing more than a courtesy; of course we'd be there, barring a natural disaster or a damn good excuse. Hurricane Josephine had passed over, and I didn't think there was much likelihood of another one brewing so soon.

We'd be there because Bob was a wonderful man and a

great father.

I reached down and grabbed the phone, wondering what on earth possessed me to drop it on the seat when it's just as easy to put it back in the cradle.

I pulled back into the lane and carried on my merry way. Only it wasn't so merry all on my lonesome. Five miles on, I came across a car stopped right on the edge of an industrial park. I slowed and saw a woman on the side of the road in a Ford Expedition, with what I thought could be two small children still in the car. I could see the outline of child car seats. Not something I could ignore. I felt a momentary twinge about being followed and I allowed myself to recall the last traffic incident we stopped at, which proved to be a chlorine-filled act of terrorism. The woman and kids won out.

I flipped my grill lights on, pulled over, clipped my badge to my belt and walked back to her car.

"Hello, everything all right here?"

The woman was standing next to the truck and was shorter than me by about four inches, which made her around the five feet five mark, blonde, green-eyed, seemed frightened or maybe timid and nervous. Inside the truck I could see children: a baby and a toddler, both upset.

The passing traffic was loud. I noted a few rubberneckers, obviously drawn by my car's flashing grill lights. They slowed long enough to stare. I stopped watching traffic slow then speed up; it was distracting.

The woman shuffled her feet. I didn't know if she'd

heard me above the traffic so I repeated my question. "Everything all right here?"

She swallowed. Nerves? Was I that intimidating? I didn't think so. Something felt hinky. I plunged my hand into my jacket pocket and palmed one of the business cards I kept in there. I didn't know if I could give it to her unobserved but I had another idea. I dropped the card while listening to the woman. Another car slowed as it passed us; I caught the movement in the corner of my eye and looked over in time to hear the car braking on the roadside gravel.

She spoke; her voice shook and snagged my attention. "The truck overheated, I've called Triple A."

I stepped sideways, covering the card with my foot.

"You want me to wait with you?"

She hesitated, her eyes flicked sideways. I looked at her car and my stomach turned over. A reflection in the window moved, the door opened. Suddenly a large shadow crossed my peripheral vision and I found myself airborne.

I landed on my back near a ditch.

"Get in the car," said a man. The voice was unfamiliar and not Russian. He was an American. There was no time to feel relieved. As I stood up, I caught sight of a black object coming at my head.

I yelled, "Not my head."

Too late.

The impact felt dull as the grayness embraced me. It never quite became blackness, for which I was thankful.

Why did no one ever listen? You'd think someone would listen just once and not smack my head. Was I invisible? If so, it's a noisy invisible place. I could feel a thump of air from speakers as Bon Jovi's 'Bounce' pounded from a stereo. I was sure someone had started my car and I was in it; the last thing I'd heard before stopping to help that lady was Bon Jovi. The reflection in her car window now took shape. Someone had been hiding in the car with her kids. No wonder she was scared.

I could feel movement and hear traffic. Definitely not good at all. I took stock of the situation and determined I was in the back of a car, which could be my car. My hands were fastened behind me, possibly with PlastiCuffs – it didn't feel like tape and I couldn't feel metal on my skin. There was something over my mouth. I pushed my tongue against the gag. It felt slightly sticky. Duct tape maybe. I tried moving my feet but they were restricted by something and wouldn't move independently. Who was driving I did not know. I couldn't see but knew I wasn't blindfolded; nothing touched my eyelashes as I fluttered them. There was something over me. I could smell a sweet, sunshine smell. Laundry powder. I was covered by a blanket I kept in my car. Made sense really: I was pretty sure I was in my own car. What had Caine said about things going horribly wrong? I hoped the woman would pick up my card and call the FBI.

Please don't let her and her kids be hurt, or worse.

My eyes closed; there was no point expending effort to see when there was nothing to see. I'd often wondered what it was like in my head. Mac had always told me it was a scary place; so far it wasn't so bad. I just couldn't seem to get out. It was a bit dark and there were long shadows, nothing a light bulb wouldn't fix.

I saw a cord hanging from mid-air, right in front of me. When I pulled it, light flooded the area illuminating faces of dead women, orbited by little moons. The moons evolved into children.

Faces zoomed in and out of focus so quickly they made me feel ill. I concentrated and slowed the movement. The victims parted, revealing a blonde woman with her back to me. She slowly turned until I could see her face.

"Mom?"

"You're in trouble again, Gabrielle."

"Just a hiccup, Mom, nothing serious." It struck me as amusing, speaking to mom as if she were here, knowing it was impossible. I remembered doing the curfew check before leaving Richmond. I definitely felt a mixture of amusement and relief. The relief came in knowing she wasn't real.

"Gabrielle, look at me."

The woman even irked me from beyond the grave. I waited for some form of accusation to be leveled at me, her usual pattern in life.

Instead she said, "You need to call Mac, it's dangerous here."

A bright light glowed behind her. What did she mean by *here*?

"It's not your time, Ellie. Go back, call Mac."

It wasn't my time for *what*? I had to meet someone to get some information, that's all.

"I can do this, Mom."

She'd never had any faith in me, not ever. All she'd wanted was for me to get a man and it took long enough to find one that she couldn't scare off; guess it helped that she'd only met him once and his mom was no prize.

And for what, so she could nag me from beyond the grave to call him? Why didn't she have some cool otherworldly wisdom to impart that would break this case and save my neck?

Mom began to fade into a halo of golden light. "You did good, Gabrielle. You will be a wonderful mother, not at all like me."

Real helpful, Mom, thanks.

A dull ache droned in my head. I knew that if I could feel pain then I was still alive and this mother of an hallucination would disappear. Whoever was in the car with me didn't need to know I wasn't fully unconscious.

I remained still and listened. The road noises had changed. The car slowed and came to a stop. My whole body tensed. Was this it, the end of the road? I breathed slowly and refused to let negative thoughts take hold. I needed to remain alert. The driver's window buzzed down. I felt a warm breeze tug at the edges of the blanket.

A male voice spoke. "Only cars bearing DOD decals are allowed through this gate." He stopped talking. Maybe he was reading something. Then he said, "Sorry, sir, didn't recognize you. New car?"

I waited for a response, hoping for some idea of who was driving my car. I was guessing but I thought we could be at one of the gates to Fort Belvoir. Not Tulley Gate – Tulley is the one people without DOD decals have to use.

"A loaner," said a male voice. There was a slight accent; I needed him to say something else.

"You should get a decal for this car if you're going to be using it for a while, sir. You might not get me next time ... would be inconvenient to drive around to Tulley."

"Thank you, Corporal, I don't think I will be using it again."

Corporal? The mention of Tulley Gate meant my car had stopped at one of the gates to Fort Belvoir. I knew that accent but not the voice. I knew it. Faint though it was, I determined the driver of my car was from Texas, or had spent a considerable amount of time there.

I held my breath, hoping for a returning rank from the voice outside the car.

"Sir," the corporal replied, a little too casually, which confirmed my suspicion that they knew each other. Chances were the driver wasn't in uniform. But he could be an officer and one stationed at the Fort. That really narrowed it down – not. "Drive carefully." Then he spoke again. "I see your other car pulling in now."

I wished he'd said who was driving it but having it pull in behind us meant it had a decal. Department of Defense.

I thought about the possibilities. Why would someone take me onto a base? It seemed risky. Unless of course he felt secure here, as someone who worked and even lived on the base would.

Great: that narrowed it down a heap more. Fort Belvoir was an interesting army base. He could be Army, National Guard, Army Reserve, from one of twenty-six Department of Defense agencies, Air Force, a Marine, or even from Treasury or maybe a civilian. A lot of civilians worked on the base.

Semi-conscious and drifting I tried to recall everything I knew about the base we were on. Dad was stationed here once, before he joined the naval criminal intelligence service and we'd moved to Newport.

We'd lived at the fort. All I wanted was a memory I could use and all I saw was mom.

The car lurched forward. I almost fell off the seat. I concentrated on external noises, trying to identify something that would give me a bearing. A helicopter flew low overhead. Distant gunfire: a firing range perhaps? Children playing. Asphalt suburban-type road noise. The car swung around several corners. I attempted to tuck up my legs to stabilize myself – which didn't work.

We stopped on what sounded like gravel.

The driver's door opened. I listened and heard the second car stop nearby, stones crunching under the tires. Whoever was driving my car, rocked the car as he alighted. I breathed slowly and calmly, using my breathing to control the surge of adrenaline as I waited and anticipated what would come.

Suddenly the door popped open, by my head. The

blanket disappeared. Sunlight hit my eyes; it hurt. My eyes don't like sunlight at the best of times. Hands grabbed at me, hooking under my arms and pulling.

I kicked out but I had no idea why – there was no one near my feet.

A man laughed. The hands let me go with a shove. I landed roughly and confirmed the presence of gravel on the ground.

I lay bound and gagged, though I could see. There wasn't a lot to see from ground level: two pairs of legs. One set wearing Marine desert camouflage and coyote-brown, temperate weather, Marine Corps combat boots. The other wore black dress trousers and polished black shoes. They were facing each other and talking quietly. The man in the fatigues held something in his hand. Metal flashed in the sun. A knife.

I twisted my wrists, hoping there was some movement in whatever bound me. I rolled one wrist. It moved. Then the other. I wriggled one hand free. The men continued talking. I checked my feet. Same deal. They weren't PlastiCuffs after all, just some kind of plastic coated wire and not secured. Whoever tied me up didn't do a very good job.

Yay for stupid people.

I doubted the Marine was responsible. I untwisted the wire from my ankles as quickly as I could.

Free.

I scrambled to my feet and ran. As I ran I ripped the tape from my mouth. I didn't know where I was going. I could see the cars, a concrete bunker, then another bunker and the road.

Someone shouted behind me. I ducked behind the far bunker then raced for the road.

My face hit the dirt, as someone landed on top of me – all the breath in my body escaped in one gasp. I clenched my fist and jabbed my right elbow backwards. He groaned and moved slightly, trying to grab at me. I rolled over, pulled my legs up and kicked. Both feet hit his lower abdomen. He snarled and tried to grab my feet. His voice rasped under the exertion, "Come here, bitch!"

I rolled out of reach and stood up. I could see him properly. It was the soldier, on his feet. Metal flashed. The knife again. I couldn't see the other man but assumed he was close by – I wasn't about to take my eyes off the guy with the knife to look for him.

I watched his shoulders and eyes for his next move. The knife moved back and forth in his right hand. I backed away. A hand in my back shoved me forward.

So the man in the black pants was behind me. Good to know.

Enough playing around. I raised my forearms to cover my body and watched the blade. As the blade rushed down I stepped inside the path of his knife and it caught my forearm. I punched him as hard as I could in the side of the neck. Using both hands I grabbed his neck and his knife hand, pushing the knife away from me while grasping his neck firmly. With a step backwards I forced him to the ground, shoving his face in the dirt.

I whispered in his ear, “Don’t fuck with me, Marine.” I straddled his back and dropped my knees onto his biceps. As I reached down to pry the knife from his hand, I remembered the other guy.

Someone hit me in the back. Once. Twice. I slipped sideways trying to take the knife with me. I couldn’t hold it. My hand stopped working. I looked down at blood.

Something hard hit the back of my head turning the scene in front of me blue, then black. The now-faint motherly voice in my head whispered, ‘Hold on, Ellie, just hold on.’

Chapter Twenty-Two
Last Chance Train

My head turned slowly. A gun came into view lying on muddy stones, just out of reach. How did a gun get there? Where was the knife?

My right arm lay bent in front of me. A pool of sticky red oozed from underneath, spreading out among the pebbles in the mud. There was considerable resistance as I tried to lift my arm, so I rolled my arm and hand, palm up, to inspect the damage. A deep wound ran at least four and a half inches down the inside of my forearm and blood flowed freely. That was going to smart a bit. The absence of overwhelming pain told me I was in the grace period between trauma and pain. If I didn't move now I never would. I knew I was looking at a defensive wound. A fight. The two men who kidnapped me. There was a fight, and for whatever reason I was still alive.

The fingers on my right hand twitched. I covered the gaping wound with my left hand and pressed hard, hoping to stem the flow of blood. I needed the gun: to achieve that I needed to exercise control over that arm. I made a decision to do it A-sap before the pain started. I had to let go of the wound to reach the gun. My hand scraped the muddy dirt, raking up stones, scrabbling in sandy muck. As my fingers inched towards the gun, blood spread like gravy onto the stones.

It seemed my hand was capable of reacting only to

every other instruction from my brain. It wasn't moving properly nor were my fingers capable of grasping. It felt like someone had turned off the power but rogue current was still filtering through at random intervals.

A shadow moved. Shit.

I half closed my eyes, letting them roll back a little in my head, barely breathing and hoping to go unnoticed.

Don't let him take the gun.

The shadow moved away. I waited, then carefully focused on where it had come from. About six or seven feet from me, I saw legs, the backs of legs wearing dirty denim. I willed the person not to turn around. I breathed in deeply and smelt bourbon. Why was I still alive? Why hadn't they killed me outright?

Every ounce of energy and determination coiled into my good arm. I knew I had to roll to grab the gun. The damage to my right arm was too great, and I would never be able to grasp, hold and shoot. Assuming I could roll and there weren't any other injuries. One chance: roll to the right, snatch the gun and shoot, before he turned around. I didn't have the energy to fight. I took my only chance. One, two, my arm flung over my body, taking my shoulder with it. I felt the rubber as my fingers wrapped around the grip, index finger sliding onto the trigger.

I leaned heavily on my elbows; my blood-covered hands made the grip slippery. He was talking on his cell phone. I hoped I could hold the gun steady for long enough to find out what was going on.

I croaked, "FBI. Put your hands up."

The man spun to face me. His face first registered surprise, followed by anger. He ran towards me, drawing a weapon.

I squeezed the trigger. The first shot hit him in the middle of the chest, the second in the forehead, moments before he fell face forward. He and his phone hit the dirt at the same time. Firing sent shock waves of pain through my arm and left a bloody splatter as my elbows gave way and my arms hit the ground. Grace period was ending. I needed his phone. I scrabbled to my knees and then my feet and staggered as I tried to walk upright, the gun still in my left hand. I kicked his gun as far away as I could without losing my balance. I shoved my gun into the waistband of my jeans, half fell, half knelt down, picked up his phone and looked at the last number dialed.

The voice in my head said, remember that number, Ellie. I nodded. Then another voice told me the number would stay in the phone's memory anyway. It was a relief to know I didn't have to squander brainpower. Using the phone in my left hand, I pressed 911. My knees wouldn't let me stand. I toppled, falling back hard. Automatically, my right arm went down behind me to protect me from the fall. Violent pain erupted. It skipped my arm and went directly to my head, as a robotic-sounding voice spoke in my ear.

"What service do you require?"

I cleared my throat, my mouth was dusty and dry and I don't even know if my voice was audible, "All of them."

"Ma'am?"

"Special Agent Conway, FBI. I need help."

The robotic voice became softer, "Agent Conway, where are you?"

All I could see was sandy dirt and dust and almost-dried muddy puddles. "Between reality and a dream."

"Keep the cell phone turned on; we're trying to get a fix on your position."

Yeah, great, good luck with that.

I wondered if anyone had noticed I was missing. Had that woman called to say what happened? Where was Mac? Where was Lee? What happened to Sam? I never went anywhere without one of them. Even seeing Praskovya would have been comforting about now. In front of me, there was a car. It looked like my car. I couldn't see the tags. The phone beeped. I glanced at it. Low battery. It slipped from my hand as I struggled to my feet. Once erect I knew I couldn't pick it up again and I left it on the ground. With my right arm cradled against my body, I walked carefully. I leaned on the driver's door and peered into the closed window. That was my jacket on the passenger seat. The doors were unlocked. I opened the door and eased into the driver's seat. My brain kicked in. I had GPS; all was not lost.

I will be okay.

The keys were in the ignition. I turned the key, bringing the onboard computer to life. There it was on the screen, my coordinates, even the name of the road. I hit the central locking button on the driver's door, then locked my door. Why didn't my driver's door automatically lock like the other doors? The car phone sat idly in its cradle on the dash, watching me. Finally I registered that the little blue light was flickering. My phone was on standby waiting for instructions. I stared at it then remembered the voice tags and heard mom's voice loudly in my head. "Call Mac!" I said, hoping my voice was stronger than it felt.

I wrapped my left hand around the wound on my right arm. It didn't help much.

Mac answered on the fourth ring, "Ellie?"

"I made a 911 call but I have my car now and I know where I am."

"Jesus." I pictured him running his free hand through his hair. "Where are you?"

My lips had stuck together, making speech difficult, "Will send directions to your truck and to EMS."

There was a long sigh from Mac. I'm sure he didn't want to hear the EMS bit.

"I'm on Deakyne Road, Fort Belvoir."

I let go of my arm. It throbbed. I sent the directions then opened the glove compartment and fumbled out a bottle of water. I took small sips of the warmish liquid but could hardly swallow. My throat hurt. "Please hurry, Mac."

My shirt was stuck to my back in places. I leaned forward; it stayed stuck but didn't hurt. I decided it was sweat and refused to pursue any alternative lines of thought.

The man I'd killed was not either of the men who had

abducted me. Where the hell were they? I thought back and remembered the woman and the children on the side of the road. Why take me? How had anyone known where I was going? I was supposed to meet McNab. It was a trap. Was the dead person something to do with the case? If this was our Unsub, why was I still alive? From the relative security of the car, I could see a half-full bottle of bourbon lying not far from the marks I'd made in the gravelly sand. The sight of the bottle sent a chill up my spine. I looked at my bloodied forearm. I reached under the seat and dragged out the first-aid kit. I heard Lee's voice, as if he were there, telling me to apply pressure, so I lay a thick pad of as many wound dressings as I could on the gash and bound it tightly with gauze. Not a bad field-dressing attempt. Blood began seeping through almost immediately. I scrabbled one-handed in the first-aid kit looking for the telltale foil hemostatic sponge packets and found one. I ripped it open with my teeth, removed the soaked, now dripping, bandages and shoved the sponge into the wound.

With a roll of hemostatic gauze, I wrapped the entire site, applying as much pressure as I could. Then took a triangle bandage and made a sling. My theory was if I could hold my arm against my body with my hand up on my shoulder it might help. It certainly helped with the throbbing. For the second time in a week I was pleased that we had decent first-aid kits and that the government had sprung for QuikClot trauma packs. I reclined my seat a little, making it harder to see me. Just in case there was someone else around.

Whoever the man was, he'd been talking to someone before I interrupted him. The number popped back into my head. I dialed it on the car phone. It was the best way I could think of to keep it safe. A man with a Russian accent answered. I hung up. Another Russian? I was starting to feel that we lived in Eastern Europe, not Northern Virginia. I felt safe in the knowledge that my car phone number was permanently withheld and confidential. It would not show up even with caller ID. Wouldn't even show on his phone if he tried to call me back.

Where had my charming abductors gone? When did the dead guy arrive? I had no memory, not even a glimmer that explained those things.

A low-flying Apache helicopter stirred the water in the bay, whipped up sand and rocked the car. For a second, I thought it was the cavalry coming to save me but it flew on over. My eyes wanted to close. I needed to take a nap, just a little one. I checked the door locks again.

I forced my eyes to remain open just long enough to look around the area. Two bunker-type structures: I'd seen them before. No sign of life. I thought back to the reason I'd set off from Washington alone.

I was supposed to meet someone at Tulley: McNab. Had he set me up? Was this what was so damned important? Setting me up?

I knew I needed a pass to get onto the base but I hadn't planned on being on the base until after the meeting, and had intended to use Tulley Gate, like all visitors. Yet I knew whoever had brought me here used a different gate and the other car had a Department of Defense decal.

My everything hurt. I turned my attention back to the outside and surrounding area.

What could I see? Another car but not the car I'd seen when we'd first arrived here. The body of the man. A bottle of bourbon. I couldn't see anyone else and as my eyes closed I wondered how long it would be before the person on the other end of the phone turned up to find out what happened. The need to know the identity of the Marine who drove the other car gnawed at me.

Chapter Twenty-Three
I Get A Rush

A loud bang jerked me awake. My vision was still slightly blurry. Someone was banging on the car window: a dark-haired male. I blinked. I heard my name. The door unlocked before I was conscious of actually unlocking it.

"Come on." Mac helped me out. "You okay?"

I knew I smiled as I said, "Yeah, I'm okay." Tired but I think I'm okay. No, better not to think, just be okay.

"Let's get you out of here." Mac's arm slipped around my shoulders. I was safe.

Lee yelled, "We got company coming!" He was facing away from us, down the road. "Two cars maybe."

I couldn't see anything but a cloud of dust.

"Could it be EMS?" I asked.

"They're not on base yet; they're waiting for our okay."

I did a mental head slap. Of course, they'd secure the area first. Mac and Lee would have overridden my EMS call until everything was secure. "Hey, wait a minute, this base has a hospital." I swallowed a surge of panic; I didn't want to be trapped anywhere within the base. "Do not let them take me to the base hospital. We need to get out of here."

"I won't."

Mac steered me towards a Ford Expedition parked twenty feet away. The familiar black-tinted windows and shiny black exterior was a comforting sight. A loud engine noise from behind made us both turn. I knew instantly it was too late. Mac turned back to the truck and in that split second something whizzed past my head. I looked around and Mac was gone. He lay sprawled face down in the muddy sand.

Lee yelled from my right, his voice grew louder as he came closer. "Do not do this, Mac. Cowboy – the fuck up! Do you hear me?"

I heard him. Mac lay motionless. I doubt he heard him.

"We gotta get out of here, Ellie."

I heard him. I grabbed Mac's shoulder with my good arm and shook him hard. "Wake up!" My knees sank in the mud, my hand slipped on his muddy shirt. "Mac, get up!"

Large hands dragged me up and stood me on my feet. Those same hands stopped me from reaching Mac.

"Praskovya, take her." I felt my body move quickly backwards. Another set of hands grabbed me and pulled me close.

A shot rang out. The bullet ricocheted off a metal door ahead of us and again, I was in the mud. It was dark and hot under Praskovya's body. His cologne removed all traces of the bourbon smell from the ground. I knew the scent. A heady musky aroma; Mac wore the same one. From under Praskovya's arm, I could see Lee shielding Mac with his body. More gunfire erupted. This time the bullets hit the ground, little puffs of sand and dirt jumped as the rounds hit, moving closer and closer to Lee.

Lee spoke over his shoulder, "On my mark."

Praskovya moved an arm. I heard a click, as he chambered a round. An indefinable calm settled over me as it occurred to me that Mac and I were with the best two people to keep us safe. I trusted my instincts that told me Mac was alive. I'd have known if he wasn't. I would just know.

"Mark."

Praskovya rolled, dragging me with him. Mud and Lee's boots flashed past my face. There was a loud clang. Then silence.

I found myself suddenly propelled into a dark and dank space. I blinked and squinted, trying to adjust my eyes as quickly as possible. Slowly, in their own time, my eyes allowed me to see. I stood in the middle of a room. It smelled as if the sun had never reached it. Lee propped Mac against a far wall. The hands that restrained me earlier dropped away. I was free to go to Mac.

Guilt flooded forth as I leaned down a little and tried to wipe the mud from his face with part of my shirt. I smeared more than I cleaned, but it was the best I could do.

"I'm sorry," I whispered in his ear.

His eyes flickered. A smile crept onto his dirt-streaked face. His voice croaked, "You're okay."

"So are you."

"Concrete head, you know that." He blinked a few times. "Dark ... where are we?"

I straightened up and ran my good hand through his

hair looking for an injury. It was too dark to see where he'd been hurt. My fingers searched his scalp, finally settling on a wound about three finger-widths long and one wide. "Found it."

"Found what?" Lee asked.

"Head laceration, I think a bullet skimmed Mac's head; it cut a fairly deep trail as it went."

"That's going to look messy later," Lee commented. He seemed to be a long way from us. I guessed he was by a door and listening for activity outside.

"Where are we?" Mac asked again. His hand followed the path my fingers took, as he felt the wound in his head.

"I think it's an old ammunition bunker, or something similar."

Mac grabbed for my hand but missed and got my leg. "Are you hurt?" he asked, struggling to his feet.

"Hurt?"

"Injured, Ellie," Mac spoke slowly, "Did he hurt you?"

"Who?"

"The dead guy we found?"

"Nope, no idea who the hell he was but he called someone who sounded Russian. He wasn't one of the two who snatched me."

"Are you hurt?"

"My arm."

Lee spoke, "It's a defensive wound, Mac."

I heard what Lee said but had no desire to elaborate on the fight I'd had with the Marine. I was struggling with what I thought I knew. A Marine? It was so wrong and it didn't sit at all well in my gut. Every time I moved, my shirt didn't; it was really starting to annoy me. I wished we were in my car and I had a clean, dry shirt.

I heard Lee speak again, this time it was to me, "You hurt anywhere else, Chicky?"

A volley of gunfire hit our shelter. I didn't have time to answer, which was a good thing because I didn't know what to say.

"They're not going to give up," Mac said.

Lee's cell buzzed. He answered quickly, "We're under fire here, Caine. We need some support."

For a second I thought he was going to call in an air strike. It wouldn't have surprised me if he had. I listened to his conversation, one-sided though it was.

"We are in some kind of bunker at the end of Deakyne Road, right inside the military reservation."

As soon as he said that, I flashed back to my childhood. Funny I hadn't made the connection before; I was sure this was where we had played as kids.

"Someone got a light?"

"Yeah, in the SUV along with my backpack," Mac replied, "Wanna go get it?"

"I'll pass, smartass."

Praskovya threw me a Zippo. It bounced, sparking across the concrete floor.

"Thanks."

I lit it and carefully began searching along the back wall. Mac joined me.

"What are we looking for?"

"We really did play hide and go seek here."

"Here, here?"

"We're by the bay aren't we?"

"Yep."

"Then yes: here, here."

"Don't tell me there is another secret tunnel."

I have a thing about tunnels. I love tunnels, always have. Once before, my love of tunnels enabled Mac and me to slip in and out of Washington, D.C. undetected. This time I hoped it'd get us out of harm's way.

"I remember a bunker joined to another bunker via an underground, well, tunnel."

"Tunnel?" Lee asked.

"Maybe," I said. No sense getting all excited yet. Might be I hadn't remembered it correctly, or this wasn't the right bunker.

Another volley hit the exterior wall.

Drums and wooden crates were stacked five or so deep and three high in the furthermost back corner. It was starting to feel like a prison cell in a third world country. Mac pointed out scuffmarks on the floor. The crates and drums hadn't always been there, maybe even placed there recently.

"What if we aren't the only ones who know about this?" Lee said. "They were out here for a reason, why would anyone come way the hell out here?"

"You want to wait and find out? Sooner or later they're going to try and blow that door." I replied, inspecting the drums and crates for something usable. Time to cowboy up. “We’re going to have to move this out of the way.”

“Step aside, Miss Ellie. Let us menfolk handle the heavy work,” Mac said, mock-tugging his forelock and bowing. Blood dripped down his face.

“Not you, sunshine. Praskovya and Lee can handle this.”

Mac grinned. In the dim light, the flame from the lighter made his eyes seem more gold-flecked than normal.

The dirt streaks down his face were a mixture of blood, sweat and mud. In the flickering light he looked as though he belonged in an old war movie. I guessed that I would look more at home in a Wes Craven horror flick. Gunfire periodically hit the walls outside, a nice reminder that they weren’t going to give up. I watched Lee and Praskovya move everything out of the way. When they finished they stood staring at a small door.

“Who is going through that?” Lee asked.

“We are,” I replied. It was smaller than I remembered – a lot smaller than I remembered. Funny how things seemed bigger when you were a kid.

“This is white rabbit territory,” Mac commented. “Real people won’t fit.”

“Just open the door.”

I could hear the rabbit. I could even see him running for the door saying, ‘I’m late! I’m late!’ I kept that to myself.

Praskovya moved back to the main door. We could hear voices every now and then. Lee worked on opening the small door. No amount of brute force made a scrap of difference. It was stuck fast.

"Next?" he puffed, sliding down the wall.

"Go out the front?" I replied. Yeah, that was really an option.

"Any ideas that won't get us killed?"

Raised voices outside interrupted our discussion.

I turned to Praskovya. "Cavalry?"

"*Nyet*," he replied. "Dissension in the ranks, they're arguing about us."

"Saying?"

"The Russian wants to blow the door. The Americans say it will attract too much attention."

"Good, let's hope they dissuade the Russian."

"How many out there, Praskovya?"

"I don't know, more than three ... I have the impression there is someone out there who is not speaking." Praskovya hurried across the room to Lee. "We need to open this door."

"Any ideas?"

Both men crouched by the door, inspecting it. Lee called me over and asked, "What is in the crates?"

"I saw a lot of packing material, but nothing else."

"We need something to use as a fulcrum."

Mac was already poking through the crates, pulling out packing material by the handful. "Shovels!" he called out. "There are shovels in here."

Praskovya joined him and removed one of the shovels. "Here's your fulcrum," he said, handing a shovel to Lee.

“Thank you very much.” Lee set to work opening enough of a gap in the small doorway to wedge the shovel in.

I took the opportunity to talk to Lee quietly as he worked. “Lee, whoever drove my car onto the base works here. Could even be an officer. The guard at the gate – and I don’t know which gate, but it wasn’t Tulley – knew him, called him ‘sir’. He let him through without the DOD decal. Someone else drove another car into the same gate, and that car had a decal. He could be a Marine.”

“You were kidnapped by military personnel?”

“Yes.”

“Those idiots outside, trying to get in here ... maybe active military?”

“I tussled with a Marine – or with someone wearing a current Marine desert-camouflage uniform.”

“Seem to be a lot of military connections surfacing.”

Those words rolled around my head while Lee jimmied the door. I went back to Mac. With Lee and Praskovya working on the door, it didn’t seem to take long to pry the thing open. Light suddenly flooded in. My heart sank and all thoughts of the military connection fell from my mind. If it went straight to the outside, it meant trouble and gunfire. Not to mention imminent death.

“Ellie,” Lee whispered. “Get over here.”

“What?” I whispered as well, only because there was so much light I was sure they would find us any minute.

“We could be heading into serious trouble: this doesn’t lead outside, it’s a lit tunnel. On the other side of this small doorway is a proper-sized tunnel."

"Do it."

Praskovya looked at me. It was one of those long penetrating looks that members of my team liked to use. He was starting to fit right in. He followed it with a question: "How much of that is your blood?" Carefully his fingers reached for something on my shirt. He pulled back with a sticky, bloodied Post-it note in his hand. I saw it and wondered how sticky those things were to survive what I'd been through, although most of my mind was still trying to decipher what he'd said to me.

"Of what?" We didn't have time. We had to get out of there.

His voice was more gentle than normal. "Ellie, your shirt is soaked through, that bandage on your arm is soaked through."

"Let's not worry about it; let's get through this door into wherever the hell it leads." Everything seemed distant. It felt like the kind of distant that wasn't good. Everything slowly drifted out of focus, until I could no longer make out clear shapes through the haze.

Mac touched my shoulder. I knew it was Mac, 'cos that's what he did to get my attention; he always touched my shoulder like that; gently. "Mind your head," he whispered. "Follow Lee."

I did, we crawled through the doorway into the more spacious tunnel beyond. There was a brighter light coming from the end. I expected to see mom again. As we stepped through the opening at the far end into the brilliantly-lit room, a voice echoed back down the tunnel, creating waves in the light.

"Medic!"

I'd stepped through into a movie set. We were in a war movie. Yes, that was it; we were in a war movie and had just escaped from *Stalag 17*. I turned to see Mac. His makeup was so realistic. Whoever they had doing the makeup on set was amazing. His head wound was so real and the blood was super realistic. I wondered what they made the blood with; it had to be some kind of non-toxic substance that reacted just like real blood. What an awesome movie. Someone called my name. I just wanted to see how this movie ended before we left. I heard my name again. Then again. This time it was more insistent and followed by an instruction.

"Ellie, wake up!" Someone said something about a cowboy.

No, they were wrong, it wasn't a cowboy movie. It was a war movie. All I asked was to see the end. The light faded, dammit, I was going to miss the end. One word escaped the dimming light and found my ears. "Goodnight."

Chapter Twenty-Four
Flesh And Bone

I sank into the misty place between reality and the dream world. I've been here before, I thought, as I stood on top of a cliff. From my vantage point, I viewed the surrounding countryside. Teetering on the brink of sliding down the cliff, I grabbed a branch from a ragged dogwood next to me. It creaked ominously. I sat down on a rock. It felt safer to sit. A river meandered below, curving gently between the hills and fields.

Memories mingled among wild flowers; straggly dogwoods poked spindly branches at the more robust rhododendrons. Old oaks sprawled gnarled limbs into a makeshift canopy. Underneath the oak, violets nodded in the welcome shade.

I breathed peace.

Insistent voices reached me. They floated on the warm afternoon breeze. I couldn't see anyone walking up the steep incline. I chose to ignore the voices. I didn't want to leave this place.

The breeze rippled the water and tousled the wild flowers. I watched in awe as it tipped and nodded through the fragrant field, leaving in its wake a list of the dead, written in pretty purple flowers. I read each name, mentally ticking it off against my memorized list. The wind wrote three names I hadn't seen before. Carefully, with much concentration, I visualized a black marker pen and blank white paper. The pen began in the middle of the paper and wrote the new names. A blue bloodied note poked out from under a patch of violets and I read the words, 'People like you shouldn't procreate.' I hadn't seen that note before. Slowly the violets grew over the note, covering the words in a purple shroud.

The voices from before grew louder and more annoying, telling me to return to where I belonged. I listened to the louder, more commanding of the voices as it instructed my being to return and awaken. I stood, using the dogwood for support, while the wind tore across the surface of the river, swirling the water and blowing across the meadow, destroying the names. Leaves flew from the old trees, whipped to a muddled frenzy by the wind.

There was little point in staying.

Carefully, watching my footing, I made my way back down the narrow path to the growing voices.

"Ellie?"

I felt warm, firm pressure on my hand. I didn't need to open my eyes to know Mac was holding my hand.

"Ellie."

I didn't want to open my eyes but I knew Mac needed me to. My eyes flickered, I caught sight of Mac. My eyes flickered again; it was hard to catch them open and make them stay that way. Nausea rose in waves. I liked it better in the dream place. My left eye opened. Mac sat next to me holding a white container.

I smiled. He knew I'd feel sick. I must've had an anesthetic. Mac smiled at me. He nestled the container next to me, then gave me a sip of icy water from a plastic cup.

"Thanks," I think I said. I hope I spoke.

"You'll feel better soon."

My eyes closed; there was something I had to remember. The piece of paper. I searched my dream for the piece of paper and the names. I hadn't felt any urgency before, in the field of violets, regarding one of the names, but I did now.

"Stacy Eberhart," I hoped I was right.

"Who is she?"

"Find her, Mac, before the Unsub does. She's next."

He stood up and left the room. I listened to his footsteps fade as he walked away. I focused inwardly, recalling the other two names from the list. Hoping Mac would hurry so I could tell him who they were. While I waited, I inspected my arm. A clean white dressing covered the wound. I lay still, trying to decipher the messages my body was sending. They weren't pain messages; discomfort seemed to be the closest description. Yes, that was it, my back felt uncomfortable in a few places. Why would my back feel like that?

Footsteps approached, I looked up to see Mac at the end of the bed and realized the dirt and blood were gone. He no longer resembled an actor in a war movie.

"Lee's working on finding the woman," he said.

"There are two more: Andrea Coleman and Cynthia Cobham."

Mac wrote the names down without batting an eyelid. It was easy working with Mac. He never showed any great surprise at the unorthodox ways by which I came by information. I'm sure it could all be explained logically. I just wouldn't know where to start.

"I'll have someone track them down. About the first woman, you got anything close to a location?"

"No. Run her name through the Foundation, I think you'll find her there."

He nodded and smiled. "That's what I told Lee already."

"I got questions." I held my hand out for the drink I saw on the night stand next to me. Mac held it for me, I sipped the cold liquid through a straw and it soothed my raw throat.

"Ask."

"My back: why does it feel peculiar?"

He sat next to me, put the glass down and then spoke, "You had two deep stab wounds, and by sheer luck you escaped serious internal organ injury."

I let the information sink in. It wasn't easy getting my somewhat befuddled head around two stab wounds. I tried recalling the events from the drive to Fort Belvoir until Mac found me. I couldn't; there was nothing there.

"Stab wounds."

"Yes."

"The war movie?"

He laughed warmly. "I wondered what your mind would conjure upon seeing soldiers and medics."

"No movie then?"

"No. Caine had someone triangulate our position from

the GPS in the cars and our phones. He called the base, told them there was a problem ... that we needed access to the base and were bringing EMS."

I knew there was something really important I needed to ask but it wouldn't come. "Say that again?"

Mac repeated what he told me.

"I can't remember as much as I should be able to," I confessed.

"You will."

I did remember being shot at and not enjoying it very much. "Okay. So what happened to the people who were shooting at us? Random shootings aren't supposed to happen even on a military base ... someone must've seen them?"

"There was apparently no sign of them when the Military Police arrived. They did find spent shells."

I leaned back on the pillow, putting light pressure on my upper back. It throbbed a bit.

"And presumably the man I shot?"

"Yup."

More memories kicked in. "I don't get how they disappeared from the area. They had to go back the same way they came in because sooner or later the roads converge at one intersection."

"There was a military checkpoint set up at the intersection of Deakyne, Swift, Johnson and Warren."

"And they disappeared? Two cars and at least three armed men cruised through a checkpoint set up precisely to stop anyone leaving the area? What are the chances that someone on that checkpoint knew them and waved them through? Or at least one of those men was an officer? Maybe even the person who drove my car in."

"We're on it, Ellie. Fort Belvoir is conducting a full investigation and has agreed to keep us informed."

Even so, I was not filled with confidence. At least two people from the base were involved, possibly more.

"Did you find out which gate they took my car through?"

"We have someone talking to all the duty personnel at each gate. We will have a list of all traffic on and off the base within the hour."

I smiled. "What do you need me for again?"

Mac kissed my cheek. "We'd be lost without you."

"You okay? How's your head?"

"I'm good, a few stitches, nothing major."

Leaning back wasn't helping. I sat up too quickly, and then waited for the spinning to stop. With the spinning under control, I swung my legs over the edge of the bed.

"What are you doing?" Mac asked.

"Getting up." I thought that was obvious. "This is not comfortable and I have things to do." I looked down at the hospital gown I wore: not the best thing to be walking about in. "I need clothes."

"Oh, no, you don't."

"Fine, I'll go like this." Tentatively, I planted my feet on the cold floor and stood up. Both wounds in my back pulled. At least I knew where they were now. Slowly I straightened up properly. It felt good.

I grasped the back of the gown closed with my left hand, trying not to become tangled in the tubing that ran from my arm to an infusion pump next to the bed. "Can I at least have a jacket?"

"You are staying here," Mac said. He sounded like he meant it.

"No. I'm going to the office." I had the most eccentric thought: I didn't know where I was. I considered in all reasonableness that it might take me a while to get to the office, being lost an' all. It was going to be tricky negotiating obstacles like getting in and out of the car with this infusion pump dragging along behind me.

Footsteps sounded outside the door and stopped. There was a knock and the door opened. Lee poked his head around the door. "Hey, get back into bed!"

"No," I replied. "What do you want?"

"Mac," he said.

"Well, come in and talk to him then." Just what I needed: a diversion.

Lee ambled in, closing the door behind him. "You got your work cut out for you, Mac."

"Seems so. How can I help?" Mac positioned himself between the door and me. Sneaky. Trapped!

"There isn't a Stacey Eberhart registered with the Foundation. I've run her name through everything I can think of and no hits. I've searched all the sound-alike variations ... then I tried running the name Stacey. There is a Stacey Averhart ... did you mean Averhart? Is that who you meant?"

Dammit! Did I say it or spell it correctly when I told Mac? Maybe there was a different spelling. I focused on the piece of paper in my dream. The names jumped off the page in bold, black lettering. Duh!

"Sorry, I'm an idiot. It is Averhart."

Lee pulled his phone from his pocket. "I'll be back." He hustled from the room, phone poised, to make his call. I knew he wouldn't be going far, just far enough to use his cell phone but close enough to get back here if required.

I stepped back closer to the bed, leaning my hip on it. "I got it wrong!" I'm almost never wrong. How shitty was that? I'd risked her life because I didn't get her name right.

Mac's arms encircled me ever so gently. "You've just come out of an anesthetic. It's hardly surprising you got the name a little screwed up."

I got it wrong and wasted valuable time. She could die now, because they didn't get there in time.

"Where are we?"

"Get back on that bed and I will tell you."

I fought a horrible sinking feeling and scanned the room, looking for familiar curtains and paintings. I didn't recognize anything. Whew! We weren't at Mac's parents' house. As I sat back on the bed, I acknowledged what a huge relief that truly was. The walls and medical equipment suggested we were in a medical facility of some kind.

"Tell me!"

"We're in a medical center in D.C."

"Not military?" That was real fear in my voice. I really didn't want someone coming after me unchallenged.

"No." He smiled widely. "Normally I wouldn't consider this to be a safe place at all, but it's not military and we were short on options."

Intriguing. "Where in the District are we?"

"In a small southeast medical center."

Now I was smiling. "It's doubtful they'd look for us here." It was hard to miss the humor in our situation. Even the police didn't like coming here. People who lived in the southeast of D.C. didn't like walking around alone during the day, let alone at night.

"If that tickles you, you're going to love the next bit."

"Tell."

"The local gang has set up a perimeter, just in case. Seems the FBI have done some good things down here."

Gingerly, I lay back. It was a long time ago. Back when I was new on the job, my very first case with Delta, I investigated the disappearance of five young girls in the southeast. D.C. police were getting nowhere; the parents accused them of not caring and doing nothing. People were scared and believed no one would investigate because their kids weren't important enough. Police called us and we stepped in. Until then they hadn't even linked the disappearances. And there I was all new and fresh and believing I could change the world. I waded in and did my job. I got to know the parents, the families and the kids; I went to the funerals and I cried.

"We did a job is all."

"No one here has forgotten, Ellie."

Just as I considered our fate, the door opened again. A pretty woman with short, tightly-curled hair and wearing pink scrubs entered.

"Agent Conway, good to see you've joined us on this fine Saturday morning."

I knew her. It took me no more than a few seconds to recall her face, name and how I knew her.

"Tallulah."

She smiled as she checked my pulse. "We never thought we'd see you back here. Guess we hoped we'd never have to." She checked my temperature, blood pressure and dressings.

"Any chance you can remove this tubing?" I caught movement from the corner of my eye. It was Mac trying to tell the nurse to disregard me.

"Yes. Your vitals are stable and your color is coming back." She ignored Mac and took a kidney-shaped dish from a cabinet on the counter. Within seconds, the canula was gone from my arm, replaced by a piece of cotton wool stuck down with Micropore tape.

Freedom! "Thank you for the hospitality."

She squeezed my hand. "We have one less evil to worry about because you cared."

She left the room, leaving a hint of a floral perfume and the memory. Her daughter was one of the missing girls. We found her dead and beaten eleven-year-old body stuffed in a sewer pipe. I was the one who'd told Tallulah. That case took several months to bring to fruition. We'd had a higher-than-expected level of cooperation from local residents. During the case we even dabbled in voodoo at the insistence of one panicked parent. Maybe it was desperation, but I was willing to try anything. Something worked and led us to a fifty-year-old white male, who worked as a sales representative or account manager or whatever the term is now. He was a candy company representative. Candy. I don't eat chocolate bars anymore.

I blinked away the memory.

"Have we got somewhere to work?"

"Yeah, in the doctor's lounge."

"Clothes?"

"You're not going to try to leave?"

"Nope."

"I want you to swear on my life." Mac paused. "Show me your hands, I want your hands in plain view before you swear."

Wow, he's playing hardball. "I can't believe you'd think I'd try crossing my fingers."

"Show me and swear."

I placed both hands on the bed, fingers spread. "I swear!"

"Thank you; your clothes are in the closet. I had Praskovya go for them while we waited for you to come out of surgery."

Always thinking ahead, that's my boy. The closet as it turned out was more of a locker, but it did contain my clothes: fresh jeans, a clean shirt, a small bag with toiletries and underwear.

The thought of Praskovya rifling through my drawers picking out clothing and undergarments made me feel a little uneasy. It's not that I thought he was the type to linger where he shouldn't or anything. He was a professional. He was just like us. I was failing at convincing myself. It did feel wrong. Even if it'd been Lee or Sam it would feel wrong.

I felt better once dressed. I pushed aside any lingering thoughts of Praskovya and my underwear. I was feeling more like me and less like an invalid.

The whole time I was dressing, with Mac's help, my mind was running nineteen to the dozen, replaying scenarios, trying to figure out how things went so wrong, how this got so out of hand. Questions came quicker than any sort of explanations. Where did the men go? I was sure they'd sailed right through a military roadblock, so again the poser: how did that happen? Why was I grabbed? What was the point of leaving me alive? Although, I didn't for one second think that leaving me alive was the plan. I think he was interrupted by the phone or maybe he'd expected the call and had waited for instructions. There was a possibility he was the Unsub. Did I shoot the Unsub? How did this become so seriously scary that my team needed to hide me in what amounts to gangland?

I think Mac knew my mind was fully occupied, and left me to my thoughts. I started thinking about the crime scenes. There was no sense to be made there. The notes, the bodies, the poem, gold ribbon, chlorine, the bourbon, the choice of victims; everything so meticulously staged. To what end? And why did he break his rhythm? One death per day, then suddenly we had two; that didn't make sense. It must mean he'd used prior surveillance to determine when the victim would be alone. That was logical. I'd happened upon names of possible victims. They were chosen ahead of time. It was possible there was another party, another unknown subject who provided surveillance.

"Mac?"

"Yeah, babe."

"What's really going on here? What is it our Unsub is concealing?"

"Bodies?" Mac replied and sat on the bed.

"He didn't really conceal them." He is such a smartass and, for once, I didn't feel smart-mouthed. "The crimes feel so contrived. He couldn't have left more things for me; the presence of cameras and listening devices tells me he's getting his kicks watching us work, knowing we're not going to figure it out. There's something he's hiding. It's as if the real crime is being masked by these terrible acts."

Mac immediately adopted his tried and true thinking mode. He dropped his feet on the ground and began wearing a track in the linoleum between the bed and the door. Five minutes later he opened the door and stepped outside. There was one long whistle. He came back in and closed the door. Lee and Praskovya appeared in the room. I don't even think I noticed them come through the door.

"What's up?" Lee asked.

"Tell them," Mac said. "Exactly what you told me."

I repeated my earlier spiel about how contrived the crime scenes were. Both men stared at me as though I'd grown horns. I was used to that look. Didn't mean I liked it any.

"Comments? Thoughts?" I asked.

Lee rubbed his face. Praskovya scratched his head. They rubbed and scratched until I threatened to have them deloused.

"You're serious, ain't ya, Ellie?" Lee asked.

I nodded, knowing he wasn't talking about me having them deloused; they *knew* I'd do that in a heartbeat. "He's pushed us so hard we're still processing evidence from the first crime scene. There's no let up – we're struggling to process all the evidence – we haven't even got all the autopsy reports. We're backlogged in all areas. He could know that."

They nodded their agreement.

"The notes, despite Caine trying to downplay the content, were addressed to me personally."

Again, a round of silent accord.

"My poem was butchered."

Another collective nod.

"The Foundation hacked."

You could've heard a pin drop. They too saw a pattern.

"My kidnapping – which, by the way, opens a whole

other can of worms – we'll get to in a minute." I paused while Mac sat down on the bed. "Why is someone going to such extreme lengths to draw me in then make it look as though I am a target?"

Ah! A joyous array of blank looks.

"And, how did those men know I'd be on the road, alone? The time frame and that I'd stop? What happened to the woman with the children? And who did I shoot?"

Relief flooded Lee's face as he spoke, "The woman and kids, they're all fine. She called the number on your card as soon as they took you. We checked with Triple A ... it was a legit breakdown. Just unfortunate that they became part of your kidnapping ... opportunistic of our Unsub." He looked at me. "We have a name, the dead guy is ..." he sounded almost happy when he said, "... Christopher Sadler."

"What do we know about him?"

Lee flipped open his notebook and read his notes out loud, "He's ex-army, spent several years in Europe."

I interrupted him, "How ex?"

"Discharged seven years ago." Lee pulled his pen from his pocket. It was as if he knew I was going to give him instructions. There's something fabulous about a man with a poised pen.

"I want to know who he knows at Belvoir – he must have connections to be on the base – I'm not liking this whole military involvement aspect of this case. I want someone I can talk to. It's my feeling that one of my attackers was a Marine; I'll have a chat with someone at

Naval Criminal Investigation. Europe: where, when and doing what?"

"Interpol has him on a watch list, suspected human trafficking. He's associated with a group of known traffickers."

"So you're saying I did the world a favor?"

"Yeah ... fuc'n good shooting."

We grinned at each other.

"Where in Europe?"

"He was living in Germany, with frequent trips to Russia, Ukraine, Romania, Serbia, Bulgaria and Turkey. There are records of him traveling to Iraq, Iran and Libya. His most repeated trips were to Spain and Morocco ... always after a trip to the Ukraine or Russia."

"He gets around. When did he arrive in the U.S.?"

"Twelve days ago."

"I want his prints compared with any unidentified prints from all of our crime scenes."

Lee scribbled frantically.

"Added to that, Lee, I want a list of associates. I want a timeline of his movements since his arrival on U.S. soil."

Lee looked at me, pen poised above the page.

"I want to know where he ate, drank and crapped. Get him on a camera somewhere, time stamp him, preferably with a live friend." I needed to chat with someone who knew him.

Praskovya remained silent during this. I noted he had stopped scratching sometime ago. A cold, clawing, gut feeling told me he knew of Christopher Sadler. The feeling matched the dark cloud of tragedy that enveloped Praskovya.

"Praskovya, do you know the deceased?"

He raised his eyebrows, not in surprise but in affirmation. I waited for him to speak. Visions of hell freezing over danced in my head, as I suppressed my impatience.

He almost spat the words, "I know of him. He evaded our police last summer. Fourteen teenage girls died trapped in a shipping container. He left them to die so he could escape."

Another person not sorry that I'd shot Sadler.

"Does he know Selena?"

"Yes."

"Do you know why he was here?" I watched his face carefully, fearing he wasn't about to tell me the truth.

"No."

Too slow! I made eye contact with Mac, letting him know I was ready to let him take over. Lee's phone buzzed. He answered and headed to the door.

A few minutes later, his hushed murmur stopped and he announced, "Ellie, we got another one."

So the Sadler guy wasn't the killer, or there is another one out there. "Name?"

"Cynthia Cobham."

"Dammit, Lee, she was on the list!"

"I know. I'm sorry. We found the other two."

Chapter Twenty-Five
Raise Your Hands

It was my turn to rub my face. "I want some information. I want to know what rumors were floating around the street. You know, stuff like how much I was worth and why me?" I stopped abruptly and looked at Mac. "Who's outside?"

"Some big dude, goes by the name of Caps."

I smiled. "Does he by chance have a smaller, more heavily tattooed, version of himself close by?"

"Yeah."

"Excellent." I said to Lee, "Ask them to come in, please."

Lee left and Mac asked, "What are you scheming?"

"A fishing expedition; these boys know, hear and see way more than you'd think; if something went on in D.C., they'll know."

Mac eyed me with suspicion. "Will they tell you?"

"They'll tell me the buzz." Did he really need me to say the exact words? I didn't want to say them. I barely wanted to think them. I wanted to know how much time there was before I became a dead Fed. I had the feeling that this was what this Unsub would like happen. Why, I didn't know.

Upon hearing footsteps outside the door, I cautioned Praskovya to remain quiet.

Lee poked his head around the door. "Okay to come

in?"

"Yes."

Lee entered in silence with the two men, who bowed their heads in respect.

I went to extend a hand; they made do with my left hand. "Caps, Tats, thank you for coming, and thank you for your hospitality."

Caps spoke. I didn't need to look at Mac and Lee to know they were surprised: there wasn't a trace of Cap's usual Ebonics. This was a relief because I struggled to grasp the meaning in words like 'shizzle' and 'fizzle.' About the only thing I did understand was that 'Yo, G, you frontin' me?' basically indicated the beginning of a fight. He spoke in a quiet and cultured voice, "You're always welcome here, Agent Ellie."

Tat's wide grin revealed gold dental work, but he said nothing.

I smiled at them both. They were imposing in stature and, I'm sure, terrifying in the wrong circumstances. "I need to know what you know, Tyrone."

Caps smiled a perfect, gleaming smile. "I haven't heard my name in a while, Ellie."

"That's a good thing; means you haven't been hauled in by the police in a while." I was sure it meant only that he hadn't been caught, not that he was keeping entirely out of trouble. "What can you tell me?"

"There's talk of a crazy killer. Some say he's Russian or German. Some say he wants to take a female FBI victim."

"He almost did," I commented.

Tyrone dropped a large protective hand on my shoulder. I felt the room pressure change subtly as my men collectively breathed in. "No one gets past us. You're safe here."

I didn't doubt that for one second.

"I appreciate it. I'm going to be leaving soon. There's been another murder."

Mac chimed in, daring with so much testosterone in the room, "Send us. No need for you to go. He won't stop until he gets his FBI agent."

Tyrone agreed, "Listen to the man."

Yeah, yeah. I semi-dismissed his comments knowing that it was Mac, my husband, speaking, not Special Agent Mac Connelly. "Heard anything else?"

"An agent got knifed, that black dude who came here with you, long time back. He okay?"

"Sam will be. Anything else?" I sensed Tyrone wasn't done yet.

"This killer, he's not alone. Word is he was recruiting ... wanted someone to run surveillance ... said it was legit."

"What kind of surveillance, Tyrone?"

Tats spoke, " 'S'up, Agent Ellie?"

"Trying to catch a bad guy; 's'up with you, Tats?"

Tats grinned. "We heard he wanted some women watched. Like five-o stuff."

I wished he hadn't said that. The theme song to *Hawaii Five-O* soared through the space between my ears. I waited for Detective Steve McGarrett to deliver his famous line to his sidekick Detective Danny Williams. He did. Upon hearing the word 'Danno,' the interlude ended.

I focused again on Caps and his information. Please don't let him mean there was police involvement.

"Is he police?"

"Nah, he weren't no five-o."

I kept my relief to myself. "Private investigator surveillance job? More than one woman, yes?"

He nodded. "Yeah, that PI shit. That's what they're saying."

"Who'd he get?"

Tyrone spoke, "No one from here, they said he sounded too strange. No one liked his fucked-up accent."

"Do you know of anyone who actually saw him, who had face time with him?"

"Maybe someone has, people spoke to him; could've been by phone but maybe ..."

"Please find me someone who spoke to him in person."

"We'll ask around."

"Thanks."

Then came Tyrone's firm advice, "Stay here. You are in danger as long as you're out there."

Mac said, "She's staying; we can handle it."

Handle schmandle. I worked my own cases. It wasn't the first time a case has taken an unexpected turn for the worse and likely won't be the last. Husband or not, I didn't like being dictated to.

I raised my eyes to meet Mac's and said, "I give directives on this case."

He said nothing. I knew damn well Lee could've taken over the case but for whatever reason, he'd chosen not to. So I was still in command. It was still my team.

Caps and Tats fell silent.

"I cannot work this case with my hands tied. I need to be on scene and that is where I am going to be."

I turned to Lee. "Her name was Cynthia Cobham, right?"

"Yes," Lee said.

"Have the Cobham scene swept for bugs and cameras."

He nodded and waited.

"I want the area cleared of all non-essential personnel. Any onlookers are to be removed."

"You got it, boss."

"And one more thing ... drape the scene. I want to be sure no one can see us while we're working." I thought for a minute. What if he was using a directional microphone of some description? "Counter surveillance measures ... Lee: a noise curtain, I don't want him eavesdropping from a distance, or at the very least, I want to make it harder for him."

The corner of Lee's mouth twitched into a smile, "That should piss him off."

"That's the plan. If he can't get in, if we cut him off, we might be able to draw him out. Get someone to find the note and get it to us. I don't know when we'll be able to get to the scene ourselves. A photo of the note to one of our cell phones will do for now."

Mac found his voice again. "Meanwhile?"

"Meanwhile," I whispered so only Mac heard. "I want Praskovya here to start talking." My arm ached. My head ached. Nausea wafted in and out, peaking simultaneously with the pain in my head. I adjusted my focal point, hoping to dislodge the fuzzy edges of my sight. It worked. I didn't need another migraine. With my vision stabilized, I let my mind drift and it wrapped itself around words. It chanted them repeatedly, 'Expose the truth.'

There was something I'd been shown when I worked my first case down here. I couldn't remember if it was Caps or Tats but one of them had an aunt who practiced voodoo. She taught me how to use some herbs and in particular, a resin called copal. There was a spell she wrote for me to uncover hidden truths, which involved burning copal. She declared the spell helped uncover the murderer and she could be right. All I know is we did it together and I found her daughter alive with the candy-bar killer.

"Tats, do you know what copal is?"

He shook his head. Wrong person. It must've been Caps with the hoodoo/voodoo aunt.

"Caps, your aunt who does the voodoo, is she still close?"

He nodded, "You need that copal stuff? How much?"

"Tell her I need to burn a little. Couple of pinches should do it."

"For you, no problem. I'll get it."

"Thank you."

Lee, Mac and Praskovya all watched me as if my head

were about to spin and spray green vomit all over the room. "What?"

The door closed quietly as Tats and Caps left. The room pressure equalized.

"Copal?" Mac questioned.

I readied a fabricated answer, "It might clear my head." Moreover, it will expose any lies and half-truths told in this room.

I remembered the old spell, yes, that's right, a spell, a witch-type spell. This spell uncovered hidden truths and I believed that Praskovya was withholding information. Not lying exactly but not telling all he knew, either. I didn't think I needed to share my idea with anyone else. How the hell I could burn copal in a hospital room I didn't know. I'd figure that out when the boys got back with the resin. A dawning: my God, I was actually intent on chanting a spell and burning copal to get to the truth.

Did I think this madness would work? Oh, this was much worse than hearing country music or having the world become a television show around me or seeing scenes from a Mills & Boon novel. This last anomaly really amazed me. I'd never read a Mills & Boon, but I have seen plenty of covers in stands at the grocery store. Apparently, all I needed was a cover and I could construct pure lunacy.

Mac eased up onto the bed next to me. I watched Lee gesture to Praskovya. They slipped from the room.

He leaned in close. "You feel all right?"

"I'm okay." That was a stretch, but it felt good to be

back with the familiar 'I'm okay.' His fingers gave my shoulder a squeeze.

"Course you are ... and now the truth."

With that, the floodgates opened; there was no shutting them.

"I feel sick. I don't know how the Unsub knew about my informant. I think Praskovya knows more than he's saying." I dragged a ragged breath inwards. "I know I've become a target, what I don't know is why ... and I'm not sure I care."

"Sweets, we'll get this prick." I heard his confidence and appreciated it.

"He's killing too fast and I'm in here recovering from stab wounds!" My voice took on a tetchy edge, "Which could have been inflicted by the Unsub, which means he's military, and there are at least two of them. I killed Sadler, how many more are there? I think I'm only alive through sheer luck. I have no idea how many Unsubs we have running about killing women – what the fuc'n hell is going on? Who the hell belonged to the voices at the bunker?" I sighed. "I need to get back to work. Where's the note Lee took off me?"

Mac blanched; guess he didn't think I'd remember about the note so soon.

"It's in evidence," he said.

"What'd it say?"

" 'I hear you knocking,' " Mac said. Slowly.

"Does that mean we're getting closer or what? Before I woke up," I said, then paused to consider the entire thought. “I saw a note which said, ‘People like you shouldn’t procreate.’ ”

“That’s not one we’ve found yet,” Mac replied.

“Can I have your phone please?”

He handed it to me. I called my father. His phone rang and rang. I’d started to think he was out when he answered, breathless.

“You okay?” I asked, foregoing the usual greeting.

“I am,” he replied. I heard a female voice in the background.

“Company?”

“Making lunch ... for a lady who moved in down the street.”

“Go, Dad,” I replied, happy for him.

“How can I help you, Ellie?” Much amusement in his voice.

“I had a problem with a Marine yesterday. I need someone at NCIS. Who should I call?”

“I know your type of problem,” he replied. “Call Special Agent Noel Gerrard.”

“He good?”

“I trained him.”

I felt a TV show brewing. “He doesn’t resemble Jethro Gibbs by any chance?”

“I don’t know Gibbs.”

I silenced the *NCIS* episode before it took hold. “Never mind – just one of my better interludes encroaching.”

“Call Gerrard. He’s a good man.”

“That’s all I need to know.”

"All right, Ellie. I have lunch to cook. Take care; say hello to Mac."

"Bye, Dad." I smiled at Mac. "Dad says hi, and he has a lunch date!"

He replied, "Go, Simon. Looks like he's getting on with life."

It was good news. We all thought it was time dad moved forward after mom's death. So far he'd thrown himself into running our Foundation and didn't seem to want to date or meet anyone.

I handed the phone back to Mac. "See if you can get Special Agent Noel Gerrard over at NCIS to meet with us."

"If he resists?"

"Tell him who my father is and, that I want to press charges against a Marine."

Mac walked to the far side of the small room and made a call. I listened as he asked our switchboard to put him through to NCIS; that way the call couldn't be traced any farther than the FBI. Seems he didn't trust the military either. A few minutes later he smiled at me and nodded.

He hung up and sat on the end of my bed. "He'll meet with you, whenever you're ready."

"Excellent, thank you."

My door opened. Caine stormed in, followed by Lee and Praskovya.

"You okay?" he asked.

Mac jumped to his feet. "Caine."

"Mac, sit. I want a quick word, then I'm out of here."

I guess I looked bemused.

"Ellie, did you really think I wouldn't find out where you were?"

He looked fierce. Quick, answer him. "Um, no."

He squinted out another characteristic gaze. "You capable of finishing this?"

"Yes."

"Good." He spun on his heels and evaporated into thin air.

I was left waiting for the other shoe to drop. The silence was deafening for almost two whole seconds, then bam, the music started in my head.

My first reaction was to slap myself upside the head, good and hard, to dislodge it. But my slapping arm was bandaged and oozing so it wasn't an option. I was trapped listening to Bruce Willis singing 'Swinging on a Star.' I remembered Hudson Hawk and I knew exactly how long that song lasts. I sighed as the third verse started.

"Ellie?"

I looked up to find Mac's questioning face. "You're sighing."

I wanted to tell him about the song without Lee and Praskovya hearing me, or thinking I was suffering from a head injury. They might mutiny. The thought of mutiny almost caused me to laugh aloud; that's not Lee's style. Mac was still waiting, and the damn song kept on.

"Ellie?"

"Remember Hudson Hawk?"

He nodded. He moved closer to my ear and whispered, "Let me guess: you have 'Swinging on a Star' stuck in your head."

"Yep, and it's just started again; thanks to you I now have another five minutes and thirty-two seconds of hell to listen to."

"That means something, Ellie."

He was right, mostly the songs meant something. So what was it I needed to glean from this one? Swinging on a star, Hudson Hawk, or a time value? This didn't mean I thought Bruce Willis was an Eastern European serial killer.

Praskovya and Lee stopped their conversation and joined ours. I don't know how much they'd heard; we kept our voices barely above a whisper.

I decided to ask the group questions.

"Do the numbers five, three, two mean anything?"

This drew blank looks.

"How about as a time? Five minutes thirty-two seconds?"

Nothing. I moved right along. Maybe it wasn't the song length. "How about the name Hudson Hawk?"

Praskovya leaned forward and repeated the name as if he hadn't heard correctly, "Hudson Hawk?"

"Yes."

"You came up with the name Hudson Hawk by yourself?"

"Yes." Parts of the movie circled slowly overhead like Leonardo Da Vinci's flying machine. "What are we expecting here? A Vatican robbery ... the CIA ... alchemy ... a nun? Did the fuc'n butler do it?"

Praskovya shifted his weight from his right to his left foot, he looked perplexed, and then he spoke, "A few years ago that name came to our attention."

"Our?" And now he talks.

"FSB."

"Carry on."

"Someone by the name of Hudson Hawk was giving large sums of money to orphanages across Europe."

"Large?"

"Millions of U.S. dollars."

"Generous man, this Mr. Hawk." I resisted the temptation to ask if Hudson Hawk had his pal, Tommy 'Five-Tone' with him.

Praskovya nodded. "Exceptionally. No one knew who he was, or is, but over a five-year span he was a benefactor extraordinaire, giving nearly twenty million dollars."

"And?"

"The money stopped a year ago."

"And the money, how was it transferred?"

"Always contact was made through a third party who contacted the orphanages in question to obtain bank account details. The money was transferred from a numbered Swiss account to the orphanage account overnight."

"How did you find the name?"

Praskovya smirked before replying, "He sent cards signed Hudson Hawk. The cards arrived in the next mail delivery, always after the money. They said 'Merry Christmas', even though he never transferred any funds during any Christmas period. All the transfers were made during summer months."

"Any theories as to why they stopped?"

Praskovya shrugged, "He could be dead, in prison on an unrelated matter, or he may have given away all his money."

"Yeah ... maybe." On the other hand, he could've left Europe.

Praskovya leaned against the wall. "Why do you ask about Hawk?'

Now that was something I didn't want to answer. I fumbled about in my head looking for something reasonable to say. "Call it intuition. I think someone using the name Hudson Hawk has a connection to this case."

"And you pulled that out of thin air, with this intuition you speak of?" Praskovya radiated incredulity; even his long black coat draped over a chair seemed to confront me with a large dose of skepticism.

I watched Lee's face contort as he considered what had been said and, probably, Praskovya's reaction. Finally he said, "More spooky shit, yeah?"

I nodded. One glance told me Praskovya was lost. And I didn't want to explain to him what Lee meant. But it didn't look like I'd need the copal or to play with voodoo and magick spells after all.

Mac spoke, "What if Hawk, Selena, Unsub, Sadler, the Marine and the mystery military man are all part of the same cell?"

I picked up on his drift. "And the money he was giving wasn't so much a gift as insurance, making damn sure he or they had a safe house. Who would look for criminals in an orphanage?"

"You have a point," Lee concurred. "And they'd be fairly comfortable places with that amount of cash pumped into them, if indeed it went to the orphanages and not a particular person."

I smiled. "I thought I had a good point but it is speculation and gets us no closer to the Unsub, or even an idea of who he is. People are still dying."

Praskovya stood up. He paced the confines of the small room. "It may." He picked up his coat and plunged his arms into it. I thought he was going to leave but he pulled his cell from his coat pocket and punched in many numbers. Several minutes later, he spoke in Russian. I sat mesmerized by the beauty of the language. Three more phone calls followed, then finally Praskovya spoke English to us.

"A woman and four men visited three orphanages on our list, at different times, staying for approximately two weeks at each place over the course of several years. There was an increase of murders in the areas during those times, mostly vagrants and prostitutes – this was recently discovered. We have identified only one man by name."

I was barely breathing. "A name?"

"Christos Von Crichton."

Lee was already on his laptop, running the name through Immigration, as well as airport security. Praskovya called another number, speaking Russian again. Moments later he said, "A photograph is being faxed to your office."

"Was anyone ever charged with any of those murders?" Questions bubbled up inside me. I wanted to know the exact details of each murder.

"No, in one town the police suspected a farmer who had a history of alcohol-related violence. His death coincided with the cessation of the murders."

"Signature?"

Praskovya leaned back on the wall by the door, stepped forward, removed his coat and draped it casually over the end of the bed before speaking. His actions made me wonder why he'd put it on to start with. I stifled a smile: maybe it was a quirk. Perhaps it was something he felt he had to do; wear the coat to access the pockets. Could the Russian dark horse have quirks like a regular human being?

Praskovya spoke, freeing me from the ramblings about his quirky coat habits. "All the victims were women and all stabbed; the bodies were found in pools of vodka or Slivovitz, depending on the town."

"Slivovitz?"

"A plum brandy made in Serbia from blue plums. It is quite delicious. I will bring you some when I get a chance."

"Why use Slivovitz in Russia?" My immediate response

was to wonder if the murders were in Russia, but surely they wouldn't be in Serbia if the FSB were investigating. Hang on. Where had Christopher Sadler traveled to? "Praskovya, didn't you say Sadler took trips to Serbia?"

"*Da.*"

My thoughts flowed on, verbally, "Don't you wonder if he brought back the brandy? Unless it's a normal drink in ... where were the murders involving brandy?"

I was trying to determine if he was using alcohol that has a geographical connection, rather than it having a particular message.

Lee waved a hand to get our attention. "Von Crichton arrived in LA two months ago, flew out of JFK in New York four weeks ago to Canada and then into Dulles two after that."

"From?"

"Toronto."

"Get a bulletin out on him: wanted for questioning, considered dangerous. Let Customs know. I want him stopped. I want the borders closed for Von Crichton. Add Hawk to that, too, for all we know they're the same person." I thought for a minute. "Can we get media liaison involved and get his freaking face all over the news channels? He can't hunt if everyone knows who he is." I stopped myself. "Scratch that. We can't warn the public until we are sure it's him. Unless we can prove this is a national security issue? And who is to say he's making first contact with these women?"

Lee and Mac shook their heads. Lee spoke, "We can't

connect the dots; wanted for questioning is the best we can do."

Mac touched my shoulder. "But you can have your dad put the photo up in the members-only area of the Butterfly Foundation website."

That was something at least and, I could do more than that.

"Also, Mac, send a bulletin to every member with the photo of Von Crichton, with all our contact numbers. Try not to scare the kids but word it so they know something is going on; include everything we know about Selena. We know she was in the chat room. There must be a photo of her. You must have one, Praskovya. Have it put up on the website. Tell them she's dangerous. That will make everyone take notice; then add that anyone who has seen either of them should call us immediately." I found myself thinking we should probably get hold of that fax and get copies of the photograph made first.

"Lee, have someone pick up the fax, scan it and put the image on a flash drive; make photocopies of the original fax. I want the original added to the case file and the copies and flash drive delivered to you."

Lee was thinking while he made notes, "You want me to have a bulletin circulated through the network with a description and the pictures of Von Crichton and Selena?"

"Yes, please. Send out a BOLO with as much information as we have. Add, 'Considered dangerous – apprehend with caution' and make a note: I want to be able to speak to these people – dead won't work for me. Call the office, have Chrissy get on it. Tell her to meet you somewhere to hand over the documents and flash drive." I was tempted to have the picture copied to CD but flash drives are so cool and small, and I love technology. Then I had another thought. "Can you ask Chrissy to please use two new flash drives, put the picture on both. I want one given to my dad."

Lee smiled. "Wouldn't it be easier to email him the picture?"

"Nope, we're dealing with at least one hacker. Physically pick up those drives and I'll have dad meet us for the handover."

Lee didn't look up as he scribbled some more notes. "Have you considered the hacker is already inside the Foundation?"

"Yes. Let's make that Mac's problem."

"Thanks," Mac replied, "Good thing I came along."

Praskovya spoke, "What is this BOLO you speak of?"

"It's a notice to all law enforcement to Be On the Look Out." I replied, "It's Agency speak."

Praskovya nodded. "We have similar thing in Russia."

Lee stepped up to the mirror over the sink. "I'm going to set up that meeting with Chrissy," he said, smoothing his short hair and straightening his clothes. He fiddled with the collar of his shirt until it sat exactly how he wanted it, then gave his shoes a quick shine with a paper towel. He likes Chrissy McQueen. Most red-blooded men do. She brought out the man in men.

"Mac, have dad make sure everyone logging in receives a message with a photo. Splash the word 'dangerous' across the picture. That should get everyone's attention."

"I'll write the message and add the photo myself, as soon as Lee brings us back those flash drives."

I wasn't done yet. "I want someone to show the photographs to the military personnel on gate duty; let's see if they recognize Von Crichton. Scratch that: I'm meeting with someone from NCIS. I'll have him do it. They'll be more willing to talk to one of their own, plus he can liaise with his army equivalent."

"What kind of name is Von Crichton?" Lee asked.

Praskovya replied, "Austrian."

"Like Hitler?" Lee said.

I attempted to head off the evil pictures building in my own mind and said, "Like Von Trapp from *The Sound of Music*."

"Much nicer image, thanks, Ellie," Lee replied. He looked up from his phone. "Office says the photograph is being circulated to all LEOs."

"Go get our picture, Lee."

Lee grabbed his jacket, threw a grin back into the room, and headed off to meet Chrissy.

Chapter Twenty-Six
Temptation

I looked around the small hospital room. Safe; yes, but also constricting. I needed to go back to the office, or I needed an office.

"We need desks, computers and a more conducive work environment."

Praskovya stepped forward from the wall he leaned on. "There is a temporary office down the hall, it has desks."

"Excellent."

Mac, Praskovya and I walked down the corridor to a waiting room already converted to a reasonable work-space.

I felt stranger than I ever had, which was saying some-thing. The whole case to date smelled of something else. I'd missed something. We'd missed something. I sat at a desk with a laptop on it. The desk I chose faced the other two desks. Praskovya and Mac slid into chairs. I could hear them talking quietly as I opened the laptop and switched it on.

By the time I had opened the case files my fingers were drumming a beat on the desk surface and my mind rock 'n' rolled over fresh ideas, hoping I could secure a new perspective.

Frustrated with the lack of answers I danced around inside my own brain until Praskovya spoke loud enough to shake me from myself.

"Ellie?"

"Uh-huh?"

"Can I help you?"

What an odd thing to say. I was busy – lost in my thoughts – and he thinks I need help. Meddlesome man!

"I don't think so."

Mac gave one of his knowing looks. As if that was necessary. I knew he knew I was struggling with this case.

"Tell him!" Mac said.

"What?"

"Whatever it is that's bugging you. It's not going to go away unless you face it."

I took a breath and let it rush out of my body. It was useless to deny anything was wrong. He wasn't just my friend, my colleague, he was my husband. He had a way of reading me, a damned annoying way of knowing me better than I knew myself.

Suck it up, chucklehead, tell him what it is.

"Usually I get a feeling in any given situation – a signal from my gut – that tells me what's going on ... then I just have to prove it." I couldn't help but smile, knowing that was the easy bit.

Praskovya spoke, "Why not this case?"

"Why any case?" I asked.

He tossed it back at me. He wasn't going to fall for my tricks.

"What's special about this case?"

Then he surprised me. "Shut your eyes, Ellie. Take a deep breath and let me ask you again."

"What the hell for?" Interfering wretch.

"You are a difficult woman. I can help. Shut your eyes."

"I am not difficult. I do not take orders from you and if you can help, then start talking!"

I knew Mac was smiling. "She's not difficult, Praskovya. She is, however, contrary."

I flipped him the bird.

"I can help. You have the answers, you have more than you know inside," Praskovya said, tapping his head.

"Why do I need to close my eyes?"

"It will help you focus."

"Mmmm ..." Skepticism lay heavy in my voice. Possibly because Praskovya had suggested it and not because I thought he was full of crap. I sighed as loud as I could. Contrary?

"How exactly are you going to do this?"

"I learned a relaxation technique a long time ago; it helps unlock things we do not realize we know."

"And this works?"

"On some people. I think your mind finds meaning where other people can't."

Mac tapped my hand. "It can't hurt."

"Fine," I said and, with great reluctance, closed my eyes.

Moving pictures folded like cloth as Praskovya's voice took me to the seashore and a yellow, sandy beach. Sparkling white-capped waves rolled onto the sand. A heat haze hung over the water, making the world shimmer. Seabirds whirled above, squawking loudly. Their calls interspersed between Russian and English as they dove at the sand. Pulling and pulling. Four birds in a row tugged a cloth from the sand, stretching it between them like a canvas. The images settled.

Still life, exquisitely painted like the gilt-edged scenes on a Fabergé egg. Fragile. Pictures captured by a dream. One by one the images told a story. His words brushed over the canvas illuminating the recesses. It was all so clear.

"What's special about this case?" Praskovya's voice powered its way into my consciousness.

I opened my eyes and looked straight at him. "There is definitely more than one Unsub, maybe even more than one actual killer. I think a minimum of two people are killing."

Praskovya smiled. His dark cloud parted briefly and I saw a man who didn't always take life so seriously. Someone who was real, not a misplaced character from a cheap romance novel.

"More than one," he repeated. "More than one killer." He tapped his fingers on the desk. "We know he has associates. Why do you think they're a part of the killings?"

"He could not have carried out all the surveillance, or picked the victims. He arrived in the U.S. only two weeks ago. Everything was already set up. He came to kill. He came to get our attention," I replied, maintaining eye contact.

"And?"

"And he has it," I said.

"Why?" Praskovya pushed onward.

"It's a mask."

"What for?"

"That's what I don't understand. Why blow smoke up Delta's ass? What don't they want us to find? We're being played."

"Delta's directive is what?"

"Serial crime."

He nodded.

"I still don't understand why they want us tied up." I left my words out in the space between us and let my mind run over the rest of my thoughts.

It made no sense. Human trafficking in Europe isn't under our directive, so that can't be what they're hiding. Why would they kill mothers connected to the Foundation? Why target me? Why make this personal? What if ... this ... was ... about ... American kids? The vulnerable kids of bipolar mothers. Nah! Can't be. Ninety percent of the children involved in the Foundation had fathers in their lives. They're not easy marks and would be too easily missed.

What if *that's* what they're covering up? The real crimes could be the kids who *are* easy marks. Those no one would miss.

My stomach sank as I realized what could be happening.

Praskovya spoke, "What are your thoughts?"

"They're not good," I said, "Is it possible that he/they kept us busy with crimes that covered up what was really happening." I paused, letting my thoughts roar. "Mixing the underlying crime with a heavy coating of bloodied murder victims so we become overwhelmed and desensitized?"

"What are you saying?"

"That a few more bodies turning up would be lost in the abundance of crime scenes; we may not notice in time that children are missing."

Mac asked, "Why the kids?"

Praskovya looked at me. In his eyes I saw a shadow of knowledge he'd rather not have. He spoke to Mac, "They could be filling an order."

I tapped at the keyboard intent on finding out how many daughters were untraceable after the deaths we were investigating. Five children were missing, presumed out of the area with extended family. No one had found them yet. Five that we knew of.

"Fuck! I've handed these perverts a *smorgasbord* of vulnerable exploitable kids."

"You didn't do this, Ellie," Mac said with his usual calmness. "We did."

I shook my head. "Yeah, I did. In my efforts to help I managed to help these boys and girls right into a pedophile's bedroom."

He started to argue again. I held my hand up to signal him to stop.

Silence fell.

"There is too much information here," I said.

The silence continued.

"I need the pictures. Victims. Kids. All of them."

Mac pulled them all from a file he had near him and handed them to me. I touched each picture and then laid each victim on the desks with the corresponding children. I moved away from the younger children – the children I knew were safe – away from Dakota's deep brown eyes.

Five children were left. The youngest was ten years old; the oldest twelve. The only children with no immediate family. "Where are they?"

"Everything we have says they were picked up by relatives."

"So why can't we find the relatives?"

"They're out of State," Mac replied. "Schools were notified that the kids were spending a week away with relatives."

"Any of those schools query who the relative was?"

"No."

No one looking. No one demanding FBI involvement and screaming about how they were good kids and someone should find them.

"Did anyone even get a contact number for any of these so-called relatives?"

"Not that we have found," Mac said.

Rage rose in waves at the realization that schools didn't care enough about their charges to ask a few basic questions. I chewed my lip and considered a plan of action. I directed my response to Mac. "Get Chrissy to work on something for me. I want the names of office staff and principals of the schools these children attended." I was fuming and trying really hard not to sound mad at Mac but, damn, the thought that no one cared about the pupils at these schools really ticked me off. "These schools need better security measures and some basic safety practices in place. They obviously have no fuc'n clue how to safeguard their pupils so we'll *help* them."

Mac wrote my instructions on a pad. "Anything else?"

It wasn't easy curbing the desire to tell to him that if and when we had babies, I'd be giving up work and home schooling them. Them? Jeez, now it was more than one. This thinking about babies thing had to stop. I thought for a second or two while he waited for more instructions.

"Ask Chrissy to get someone from the Crimes Against Children program to contact these schools and express our concern." Before I go in there and express myself through the medium of a closed fist. "While you're at it. Get her to fire up legal ... find some charges we can threaten them with. I want something to scare the fuck outta these people."

"I'll get it done."

"I don't believe they're with relatives. Why don't we have something, anything that says these kids have family somewhere? We don't. All we have is the schools being notified by someone other than the parent and no contact phone numbers or addresses." I was aware that I was starting to rant. "These are the children I think we've lost." I spread their pictures out across my desk. "These and how many others, I don't know. We have to find them."

Praskovya cleared his throat. "There are so many ways to leave, but they may not always leave. Sale could be arranged here within the United States."

I nodded. "And so many places to hide, right here."

"Why the fort?" he asked suddenly. "What's so special about the fort? Why did they take you there? Where is your informant?"

Lee swung the door open. "It's taken care of," he said. In his hand was a manila folder, and from it he pulled some photographs. When he slapped the first photograph on my desk I knew he'd heard Praskovya's question. "McNab was drowned in the bay, about a hundred yards from where we found you, Ellie."

I picked up the picture. Dead.

"How did they know?" I struggled with the knowledge. "How did they know who my guy was?"

They knew better than to answer. I thought and thought. The only thing I concluded in the short term was that McNab had set me up and it all went pear-shaped on him. I hope he was paid well, that it was worth dying for. The whole scheme was well planned.

Kids targeted.

Planned.

Someone else helped set this up: it wasn't just McNab. Someone who could conduct surveillance on me as well as on the Foundation, and set up safe houses; someone who could get around Fort Belvoir with no questions asked.

"He's watching and listening at crime scenes. How else could he get information?" I said.

"Your computer, your cell phone ... car. If he's as well organized as he looks to be ... bugs in our homes and offices. We know at least one operative is Spetsnaz trained, plus two other military types involved. We could've been tailed. The cell could be bigger than we know," Mac replied.

"This could've gone on for months." I looked at Mac. "Take what you need, go back to my room and see what you can uncover. And get Noel Gerrard to come meet me here. Have Caps and Tats bring him in from their outer perimeter."

He grabbed a laptop and disappeared.

The penny dropped, spun and came up heads.

"Last Saturday – missing Dutch kid. The Albanians."

Praskovya looked baffled but Lee caught on. As he would; he was with me on Saturday.

"A test to see how we would react? How deadly our response is ..." Lee said, slowly shaking his head. "Damn!"

I nodded. "It feels like that and what a great opportunity to see who responded."

"To snatch a look at the lead agent," Lee said.

"Finding the girl we were supposed to find."

"Go team," Lee murmured. "We were played."

Praskovya interrupted. "Excuse me. The note – the first victim – did it have your name on it?"

"Yes."

"They were hoping for you to take the case ... then tested your responses just to make sure you were available?" Praskovya asked. "Or was this fluke of timing?"

I shrugged. It seemed nuts. Mostly that's how it goes with my job. "I doubt it was me they wanted. But they did want a name, a lead agent, someone they could taunt."

Lee added, "Those rooms, the building where we found the girl: probably bugged."

"That's how they knew my name. If anyone had overheard my conversation with Caine they'd also know all the other teams were involved in cases and we were the only available team," I replied. "That would explain the mystery of the notes addressed to me. I wonder, did they let that girl escape on purpose?"

I sank into the chair behind me. From beginning to end we had been under the microscope.

"Most probably," Lee replied. "I would say they most certainly unlocked the door and left the room on purpose, sending the bait running off to trap us. And then it wouldn't take much research to find out you're the FBI poet everyone's been talking about. That makes you much more likely to receive taunts than say, me or Sam."

"Where would these kids be?" I asked, burying the Post-it notes, pushing aside the death of my informant and mentally uncovering the faces of the missing children.

We all reached the same conclusion. "Fort Belvoir."

"They got me through the gates with no problem whatsoever and I'm an adult. It'd be much easier to conceal a kid in a car," I said.

“Could we have been so close to those kids and not known to look?” Praskovya said.

“But why would they take me to the same place?”

We were interrupted by Mac at the doorway. “Gerrard is on his way now; he’ll be here in about twenty minutes. Caps and Tats are the welcoming committee.” Mac went back to what he was doing, leaving us to continue the conversation.

I heard Praskovya speak softly, “She goes where she is comfortable.”

“Who?” I asked.

“Selena,” he replied. “Most likely place to hide?”

“Somewhere out of the way, a private house, an army house, an old bunker on a military reservation. We’re talking about a big area. We need to narrow it down.”

“What was that road? Deakyne?” Praskovya asked. “Where you were.”

I nodded. “There was another building before the bunker, close but not too close. It was large and concrete. That could be what they were protecting.” I remembered seeing both structures. The car driven by the Marine was parked near that building. “I need to meet with NCIS. Hopefully he’ll agree to get us on base and we can check out that building.”

We all scoured the notes, case files, every scrap of information we could find while waiting for Gerrard to arrive. I was hoping something would jump out and declare itself irrefutable proof of my theory regarding snatched children.

Eventually, several sets of footsteps approached the door. Someone knocked.

"Come in," I called.

Tats swung the door open.

"Visitor for you, Agent Ellie."

"Thank you very much."

Noel Gerrard stepped into the room. Caps poked his head in and made eye contact with me. "Do you need the copal now?"

I'd forgotten all about it. "Oh, Caps ... it's worked out. Please thank your aunt for me. Maybe I just needed to know I could get it."

"You sure?"

"Yeah. Thanks Caps."

He pulled the door shut, indicating they would be outside waiting.

I stood up and moved to greet my perplexed visitor. He was clean cut, about six feet tall and stood strong and straight. His eyes suggested he missed nothing. "Special Agent Gerrard, pleased to meet you. I can't shake your hand. Sorry."

He glanced at the bandages.

"Good to meet you, SSA Conway."

Lee moved a chair over to my desk for Gerrard.

"Have a seat. Call me Ellie," I smiled and introduced my roommates. "This is FBI Special Agent Lee Davenport and FSB Officer Misha Praskovya."

He nodded and greeted the men.

"You wanted to see me?"

"I do. I had a little run-in with a Marine out at Fort Belvoir."

His expression didn't change as he asked, "Would this have anything to do with the shoot-out yesterday on Deakyne Road?"

I smiled and inclined my head. "The Marine I'm referring to assisted in my kidnapping. He also attacked me with a knife."

"Your arm?"

"Yup. I have nothing. No name, no rank, no nothing. Except that he was with another man – possibly military or at the very least a civilian working on base. What I can tell you is that he's hurt."

"Hurt how?"

"I cut his right hand, while trying to pry the knife from him. Before his buddy stabbed me in the back."

"Bad enough that he'd show up on sick call?"

"I think so."

"Shouldn't be too hard to find him, then. I'll look for recent injuries reported at the base hospital, and for anyone on sick call. How good a description did you get?"

"White, five-ten, light brown hair – not thinning – medium build. His hands were kind of soft. Not what I expected. I did my best to get a description but I was fairly preoccupied with survival."

Gerrard smiled. "I'll investigate this. Is there anything else?"

"Can you get us into Fort Belvoir without creating a stir?"

He grinned. "Sure, why the hell not? When?"

"Now."

"What are you after?"

"We think there are missing children being held out on Deakyne Road. We don't want anyone on base knowing we're heading out there."

"So I'm taking you." He swept his arm around the room. "And no one's supposed to know?" His voice held a hint of sarcasm.

"Uh-huh."

He pulled a phone from his pocket and made a call. "Get your gear, you're heading south. Meet me at the intersection of Fairfax Country Parkway and Route 1."

He closed the phone and put it back in his pocket. He looked at me. "You might need help. My team is coming."

"Let's do it," I said. I looked around for my badge. Lee pulled a hand out of his pocket and passed my badge over. I stuck my head out of the door into the corridor. "Yo, Mac. We're moving out."

I pulled on my jacket. Praskovya helped. Pushing my injured arm into my sleeve wasn't easy. Mac arrived at the door and spotted Noel.

"This is Noel Gerrard NCIS," I said. "Noel this is SA Mac Connelly."

"Good to meet you, Mac. We spoke on the phone?" They shook hands. Mac turned to me. "Where we going?"

"Fort Belvoir," I replied. "Find anything?"

"I found crap-loads. GPS tracking devices ... there are keyloggers and spyware on the computers belonging to

Delta and on your PC at home."

I sighed. "I hate having technology used against me."

"Then you'll hate this ..."

I braced myself mentally. We were all walking down the hallway to a door that led to a small parking lot. "Tell me the worst."

"The cars are being swept for bugs. I have teams going through the garages. So far only the cars assigned to Delta have devices, but they did those first."

"Then we need to search our cars here before we leave. They may know where we are."

"They probably know where we live." Mac said.

Lee strode ahead. "Wait. I'll get Caps to lend a hand."

We all stopped walking. Lee pushed through a set of double doors. Through the glass we saw him beckon to someone. Caps came into view. They both gave us a backward glance, then vanished.

Ten minutes later Lee and Caps came back. Caps stood by the door.

"Clear, now," Lee called.

As we joined him by the main entrance I asked, "What'd you do with the devices?"

He grinned. "Caps here came up with an idea."

I wasn't sure I wanted to know; the devices were evidence. "Do I need to know this?"

"Probably not," Lee replied.

A dog ran past. Caps hooted wildly. The dog scampered off down an alleyway. Lee and Caps watched him go, beaming at each other. The high five was completely unnecessary.

"I'm glad I don't know anything about that," I said. "Let's go."

Caps slapped on the car roof as we pulled out after Gerrard. He stood, like a sentry, watching us leave. A hundred yards down the road, Tats did the same. And a hundred yards later another young man stood. This carried on until we were out of their territory. Either they wanted to make sure we had gone, or they wanted to make sure we had gone safely. I wanted to believe it was safely.

We drove in silence. I didn't know what the hell we thought we were doing trying to find the kids, just us and Noel's small team, but we didn't want to call the cavalry, so to speak. I had nothing that suggested the kids were at the fort.

Far be it from me to be the girl who cries wolf.

Gerrard pulled over just before the Fairfax Parkway and Route 1 intersection. An SUV bearing the NCIS insignia was already waiting. We pulled up behind them. Gerrard ran back and tapped on my window.

"I'll lead ... then you ... then my team."

"Okay."

We checked through Tulley Gate with no problem. At the beginning of Deakyne Road we swapped places because we knew exactly where we were going and they didn't. We led, Gerrard followed; his team came up last. Mac was driving and slowed to a crawl as we moved down the road, ever watchful.

"No one around," Mac said, flipping the window wipers to clear drizzle from the windscreen. "You'd think there'd be someone."

"Yeah, maybe," I replied. "He likes cameras; the whole place is probably rigged and streaming live to someone's computer. Pull over."

He did as I asked. The sound of rounds being chambered surrounded me like a deadly chorus. Everyone pulled out their phones and switched them to silent.

Mac opened his door, with a tentative look at me. "You coming?"

"Is your brother a moron?'" I replied with a grin.

From under the passenger seat I pulled out a bulletproof vest. I climbed out of the car and pulled off my jacket. "Suit up."

Lee and Praskovya shut their doors with little more than a click. Mac grimaced but opened the truck and pulled out three more vests. He handed them out. I needed help to fasten the Velcro on my Kevlar vest and to put my jacket back over it. Gerrard and three men arrived, already wearing Kevlar under NCIS jackets. We headed for the building: the one in front of the bunker we'd been trapped in the day before.

We ran in single file, separating as we neared, and circled the building. All the windows were boarded up. I counted two doors. One front and one back. It didn't mean there weren't tunnels underneath. I was at the back with Praskovya and one of the NCIS guys, scanning the exterior for cameras or anything that indicted the cladding had been interfered with recently. It seemed sensible to let Mac, Lee and the others take the front.

I was going to have to shoot left-handed if needed. Been there, done that, and it ain't pretty.

Lee called my cell.

"No sign of any cameras out front."

"Okay. Let's get in there then."

I wondered for a moment why there were no cameras. He liked to watch everything else. Why not watch the building? The thought occurred to me that we could be wrong about it being the stash point for the missing kids.

I heard Lee call out at the front door, announcing us as FBI/NCIS. It pays to announce. Listening intently, I discerned no reply.

The next sound was crunching wood. I guessed Lee and Mac had opened the door.

Mac hollered, "Ellie, come here!"

I ran around the corner with Praskovya close on my heels. Puffing from the exertion and wincing from the reminders emanating from the sutures in my back, I found Lee outside. He was on his cell phone. He looked at me, winked and smiled. Filled with positive vibes, I left him to it and hurried to see Mac.

He was smiling too. It didn't take me long to see why. He dropped to his knees next to a mattress and grinned at me. Gerrard and his men were standing by.

"You were right," Gerrard said.

There were sleeping kids. I hoped they were sleeping. I bent over and touched each face as I counted. Six. They were warm.

"Sleeping?"

"Drugged, I think, not waking," Mac replied. "And we weren't quiet coming in here."

Praskovya was smiling. I glimpsed the relief in his eyes. "You found them. You found them," he said, his voice crumbling at the edges.

"Six kids. We only knew about five. Are they okay?" I asked.

Mac was checking pulse rates and trying to wake them. "Six ... an extra kid. Wonder who she is."

The kids were huddled together under a thick comforter.

"Lee's calling for ambulances and backup. They wouldn't leave these children for long, not that they could get out. But whatever is keeping them asleep will need topping up."

I looked around the room. It was one large, cold, concrete room. No windows. There was light and electricity. I carefully checked every inch of the room, looking for anything that could conceal a camera or microphone. A bucket in the corner with a towel over it; a roll of toilet tissue on the floor next to it. I lifted the towel and wished I hadn't. A small sink. I turned on the taps and checked the pipe underneath. Tiny surveillance cameras can be hidden almost anywhere these days.

Sirens whined in the distance coming ever closer. Lee and Praskovya took up positions on either side of the doorway. Partially hidden from outside, they were our defense should the traffickers return. Nerves yammering, we waited for medical help for the kids and our backup.

My cell rang. I fumbled it from my pocket, heart pounding, and almost dropped it. Aidan's voice met my ear as he said, "Ellie, I have a kid online asking for help; her mom hasn't come home."

This felt very important. "Get her details. Is this the first one who's asked for help?"

"Yeah. I would've mentioned it earlier if any others had."

My brain raced. So far, we'd found all the dead women in their own homes; more specifically, in their kitchens.

"Where's the kid?"

"At a friend's house."

"Good. Get an address." Adrenaline raced through my body. I knew we had to get to the child before they did. I hated being right but we'd caught a break; we had a kid who hadn't disappeared yet and the five plus one missing kids. Now we just needed to keep this new child out of harm's way.

"Ball park on her location, Aidan?"

"Georgetown."

I paced up and down the room. Willing the sirens to hurry. I wanted to get to the girl before she disappeared. Gravel crunched under tires.

I leaned back against the wall in the shadows and whispered to Aidan, "We're heading out as soon as we can. Get that address. I'll call you back."

"Sure."

I hung up and pushed the phone into my pocket. “Lee?”

Lee was moving back into the room, he said, “Three ambulances and I hope our backup, Chicky.”

“Praskovya?” He didn’t answer right away. “Misha?”

“I see paramedics.”

Pfft. Dust rose from outside the door. *Pffft*. More dust. *Pffft*. Something lodged in the broken door. Praskovya jumped back. “Shots.”

Lee dove back to the doorway. He peered around it. A bullet hit the door jamb. The kids were safe enough, unless our attackers were firing something that could penetrate concrete. It felt like massive *déjà vu*.

Mac hooked my leg with his arm and pulled me closer to him and the children. I sat down on the mattress. “Stay over here, they won’t want to lose the kids.” He then scuttled away, gun in hand to take a position lower than either Lee or Praskovya. I listened to the firing. Tried not to jump at every hit the door and doorframe took. Wishing I could be of some use.

“How did they know? I haven’t seen a camera,” I asked, as Lee fired a few rounds. Then looked at Gerrard.

He shook his head. “Don’t even think it. As for my men, they didn’t know where we were going until we got here. No one has used a cell phone. And they’re *my* men.”

I didn’t mean to think it, and once upon a time it would’ve been the farthest thing from my thoughts. Once upon a time when I believed in Santa Claus, the tooth fairy and the honor of the Marine Corps. And I wanted to again.

"Maybe it's checking time?" Mac replied. "See if any of them look like they're about to wake up ..."

"That's the last thing we need right now." I looked at them all, one by one. A couple showed signs of waking, eyes moving inside closed eyelids. "Damn, it's a good thing we arrived when we did, any later and we'd have walked into a hornet's nest."

Mac looked over at the kids and me. "Any chance we can wrap this up before we have six hysterical tweenies?"

Lee was on his phone again. "We do have backup coming, they're two minutes away and running silent. Should be on the shooter any minute. Guess they didn't think of that."

"Where are they anyway? Is it even 'they'?"

"From the shots fired I suspect one person with a rifle, probably behind the ambulances somewhere."

I nodded, more to myself than them; all eyes focused out the door. "Guess it doesn't take more than one person to administer more whatever-it-is that keeps them asleep."

More gravel crunched under heavy, moving tires.

Pffft. Pffft. Splinters of wood flew into the room.

A male voice called out, followed almost immediately by a single gunshot. Running booted feet headed our way.

Lee called out, "About time!"

"Gunman neutralized," replied a deep voice.

Two men in FBI SWAT gear hustled through the door. The first man in asked, "Anyone hurt?"

"No," I replied. "Paramedics?"

"Luckily unhurt, ma'am."

"Can we get them in here then, please?"

"Yes, ma'am."

I couldn't see his face but his voice was comforting. Paramedics ran in, carrying their bags and looking shaken and more than a little stirred. I half expected to see a tall, suave, tuxedoed man emerge from an ambulance, dust himself off and offer me a martini. Bond, James Bond.

SWAT surrounded the building, lending a much-needed feeling of security to the area. Half an hour later Caine walked in. I doubt I've ever been so pleased to see him.

I held up my finger indicating I needed a minute and called Aidan. I kept him on the line and spoke to Caine.

"We need to go, we have another kid. I think she's about to be snatched. Can you stay and deal with this?"

He nodded. Kids were slowly waking and crying.

I waved my arm in the direction of the mattress. "We expected five and have six. Getting the identity of these kids confirmed is priority. I'm picking there's another body we haven't found yet. Number six's mom."

Caine's mouth twitched, his gruff voice crackled with amusement. "I can handle it, Ellie." Caine took charge of the scene.

There was a smile on my face when I turned to Gerrard. "Thank you for your help. Let me know if you find my Marine."

"Will do. Tell your father I'll be by to visit soon."

"You knew who I was?"

"Little Gabrielle Conway. I remember you when you were at college."

I smiled. "Thanks for not saying that earlier."

Motioning to Mac, Praskovya and Lee to leave, I walked to the car and waited for Aidan to give me a current address. I heard music. I held the phone away from my ear and I still heard it, so it wasn't the phone. It was in my head. I could hear the Rolling Stones singing 'Lady Jane.'

"Her mother is Jane," I said, to no one in particular.

Aidan replied, "How could you know that? I just asked the kid her mother's name."

"I just do. Give me a location and an adult to talk to there."

Praskovya and Mac stood by the car door, they were waiting for me. Lee was already in the back.

I held out my hand, Mac dropped his cell phone in it. While Aidan called out the number where the kid was, I punched it into Mac's phone.

We were in the car and heading back along Deakyne Road before the phone was answered by an out-of-breath woman. "Hello?"

"This is Supervising Special Agent Ellie Conway with the FBI; do you have Carla Torres with you?

"Yes, I do, she's a friend of my daughter's. Is there something wrong?"

"I'm on my way to your address, ma'am, please keep Carla with you until I arrive. She is to stay in your care.

Do you understand?"

"What if her mother comes for her?"

We hit Tulley Gate with our grill lights flashing and were waved right through.

"Can I have your name?"

"Sandra Boyd."

"Sandra, I doubt if Carla's mother will come for her but, even if she does ... I do not want you to release her to anyone but me."

"There's something wrong, isn't there?"

I know I took her by surprise and everything, but come on! What did she want me to say? No? The FBI called her up and told her to detain a child, for fun?

I took a moment to tell myself off. Stop it, Ellie! I wasn't being fair. It was getting late and Mrs. Boyd sounded harried to begin with.

"Agent Conway?"

"Sorry, Mrs. Boyd, we're on our way to you. And yes, there is something wrong. Just please do as I ask."

"How serious?"

"Serious enough for the FBI to be involved, ma'am; it doesn't get much more serious."

"What should we do?"

"Lock all the doors and windows. Draw the curtains. Do not open the door for anyone but me. I will hand you identification when I arrive and a card with a phone number. Call the number and check that I am who I say I am."

The woman's voice shook as she replied, "All right."

"Ma'am, I will have three male agents with me. Two American and one Russian."

"We'll be waiting."

"We're on our way."

Chapter Twenty-Seven
Nobody's Hero

I leaned my head back onto the headrest. The movement of the car and sound of the engine lulled me into a waking trance-like state. Standing on the edge, I stared into the black beyond. One foot toyed with the notion of stepping into space. The other firmly planted on the ledge. Noises that became voices and cries floated up from the dark. I looked harder, trying to make out the origin. The ground under my foot shook, threatening to send me tumbling into the unknown. My balance was now precarious at best, treacherous at worst; I felt my foot slip forward. A thought entered my head, how bad could it be to fall? One foot already wavered over the abyss below. How bad would it be?

Faces of the dead swirled into focus; one by one I saw their calm, peaceful faces. With no warning, piercing screams shattered the calm. Each pain-contorted face stayed for a few seconds, then vaporized in a ball of flame.

As horrible as it was to witness, knowing that I hadn't stopped it was worse.

I needed more help than my team could provide. I pulled my cell phone from my pocket and from memory pressed in a number I hadn't used in a long time. I could imagine the surprise on Caine's and Owen's faces should they learn who I'd called. Talk about jumping the chain of command.

Within the second round of ringing tones a familiar voice said, "O'Hare."

"Director, this is Ellie Conway."

A pause ensued. I waited.

Cait O'Hare spoke in a soothing tone, "I have a file on my desk, Ellie, sent over by EADC Owen regarding the case you are working now." At least she'd heard about it. "What do you need?"

"Cooperation from Homeland Security, Customs, Immigration," I replied. "If it's an alphabet company I want it on my side."

A Steven Seagal moment flashed *The Patriot* onto my internal screen. Not to be confused with Mel Gibson's *The Patriot* which portrayed a very different time. Steven Seagal removed the images of Mel Gibson with a swift kick. No room for short men in my life, not even in the movies. There was no need to explain alphabet companies to O'Hare. I'd heard her refer to CIA, NSA, USSA, CBP and the rest as alphabet companies more than once. She was the ultimate Seagal fan.

"What's happened?"

"We've got a terror cell operating and they're making money by selling our children."

"Owen didn't mention a cell."

"Owen doesn't know, it's only just become apparent. There is a military aspect. I don't want to hand this on. These kids are the priority, if I hand it over ... we've recovered six but I believe there are more."

"I'll speak to the relevant directors." She paused then said, "I may leave out some pertinent information regarding terror cells and the military. Let's call this child trafficking for now."

"Thank you."

"You get those bastards and bring home those kids," O'Hare said. "Whatever it takes, Agent."

"Yes, Director."

Her voice softened as she said, "You owe me dinner."

"Ruby Tuesday's, when this is over?"

"Sounds like a plan."

I heard a hint of amusement in her voice. Ruby Tuesday was an inside joke from a case I'd helped out on a few years previously. A case involving an award-winning novelist; a stalker; a bomber; a kidnapper; songs with the word Tuesday in the title and Director O'Hare. Good times.

I hit the end button and pushed my phone back into my pocket. I saw Praskovya and Mac exchange glances; neither said boo.

Smart men. I sure didn't want to explain the phone call they'd just overheard.

Chapter Twenty-Eight
Real Life

"Mac?" I hit his arm lightly to get his attention. I showed him a picture on my phone that I'd just received from the Cobham crime scene. We hadn't made it to that crime scene. As soon as we'd rescued Carla, that's where we'd head. Mac took my phone and viewed the picture of a blue Post-it note with the words, 'I am invincible' in black ink.

"Nice, is it new?"

"Yes. From the Cobham scene."

"Interesting words." He handed my phone back to me.

"This means we're right about there being more than one killer." I was absolutely sure. "Why would a guy leave a note that says 'I am invincible'?"

Mac frowned. "Because he thinks he is?"

"No, no, no. It's from 'I Am Woman' by Helen Reddy. It's a chick song."

"You think his accomplice is the chick from the car, the one Praskovya here is chasing?"

Duh! Where had he been for the last few hours?

"Those crime scenes were totally scripted. She was in the car crash – her traveling companion was in Richmond. That, at the very least, suggests she may have been in Richmond also. I think she's killing too ... she's the other killer. The Richmond victims were not raped."

Praskovya swallowed so hard I heard him. To his credit he didn't interrupt me.

"They're blowing smoke up our asses and grabbing youngsters from right under our noses. She is involved. Hands-on killing – just like him. Two of the notes are hers. I need Questioned Documents to verify."

I heard Lee's phone flip open. Seconds later he asked someone at Questioned Documents to compare the notes and determine if there were one or two authors.

We were pulling into the driveway of the Boyd's home when his phone rang.

"Ellie, lab says two notes were written by different people; they're now analyzing the scene writing again and will check the latest note when it arrives in the lab."

"Excellent."

Mac gripped the wheel. "Does this help us at all?"

"It may do."

I flicked through the photos in my phone until I found the passport photo of the missing woman. I put my hand on the door handle and said, "Let's go get the kid."

Praskovya was out the car and had opened my door before I could reach the handle. More Russian charm.

Lee knocked on the front door of the house.

An adult female voice called out, "Who is there?"

It's me, the big bad wolf. I'll huff and I'll puff.

"FBI, Mrs. Boyd."

"Hold your identification up to the peephole."

Good to know she could follow instructions.

Lee did as commanded. I got the feeling she wasn't expecting a large man at her door; probably his movie-star good looks threw her too.

Mrs. Boyd said, "It was a woman who called me. Agent Conway?"

I stepped up to the peephole, then stepped back and said, "Right here, ma'am."

The door opened two inches. "Pass me your identification."

I did.

We waited. It was a small price to pay for the security of a child.

Two minutes later the door opened. I saw the phone in her hand. She really was smart. She'd checked. I couldn't help but wish more people would make that phone call.

I stepped forward with my left hand outstretched; it was a rather awkward handshake.

"Supervising Special Agent Conway, ma'am. Where's Carla?"

"Follow me."

We filed through the door. Praskovya was last and closed it firmly behind him.

We followed the woman into the house. I glanced around. No shortage of money in this home but appearances can be deceiving. In this case no one is above suspicion, not even apparently caring mothers who take in a worried child. Trust no one.

She stopped outside a pale pink door and knocked. "Girls?"

She opened the door. Three young teenage girls looked up from the computer they were gathered around.

"Carla Torres?" I asked.

A cute brown-eyed blonde raised her hand. I asked the mom for somewhere to talk and she suggested I use the sitting room down the hall. The hallway could've been another room in its own right, it was so spacious.

"Come have a chat with me, Carla." I ushered her out the door. "I'm Ellie."

"Hi."

We stepped into a living room and sat down.

"Where's my mom?"

I held my phone out, showing her the picture on the screen. "Have you seen this woman before?"

Her eyes lit up with recognition. "Yes. She moved into our building. She has the coolest accent. Russian or something."

"Do you remember when she moved in? ... Which apartment?"

"Last month and she lives in 7A," Carla said. "She is at our place a lot. She and mom go swimming together. Some kind of fitness class."

"Swimming," I repeated. Swimming. Chlorine. They went swimming. How many others went swimming? This chick really likes chlorine.

"Where's my mom?"

How do I say, I don't know but I think she's dead?

I ignored the question and showed her another picture, the man from the crash. "Have you ever seen this man?"

"No." She passed the phone back. She was telling the

truth. I never could understand why no one liked working with kids.

My phone rang. "I need to take this, then we'll talk some more." I stood up and walked to the window as I answered the call.

"Conway."

"It's Agent Simmons. We have the mother."

"Condition?"

"Same as before."

"Where?"

"In her home."

"One second."

I turned to Carla. "When did you go home?"

"After school."

"How long did you wait?"

"It was nearly seven. Mrs. Boyd always told me I could come here, if I got scared or worried. I kept calling and calling but mom didn't pick up her cell."

"Thanks." I turned back to the window and my call. "Did you get that?"

"It's ten fifteen. She's still warm."

I whispered harshly, "Seal the scene, sweep for cameras etc. And lock down apartment 7A."

"ETA?"

"Within the hour," and hung up.

"Carla did you leave messages for your mom on her voicemail?"

"Yes, lots. I told her I was at Sally's and I was okay. And she should come get me."

I smiled at the worried girl. I'm sorry about all this, Carla, I'll be right back."

I hustled from the elegant room to find Mac, Lee and Praskovya. My arm began to throb.

"Lee ... Child Services. This kid needs protective custody until next of kin are found."

Mac asked, "Mother?"

"They found her – still warm."

"You think someone's coming for her?"

"Oh, hell, yeah. And I'll be real surprised if we find any next of kin," I said.

"This sucks out loud," Mac hissed.

"If they want this kid, it's not going to be difficult. She left messages on her mom's voicemail, saying she was at Sally's house. Like a good kid."

We stopped dead as a cell phone rang in the sitting room.

I ran.

Carla flipped the phone open before I could stop her.

I mouthed, 'Who is it?'

She shook her head and said, "Hello?"

I indicated that she should put the phone on the coffee table and mouthed, 'Speaker.' She pressed a button and set the phone on the table.

"Hello?" the voice replied. A distinctly female Russian voice. "Carla?"

I nodded.

Carla replied, "Yes."

I stepped to the doorway and whispered to Mac, "Get

this call traced, it's incoming to Carla's cell phone."

"Number?"

Mrs. Boyd coughed. "Here," she said and wrote the number on a pad.

I moved closer to Carla to hear the Russian.

"It's Selena. Your mother asked me to fetch you."

"Is mommy home now?"

"Yes. She's not feeling well. I'll come get you."

"Sally's mom said I can stay."

"She wants you to come home."

I wrote a note to Carla on my notebook, telling her to keep the woman talking. She nodded at me.

"Okay. Can I finish the game we're playing?"

"It's getting late. You have school tomorrow."

"I suppose," Carla said, with the resignation of a child who really doesn't want to do something.

"I'll come now, Carla. What is the address?"

Carla looked at me, unsure of what to say. At that moment, my phone vibrated, with a text message saying where the phone call originated.

I picked up Carla's phone and ended the call. While I talked to Dave Simmons, I switched off her phone. She stood watching me.

"Dave, a woman called from that apartment block, a phone in apartment 3A. Don't let anyone leave. She's dangerous. Consider her armed. Backup on the way."

I called out to Lee, "We're going."

"The girl?" he asked, as he turned toward me.

"One of us stays here with her," I replied.

Carla stamped her foot and yelled at me, "Where's my mommy!"

Shit!

"How old are you, Carla?" She looked eleven or twelve tops, maybe ten.

"Twelve and a half," she said with a defiant look. "Where's my mom?" Her voice climbed an octave or two. "I want my mom!"

I looked at Lee. I hoped he had some kind of brilliant rescue plan.

He didn't.

Carla yelled louder.

He tapped his watch.

Didn't I look desperate enough? Shit.

"Who is staying?" Lee asked.

"I'm coming!" The kid squawked. "I want my mom! Don't leave me here!" She stamped her feet as tears poured down her face.

"Calm, Carla. Be calm." I grabbed both her hands and held them. "Listen to me."

Her mouth opened to let loose another scream. Lee clapped a hand across her gaping mouth and said, "Listen to Ellie. Shush now." Soothing her.

I watched her eyes and saw her relax. I nodded. Lee released her.

"I'll take you with us, Carla. Let us do what we need to do. On the way I'll tell you about your mom."

It was a bit of a squeeze in the back of the car. Carla sat between me and Mac. Lee drove. Praskovya, who'd remained silent, rode shotgun.

I admitted something to myself with the kid safely ensconced in the back of the car. I was that kid. I was almost that kid.

Dad was at sea when Aidan and I got home from school one day and found mom was gone. I was eleven years old and had to take care of my eight-year-old brother. I called all the places I knew she went and didn't want to call dad. Eventually I decided we were better off not reporting her missing. She turned up a few days later, stinking of booze and cigarette smoke, wearing the same clothes she'd worn when she waved us off to school.

I was that kid. Time after time, I was that kid. I waited for what I considered to be the inevitable: mom's death.

The confusing part was the conflict. I wondered if Carla would feel it too. On one hand the relief – no more hell – on the other, better the devil you know.

I was procrastinating.

We crawled up Carla's road. The line of vehicles and flashers in front of the apartment building lit up half the road. How did the Russian miss all the activity in the apartment block once the mother was discovered? Did she think she could still take the kid and disappear, with cops crawling all over the building?

People gathered around the taped section. Gawkers. Morbid rubberneckers hoping for a glimpse of something dreadful. Something that would make them the center of attention at the water cooler in the morning.

"Why are the police at my building?" Carla asked, pensive, almost as if she knew the answer but the realization was too awful for her.

I saw the medical examiner's car parked near the ambulance.

First rule when dealing with kids: age-appropriate simple truths.

I turned to her. It was time.

"Carla, we found your mom. I'm very, very sorry but she was already dead when we found her."

Tears welled in Carla's dark-lashed eyes. I watched as she fought them back.

"Mommy is dead?" Disbelief rang in her young voice.

"Yes." I struggled with the knowledge that my words had collapsed her world.

"She's at home?"

"Yes."

"Can I see her?"

"Not yet. I need to do my job first. When we're done."

"Why were you talking about Selena?"

"We've been looking for her." I watched Lee and Praskovya leave the vehicle and speak to a uniformed officer. "I need to go inside now, Carla." I looked at Mac. "Mac here is going to stay with you."

Mac smiled. "Yes, ma'am."

She nodded, tears flowing down her cheeks. I think she would've agreed to anything at that moment. I slipped out of the car as she turned her attention to Mac.

I recognized Josh Konstram at the door.

"Ellie," he said with a smile. "This is getting to be a

habit."

"Josh. What have we got?"

"Dead woman: Jane Torres, in 7B. A Russian woman held for questioning in 3A."

"Excellent."

Praskovya and Lee caught up with me and waited just inside the foyer.

"Let's go, "I said. "View the body then we'll question the woman."

Josh spoke, "The Russian says she has legal guardianship of the girl."

I bared my teeth in a mock smile. Finally. "Now I know how they get the kids out of the country; brilliant. Josh, keep a close eye on my car."

"I sure will."

I walked between Praskovya and Lee.

"They're getting guardianship before killing the mothers. This is the break we needed. Lee, first thing in the morning hit the courts and find out how many petitions for guardianship have been filed recently."

"This case has reached tipping point," Lee muttered.

"Yes, it has. It's going to go like Topsy any second."

Lee stared at me with a mystified look on his face. "Go like Topsy?"

I shrugged. "Dad says it. Don't ask me where it came from; all I remember is that she grew and grew, but it fits."

Praskovya spoke, "How do they get this guardianship and what does it mean?"

"You can appoint guardians for your children, in case you die; that person is then legally responsible for the child."

"Is there some proof required, a death certificate?"

"Yes, if the mother is declared dead. I don't think they're making any declarations. I think they are having guardianship papers signed, like maybe you would if a child was attending a boarding school. So that in the event of an emergency, the school can consent to medical treatment but also the school is responsible for the child on field trips and camps."

"They can take the child, get a passport, and leave the country?"

"I think that's what they're doing. I'm not entirely sure they're leaving the country with passports, however."

Praskovya nodded.

The three of us viewed the body and the crime scene. I attempted to filter out the bourbon and blood smell. It didn't work and made me wonder if that was why the Unsub covered the crime scenes in bourbon. He or she was trying to mask the smell of the chlorine. I stepped carefully to Jane's head, knelt down, and sniffed her hair.

A trace of chlorine.

I touched her hand; she was cool but not cold. I whispered to her, "Carla is safe. I'm sorry we didn't get to you in time."

She looked so peaceful, as if she were asleep, not dead. Her last few hours ran through my mind. Swim, coffee, drugged, stabbed, adorned with ribbon, dead. At what point did she think this is not how her night was supposed to go? The look on her face suggested the realization never happened. She never saw death approach. Was that a blessing?

Praskovya cleared his throat to attract my attention. I stood up. He pointed to the walls. More lines of the same poem written in black pen. Lee found the Post-it note.

I read it. My eyes locked on Lee's. " 'A pig is an animal,' " I said with deliberation.

"Yes, of course it is," Praskovya replied tersely. "What does this have to do with anything?"

"Don't force me to sing," I replied.

His eyes shrouded with confusion, he shook his head from side to side. "I don't understand."

"Pig is a slang term for police, or it could be a reference to Hudson Hawk and the song 'Swinging on a Star'," I explained.

Praskovya nodded. "I see now, a sentence with two meanings."

I moved to the far side of the kitchen and viewed the body from a different perspective. Mostly it was the same as the other victims. Mostly. She lay on her back with her legs bent at the knees in a pool of blood and bourbon. Blood congealed into gelatinous lumps near her back. The bourbon was concentrated more towards her feet, thinning the blood into a shiny puddle. The first notable difference was her clothing – it was intact; she was fully clothed. The second thing was gold ribbon laced at her ankles. Crisscrossed and then wrapped, like a ballerina would lace her pointe shoes.

Lee stepped back to stand beside me. "That's freaking creative," he said, cocking his thumb at the victim.

In a quiet voice, Praskovya said, "Selena was ballerina. In her youth. With the Russian National Ballet."

"Thank you," I said. At least I had an explanation for the use of the gold ribbon this time. "Do you by any remote chance have anything to add regarding the gold ribbons on each victim – other than this one?"

"On all victims, not ones you think killed by Selena?" he asked.

"On all."

"Perhaps this is Selena's idea. Maybe for her, he does this and she for him."

"Why?"

"She always wore gold ribbon somewhere." He looked back at the victim. "Even when in Spetsnaz, she had gold ribbon tied in bow sewn inside her clothes."

That was interesting. I suspected the ribbons were messages but never imagined they could be messages between the killers. Which made me wonder if the cameras weren't so much to watch us carry out scene investigations but for each to see the other's handiwork? My skin crawled.

"Let's go. We're done in here," I said.

Outside the apartment door, we huddled for a short conversation. Praskovya began to offer more of his thoughts.

"The orphanages, the ones we think harbored these

killers, could they also harbor missing children?"

"That would be a great place to hide the children before auctioning them off to the highest bidder," Lee commented.

"Praskovya, see if you can find out if any of the orphanages have new children, foreign, English-speaking children," I said, hoping my tone conveyed the urgency of the request.

"I'll do it now. I will make phone calls from outside."

"They don't have swimming pools do they, these orphanages?" I wasn't being entirely facetious. I'd build a pool for orphans if I had millions handed to me.

Praskovya gave an indulgent smile. "You are thinking of country clubs, not orphanages."

I turned to walk down the hallway towards the front of the building and the apartment where the woman was held.

There was a pop, pop noise from outside, followed quickly by screaming and more popping. Lee stepped past me, his gun in his hand. Praskovya took my arm and moved me into a doorway. He towered over me. I was unable to see down the hall and couldn't tell where Lee had gone.

The popping stopped but the screaming and shrieking continued. I flipped my cell phone open and called Mac.

His phone rang and rang.

The ringing stopped. I heard his voice. His voicemail introduction started up.

I hung up and called back.

Same again.

I shut my phone and put it back in my pocket. Staring at Praskovya's back was less interesting than wondering why Mac didn't answer his phone.

I tapped Praskovya on the shoulder. "Let's go."

"Yes."

We made our way to the foyer of the building with care and caution. Neither of us knowing what lay ahead.

Screaming.

Shrieking.

The smell of fear.

I guessed the crowd of gawkers now had water-cooler stories that would make them the envy of the workplace for weeks to come. It was a good bet that they'd also need counseling and that the FBI would be paying for it.

Lee was nowhere to be seen as we entered the foyer, nor was Josh. Three armed police officers crouched in defensive positions near the doorway.

"What's happening?" I asked, trying not to scare anyone by sneaking up behind them.

"Two gunmen opened fire on an FBI car outside."

And that statement stopped my mind from spinning.

Stopped it dead.

"Did you get them?"

"Yes, ma'am."

"Where did they come from?"

"We think they were in the crowd, ma'am," the officer replied. "Both carried an Albanian passport and tourist visas."

Albanian. Interesting.

"Casualties?"

Before the officer could answer, Lee strode back in the door. He shook his head at the officer. Who promptly fell silent.

Lee addressed him, "Thanks, Tim."

Officer Tim Whoever-he-was nodded.

"With me," Lee said to Praskovya then looked at me and chose careful words. "You need to come, Agent Conway."

I didn't feel like arguing, mainly because I knew something bad had happened. Mac wasn't answering his phone and Lee had gone all Special Agent on me.

I tried to determine how I felt as I walked with Lee and Praskovya back out onto the street.

Numb.

From the front steps, I could see our car. The windscreen was shattered. A buzz of activity around the car drew everyone's attention. I saw flashes of white shirt-sleeves and high visibility vests from the paramedics working on someone beside the car; the police and FBI agents were standing around looking helpless. The medical examiner stood by the back of the car, near the other opened door. His face bore the telltale signs of stress and horror.

I figured the kid was hurt. Mac was hurt.

Or they were both dead.

"Lee?"

"They're working on Mac. He took four rounds to the

back."

"What happened to his vest?" I had a horrible thought. "Were they armor-piercing rounds?"

"No, he wasn't wearing his vest. He put it on the kid."

"Where's the kid?"

"In the back of that ambulance."

"Shot?"

"No, she's fine. Shaken but fine. Mac must've seen something. He used his body to shield her."

"But he'd already given her his vest!" Idiot! He should've kept it on! "Fuck! I'm going to interview the woman. Before they kill her too."

My eyes seized on the paramedics. I couldn't process what I knew was happening and turned away. There was nothing I could do to help. I wanted to shove them out of the way, to scream, to make Mac stand up. What I did took every ounce of my strength.

Praskovya and I hurried to apartment 3A. Two police officers stood outside the door. They greeted us with concerned expressions. They'd heard.

"Is someone with her?" I asked.

"Yes."

"Have you checked on them, since the gunfire started?"

Panic flared in the young officer's eyes.

"You haven't checked?"

"There's been no noise." He looked at his partner, who verified that all was quiet.

"Good thing people don't die quietly," I snarled. "Open

the door."

The officer swung the door open. He was right, it was quiet. He was also a numbskull who would never make that mistake again.

From where I stood, I could see legs. Someone wearing police issue trousers was lying on the living room floor.

"Praskovya," I indicated to the left.

He drew his gun. We swept the apartment and found an open window, a dead officer and a dead suspect. Without thought, I made the sign of the cross over the dead police officer. I moved to the suspect and sniffed her hair. Chlorine.

I don't want to be here.

Praskovya spoke, "What did you do?"

"She's been swimming, I could smell the chlorine just like on Carla's mom."

A sinking feeling hit my gut. They were cleaning up loose ends and moving out. As soon as they saw we had the kid, it was over. I flipped my phone open and pressed a few numbers.

I was in no mood for chitchat or to even be polite. "Caine, they're on the move."

"We've alerted Customs and all airports."

"What about Air Force bases?"

"Air Force?"

"Anything military that involves offshore travel. Navy. Army. Air Force. They had a link to an army base, they might use the military as an escape valve."

"Ellie, Director O'Hare called me earlier. Anything we

need, we just have to ask."

"I'm asking. Shut everything down before these pricks get out: they'll either be back or set up operations in another country; that's more kids in danger."

"Everyone is on standby. Go do what you need to do, let me handle this."

I hung up. He didn't know.

Praskovya began searching the apartment for anything that might hint at the next move. He found a laptop cord still plugged into the wall, but the laptop was missing.

The chlorine irked me.

A piece of blue caught my eye.

"Misha!" I called. "Stop."

He turned to look at me with his hand resting on a cupboard door handle.

"There is a problem?"

I pointed at his feet. He picked up a blue square of paper. He showed me. A Post-it note.

"Read it," I instructed.

"It says, 'It's been a blast.' Booby trap?"

With a sheepish smile he touched the cupboard door handle, then let his hand fall to his side. "In here?"

"Yes."

I flipped open my phone and called the bomb squad, letting them know there could be a canister of weapons-grade chlorine somewhere. Then cleared the room.

On the way out I ran my eyes around every inch of the place. The rest of the apartment held nothing of interest. It was sparse. Nothing personal in it. No pictures, no reading material, no personal effects of any kind. I ducked into her bathroom. The cabinet was open and empty. Empty?

A woman with an empty bathroom cabinet?

Our Russian woman had an empty life. A controlled life.

All that control and care, yet she still ended up with a slit throat, lying next to a cop with a broken neck. Despite what Praskovya had told me, I still felt there was much we didn't know and maybe would never know about Selena.

Then I remembered. "She has another apartment."

Praskovya stiffened beside me. "Here?"

"Yeah, the kid said 7A. She called from this one but apparently lives in the other. I had them lock it down," I replied.

"Probably rigged to explode. We leave now."

As I stood there looking at the carnage in the empty apartment, it occurred to me that we were going to lose.

The country was too damn big to shut down before they could get out. We couldn't possibly close all the gaps in time. A photo; a name; but only one man. We had no idea who else was helping him. My gut said Hawk had a safe way out and was already gone.

Screwed sprang to mind.

Praskovya took my arm and escorted me through the door and outside. Everyone was outside, the entire building evacuated. The door guarded.

Paramedics still worked on Mac.

Why haven't they transported him yet?

I pushed Praskovya's hand off my arm and walked through the throng of police officers to the car. The crowd stood silently watching. I edged my way to Mac's side and knelt on the wet road. A paramedic turned to me and said, "We're trying to stabilize him for transport."

I nodded. My cold fingers brushed Mac's hair off his face. His eyes flickered but didn't open. I wiped away foamy blood from his lips.

"You saved the kid. Now fight, damn you," I hissed into his ear. Blood came from so many places on his torso I couldn't pinpoint the worst injury. So I opted for words of encouragement. "It's a flesh wound. Fight, dammit."

I watched his face, his closed eyes, waiting, hoping and desperately wanting him to do something that meant he knew I was there.

"He needs to be in hospital, now!" I said to the nearest paramedic. "Has he spoken?"

"Are you Ellie?" the man replied, signaling to another paramedic for something.

"Yes."

"He loves you."

I leaned over Mac and kissed him. Tasting only blood. His eyes flickered, his mouth moved. I stayed close. He whispered or tried to. His mouth moved and I read the words. "I'm okay."

"That's my line. Get your own ..." I replied, squeezing his hand. He didn't squeeze back. His fingers never reacted.

Lee crouched beside me. I recognized his cologne without having to look. His hand covered mine and Mac's.

"They're taking him now, Chicky. Let him go. You and me, we'll follow."

I don't remember standing up, or getting into a police car. Not my car. My car was full of blood and glass. I knew Lee was next to me; I knew Praskovya was in the front; I knew we had a police officer driving.

There were sirens, lights. Lee spoke on his cell phone several times. I didn't listen. It all happened outside my bubble.

Outside my bubble the harsh reality of life was hitting everyone we loved and rippling through the FBI and other law enforcement agencies. The ill-fated case that saw Special Agent Sam Jackson stabbed, children and parents traumatized – their lives changed forever – and Special Agent Mac Connelly in critical condition, would be ripped apart and glued back together as we all searched for answers. We'd saved six kids and that wasn't enough. Okay, seven, I added Carla to the total in my head.

My bubble opened enough to let a question glide free. "Lee, who was that kid? The sixth one?"

"Her name is Lily Dean," he replied. His voice sounded strange. Gone was the deep smooth tone I was used to, replaced instead by misery and distress. The materialization of pain twisted his expression as he struggled to talk. "Caine's en route to the family home now. He believes Lily was the first child taken. She's in the worst physical condition."

The soothing cold walls of my bubble closed. Lee's voice faded away.

Inside my little world everything felt unforgiving and empty.

Chapter Twenty-Nine
Kidnap An Angel

"What did it feel like?" She didn't make eye contact as she spoke. Her fingers traced the seam of her jeans. I sank back into the chair opposite. A small coffee table sat between us, with a box of tissues and last week's Time magazine featuring an article about Internet safety and sexual predators.

"Which bit?" My mind was running a video clip of that day. How do I explain how it felt without feeling all over again? Simple answer: don't.

Her eyes flicked up to mine as she said, "When they told you about your husband. How did you feel?"

"What about him?"

"That he was wounded, let's start with that."

"They didn't tell me anything. I saw him lying on the road."

The psychologist coughed lightly, reminding me she'd asked a question.

I looked her straight in the eyes and replied, "I didn't feel anything."

Her gaze held. Tears prickled in the backs of my eyes. I didn't want to go over this, not ever. A lump formed in my throat; it hurt to swallow.

She pushed forward. "What did you do?"

"I carried on. I was at a crime scene and ready to interview a suspect before the Unsub got to her too."

"You carried on?"

"Yes."

"Didn't that feel unusual to you?"

"No, it didn't." I sensed her frustration at my answers. For some perverse reason it gave me satisfaction knowing she had to work for every word I uttered.

"What happened next?"

"I told you. I went back to work."

"Right away?"

My eyes wanted to roll skyward but didn't. My voice even remained level, "We were trying to stop a child trafficking ring that operated at least one terror cell. I went back to work."

"Couldn't someone else have taken your place?"

"I was the Supervising Special Agent; it was my case." And then what was I supposed to do – sit around uselessly? Get in the way as paramedics tried to save his life? Hold his hand and pretend he was going to be okay? I did that. I did that later.

I had glimpsed him as they worked on him. I pulled up the scene of carnage and mayhem and played it in my mind. No, I really didn't see much of him then, just blood and wounds. A bloodied torn body was what I saw but it didn't feel like my Mac.

A large internal sigh vibrated around my rib cage; I shut my mouth – tight – to stop it escaping and counted to five slowly. She had no idea what it was like being a field agent.

How could she possibly understand that no one had

time to assimilate what had happened until much later? My turn to ask the silly questions.

"Do you know what we do?"

"I think so."

She had no clue. We do the things no one else wants to do. We choose to do those things. She picked up her pen and wrote something on her steno pad. Probably how uncooperative I was being. She looked at me again, words forming. I could almost see them. I waited.

"When did you get to see him?"

"After I'd determined the woman I wanted for questioning and a police officer were dead and that the possibility of a bomb was high. I also attempted to get the borders closed. So it was at least twenty minutes later." I managed to remain emotionless while retelling the sequence of events.

Her pen tapped on the arm of the chair as she studied me for a few minutes.

I knew what was coming.

"Why are you here?"

"Because I have to be."

"You don't think I can help, do you?"

"No one can help."

I looked at the carpet under my feet. That Sunday replayed for me in the pattern on the carpet. Lee and Caine emerged from a doorway at the end of the hall. Behind them I saw a surgeon. They both stopped and spoke to him. Then to each other. Caine and the surgeon hung back. It was Lee who walked towards me. A noise behind me made me turn. And I saw Sam. He was walking slowly, but he was walking. Sam stepped up beside me. There were no words that needed to be said. He stood so close I could feel the air pressure change as he breathed. We waited for Lee to deliver the news. Lee told me what I already knew.

We stood, the three of us, with our heads bowed, arms around each other in a tight circle. The three musketeers. Praskovya appeared. Lee and Sam dropped their arms, shuffling followed as Praskovya joined the circle. Shoulder to shoulder we stood alone in our silence. Caine came over; he tapped my shoulder. I moved my arm down and let him in.

There were no words to be said, and no words I wanted to hear.

And I still didn't want to hear whatever it was everyone wanted to tell me.

The psychologist coughed. My vision faded back into the floor.

"Why do you say no one can help?" she repeated.

"I can't see how anyone can help."

She uncrossed her legs then crossed them again. It seemed like a pointless act.

"Why do you say that?"

I took a breath and stilled my inner grumblings. "Because it's true."

"How do you know if you don't let me try?" She wrote something else. Curiosity got the better of me. I read her notes upside down.

"You've made a spelling mistake."

She glanced from the page to me, "I have?"

"Third line, the word uncommunicative, you have two n's."

She checked the word and smiled. "Thank you."

"You're welcome."

In different circumstances, I could quite like her. I guessed her age to be close to mine, which would put her in her early thirties. Her accent suggested she was from the south, maybe Georgia. She was giving off vibes that indicated she hadn't been in Washington long.

"Why do you feel I can't help you?"

Oh, we're back to that again.

"Because no one can help. It's nothing personal. It's just how it is."

"Why?"

"He's dead."

I looked at the carpet under my feet wishing what I saw would evaporate before it cemented as a real memory.

"I can help if you'll let me."

I pushed the encroaching scene aside and smiled at her. She was working so hard and getting nowhere.

"You can't help," I replied, with gentle firmness.

"You won't let me try?"

"He was murdered, nothing can change that," I said.

"I can help you feel better."

I took a moment before responding, "Can you bring him back?"

She shook her head.

"Well, then, what I need is inside me and it will take time to work through. Talking to some fresh-out-of-med-school shrink who thinks she can cure the world is not going to help me."

I could tell right away that I had offended her. She stiffened and planted both feet on the floor.

"I'm sorry you feel that way. I am only trying to help."

"And I am only here because I have to be," I said, letting my tone convey a small apology.

She relaxed again, crossing her ankles. "What is it you do now?"

My eyes sought the clock on the wall behind her. Time was almost up; any minute now a buzzer would sound and I would be safe.

"I'm with the Director's office."

"Do you enjoy it?"

"Yes and no. I prefer fieldwork. I was ..." I made the correction, "... I am a Supervising Special Agent with Special Criminal Investigations, Delta team. The Director's office is temporary."

She smiled. I realized I was smiling.

I steadied myself ready for the buzzer. As soon as it sounded, I rose to my feet. I had a feeling that as soon as I left she would look up Delta to find out what we did and try to understand what drove us to do such a physically and mentally challenging job.

"Would you like to come back?"

"No." I had now fulfilled my division-required visit.

"It's nothing personal. I think you and I could probably be friends. I'd just prefer not to talk to a shrink."

Something changed. I felt different, lighter somehow; it made no sense to me at all but that's how I felt. The whole time I'd struggled with his death I'd had the answer and just never knew how to verbalize it. I could feel a smile on my lips.

She interrupted my introspection and asked, "Would you like to get a coffee sometime?"

I nodded. "I would like that."

She smiled. "Me too. I'm new to the area and so far have only met nuts."

I laughed to myself. "Nuts with guns, no less."

"It's a scary job looking into the inner workings of agents' minds."

"I bet." I opened the door and stepped out into the quiet corridor. "Drop by my office later; we'll grab a coffee."

She smiled. "Thanks, Ellie."

"You're welcome. I was new once." A thought popped into my head and before I could censor myself, it fell from my mouth, "Do you run?"

"Run?"

"Yes, run."

I didn't know where I was going with the whole 'do you run' thing, I just felt like I should be running.

"Not since I moved up here. I was thinking of making swimming part of my daily program, care to join me?"

I hesitated then shook my head. "I really wouldn't, but

thank you. You're welcome to join me on a run any morning you like."

I closed the door behind me and smiled.

Ahead of me stretched a long carpeted hallway with many doors. The one I needed to open was the one I'd recently closed.

I whispered to myself in the silent hallway. "Swim? No thanks; I don't like the smell of chlorine. I think I'll pass on adding swimming to my daily program. I won't have time anyway."

My hushed words floated in the air then fell apart. Tiny butterflies erupted from the individual letters. They flittered in front of me on gossamer wings. I watched in awe as they gathered into a quivering mass of color. Oranges, browns, reds, and yellows jockeyed for position. I blinked, and then suspended in the air I saw an image of Mac. Seconds later, his likeness began to dissolve. One by one each butterfly fell into the blue carpet and vanished.

Yep, I'm perfectly sane.

I headed to the Director's office. I wanted back into Delta.

It's not over until the fat lady sings and I don't know any fat ladies; therefore it's not over.

I knocked on the outer office door, let myself in, then knocked on the Director's door.

"Come in, Ellie," she called.

I smiled. I knew she monitored her outer office camera.

I opened the door to find Director O'Hare behind her

desk. She looked up with a half a smile on her lips.

"You want me?"

I met her eyes and with as much control as I could muster said, "I want back in Delta."

"You're sure?"

I nodded. She spun her monitor to face me. On the screen was an emailed copy of the psychologist's report. I skimmed it looking for the bit that said she thought I was uncommunicative and difficult. I couldn't stop the smirk that crept across my face when I found it. What surprised me was the final sentence. She'd signed me off. I didn't have to see her again.

"So I'm not nuts then?"

"She didn't go that far," O'Hare said, with a smile.

O'Hare clicked another email and showed me the contents.

It was from my neurologist. He'd written a report on my head injury and the results of my MRI and head CT. It didn't say anything I didn't already know. It said Leon was correct in his initial diagnosis of benign paroxysmal positional vertigo. I'd undergone treatment in his office and now showed no symptoms at all. The blow to my head during the Hawk case didn't do any damage, other than a slight concussion. He mentioned concern about future head injuries but he'd cleared me for field duty.

"There's something else, Agent. I received a report from Special Agent Noel Gerrard at NCIS. A Navy Corpsman was reported UA after receiving treatment for a badly-cut right hand; this Corpsman served three tours in Afghanistan with a Marine deployment. This effectively makes him a Marine."

Unauthorized Absence. Interesting.

"Does he have a name and did he travel much?"

"He is Hospital Corpsman First Class Brent Miller and frequently traveled to Germany with wounded military personnel."

"Can they link him to any of the kidnappings?"

"His fingerprints were found in the building where you found the children."

"That's a start. What was he doing at the Fort?"

"Working at the hospital with rehab patients." She placed a photograph on the desk in front of me. I recognized him immediately.

"That's the Marine who helped kidnap me and then attacked me."

She smiled. "They're working on trying to tie him to an army doctor who recently specialized in pediatrics, Captain James Chadwick. Gerrard would like you to look at this photograph and identify him if you can."

She slid a photograph over the desk to me. I spun it with a finger and came face to face with the man in the black trousers. It felt like an empty victory.

"That's him – the man who kidnapped me and stabbed me in the back. Our female victims were drugged with Thorazine; can you ask NCIS to dig into that? The doctor here may have something to do with it."

She picked up her phone and made a quick call.

"Agent Gerrard, this is Director O'Hare. Agent Conway

has identified the photograph of Captain Chadwick as the abductor and as the man who caused the stab wounds in her back. She has also identified Corpsman Miller as his accomplice and her attacker. I'll be sending a report. There's a drug supply issue regarding Thorazine that your doctor might be able to help us with."

She hung up and removed the photographs, placing them carefully back in a file. O'Hare smiled and leaned back in her chair.

"This is two-part good news, the second part is; you can rejoin Delta Team A as a Supervising Special Agent whenever you are ready."

"Now's good."

The Butterfly Song

In a glade where butterflies sing
A silver brook babbles
Oak trees grow in dappled light
Tiny acorns sprout
My prince came in chain mail armor
His arrow whistles true
In his heart the butterfly song
A dream upon a wing

Melting smiles in fading light
Drawing from butterflies within
He sets the scene in motion
The world begins to spin.
Butterfly feathers gracefully fall
Carpeting the glade in color
Fairies peek from under leaves;
Listening to the song.

In a blink my prince is gone.
Alone I am left to wonder
Why butterflies sing.

About the Author

Cat Connor is a prolific crime thriller author hailing from New Zealand. Her expertise in the genre is reflected in her engaging and suspenseful narratives, which have garnered a loyal following. Her work is known for its intricate plots, dynamic characters, and relentless pace, keeping readers on the edge of their seats until the very end. She has authored multiple books, including the popular "Byte" series, which follows the exploits of an FBI unit that investigates serial crime.

Cat's passion for crime and espionage is evident in her writing, as she strives to create a world that is both authentic and thrilling. Her meticulous attention to detail and extensive research have won her critical acclaim and accolades from readers and peers alike. In addition to writing, Cat enjoys speaking on topics related to writing and publishing. Her talks are known for their candidness, humour, and practical advice. With her unique blend of talent, expertise, and passion, Cat Connor has established herself as one of the most exciting and accomplished authors in the crime thriller genre.

Her other passions include music, reading, tequila, red wine, coffee, and chocolate. When she's not writing she can be found binge watching TV shows and spending time with her much adored animals; Diesel the mastador, Patrick the tuxedo cat, & Dallas the tortie Birman.

You can follow and contact Cat at the following places:

Website: www.catconnor.com
Twitter: @catconnor
Facebook: @cat.connor
Instagram: @catconnorauthor
Bluesky: @catconnor.bsky.social
Threads: @catconnorauthor

EXACERBYTE
By Cat Connor

Chapter One
Every Intention

My phone chirped like a demented cricket. It was the second call in two minutes. Demented crickets are never good. I pulled over to the shoulder and stopped. Cars whizzed by me. The phone chirped again.

"SSA Conway."

"Ellie, Chrissy here. Just reminding you about the high school visit."

"I hadn't forgotten – there's plenty of time yet." I checked the time on my watch just to be sure. "I'm dropping by Cassie's then I have a few things to do. I don't have to be at the school until later this afternoon."

"Tell her she's invited to my place next weekend. My turn to cook for us all."

"I'll pass it along."

I dropped my phone on the passenger seat and pulled back into the traffic.

Ten minutes later, I parked in the driveway behind Cassie's Subaru. Icy rain splattered from the gray sky as I cleared some mail I noticed poking from the mailbox. Clutching a few letters, I wrapped my jacket tighter against the cold wind and hurried to the front door.

I knocked and waited, shuffling from foot to foot to

keep warm. I knocked again. There were no signs of life beyond the stained-glass inset in the door.

"Cassie!" I called.

No reply.

I walked along the porch. The curtains were open. It was difficult to see into the room; even weak winter light caused too much glare. I cupped one hand against the window and placed my eye up to it. No one moved within. I knocked on the window as I peered. For a second I thought I saw something moving by the living room door. "Cassie!"

There was a skittering of paws on wood. Suddenly Roscoe's face appeared, pressed against the window, his huge paws on the windowsill. Tongue lolling.

"Roscoe! Sit!" The large dog dropped to his hairy backside, tongue still hanging from his open mouth. He wasn't the brightest of dogs but he was sweet.

He'd left a large reddish smear across the glass. I craned my neck to see if the dog was bleeding but couldn't see anything. I jogged around the back of the house, letting myself in the back gate. Still no sign of human life.

I pulled out my cell phone and called Cassie's cell. From where I stood, I heard it ring. It had to be in the kitchen. I hung up before it went to voicemail and hammered on the solid back door. The only noise beyond was the dog tearing across the house and sliding into the kitchen cabinets.

It just wasn't right. Cassie never left without her cell.

Her car was there. Roscoe was in the house, not in his centrally-heated dog run. I counted rocks in the garden beside the back porch until I found the hollow one and the back door key. I knocked, turned the key and handle and then called out as the door swung open.

Roscoe hit me like a freight train, knocking me back. I scrambled to my feet and wiped my slimy hands down my jeans. "Damn drooling dog."

Roscoe bounced around me, slobber flying.

"Sit!"

He plopped like a stone sending a cloud of fluff into the air. His yellow fur was stained red in patches. His large hairy feet were matted and messy.

"What's on you?" I held his collar and leaned down. There was no mistaking the smell. "Blood."

I couldn't trust the dog to stay, so with a firm grip on his collar and my Glock in the other hand I started searching the house. We were in the laundry. I followed his dark footprints into the kitchen. My eyes scanned the immediate area. My nose prickled at the smell of fresh blood. On the corner of the kitchen counter, there was blood and long strands of dark hair. Blood dripped down the front of the cabinets. I held the dog tightly, stopping him from putting his hairy feet in any more evidence.

Above the dog's panting, I heard a click. I closed my eyes and concentrated. A door clicked shut. Someone was in the house. Dog, gun, no hands left for the phone. I crouched down next to the dog and pried my cell from my belt. This wasn't going to work. I stood up and put a leg over the dog, successfully trapping his head between my knees. I managed to send an emergency call to Delta A. An open line was all I needed. I slipped the phone into my shirt pocket.

"I hope you can hear me. I'm at Cassandra Smith's home in Reston. Possible home invasion. There is blood all over the floor. Can't find Cassie. I need back-up and paramedics."

Voices jumbled in my pocket. Sam's overrode Lee and Chrissy's. "We're on our way Chicky Babe. Notifying local police."

"Good to know."

I adjusted my grip on the panting dog and wound my fingers tightly under his collar. With care I moved my leg, to stand next to him again. "Come on Roscoe let's find Cassie."

We cleared the kitchen. I noted more blood splatter on the walls and smearing on the doorframe. Drag marks on the floor led down the hallway. The blood faded into the carpet fibers.

Another click.

The dog pulled. I pulled back and whispered, "No."

My heart raced and stomach twisted. With trepidation, I opened the guest bathroom door. Nothing. I closed the door: if anyone was hiding, they couldn't use the rooms I'd cleared for cover without alerting me by opening doors.

My attention focused on the guest bedroom. Silently I opened the door. There was nothing obvious. I checked under the bed, in the closet, behind the curtains. No one. No sign that anyone had even been in the room.

Four more doors led from the hallway.

The dog whined softly as I swung open the next door. It was Cassie's home office. I breathed for a moment. The entire room was visible from the doorway. A desk, chair, overstuffed bookcases and her laptop.

Next was another bedroom, used as a storeroom by the look of it. Boxes piled high around the walls. Roscoe and I swept the room keeping an eye on the hallway the whole time. Only two rooms remained. One on the right and one on the left at the front door end of the hallway. One was the living room and one Cassie's bedroom.

The dog and I stepped carefully into the room on the right. The door was open. Nothing out of place at all. No one hiding under the sofas in the living room. No one behind the floor-length drapes.

The only place left was Cassie's room. It had a walk-in closet/dressing room and a separate bathroom. Two rooms within a room. Both with locks. Maybe she was in one of the rooms and was safe. Maybe it wasn't her blood all over the dog. I looked down at Roscoe. He was the dumbest and friendliest dog I'd ever met. This was not a guard dog; this was a seventy-pound lapdog. He was likely to lick someone to death or maybe trip him or her with his over-exuberance but otherwise, he'd never harm anyone. Roscoe whined and pulled me. He wanted to get into the bedroom.

A door slammed. It sounded close.

My stomach flip-flopped sending bile rushing toward my mouth.

I swallowed hard, took a deep breath, held tight to the dog and twisted the knob of Cassie's bedroom door. I pushed it so hard it hit the wall behind the door. The dog flinched.

Deep blue curtains billowed into the room. I checked behind them. The French doors were open; there was blood on the floor and bloody footprints outside on the porch. In the distance, sirens.

"Cassie!"

Nothing under the bed. I tried the dressing room door. Locked. I banged.

"Cassie!"

I let the dog go. Roscoe scratched at the door. Then ran to the bathroom door and scratched that.

"Cassie! It's Ellie."

I listened. Roscoe scratched and whined. "Roscoe, shush."

He looked at me with his head on one side, ears alert and goofy tongue falling out of his mouth. Then I heard her voice from the bathroom.

"Ellie."

Bathroom locks aren't that secure. I didn't know where Cassie was, so couldn't shoot. I braced myself on the doorjamb and kicked. Wood splintered. The lock groaned. The dog tried to force his way between my legs. I shoved him out of the way. He made another attempt.

"Get out of the way."

I kicked again. The door flew open.

My gun was already in my holster as I pushed Roscoe again to get him out of my way and rushed to Cassie. She was covered in blood and sitting against the bath, wooden long-handled body brush in her hand.

"Jesus. You look like shit."

"Really? But I feel so good." Roscoe dropped his big furry head on her lap. "You are the dumbest dog in the world," Cassie mumbled patting his head. "Completely useless and I wouldn't be without you." The brush clattered to the tiled floor.

I pulled a towel from the rail and pressed it against her head. My pocket was erupting with noise.

"Excuse my pocket; it's been very worried about you." I lifted my phone and spoke into it. "Cassie needs paramedics. Tell police they're going to need dogs; someone left on foot." I dropped my phone back into my pocket and concentrated on Cassie. "Who did this Cas?"

"Never saw his face ... he wore one of those scarf things soldiers wear ... shema ..."

"Shemagh?"

"A brownish color."

After a couple of false starts, she managed to tell me more. "He had the same color boots, dark blue jeans, a dark jacket. Odd eyes."

Sirens stopped outside. Heavy footsteps ran to the front door.

"I'll let these guys in, or they'll break your pretty door." I hurried away.

I called out and identified myself before opening the door to four uniformed patrolmen. I gave them a description and went back to Cassie.

The towel was soaked in places. I grabbed another and pressed it against her head.

"Odd eyes?"

"Different shades of brown."

"Excellent." I called out to the police and relayed the extra description of the Unsub's eyes, then turned my attention back to Cassie. "You hurt anywhere else?"

"He hit my head against the corner of the kitchen counter a few times; when I fell he kicked me and then dragged me up the hallway."

"I am so glad I left my scarf here last night."

"Me too." Tears escaped her swollen eyes and coursed through the bloodied bruises. "You scared him away. I locked myself in here when he went to investigate."

"Any idea who he was?"

I was aware of police hovering in the bathroom doorway, they were happy enough to let me ask the questions.

"No, he never spoke but he seemed very interested in the pictures on the fridge."

She moved and from a pocket handed me a piece of paper. "He gave me this."

It was a photo of Cassie and me, taken over a year ago, in a heated debate outside the Hoover Building. "That's an old picture."

"When we met."

We both smiled. We came from opposite ends of the

same problem and met with an explosion in the middle. Cassie was the social worker assigned to Carla Torres the day her mother was murdered. Within a week of our first meeting, she began trying to convince me Carla Torres was better off with me than in foster care. Cassie and Carla became fixtures in my life. Fixtures in all our lives. We'd all hung out together. Sam, Lee, me, Carla, Cassie, Chrissy, sometimes even Caine. She had pictures stuck on her fridge of all of us, having fun, proving that family is what you make it.

Cassie looked at me. "Dinner your place next week."

"Yeah. Dinner at my place." I wiped tears from her face with my fingers. "We'll talk before then."

"Call me." Her eyes rolled back. She slumped forward. Her hand went limp in mine.

"Cassie!"

Suddenly a paramedic was in the room. He almost threw me out of the way.

"She's unconscious," I said. "She was talking and seemed okay." As okay as someone who's been beaten to a bloody pulp can be.

She was talking.

I grabbed the dog and pulled him out of the way as the paramedics began CPR.

That's where Sam and Lee found me. With my arms wrapped around the stupid dog, sitting on the bedroom floor, while paramedics tried to bring my friend back to life. A few times while sitting there, I felt sinister eyes watching, an unwelcome feeling I knew all too well and one I'd hoped to never experience again. When I looked over my shoulder, there were only police. I scanned everything with expert eyes looking for telltale signs of hidden cameras and saw nothing out of the ordinary.

Through the bathroom door I saw the paramedics. One looked over at me and shook his head. They weren't in the business of giving up. One was bagging her, the other doing CPR. A suited man ran past me into the bathroom. I watched him drop to his knees next to the paramedics and Cassie. His head turned and eyes locked on mine. Supervisory Special Agent Kurt Henderson otherwise known as Doctor Henderson. His head shook ever so slightly as his mouth took on a grim line.

Police crawled all over the house. They found some clear boot prints on the porch.

Sam went to look. He returned with his opinion. "Combat boots. Cassie mentioned a shemagh? Military or a poseur?"

"My money's on poseur," Lee said, watching the paramedics.

"She's not going to make it." I knew the words were mine but they felt foreign. My arms tightened around the dog's hairy neck. "She has a brother in Richmond. We should call him to take Roscoe."

Lee pulled his phone from his belt and made a call. I listened to him talking to Chrissy. He wrote a number in his notebook. "Ellie, do you want Chrissy to reschedule your afternoon?"

I shook my head. "No. I'll carry on. I'd sooner be busy

than sitting around waiting to hear from police."

He finished talking to Chrissy.

I heard Kurt call out the time.

Cassie was dead.

A police officer asked that they leave her body where it was. The medical examiner was on his way.

Kurt weaved his way around people to me. "There was nothing that could be done. Autopsy will confirm but it looks like she had a massive brain bleed due to trauma."

"She was talking. I had no idea she was going to die."

"I know." His hand rested on my shoulder. "Head injuries are unpredictable."

"Thank you for coming," I said, hoping my voice didn't crumble.

"Heard your call. Figured I might be able to help." He shrugged. "Sorry."

Kurt walked away. I guessed he'd wait outside for the medical examiner.

Lee turned to me and said, "I'll find the officer in charge and see about notifying Cassie's brother and finding somewhere for Roscoe to stay in the meantime."

"I need to go home and clean up before I visit that high school."

Lee squatted in front of me. "I can do the high school visit. You could stay here with Cassie and Roscoe."

A few deep breaths later I replied, "You know nothing about poetry." In all honestly I knew about the same. I could write it but had no clue about iambic pentameter or any other device I was sure the kids would know and be able to discuss. “I can’t stay here without inserting myself into the police investigation and no one wants me telling cops how to do their jobs.”

“I could come with ...”

“Not necessary, but thank you.”

“Carla?”

“I’ll go over to her foster parents’ place after school and tell her myself.” The last things Cassie said to me rolled around my head. The air was filled with noise and I needed quiet. “I’m just going to go outside. It’s a bit claustrophobic in here all of a sudden. I’ll take Roscoe and put him in his run.”

Lee nodded. I used the dog to help me stand. He stuck close as I walked to the front door. I didn’t need to hold him. From the front porch I could see two police cruisers at the end of the driveway, three more sat across the street. Officers were taping off the front lawn and drive.

Roscoe leaned against my leg as I walked him through the back gate and over to his impressive dog run. He walked inside, whined and pushed against me. I patted his head and tried to speak to him calmly. “It’ll be okay Roscoe.” I knew he knew Cassie wasn’t coming back.

The dog dropped to the ground, his head on his paws, brown sad eyes watching me, as if his life-force had drained with Cassie’s. I checked he had water and tossed him a few dog biscuits. Cassie kept a small bag of dog snacks in a cupboard inside the run. It also contained his leash and brush. Roscoe took a biscuit into his kennel. He flopped onto his bed. I closed the wire gate and locked it.

I expected the sound of dog teeth crunching to follow me from the backyard but there was nothing but a mournful silence. By the time I reached the house the yard was filled with the saddest howl I could've ever imagined.

I leaned back on the wall by the front door and eyed the two chairs sitting on the porch. Serenaded by the dog's grief I thought about the night before. Cassie and I had sat out on the porch. It was a cold night but the sky was clear. We'd watched shooting stars, consumed coffee and righted every wrong in the world. Cassie had again broached the subject of me adopting Carla. She told me she'd written a letter and placed it in Carla's file, her recommendation for Carla's future. Our coffee cups were still on the small table between the chairs.

A mixture of blood and dog fur stuck to my jeans like a macabre patchwork.

Footsteps.

Caine stood in front of me. "Cassie?" Gruff as ever.

I swallowed, hoping the word wouldn't choke me. "Dead." I looked down not wanting to see Caine's eyes. "Did you see Kurt Henderson?"

He nodded. "Who's running this?"

"Not us. Police. I heard someone say Darren Reid was Officer in Charge."

A cop appeared behind Caine. He was tall, broad shouldered and about forty years old. I'd seen him before but couldn't place him. As it happened, I didn't need to.

"SSA Conway, I'm Darren Reid. We met at Mac Connelly's house a few years ago – home invasion."

That's how I knew him. He was the cop Mac knew.

"You found the cat and took it to Bob Connelly's," I replied, shaking his hand then introducing Caine. "This is SAC Caine Grafton."

They shook. With pleasantries out of the way, work mode resumed.

"What happened here?" Caine asked while he pulled on the shoe coverings and gloves another officer handed him.

"Cassandra Smith, a fifty-one year old social worker with Child Services was murdered. Agent Conway was first on the scene and with her when she died. We don't have a motive yet. Follow me."

I stayed where I was.

"Conway?" Caine said. I got the message and walked behind Darren and Caine into the well-known interior of Cassie's home. Hundreds of photos of kids smiled down at me from the hallway walls. Their eyes followed me. I figured I could handle those eyes watching me as long as I didn't have to acknowledge losing a friend.

I almost walked into Caine, not noticing he'd stopped outside the kitchen. Darren entered the room. Caine and I stood in the wide doorway. Last night the room had been bathed in warm light and the delicious aroma of homemade lasagna. Today it was blood splatter. I shivered.

"Okay?" Caine asked.

"Sure."

I shuddered. My eyes flicked to the refrigerator door.

Photos fixed with magnets covered the entire surface. There were photos of me, Cassie and Carla at various outdoor events over summer. Some of us hanging out in Cassie's backyard, or my backyard. My eyes landed on a picture of Lee, Sam, Carla and Cassie. I remembered taking it.

"Cassie said the Unsub seemed interested in those photographs." I pointed to the refrigerator. "He gave her a picture. This one." I took the picture from my jacket pocket and gave it to Caine.

He showed Darren and the questions began.

"You know the victim well?"

"I know Cassie very well."

"What's your connection with Cassandra Smith?"

"She was the social worker assigned to protect Carla Torres. Carla's mother was murdered." I breathed in to steady my voice. "Cassie was convinced that Carla would be better off with me than in foster care. She was my friend."

"This is where the injuries were sustained. The Unsub then dragged Cassandra down the hallway ..." Darren walked back down the hall and into Cassie's room. He pointed to a bloody patch on the floor by the bed. "We believe she was left here for a few minutes."

"That could've been when I came in the back. Cassie told me I spooked him. She used that time to get to the bathroom."

"When I came in here, that door was open." I pointed to the french doors. "Once I determined the Unsub was gone I found Cassie in the bathroom."

I blinked trying to stem the prickling at the back of my eyes. Cassie's body called to me. I moved carefully, avoiding blood and crouched beside her. Her out-of-focus eyes stared at nothing.

"Oh Cas, who did this?" I wanted a reply but none came. There was a smell of bleach by her hands. I hadn't noticed it earlier. It tickled the back of my nose and triggered a memory. I sniffed. Chlorine. Chlorine bleach. "Caine – she has chlorine on her hands."

The crime scene took on a new meaning. I scanned it for anything else that would go with the chlorine. Familiar poetry. Notes. Bourbon. Possessed by the past, I walked back through the house searching everything again with new eyes. Caine and Reid followed me in silence. The kitchen gave off the strongest smell of chlorine. My nose led me to the sink and a teacup. I sniffed and recoiled. The cup had contained chlorine bleach. I pointed it out. "She must've been soaking it to remove tea stains."

I opened the cabinet under the sink and discovered a large bottle of Clorox. One mystery solved and it wasn't sinister. I'm pretty sure the sigh that escaped me was audible.

"Do you have any suspects?"

"Only you," Darren replied.

Caine bristled. "SSA Conway was not involved in this unfortunate incident."

"I'm not in the habit of killing my friends and I sure as

hell wouldn't beat someone to a pulp then call police," I muttered at Darren. "And I don't wear combat boots. You find a shemagh anywhere? Are my eyes different colors?"

He shook his head.

"We only have the description you gave. My officers weren't able to confirm it with the deceased."

"You need to look elsewhere."

"I'm starting with what's in front of me," Darren replied.

It felt as though he wanted me to be involved. My annoyance intensified. "What else do you have or are you content to waste time with me?"

"Did Cassandra have a partner? A boyfriend? Anyone she's been dating?"

Nothing then.

"No one permanent. She dated a guy from Alexandria a few times but said it wasn't going anywhere." My brain started to kick in. "Have you looked for her day planner – his phone number will be in there."

"There was no day planner that we've found."

"It might be in her car. Or maybe she uses her laptop as a day planner. That's in her home office."

My cell phone chirped. I looked at the screen. Chrissy. I looked at my clothes. Blood soaked. Time to go home and shower.

"I have to go. I'll write my statement tonight and email it to you." I took my card from my pocket and handed it to Reid. "You can reach me anytime. Keep me informed."

He shook my hand. "Don't leave the country."

“If I were you I’d start checking for bugs and wireless cameras. Something is not right here,” I said, barely keeping a nasty edge from my voice.

“You Fed’s think everything is about terrorists and spies,” he scoffed.

“I’ll walk you out,” Caine said, turning me toward the door before I could snap a retort at Reid. My hand strayed to my hip. My fingers brushed the grip of my Glock. It took real will power to shove my hand in my pocket and not decorate the room with Reid’s blood.

“Is he for real?” I snarled at Caine as we stood on the driveway. “Don’t leave the country; it’s all about terrorists and spies. Who the does that fucktard think he’s dealing with?”

“I’ll handle him.”

“Thanks.” I looked at him. “Cassie was a federal employee – can Delta B investigate?”

I knew Delta A couldn’t. It’d be like investigating a family member’s murder. Not good to be so close.

“No reason why we can’t run a parallel investigation. I have the impression you are not filled with confidence by Mac’s old buddy?”

“Nope.”

“You sure you’re okay?”

Hell no.

I avoided the question. “I gotta go clean up and visit a high school.”

www.ingramcontent.com/pod-product-compliance
Lightning Source LLC
LaVergne TN
LVHW041059080826
845145LV00007B/1632